I0599232

A Plague On Both Houses

by

Zack Highstreet

Published by

Philadelphia Freedom, LLC

Publisher's Cataloging Information:

Highstreet, Zack.

A Plague On Both Houses / Zack Highstreet.

ISBN 978-0-6152-2284-4

Published in the United States of America by Philadelphia Freedom, LLC

Under the full protection of the First Amendment to the United States Constitution

Printed in the United States of America

Publisher's Note: This is a work of fiction. Names, characters and incidents are either products of the author's imagination or used fictitiously. Any resemblance to actual persons, living or dead, or events are entirely coincidental. Locales, establishments and names of amusement park rides and attractions are either products of the author's imagination or used fictitiously. DISCLAIMER: Although the author and publisher have researched sources and citations with due diligence, the author and publisher assume no responsibility for the accuracy and completeness of information contained in this book. Any perceived insults or slights, personal or otherwise, on part of the reader are the responsibility of the reader and not that of the author and publisher.

Grateful acknowledgement is made for permission to include the following copy-righted material:

This story is dedicated to my daughters
who live in the House of War,
furnished with liberty, equality and justice;

to Dafna's daughters who live in a land
surrounded by hate
but nevertheless live in a house full of a mother's love;

and to the Daughters of Islam,
past, present and future,
they being the first
and always the worst
victims of Submission,
confined to their quarters
in the House of Islam.

Conquest

Because he loved his religion above all things, he kept praying. Cupping his hands against his off-white thobe, he tried to put this world behind him as best he could for the evening prayer, but the excitement of the moment prevented him. He called out for Allah's blessing for the final leg of the operation, which began during this prayer.

"I thank You for my life thus far and for the great deeds I now begin in earnest.

I ask You to help me carry out Your will.

Help us, give us strength.

You alone we worship.

You alone are due the worship.

Strike down all those who stand against Your will.

Bring us through the trials to a successful conclusion.

Help us kill as many unbelievers as possible.

You alone are benevolent and ever-merciful.

Amen.

Let it be now as it was in the olden times. Make me an instrument of Your retribution, *inshallah*."

The sea began to kick up harder now and the twin diesel engines strained under the increased load. Acrid smoke enveloped him as his ship's course changed slightly to the West and into the strengthening waves of the setting sun. He squinted just enough to see the silhouette of a ship coming out of the sunset's singular, horizontal intensity. The journey had not sat well with him, but three months' duty had given him the ability to estimate the size of a distant ship if nothing else. It was the coffee freighter, which would take him into *Dar al Harb* – into the House of War.

After a time, Abdullah bin Malak al Zalam stood as best he could in the pitching seas and gathered up his Qur'an and his threadbare prayer rug. His rug these past twelve years, with its colors all faded to shades of earth and gray and black. The wear patterns from his knees and feet and the frayed edges testified to the 21,900 times he had submitted to the will of Allah and marked himself as a slave to it.

He grasped the safety rail running the course of the deck and fleetingly wondered if it would hold. The ship had many years on her, but *inshallah* she had a little more time. She had had at least four legitimate owners prior to the sheik and three pseudo-owners under him. But in truth, the Brothers owned the ship, flying a flag of convenience under Panamanian registry. Anyone checking into its provenance would find a Turkish company laid claim to it now and its current manifest declared a shipment of Spanish produce, bound for Venezuela. Abdullah did not resemble a tangerine in the slightest, but carried with him the fruit of the godless, necrotic Soviet Union. He smiled at the irony of Allah's plan. Even the godless had a purpose at times.

He took one last look at his old carpet and threw it overboard in the direction of the other ship, now growing larger. The ship's lines became more distinct as the Brothers' rust bucket carved through the warm, teal waters of the Caribbean, closing the gap between them. Clouds larger than he had ever seen plumed up behind it, making the skies darken and the sea lighten. Looking back, he watched stoically as his prayer rug floated briefly then disappeared under the next two-and-a-half meter wave. Like Prince Houssain's flying carpet in the old stories, his carpet had brought him around the world, but it had taken a season instead of an instant – a span of time far too long for a man of action with a restless temperament. Truly, he would be glad to leave the smallish heap with its stench of decay. Its size was no match for a rough sea.

He thought back to the first week of his journey and its unending stream of nausea. The hold, with its redolence of spent diesel and cancerous rust had gripped his throat in the resting times between the dry heaves.

He had passed through that test of will as he had all the other tests before it. No physical pain or disability would stop him short of the goal. Only death could do that. If death came in the end, so be it. God would provide, both then and now. As in the old saying "It is the Will of Allah; to Him we belong and to Him shall we return."

He kept his Qur'an. They all needed to keep that.

He felt the weight of the unknown settle around his thoughts. In less than an hour he would be off the ship but in the hands of unbelievers whom they needed but could never trust. Abdullah gritted his teeth hard enough for the cords of his neck to show. He objected to involving the *kuffar* from the start. The security of the mission will not be jeopardized they had said – '$10 million US Dollars of pure Afghani heroin should be enough down payment to silence an army of drug dealers' they insisted. He trusted no one outside of the brothers. *Take not the unbelievers as guides or helpers.* Allah Himself commanded this and he obeyed.

Conquest

He descended into the dank stairwell, running both of his slender hands through an oozing coat of humidity still new to his senses. *Water, water everywhere. The air itself full of it to the point where it chokes,* he thought. Too much water was a novelty but at the same time a liability.

The last fifteen minutes of the trip seemed to stretch out as miserably as the first year and a half. The closer he approached the end date the longer the idle times stretched on. Once again, he stood and waited while the inflatable canvas skiff scuttled over the patches of foam, rising and falling from peak to trough in the blustering warmth as alien to him as the infinite quantity of water surrounding them all. The hulking four-story ship that would take him into port was a mere two hundred meters away, but he would have to transact some business before he boarded it. Men wanted to be paid for their part in the matter. Men without a future always demanded to be paid in the present. He found this amusing since it would do little for them in the long run. Impatiently, he shifted his weight back and forth in the steel-toed boots he now wore. He had on the clothes of a crew member: a matching cotton twill shirt and pants in the same camel-dung brown as the water from the ship's faucets. He strapped a Mae-West style life preserver around his neck and chest. He never learned to swim in Buryadah, but then again coming from the middle of a desert few people did. No one he knew could swim.

A couple of the Brothers began to lower him down onto the netting. He carried a steel case in each hand, for he had never allowed anyone else to handle them. He insisted that they help lower him by rope so that he could do this. He took the plastic bench at the front of the boat, placing the cases to either side. The little boat banged against the hull, making a shallow scratching sound as canvas rubbed against the flaking steel. The boat hands spoke Spanish in short, clipped sentences and only when necessary. The sea made them nervous.

He shouted up in Arabic for the rest of his bags, deepening his register and separating his words more than usual to compensate for the din of the sea, the clanging of the two cycle outboard and the thunder, now not so distant and building in power. Abdullah waved to show he was clear and pinned the drugs between the bench and his feet. He grabbed at the lip of the bench as the motor swung the bow away from the freighter hull. He breathed in a large amount of storm air and set himself hard against the bench. They now began to move toward the freighter and a yacht, which had come between the two ships and gleamed each time the lightning flashed. They came alongside the 52-foot Viking and maneuvered toward the stern, where a couple of Hispanics paced back and forth with thick, nylon lines ready to cast them at the little raft. They had to try three times to moor it because of the rough conditions.

Abdullah grudgingly opted to hand over one of the cases, conditions as they were, but carried the other one up onto the swimming platform, extending out from the gunwale. The name 'El Cid - Caracas' flashed at him in large, stylized letters. The name of the accursed barbarian who drove the Moors from al-Andalus and plunged that country back into the Dark Ages of Christianity with its Inquisition. His thoughts had been confirmed. *The brothers are misguided,* he thought, *This alliance has to be one of convenience -- one of utility and nothing more.*

Abdullah gained his footing and stepped onto the stern deck. Getting onto the coffee freighter might prove dangerous in itself, unless he could conduct this transaction quickly. He stood by the table, waiting with the enforcer from the skiff, who wore two shoulder holsters filled with what looked like .40 caliber Smith & Wesson semiautomatics.

The lower cabin door opened and three men came out into the night. The first one looked to be another bodyguard type, tall and muscular but blank in the eyes, carrying a stubby machine pistol on a sling. The second man had a good fifteen years on the first one and looked well fed. He had several gold chains around his neck, the thickest pulled down by an obscenely large cross underneath. His face was decorated in the easy, sly smile of a crooked merchant from the market; the kind who would load the scales at first opportunity. He was the contact, judging by the others' deference.

At this point, the noise of the outboard motor rose in pitch and Abdullah looked back to see the little boat heading in the direction of the freighter. This disturbed him. He hadn't expected to be stranded like this but didn't let this show in his expression.

"I am pleased to meet you, Sir," the heavy one said in English. His tone and delivery were generous. "You must be one very important person. The price of your safe passage says that much. " The chains around his neck clanged together like a hateful church bell.

"Thank you," Abdullah lied.

"Would you like to take care of the details inside where it's dry and more conducive to business?"

"I think it best to finish this as soon as possible. Pardon my rudeness, if you will. I'm afraid the sea will bring more trouble should I accept your kind offer."

"Please call me Pepito," he smiled, slightly bowing his head, "Very well then, if you would be so kind as to hand your 'gift' over to my assistant. We will test its purity and then you may be on your way." His voice smiled, as did most of his face, but the eyes never lie. They followed Abdullah with every movement, unblinking, like those of a prince's hunting falcon. A thin man with patchy facial hair took the drugs from him. His complexion had an ill-tinged pallor even in the intermittent light from the thunderstorm. *He must sample the drugs himself*, thought Abdullah. The fellow took the package into the cabins without comment.

The hawk eyes kept watching him.

"Please send my regards to your associate Muhammad. I always enjoy the arms shows in his company. The man knows how to party, I am a witness to that. He has indisputable taste in French wine as well as French whores," Pepito laughed.

Abdullah pursed his lips, disgusted at the slander. He said nothing.

"My brother and I always call him to see if he will be attending. It's just not the same without him."

"When I speak with him next I will pass on your good wishes." He forced a diplomatic smile.

"Now, about the matter at hand; we will receive the other half of payment once we have you safely ashore, true?"

Payment…always payment…Payment being of primary importance to mercenary drug and arms dealers like Pepito Arravanchía and his brother Jorge, but this was of secondary concern to a believer like Abdullah bin Malak al Zalam. They might control a vast empire on this earth, built on the weakness of men, but it meant nothing in the end. People such as this were weak and could be bent to the cause of Allah -- the Ultimate End – they could be instruments of Allah's will.

"When I am safely delivered I will notify my ship and will send the coordinates and time for the final payment rendezvous."

"My intentions are honest here, sir, but I need some reassurance that will receive the other 25 kilos as promised. I don't agree with my brother's conviction that a promise is enough in the matter of $10 million U.S. dollars." He shifted his weight to turn and faced Abdullah toe to toe, "we can stay with you until you are comfortable in port. That will make *me* feel much more comfortable with this arrangement and will guarantee your successful arrival. Our added protections can expedite the exchange as well. Don't you agree?" Pepito insisted.

Abdullah heard the unmistakable clatter of the outboard in the distance. He looked over starboard and saw a small, dark shape cresting the top of a wave, blocking the reflected light of the white caps. The skiff was returning to pick him up. He exhaled stronger than before.

"That was no part of the agreement I understand. You have the first 25 kilos right now and I would rather be left to my own devices once we make landfall." He wanted to be anonymous, alone. "But if it would give you peace of mind, so be it. Your men can escort me up until the point where I reach my safe house,' smiling. He saw no merit in arguing the finer points while at a disadvantage, but it would not play out as Pepito Arravanchía wished. He would abide by the original agreement – they would get their heroin. But it would be on his terms and under his discretion. He recalled his evasion training.

At this point, the drug tester stepped out of the cabin door and nodded.

"It's nearly pure; the best I've seen in a long time."

Pepito smiled the first genuine smile of the evening. His face lightened, looking like one who is privy to a revelation.

"Let's not keep you from your appointment with destiny," Pepito laughed. *Just, let it pass*, he thought. *They will all suffer the same fate; it being only a matter of time and place,* Abdullah thought.

The ferryman came up alongside the stern. Abdullah reached down for both cases, but stopped at the halfway point when Pepito shook his head.

"Wait, my friend, we have one last thing to take care of for you. Just wait. Come over here." Pepito motioned with his chin to the spot where one of his enforcers had stood, near the center of the three by four meter deck. Three weather-beaten young Latino men clambered up from the skiff and stood in a loose linear grouping opposite of Abdullah and Pepito.

"Which one of you is Jesús Cansadas from Lake Maracaibo?" Pepito said in Spanish. He reached for something under the Armani sport jacket he was wearing.

The fellow in the middle mumbled a few words. Abdullah knew Spanish, but couldn't hear him properly under the conditions. This fellow stood approximately the same height as Abdullah and had the same build. He looked up to see the man's expression change from that of slight confusion to that of sudden terror.

Abdullah involuntarily jumped each time the Glock 17 in Pepito's hand reported another slug tearing through the cotton twill covering Cansada's chest. The man staggered backward, arms flailing and torso convulsing. The blood oozed as black and viscous as the crude oil from the wells back home. The man fell against the support columns for the bridge deck and his body wedged itself between a column and the corner of the safety rail. Pepito put another round in his trunk, destroying the heart within and snuffing out any meager dreams the sailor might have kept there.

Pepito evaluated the gun, turning it to various angles. He nodded approval. Then he glanced one last time at the body of Jesús Cansadas while saying, "Manuel, give the papers to our guest. We wouldn't want the ship to be short a crew member." He grinned.

The drug tester handed Abdullah a leather bi-fold case the size of a day planner. He opened it and thumbed through the documents. A Venezuelan passport, international driver's license and map of New Orleans in Spanish were among the items, as well as various photos of someone's girlfriend and some small photos of children and a family.

"This is your life -- Jesús Cansadas. I hope you're making the best of it," Pepito said, between spasms of arrhythmic laughter. "You might need this too." He held the semiautomatic by the extreme end of the grip and flicked it over. Lunging with both hands, Abdullah trapped it between his palms, immediately trying to orient it downward. The barrel gave off heat.

When he regained his composure, Abdullah began protesting about his new identity, "Why do you give me the Christian name of the prophet *Isa*? This is offensive to me. People will think I associate partners with God. There is no savior or partner with Allah

– He alone saves who He will and damns who He will. This name is an insult. You are insulting my religion by giving me this name."

"Look, my friend, I want the heroin, not a philosophical discussion, okay? My motto is: to each his own. And my 'own' is to own my own -- my own fast cars, haciendas, mujeres and so on, *comprendes*? Religion bores me." Pepito broke the stare and pointed his chin at the one with the pistols. Manuel, give our friend a couple of extra clips and a box of 9 millimeter rounds. Everyone carries a gun in America – we wouldn't want a poor Venezuelan like Jesus here to be left out of the fun, no?"

Abdullah stared at the body again. It was still pinned up by the arms. One hand limply shook in the breeze like a palm frond about to fall from the tree. The other was raised to heaven with fingers curled as if in supplication. He looked at the expression on the face: the wide, fixed eyes and mouth futilely screaming at the seven heavens.

Heaven did not answer. Allah doesn't listen to unbelievers.

He is the first of many in the days to come, noted Abdullah.

Chapter 2

The insects had been buzzing around his face the whole time he'd been in the garden and now the pager buzzed against his appendix. He dropped his shovel and left the flower bed. He'd been waiting a month and a half for this and couldn't wait to get started. He stopped at the work sink in the garage to wash his hands, stained a dark henna color from the earth. Since last Fall, he had worked ten cubic yards of humus into the beds and the effort was going to pay off in roses this year. Roses and gladiolus and lily and many other flowers, to be exact. Since they had moved in last fall, Ben had been working up the side and back yards beds, putting in many bulbs for the splashes of color a white house with a white picket fence needed. He had sat many hours over the winter, selecting plants and drawing up an arrangement which would maximize the bloom times and would spread the color all around the yard. But the pager pulled him into a different project. The bulbs and dirt would have to wait.

He bounded down basement stairs and closed the French doors to his study. He logged into the laptop humming on his desk. Ben's fingers jumped up and down the keys. He hummed too. In fact, everything was humming along quite nicely. Ben now owned the domain www.almuminum.org. The trap he set back in May came off flawlessly. When technology actually worked as advertised it was a beautiful thing. He owned the domain name of an important, pro al-Qaeda website. He controlled the access and the content on the site. He smiled one of his trademark, crooked smiles. *How's the old saying go? Revenge is a dish best served cold?* he thought. Back in the last week of April he had enlisted one of the automated registry services to grab the domain name from the terrorists. It had been waiting all that time, never sleeping, never distracted – waiting for the term on the name to expire. It had been waiting a month and a half, waiting silently, relentlessly, for the domain name to be vulnerable and available.

As soon as it did, Ben snapped up ownership of the name, like a crocodile dragging its catch back into the murky shallows. He owned the rights to the name for a year now. He registered it under the alias 'Ben Zona' of Plano, Texas, supplying a false mailing address and benzona@NetMail.com for the contact information. Everything was fake except the credit card number he had to use for the registration fee.

The cooling fans on the laptop and his custom desktop were both working overtime. They were putting out enough heat to make the air stuffy in Ben's office. He knew conditions like this tweaked his claustrophobia, so Ben worked quickly. He also knew that the risk of being discovered as a fraud diminished if he could get the fake www.almuminum.org site up as soon as possible. The fans in both computers ran continuously now. Ben's hands felt the warmth coming from the core of the laptop. It reminded him of the warmth he felt from the small of Grace's back when he held her close. He would be horny tonight. The excitement of hacking al-Qaeda revved up his libido. But sex would have to wait; his fakery didn't have a moment to waste if it was going to work as planned. Besides, over the last few years with all of the family commitments to school and church and work and keeping up both the houses now and all the rest of it, sex had began to resemble the weekly televised Missouri lottery drawings. It wasn't riveting entertainment, but it was fun and happened on a regular basis. It promised a potentially big payoff, but the person grabbing the balls did it mechanically – with no expression of excitement in her face. So much for spontaneity.

Ben pushed the Cold Fusion code out from the laptop to the more powerful desktop through the 100 Meg network he ran at home. He did a little freelancing as a web developer to keep him up on the technology and to supply beer money for the Cardinals games.

Ben put a maintenance page up on the site, which asked the faithful to be patient due to technical problems. The apology was all in Arabic for authenticity. Ben struggled with the wording for a couple of days, but found a free translation service out on the web to help. He had forgotten most of what he'd learned.

Ben worked as fast as he could. The longer the site stayed down, the greater the chance he would be discovered.

Ben's mocked-up almuminum.org pages matched the real ones. Just like the real site, he had pages of editorials attributed to Imams and the quotes and writings of bin Laden and Ayman al-Zawahiri, second in command. Many articles appealed to the Islamic world for action. Some of these writings advocated terrorist violence, justifying it according to specific verses of the Qur'an. Much of the verbiage was in English. They had some good stuff -- audio files of Osama bin Laden's rants against the West and video clips from terrorist training camps. Another page offered thirty-two JPEG files to budding young terrorists, who could pull them down and use them as wallpaper on their own PCs. Nice pictures. Ben placed a tag or marker on as many of shareable files as possible. That way the FBI could use them as evidence after they busted the terrorist wannabes. He had put the pages together over the last three weeks. The only thing he'd be missing were the blog entries from the last couple of weeks, but he didn't want to risk taking the time to update what he had. It was more important to get the site back up under his control. He could update over the next few days. He'd have plenty of time, since Grace and the girls would be at the Lake for the next week. Besides, he needed to finish the work in the flower beds before it got too dark to see. It was just a few days before the summer equinox, but he didn't have much light left. He needed to clean up the mess out in the flower beds before it got dark.

Ben Adams thought no one would notice his changes when the almuminum.org website reentered the ether space at 20:35 CDT Wednesday June 26th, 2002. *Al-mu'minum means 'True Believers'* he thought, *The believers might be true, but from this point the website would be false.* The idiots who chose to throw turds into his sandbox had Hell to pay. He had outsmarted them and now he was going to mess with their minds, frustrate them and do everything he could to disrupt communications among them. It was a small thing, but it was some payback for his brother as well. He owed Nick at least that much.

Ben Adams had it all. He lived a quiet, suburban American life with all the comforts, privileges and access that reality brings. Like the original Adam, living in the garden wasn't quite enough for him. Like the original Adam, Ben had to eat the fruit of forbidden knowledge. And like the original Adam, his world would never be the same. Unlike the original Adam, however, Ben's expulsion from the garden would help, not hurt, a great number of people. The Adam of Genesis gained knowledge through an Apple. For Ben Adams it wasn't an Apple since he was a PC user. His knowledge came through a Dell Latitude running at 1.2 Gigahertz.

Chapter 3

Ben sat at one end of the oval, oak table in their kitchen. He ate a solitary, catch-up dinner of cold fajitas and cold, yeasty-smelling microbrew. He added five dashes of cayenne pepper to the mix, rolled up the tortilla and chewed. His face flushed with the rush of spice. Grace walked by, looking sexy in a disheveled co-ed sort of way with a pair of shorts which barely hid the curvy cheeks of her ass. She smelled like summer sun and grass cuttings. A few fallen locks framed her heart-shaped face in the golden-brown highlights of summer. She still had it and Ben still wanted it. But their sex life had all the spice of a federal income tax form since the girls had come. Most of the hot stuff he got these days came from a bottle of Louisiana pepper sauce.

"Why do you have that shit-eating grin on you face?" she asked over her shoulder. Her form-fitting top was in a nautical red and white stripe and the fallen spaghetti strap exposed the smooth, fullness of her shoulder and the day's tan line.

"almuminum.org. I *own* it, baby," he said. He gave her a mischievous, crooked smile. One of his dimples showed.

She turned and cocked her head slightly to the right. Her breasts jiggled in a very healthy way when she crossed her arms under them. A misting of sweat decorated her cleavage, now taking on the delicious freckled caramel color of summer.

"What do you mean?"

"I took over an important terrorist web site. It's named almuminum.org, translated 'The True Believers'. I'm going to wreak havoc on those mealy-mouthed bastards."

An incredulous look swept across that sweet face of hers.

"What kind of stupidity are you getting yourself into? Do you think you can change the world by faking a website? Haven't you had enough of this? What about Nick? Isn't that enough for you?" Always the voice of practicality.

His grin diminished in turn. She didn't understand his motives.

"Look, Nick *is* the reason for this. I can't just mournfully take his estate and that be the end of it. Someone needs to pay for this; someone needs to suffer, however insignificant that may be. At least I'm doing something for him. It helps me too."

"By being nothing more than a pest?" she answered, "stirring up some shit for a bunch of internet posers won't change the world. It's not going to make a bit of difference in the long run."

"They killed my brother. I have to do what I can do. I'm a father and a husband and I'm thirty-three. I can't go out and do a Rambo on them. But I can frustrate these *jihadi* sons of bitches and disrupt the hate mongering communications I see on these sites. I've got to do something."

Her eyes flared and nostrils twitched. "Fine. Play the fool for the Islamic world then. You're not doing anything you can get into trouble for, are you?"

The smile returned to his face. "What I've done is perfectly legal. I just took over the domain name at the end of the previous contract term. That's all. Nobody will get hurt over this. I'll have some fun with it for a couple of weeks. I'll redirect some of these guys to the Pork Producers Council website. Stuff like that. They hate pork, you know, that'll drive them ape-shit." He wasn't getting anywhere. "Okay, I know can't really do anything harmful to them anyway. I just want to put them in their place and make them pull the greasy, black hair out of their chins."

"I'm afraid some freak will figure out who you are and mess you up over this, Ben," she said, with a look of doubt and concern. "I don't want anything to happen to you or the kids over a vendetta. It's just not worth it. We have a wonderful life here, Ben, you know it?" *She had petulantly pouty lips. Juicy.*

"Nothing is going to happen Grace," he said, picking up the last of the fajita and taking a bite, " Finding me would be too difficult. These guys are religious fanatics, not techno-geeks."

Chapter 4

Ben tucked the fuzzy cotton cover around the arms and shoulders of his youngest daughter, Sarah. She wore a flannel nightshirt decorated with purple stars and yellow moons. It was summertime, but she liked the feel of flannel and Ben liked to pick his battles. The sun had been down long enough by nine o'clock to finally have a darkened room.

"Let's pray," Ben said.

They both made the sign of the cross as Ben began the prayer they had been saying since before Sarah could say all the words

"Angel of God, my guardian dear,

To whom God's love commits me here;

Ever this day, be at my side,

To light,

To guard,

To rule and guide."

Ben added, "Lord. Thank you for our lives and all of the good things in them. Please help us and protect us from harm. We pray for Uncle Nick and all of those people who died on September 11th. We also pray that the terrorists see the mistake they're making before they hurt more people." He prayed this for his daughter's benefit – he didn't see much hope of a sea change any time soon, if ever. He didn't see much chance for the people of this world to ever improve themselves. He had read enough of the Bible and of history to know that people hadn't changed in 5,000 years, but he prayed for his daughter's sake.

"Why did those people kill Uncle Nick, daddy? Was he doing something bad?" she asked.

"The terrorists think that they are doing God's work. They think that we are bad and they are trying to please God by punishing us."

"What did Uncle Nick do?"

"Nothing, honey. He just went to that building to work like he did every day. He did nothing wrong."

He saw the confused look on Sarah's face but couldn't explain something that he hadn't come to terms with the past nine months.

She moved on.

"Daddy, are we going to Disney World soon?" she asked. She looked up at him with the clear, bright eyes of a five year old and smiled with the pure, innocent trust of a child.

"Yes, honey, we'll be going soon. We're leaving July 3rd. I have the airplane tickets and I think the park passes should be coming any day now." She grinned and squeezed him around the neck. He smiled and brushed the silky ringlets of hair from her face. He looked at her in that glowing, diffuse light fathers see around their daughters.

"Your fish tank needs cleaning," he said. The fish had begun to settle once again and the air pump kept producing bubbles and a calming white-noise hum. "Good night, Sarah."

"Good night daddy. I love you."

"I love you too."

"How much?"

"You know how many drops of water are in the ocean?" he said.

She scrunched her lips, crinkled her nose, knitted her brow and nodded 'yes'. Her nose bent slightly to one side when she put on her 'concentrating' face.

"I love you that many and then one billion trillion more." He kissed her on the forehead and gave her a good squeeze. "Good night, Sarah."

He walked out of her room thinking that her world needed protecting. He had to protect its potential but he knew his limitations. He couldn't do much by himself. Disrupting internet communications and irritating some hot heads amounted to squat, but at least he could that, right here and now. He owed her at least that. He owed his brother at least that much.

Conquest

Chapter 5

The noise pulled him out of the newly-discovered luxury of deep sleep. He found the top of the new alarm clock and rested his meaty hand on the snooze bar, covering it entirely. The ringing continued. It must be the telephone then. He hadn't fully acclimated to the United States. He had only been in-country for two weeks. The ringing pattern of American phones sounded nothing like Israeli phones and that fact still caused confusion.

"Shalom – hello?" Ofer mumbled.

"Ofer, this is Eitan," the voice spoke in Hebrew, "I need you to come down here in about an hour." The line clicked dead. The latest clerk in the long fools' parade had started disturbing his sleep with just two weeks' tenure. The last one had almost gotten him killed in Uzbekistan and then again in Turkey, forcing him to take this assignment to lay low for a time.

Ofer shuffled to the bathroom and stood under the shower until he'd soaped all of his hairy parts. This took a while since he was thickly covered. Fifteen minutes later, he picked up the satchel containing his laptop and other work-related items. It had been on the table, the only piece of furniture in the apartment besides his bed. The place was twice the size of Israeli standards. It would take a lot of things to fill it, but he wouldn't be staying long enough and had no interest in doing this regardless.

Ofer yawned while turning the key to the ignition. The clock reported 0430 in bright, green letters. What was so damn important in this town that couldn't wait until a more reasonable time? His sleep patterns had just synchronized with local time and that bureaucratic asshole was screwing with it already. Ofer didn't think much in Saint Louis would warrant coming in before nine. It was a safe, quiet, predictable place where nightly news programs spent four minutes on pertinent issues like determining the proper diet for pet dogs. *Four minutes* on this subject. As soon as Ofer saw that, he knew he could stop looking over his shoulder, reflexive after the years of bombings and hostility. Ofer decided it would be better to continue in his usual mindset anyway. He would need it when he returned to Israel.

He drove down the nearly-empty middle lane of U.S. Highway 40 under a fullish moon. Funny how it looked the same everywhere he'd been; in all the different worlds. He didn't have to concentrate much on the road – very straight. Americans built good roads. The roads were all clearly named and marked at every intersection. With a map and a little experience, it wouldn't be necessary to memorize anything here. The junctions didn't have the names – the individual streets did – that took some getting used to, but many of the little worries in life disappeared in this country. It amused him to hear the complaints anyway. They knew nothing of the curse of history and its weight. They had the present and the shining future to think about. They limited their past to a couple of holidays. They didn't know how good they had it without its burden.

He finally reached the fifth floor doors after mugging for the closed-circuit camera in the elevator and swiping his magnetic ID badge twice. Ofer trudged past the half-lit and empty cubicle rows where the Americans worked during business hours. He kept going towards the end of the hallway, where the greenish-yellow light cast the shape of Eitan's doorway. He entered without knocking and his boss greeted him with the customary scowl.

Eitan spoke in Hebrew. They could do this as long as no Americans were around. The rule stated English Only in mixed company, but it didn't apply at 5:03 on a Monday.

"Ofer, I just finished talking to our colleagues at the Home Office about a very interesting development here in Saint Louis."

It would have been just after midday in Tel Aviv. A much more reasonable time to mull over the day's bullet points.

Eitan continued, "One of the web sites we monitor has been hijacked. Someone in the United States took over the domain name for almuminum.org and has put up a spoofed site in its place. Our colleagues are concerned about this. It could delay the transfer or put off the operation for some period of time." Ofer fidgeted. The space between his chair and Eitan's ponderous desk prevented him from anything but keeping his legs straight out. The desk took up at least a third of the room and Eitan had pushed it toward the door so that he had plenty of space behind it.

"What else does The Office know?" Ofer tried to cross his legs and bumped his knee against the serrated edging of scars and peeling laminate. The desk fit Eitan perfectly in Ofer's estimation: it being ill fitted to the situation, damaged over the years and of lower-than-average quality.

Eitan continued, "They say that the IP address came from the ISP we have here in Saint Lois – *Louis.* Tel Aviv wants us to take the lead. They are asking our colleague at the telephone company to review the logs and send us more information by ten this morning."

At least someone else had to get up too.

"Am I supposed to be involved with this?"

"Tel Aviv insists. You're the one with a history on this. Your resume fits hand in glove with what is needed here. The handler here is very pleased with your credentials."

History, always the curse of history. It kept him in work, however. Ofer rolled his eyes and let out the world-weary sigh of a man who, in the words of Yogi Berra, had déjà vu all over again.

"Don't they know I'm supposed to be on vacation. Fine, whatever." he crossed his arms and grimaced.

"So this 'hijacker' is a local? We know that much?" Ofer asked

"Yes, we'll know in a few hours who it is. He used the alias 'Ben Zona' but had to have a legitimate credit card for the domain registration fee. Our man in the billing system over there will get us the number and we'll do the trace. In the meantime we need think about developing a couple of contingency plans. At ten we'll meet with the boys on the third floor and go over our options." *Decisions by committee protect clerks but end up getting people like me killed*, thought Ofer. He had only worked with this cautious bureaucrat for a couple of weeks, but had done some checking. Eitan had had a long and unremarkable career on several desks at the Institute.

"Ben Zona -- do you think the hacker is an Israeli or an American Jew?" Ofer said. He wasn't a gamer but would play along for the time being.

"Why does he have to be either?"

"Who else would use the Hebrew term, 'son of a whore', for a registration alias?"

"Who knows? Look at all the Americans in this building. They would know what 'ben zona' means. Those words would be some of the first an American would learn working here. You always learn the dirty words and insults first, they being the most useful."

Chapter 6

The minivan, fully loaded and doors opened, idled beside the convertible. Grace and the kids would be leaving in a few minutes for a week at the lake house. They had stretched themselves to buy it two years ago, but had paid it off with cash from Nick's estate. It belonged to them now, as free and clear as the promise in an early Summer morning.

Kristen came out first, carrying a pink overnight bag with wheels and extension handle. She had her books, some toys and from the look of it, a pair of 16-pound dumbbells packed inside. She strained to clear the threshold of the door and dropped it with a thud onto the garage floor. She took up the handle and quickened her step towards Ben. She smiled.

"Goodbye Daddy. I love you," she said.

"I love you too, sweetie. Will you be good and try to help Mommy while I'm not there? Please listen to what she says and be a good girl, okay? Don't drive her crazy about swimming off the dock all the time, okay?" Ben saw a gleam in her eye when he mentioned the word 'swimming'. At the lake, Kristen tried to speed up evolution and become a fish by spending as much time as possible in the water.

"Grandma and Grandpa will be there too. Can I drive them crazy about swimming?" Kristen showed her mix of baby and big-girl teeth. She had the two big ones in the front. They still had the serrated edges all incisors have in the early days.

"Well okay, you can bug Grandma as much as you want, but she's the only one." Ben and Kristen laughed from the belly. She had his laugh. He bent down and gave her a kiss on the lips and a bear hug around the middle of her chest. Sarah came around the corner with her arms already extended.

"Daddy, Daddy, don't leave yet! I haven't got a hug yet!" She shouted.

"Oh Sarah, I wouldn't leave without getting a big hug from you. Give me your best one, because it has to last two weeks. That's too long for a Daddy to go..." he pursed his lips, putting on his best pout.

He squeezed her in a bear hug and rocked back and forth and from side to side for a little while.

Conquest

By this time, Grace had poured herself a cup of coffee, locked the back door and got in line for a send-off hug and kiss. Ben stood up and grabbed her by the hips. He growled throaty noises. He pulled her close, so that they pressed against each other, but couldn't go into the ol' bump and grind with his daughters both watching. They picked up on everything.

"Goodbye Grace," he said softly, "I put the cooler in the van already and the other things you had stacked up out there. Do you need any more help before I go?"

"No dear, we're ready now. We'll see you on the thirtieth. I love you. Are you going to call? Tonight?"

"No, I think I'll just stay downtown and catch the game. I'll call you tomorrow night. I love you too, honey. Be safe, it looks like rain this morning."

He kissed her. She tasted like salty coffee au lait.

"What are you going to do with your time?" she asked.

"The grass needs cutting. I don't know, I'll think of something, I'm sure. I think I'll mess around with the website I took over. I think I'll disturb some shit. Sound good?" he grinned.

"Is that really necessary? Ben, I don't think it's wise to screw around with those people. The world is full of crazies. I think you're asking for trouble."

He looked in through the glass and saw Kristen and Sarah side by side, their heads moving back and forth as if they were taking in a ping-pong match.

"Let's not fight about this, okay? Nothing's going to happen. This is Saint Louis. We're safe here. Look, people don't follow this like I do. They don't know how dangerous these people really are. I do. I've studied it . People are beginning to forget 9/11 too, if you can believe that, but our trouble has just begun. We're talking about world war four here.

"You say you understand, but I don't think you do. These people are more than dangerous - don't mess with them. They're worse than anything we know – they kill everyone – women and kids included and think nothing of it. Even I know that and I don't pay attention."

"They think killing is good, actually," Ben said, "Their scripture commands them to kill and subdue all unbelievers throughout the world. That's you and me and *them*," he said, pointing in at the girls through the minivan's tinted glass. "How can you say I should forget about it and do nothing? They killed my brother -- the only family I had left. They'll kill the rest of us if they get another chance."

He broke her hold on him and walked around the back of the van, closing the back gate with a thud. Grace shook her head, her pretty face clouded with wifely concern and annoyance. He walked around the back of the convertible and opened the door. He waved goodbye. The two miniature silhouettes in the rear waved back. The driver's window came down.

"Ben, don't have any wild bachelor parties while we're gone, all right? I want the house in one piece when I get back." She stuck out her tongue at him, but then waved goodbye.

The Metrolink train accelerated away from the DeBalivier station bound for downtown Saint Louis and from there beyond the river to Illinois. Except for the occasional group of rowdy teens or drunks heading home from the baseball game or the stray schizophrenic, the train was a quiet, safe and predictable way to get downtown.

Ben's wet shoes squeaked against the black rubber floor. It shined from the tracks of water earlier riders brought in during the morning drizzle. The moist South wind had brought up an uneven gray sky that belonged more to an April morning than middle Summer. He sat next to the window, placing his bag in the empty seat. He unzipped one of the compartments and pulled out his copy of the Qur'an. He opened his laptop, bringing it out of standby. The logs from the website appeared as the monitor blinked to life. He had kept all of the postings to look for the worst offenders to flame and harass. Most of them seemed to be young and foreign, based on the bad English grammar and the use of Internet chat room short cuts- like 'U R noisy and childish'. The majority of it amounted to puerile crap, nothing more than the rantings of homesick Muslim boys needing an outlet for their feelings of frustration and alienation. People were predictable even in their anonymous threats. They would tone the rhetoric down and acquire some balance and perspective as they took degrees and jobs and wives and settled down into meaningful lives. Most of the postings amounted to political masturbation, aimed at the biggest target left standing after the Cold War. Uncle Osama on one side; Uncle Sam on the other. Most of the posters were probably just lashing out at the most convenient target, which was funny since many of them actually enjoyed the benefits of the United States. They protested and vilified the country whose very freedoms they enjoyed while being educated in its universities on oil money grants back home. But Ben knew he was fighting from outside. He was kuffar – a Christian unbeliever. His words would never count to believers. He read *surah* 4, ayat 144:

> "Believers, do not choose the unbelievers rather than the faithful as your friends. Would you give Allah a clear proof against yourselves?"

At best, be could slow the spread of malignancy. Maybe the effort would be worth it if he could delay their success or diminish their chances at victory. Frustrate them – make it difficult. Ben scanned through the text, looking for posts which showed a more mature and dangerous malfeasance.

The train rolled on, picking up speed. The electric motors' whining increased in pitch and the scenery began to blur. He returned to the logs. He debated whether he should put all of this back on the site, since he'd have a two week gap in the blog threads. Someone paying attention would see the difference in his pages and the original ones. He found a post that got his attention:

> Brothers, a good word to you. I have some readings that will be the key to your success on this Hajj.
> 2:289,9:54,5:77,43:29,6:18,63:128,140:21
> for your right hand
> 17:33,16:88,58:247,29:89,36:126,44:92
> for the other.
> An-Nasr

Ben checked his table of contents - again An Nasr , "help" in English, was the 110th *surah*. It said:

> When the help of God arrives
> and victory,
> And you see men enter God's discipline
> horde on horde,
> Then glorify your Lord and seek His forgiveness.
> Verily He is relenting.

He decided to read the *ayats* to see how helpful they were.

Know your enemy, he thought, *the first rule. Understand how they think*. He had trouble with it in practice, however, he could not begin to understand why or how anyone could willingly die while killing innocents for a medieval garden of sensual delights. *Seventy-two perpetual virgins, non-alcoholic wine, an octopus' garden in heaven…* His three college courses couldn't bring him close to that state of mind. He didn't understand the attraction then, but later found out the two 'splendid' things to pagan Arabs were drinking wine and having sex. They would buy an afterlife of drinking and inexhaustible sex. *Sex sells – then and now*, he thought.

He looked at his reflection in the window. Did he look like a Muslim? Hard to tell. Islam is a belief system, not a set of genes. You can't really fault people for their genes. But you can fault them for what they think. A Muslim could look like him, blue eyes, light brown hair – European. They could be anyone. The ideas are the target – not the Arabs or the nation of Egypt for that matter. The difficult part of it all was the *ummah* could be translated as "the Islamic world." A nation sans borders. A belief collective, like communism. How do you kill a set of ideas? And how to you discredit "The Eternal and Unchanging Word of God Himself?" when death is the penalty in this life and eternal torture is the penalty in the next? It would be prudent to say you believe and take no chances – like many in the Islamic world do. He didn't blame them, considering the circumstances.

Ben knew he only had about ten more minutes on the train. He didn't want to investigate this at work – it might not be 'kosher' with all the Israelis around. But he still had a little time to check things out. He thumbed to the end of *surah* 2. He knew this chapter was the first of the 'living' *surah*s – revealed in Medina more harsh than the *surah*s revealed to Mohammed in Mecca. And it was the longest. He looked for ayat 289. The last one had number 286. He double checked. Then he looked up the next four references from An-Nasr. They did have matches, but didn't seem to make sense together. The sixth one, 63:128 had no match in the Qur'an either.

At this point the train shot into the tunnel next to Busch stadium. He looked at the last entry, 140:21. The Qur'an only had 114 *surah*s – the last entry didn't exist. He furrowed his brow and closed his laptop, putting it into standby and slid his books into the pockets of his bag. He glanced at his reflection in the mirror. He could resemble a Muslim, albeit a confused one *They're talking about something in code*, he thought as the doors to the train opened, *they're doing something.*

For a time, he forgot about his thoughts on the train. For a few days he could shed the weight of being father and husband and he planned to make the most of it. He was a bachelor again.

Moments like this were meant to be savored. Freedom didn't come along too often. He bounded up the flight of stairs to the street. He walked the length of an old warehouse, turned the corner and set his bearings on the towers six blocks away. He humped along the broken and uneven concrete sidewalks between derelict loading docks of the old warehouses. Ben crossed the intersection of Clark and 9th streets and bounced along the next couple of blocks, passing people shuffling along, heads cloudy from the weekend and straining to recall the lists, schedules and the minutia they left behind last Friday as they shuffled towards the office towers. Ben felt lighter than usual. He could do as he liked. He pushed along through a couple blocks of bricks and rubble, fenced off from pedestrians. All the old abandoned buildings told the truth. Nothing happens here anymore, thought Ben. Nothing big. Local people still drug out the 1904 World's Fair from time to time, polishing it up like an old grade school trophy that meant something once upon a time. But that summed up the world class events for Saint Louis in the twentieth century. The rest of the time the city busied itself wasting away and turning old buildings into piles of bricks and rubble. *When you're looking backwards at the past you trip on its rubble in the present and ignore your future direction altogether,* he thought.

He started up the next block when a shaggy-looking guy in untied high-tops ran up on him as he crossed the intersection.

"Dewd, what's up? Do you have five bucks I can borrow? Got any change?" He could have passed for a bum if not for the beer gut, the satchel and the company id around his neck. Ike was a full time bachelor, the real thing, and would probably stay that way. His parents had named him Isaiah, but he had gone by 'Ike' since grade school.

"You need money for parking? Are you on the street?" Ben said, reaching for his wallet.

"Yeah man, the lot is full and I don't feel like parking way down by Cupples Station. I've just got to remember to come out and feed the meter every hour and a half."

"Are you sure you want to do that? It you get another ticket, they'll put a lo-jack on your car." Ben reached into his pocket and pulled out the $1.50 in mixed change. They had to stop and wait for the light at Market Street.

Ike wheezed from the exertion of running across the street and Ben's walking pace. He smoked dope and had asthma. He carried extra weigh equivalent to a fetal elephant, like many IT people who spent far too much time in front of a monitor. He stood six feet two and had thick arms and legs. His prematurely gray pony tail, carefully tied in three places was the only tidy thing about him. They had to stop in the middle of the street, waiting for a couple of westbound cars.

"Another day in the salt mines," he said, still out of breath.

"You got that right. At least for the domestics, anyway. The Israelis don't seem overloaded. What do you think they're all doing?" Ben asked.

"The ones who come and go are road warriors. They're pimping the latest revisions and add-ons for the integrated tool suite, you know what I mean? And the new billing product."

"Well, that might be true, but why do we have so many of them coming and going all the time? You know we sell primarily to the Baby Bells and the smaller CLECs. I'm sure that all of the smaller cellular phone companies need attention too -- but we have around thirty to forty different people coming and going at any given time. That's too many for the three big accounts and the other five, smaller accounts we deal with here at the Development Center. What are all of those people doing? Also, have you noticed how many freakin' managers we have blocking the aisles? What are they doing all day? Our Israeli PMs don't manage their groups – they let the American team leads do that for them," Ben said, walking around a fire hydrant.

"The baby bells are big companies. Many middle managers to bullshit with."

"Dude, I just don't see it. It doesn't add up. Most of the guys in the offices don't *do* anything. I never see them involved with any of the projects. They don't keep regular hours either. What the hell are they doing?"

"Well, I do know one thing they're doing. They're taking up some prime parking spaces that I could be using," he was wheezing again.

Ben resisted the urge to suggest Ike needed the longer walks. He didn't want to bring him down. They watched each other's backs in the Development Center.

"Another thing I've noticed is that higher-level people never sit by a window. Do you notice that? People with more seniority or with rank usually get the window seat. Most of our mystery managers take the offices with a door in the center of the building, like that weasel Eitan. What does he do anyway?"

"I don't know, man, but I'm going to enjoy my window seat and its great view," Ike said sarcastically, " As long as they keep sending me a check every two weeks, it's 'yessir' and 'nosir'. Why worry about it?"

By this time they'd made it to the revolving door at the building. Ben entered first and they walked across the shiny period terrazzo that decorated the lobby. The company had spent beaucoup money renovating the red brick Romanesque building and it showed especially well in the foyer. Its style epitomized Saint Louis architecture: massive, Roman, solid and permanent. It looked like a fortress with too many windows.

They flashed their badges at the guard desk. They sat across from each other on the fifth floor, but Ben always took the stairs. He said it kept him in shape, but he wanted to avoid the feelings of entrapment that filled his imagination when he rode in the cable-coffins. He walked up to his cubicle, a window seat with wonderful views of the deserted Arcade and Paul Brown buildings across the street. Ben scanned the floor above him in the Brown building to see if anything had changed again. Ike spoke to him over the wall.

"Are you batchin' it now? How's about I get some guys together and we go over to the East Side and take in the sights? I've got plenty of singles in my wallet."

Ben stood up and walked over to Ike's cube entrance. He kept it like a fire hazard – papers piled up in random directions on every square inch of desk space. The chair had a pile on it, now over two feet tall.

"I can't see the good in spending all that money to come home frustrated."

"What about Rosé?" Ike asked.

"Rosé?"

"Rosé Palm – your old friend?"

Ben laughed like a frat boy at a kegger. "Rosie ain't invited over tonight." he said, grabbing his crotch and sticking his tongue out, "I'm thinking about going to the ball game tonight. You wanna get some bleacher seats? We could take off around 4:30. We'll get the tickets by 5:15 and then we wait over on the hotel terrace across the street and get drunk."

"I'm busy tonight."

"You got a date?" He didn't answer.

"Let's go tomorrow night. Why don't just go in and watch batting practice? I haven't done that in a long time. We can drink plenty of beer in there," Ike said.

"The beer costs too damn much to get a cheap drunk on," Ben said, " It costs $6 a cup this year. That makes it a $50-plus night, with a ticket and something to eat."

"Dude, I never said I was a cheap date." Ike said, grabbing his crotch again, "nobody but Rose ever turns out to be a cheap date." This time he made honking noises while he grabbed himself.

Chapter 7

Ofer bumped his knees on the ponderous battleship of a desk. He mentally winced at the prospect that lay before him. He would have to work out of this dollhouse of an office with the old paper pusher and his unknown handler and would be banging his knees on the desk, comically oversized, for months to come. He had relished the idea of taking a sabbatical during his time in this city. The Clerk had other plans though, as overzealous and ill-fitting as this cursed desk, no doubt. Little men often hid behind big desks and big words. He would play out the hand he was dealt and bide his time. They were looking for him all over central Asia. Probably in Israel as well.

"The world is truly a small place," Eitan began, " Son-of-a-Whore is in this city, right under our noses." His face had the shine that fishermen have when taking pictures with trophy fish. The expression surprised Ofer since all the clerks he'd worked under had shunned anything disruptive to a steady course of paperwork and over-analysis. Different.

Eitan turned to one corner behind his desk and fussed over the slender vase-shaped object sitting on a plant stand. He was putting on a show for the three of them, crowded into the room. With a measured deliberateness, he repeated the same actions in the other corner. He shifted his body around the corner of his desk and pressed a button on the base of the third.

"Ofer, would you turn the other one on?" Ofer started up the final suppressor, protecting the core of the room from electronic eavesdropping. *Fumigating*, they called it. Reflexively, Ofer pulled his chair as far as he could toward the center and the other two fellows from sixth floor Ops stepped up to the edge of the desk, their thighs pinched against its edge while they leaned.

Eitan sniffed for dramatic effect. He began, "We got lucky when he used an Israeli domain registry service. We had them change the data display so that we could see the credit card number he used remotely, in other words, they made the full entry fully readable. With that, the *yahalomin* in Tel Aviv ran the credit card number. We have our man," he glowered in self-satisfaction. "Yes, this is truly a small world after all." He made wide, sweeping gestures.

The insipid attempt at drama had not affected Ofer in the slightest. He yawned, looking at the dents in the desk where the ghosts of knees past had left their marks. The four of them pumped out too much carbon dioxide and made the air close and stuffy. Ofer saw no air vents. *The builders intended this to be a closet.*

"Could you open the door and let some air in here?"

Eitan looked disgusted. "Don't you realize what I'm saying? Our hijacker works here, in fact, he works on this floor, two aisles from that door." He furrowed his eyebrows, which resembled tangled thorn bushes, and pointed his chin at the door.

"So what? We have a great coincidence? What are we to make of that? We're in Saint Louis. Nothing happens here. We're two thousand kilometers from nowhere." Ofer folded his arms and slouched. He wondered if he was still in the cone of silence, not that it mattered.

"Ofer, the Internet is nowhere and everywhere; there are no safe places any longer. We've watched almuminum.org for some time now. As long as it has been up, in fact. It has been a conduit for al-

Qaeda and others. We have a directive to take advantage of the situation at hand. We don't want to disappoint them since this has visibility with the directors." *Always the bureaucrat*, though Ofer, *looking for political approval no matter how trivial and pointless the work.*

"What are the orders? What do they have in mind?"

Eitan paused again, leaning back in his chair, folding his hands and setting his gaze at a point on the far wall.

"They want us to turn this to our advantage. We need to do a cold approach on Ben Adams or manipulate his work to suit our needs. My handler is all for it."

"Our needs?"

"We need to get the logs from the site. We probably have less than a week before they figure out it's fake. That doesn't give us much time for results and you know Tel Aviv *always* wants results. That's why I've brought us all together. We need to come up with a plan."

"A couple of weeks won't buy us anything in this game, Eitan," Ofer said, still looking at the banged up edges of the desk, "we have to work with their timetable, not ours. And we're going to have to deal with the fact that the prime mover is not one of ours. He's an American. Shaping him into something we can use will take longer than two weeks and is usually measured in years," he said, looking up and meeting an unfriendly look of frustration.

"Look, I don't like this any more than you. You're supposed to be good, so prove it. Earn your wages. This could stand in the way of my retirement as well. I came here to serve out the last three years of my career. In my last six months I have to deal with this," he frowned and sighed as if the weight of the world were on his rounded, bony shoulders. "And I have to deal with the likes of you – a 'hot' field agent with nothing but grief for me and the task at hand," he snorted, cleaning the space between his two front teeth with his finger.

"This will be a waste of two weeks," Ofer predicted. He looked up at the other two in the room. Both young Israelis who had come over to see the States and work for Ops on the sixth floor. This office was the clearinghouse for any projects going on in the middle two thirds of the country. The Eastern and Western seaboards had their own crews. *If there were matters that mattered in this part of the world.*

"What do we know about this guy?" asked the taller one.

Conquest

Eitan's expression lightened at the position change in conversation.

"His name is Ben Adams and he works in the infrastructure group. He married nine years ago and has two daughters, aged seven and five. We also have his results from the tests and personality profiles we require as a condition of employment here. The tests indicate his intelligence. So do his performance reviews. He's doing database and systems administration and is helping out the middle tier as well, doing some web work. He demonstrates all the skills needed to run the al-mu'minum site.

As for work, He's been on time and has shown a resourcefulness in meeting his work goals. His personality profile suggests a mild streak of anti-social attitude and disregard for rules, which fits a hacker profile. To top it all off – some of our helpers here who work with him told me this morning that his only brother died in the World Trade Center on 9/11." Eitan paused, a flicker of prim smugness in his expression. He adjusted the gold-rimmed, round glasses that emphasized his cold, analytical demeanor and his angular features. His wooly caterpillar eyebrows were the only thing about him that suggested abundance.

"You're thinking we can make him an asset based on his loss?" asked the curly-haired Ops guy.

"Don't you?"

"It's a mistake to assume anyone will commit treason," said Ofer.

"I survived up to retirement age because I never assumed anything – no matter how insignificant the details," Eitan insisted, "That's why I called the two of you into this. I want you to scan his work equipment. Continue doing so until I give you word to stop. Start reviewing all the logs we keep - phone, email and web traffic. I want a daily report on this, beginning now." He looked at Ofer, shifting his position around the edge of the desk. "I want all packets coming out of his laptop and on any machine he has privileges on to be diverted through Ops until further notice. Ofer, I want you to find a way into his house and set up monitoring. Start cultivating a relationship with him as well. We need to have his cooperation as soon as possible."

"What else do we know about him," asked Ofer, "something we can use?"

"The tests indicate he suffers from claustrophobia."

"No. *Bioleverage*?" Ofer asked.

"Nothing good enough for blackmail yet," said Eitan

"Who are his friends?"

"We're checking into it now. The Israeli he spends the most time with is Dafna. One look at her and you will understand why. She comes from a good family, you see. Her mother is a beautiful woman as well. I worked with her father for many years. Like a brother to me," said Eitan.

Conquest

Scholars agree that all polytheists should be fought. This is founded on [Qur'an 8:39]: "*Fight them until there is no persecution and the religion is entirely Allah's.*"
Ibn Rushd (Averroes) (1126 - 1198)

Chapter 8

-- The Port of New Orleans

The freighter uneventfully docked alongside the quay at Leake Avenue by 3:00 p.m. Abdullah bin Malak al Zalam busied himself in Cansada's three-by-three meter cabin repeatedly touching the bulky leather wallet pushing against the sides of his pocket. He had the recurring thought that it would fall out, leaving him stranded without a false history. He thrust the few remaining articles of clothing into the duffel bag, gathering up the grommets in one hand as he reached for the nylon strap with its metal clip. He put this by the two suitcases and his laptop computer by the door. This last leg on the coffee ship suited him much better. He had no hint of nausea the last three days. Taking a circuitous route starting in the Black Sea, through the Mediterranean and out across the Atlantic had cost him a full season of time and loads of sweat, puke and bile. The rest of the martyrdom operation would be easy compared to the trial at sea. He thanked God for the end of his trials and suffering and pleaded for leniency for abandoning the prayers.

He stepped over the threshold and locked the cabin door. He decided to scout for a means to surreptitiously leave the ship. Although he had stayed in the cabin as much as possible, several times he had the feeling members of the crew watched him, including the one who brought him meals. He pinballed against the sides of the steel-clad hallway as the suitcase grips cut into his hands. He tightened his arm and chest muscles against the strain. The straps from the two bags, crisscrossed in bandolier fashion, pulled down on his light frame. He tried to be as discreet as possible, crouching cat-like up the metal stairs, wide enough to let him pass without bumping his luggage. He began to breathe hard on the second flight. At home imported workers did manual labor like this. His body was lean now, hardened by three months' work aboard the old freighter, but still -- carrying more than fifty kilograms a distance of three kilometers to the safe house would drain him. He needed to be strong and alert. He assumed the worst. Pepito would send his men along and would be watching him. Abdullah needed to make his way alone, as originally planned a year ago.

Knees trembling from exertion, he stacked his load in the deck-level utility closet. He knew he had to move quickly to get off the ship unnoticed, but he would have to rest a bit before making the attempt.

At the deck door, he flattened himself against the edges of the window, looking as far down each approach as possible. He saw no one. The intercom blared out a chorus of Spanish-speaking voices as the crew worked together to bring the ship into final docking. Working with these unbelievers was the one weak spot in the plan. The heroin didn't guarantee silence or success. He prayed the sheik was correct in the risk assessment, *inshallah.*

Abdullah leaned against the railing, taking the weight off his legs to rest them. He looked around for a moment. This great city surprised him, with its many large buildings of industry smoking and humming with a breathing vitality. From this high vantage point, the city stretched out for kilometers all around, smoking and pulsing. The sheik wisely chose this port. It would be a fine gateway to cross from *Dar al Islam*, the House of Islam, where all the people submit to the will of Allah, into *Dar al Harb*, the House of war, where *jihad* must constantly be fought until all religion is for Allah. His laws must rule over all the Earth, as he commanded for all time in the Qur'an.

New Orleans rested at the mouth of the world's busiest inland water way. More than six thousand ocean-going vessels passed through the port annually, he being an insignificant crew hand on one of many overlooked coffee ships from South America. They had Foreign Trade Zone access into a demarcated shipping area where goods came into the country without being immediately subject to the usual U.S. customs regulations. A Colombian ship and Venezuelan government contacts through the narcoterrorists had made it easy to get ashore unnoticed. New Orleans wasn't the biggest port and it deals mainly with the 'neighborhood'. It didn't have the Customs scrutiny of a New York or Long Beach harbor. And it was situated between the targets.

He decided to carry the luggage as far from the ship as he could. Then he'd look for some easier means of carrying the load to the safe house, at least three kilometers into the city.

Abdullah could see two gangplanks being set, dividing the ship's length into thirds. He slid between the upper walkway support and the safety rail, keeping himself inconspicuous. He could see no one along the length of the deck. He smelled the inviting aroma of roasting coffee beans wafting along the shoreline. The smell reminded him of good times with his father, uncles, brothers and cousins sitting on the carpets in a closed circle, dipping their hands into fiery dishes and drinking Arab-style coffee while trading exaggerations, bluster and jokes. If it be Allah's will, he would return to them after this mission. He did not count on this, however. He must succeed in this, no matter the personal cost. They would sing his praises over that coffee with or without him and this thought comforted him well enough.

He gathered himself there and after a time Abdullah decided that the bow-side gangplank had the least activity.

At this point one of the dockside gantry cranes dropped a container suspended about three meters off the deck. Shock waves from the impact ran the length of the rail Abdullah leaned against. Crew members rushed all around and Spanish babble poured from the intercom in a rapid stream. He had his chance now.

He opened the doorway and stepped inside in one, fluid movement. He stopped for a moment, focusing on the stairwell for any indication that others might be coming up to help with the accident. He heard nothing but the tinny scratching of the intercom system. His movements rushed but mechanical, he hoisted the bags around his shoulders and grasped at case handles, jerking them up simultaneously and forcing his neck tendons to jump at the effort.

He started to open the door, but pulled back hard on the handle when two ship hands ran past, towards the stern. After a couple of seconds, he tried again, this time scuttling along the wooden planking under load. He sat the weight down where the stern deck opened up. Looking around he saw no one. He picked up the cases once again and made it to the head of the gangplank. He stepped up and began his descent. Most of the workers in the marshalling yard had gathered around the problem crane. The others passed him with complete lack of interest, looking instead to the stern of the ship and the container hanging over its edge, where the railing used to be.

Abdullah bin Malak al Zalam muttered a Thank-You. He smiled, greatly strengthened by God's intervention. Allah would see him through. He humped along the quay in the direction of the city, sweating and breathing hard – the latest immigrant in a long line of immigrants. Like many nameless hopefuls, he had come to this great country carrying everything he had in his hands and on his back. But he differed from the immigrants before him in one important way.

He had come to destroy the American Dream, not fulfill it.

Chapter 9

"*Shalom*," Avi Cohen said from nearly halfway around the world. Two or three other members of the development team joined in. Ben waved at them, framed in a panel of his monitor.

"Okay – I will see you all tomorrow afternoon. Thank you," he replied. Thought it was only nine a.m. local time, they had put in a full day due to the eight hour difference and from the look of it most wanted to go home. It was good of them to schedule the meeting at the end of their day, he thought, since they all needed to coordinate their tasks for the upcoming code release and he was the only American involved in the project.

"Now, Ben, you have three items to take care of today, correct?" Avi reminded him. He sat at the end of the table, directly facing the web camera. Ben had a web camera at his desk. He and Ike were the only two in the development center to have them so far, besides management.

"Yes, I have them written down here. I'll finish them today," Ben said.

"The control tables are the critical item. We won't be able to progress tomorrow without the changes."

"You'll have them. Don't worry. I'll get the modules checked in and compiled as well, don't worry," Ben said. He liked the web video meetings better than the conference calls. Some of the Israelis had thick accents, the Russian emigrants especially, and seeing them speak and gesture helped Ben understand them better. "*Shalom*, Avi, have a good evening," he said.

He closed the web cam application and finished up his notes. He ranked the tasks in order of importance, estimating it would take the rest of the morning to get the control tables synched up using the scripts. He decided to get another cup of coffee before getting into the work.

He stood up stretched, fixing his gaze on the building across the street. He focused on a double-hung window, not directly across, but one floor up and two windows to the left. He'd been watching that window for about two weeks now. The building had been vacant for years, but one evening he had to work late and stayed after sundown. He thought he had seen movement, but wasn't sure. Behind all the street grime and dust the old, wide-slat Venetian blinds haphazardly blocked a clear view of the interior. Those blinds had been moving that Thursday, he was sure of it. Subtly moving, as if something had brushed against them from the side, causing them to pendulum back and forth in a way unlike any breeze would cause. It wasn't a breeze. All the neighboring windows were still intact. And he had noticed a light source more than once. Nothing near the windows, but a dim, dusky light farther back, like from a hallway or an interior office. It seemed random but it made him curious. Did someone finally buy the building? What were they going to do with it? Downtown St. Louis had been through bleak times for the last twenty years.

He went out to get a cup of coffee. He sat down again. He took a manila folder out of his laptop bag and went over the items for his family's trip to Disney World again. He just needed the Park passes and they would be ready to go. The rest checked out correctly. Then he began the long process of synchronizing the control tables.

His stomach growled. He put the final changes in and looking at the clock in his task bar, noticed it was past lunchtime.

"Ike, are you busy? Have you eaten yet?" he asked.

Ike mumbled something unintelligible. Ben walked over to the cube door and from this vantage point he could see Ike hunched over his keyboard, pre-occupied in the unorthodox three-finger pecking he did.

"You want to get some lunch now?" Ben repeated.

"Just give me a minute."

Ben returned to his cube, shuffled some loose papers into piles and locked his terminal. He took another survey of the windows over on the sixth floor but came up empty-handed.

Ike's head popped up over the cube wall, "Okay, man, let's hit the road. Where do you want to go?"

They walked down the aisle, passing Eitan's door on the way to the magnetically-locked glass doors at the end of the hall when Ben realized he'd left his badge on his desk. Getting back in would be a major pain in the ass since he would have to sign in twice and get a temporary card.

"Look, I'll just meet you downstairs, all right? I forgot my badge." He felt better taking the stairs, anyway. He heard Ike coming after him.

"Wait, I'll just come with you. I need to take a piss." He stopped off at the men's room. Ben walked down the aisle into his cube. He opened the drawer and the badge in his pocket. He turned to leave but noticed his disk drive chattering. He looked back over his shoulder. The green LED blinked rapidly. He turned around, confused.

Ike came out the door to the bathroom and walked to the end of the aisle. He saw Ben staring into his cube.

"Have you been paged?"

"No, come and look at this."

Ike walked down and peered over the cube wall. He looked at the PC, still chattering away.

"Did you push a patch or something before we left?" Ben asked.

"No, I was working on the latest virus update, but I didn't send it out." Ike did the LAN updates for the corporate desktop via SMS.

"What the hell is going on?"

Ben sat down and unlocked his computer. He brought up the Task Manager, clicking on the 'processes' tab. A program named aitx32.exe was taking up 67% of the CPU. Ben looked up at Ike, confused.

"What's 'aitx32'? Is it something you guys do?"

"It's nothing I know about. Dude, you're being scanned."

Chapter 10

Ike had left Ben in the middle of lunch because of a page from the system. Ben knew it had to be something critical, since Ike would never willingly choose work over food. Alone, Ben slowed down, chewing more carefully as he looked around. The day had been made-to-order: sunny, not too humid and the blue sky dotted with those round, puffy clouds the kids liked so much.

Conquest

Dafna from work walked up on him. She was Israeli and smoking hot to look at, but good to talk to as well. Interesting. He really enjoyed her company.

She asked Ben if he'd like to take the long way back and naturally he agreed.

They strolled along Kiener Plaza, down in the shady area along the sunken waterfall. The shade and the water made the air cool. He liked taking these walks with her because she made it cooler. He liked spending time with her and walked close to her, leaving only a few inches of space between them as they strolled along.

"Well, so many of Life's problems could be avoided by just staying in bed, don't you agree?" he said, grinning crookedly and keeping his gaze on the mounds of blue and pink hydrangea blossoms, some with heads as big as cauliflower.

"Are you bullshitting me again?" Her elbow nudged against his ribs, more like a caress than a jab. "If we all stayed in bed nothing would ever get done. Besides, staying in bed can still cause problems -- for women anyway. Babies for one thing." She sent an exaggerated look of annoyance his way.

He laughed. Then said, "Yeah, but does anything ever get done, really? Have people really changed over the last five thousand years? Why don't we all just call a general bed-strike until we can agree on how to get along? Maybe John and Yoko had it right after all." His mood had turned philosophical since discovering the scan just before lunch. It ruined his appetite, "I don't see how we can change things in the Middle East. People in this country have the idea that people in countries like Iraq and Syria actually want democracy. They think that if we help set up a Western-style representative government that suddenly everything will change. Well, they've been doing things the tribal way for millennia," He looked at Dafna, walking alongside him with arms crossed under her breasts, a look of consternation on her face, "but I'm sure you know that already. People here don't realize that the majority in the middle east doesn't want a democracy. Democracy is western and therefore evil. We are the devil to them. Western style rule of law is man made and therefore against the commands of their god. Islamic law is what they want: The *shar'ia*, the body of Islamic law set down by Mohammed and the clerics after him. They don't realize that Islamic law is antithetical to Western law. In the *shar'ia* the rights of the collective, the community of Muslims; in other words the *ummah* is protected from outside threat. No concept of individual rights can be found in it."

"You know a great deal about this…" Dafna said, "Have you been studying it?"

"I took a couple of semesters on middle east culture, the Qur'an and the *shar'ia* during the lost years of my college days," he said.

"Why did you study that back then?" she asked.

"I didn't want to get out of bed," he said, chuckling under his breath, "I had a policy I called 'No Classes Before Ten in the Morning', and one semester it was the only thing that satisfied my prerequisites after nine-thirty. I liked to sleep in after all the partying."

She furrowed her brow and shot disapproving glances at him.

"Well, a teaching assistant from Iraq taught the course and it was pretty easy and interesting enough. That guy was in the physics department and earned room and board by teaching the course. For all I know, he probably ended up working for Saddam Hussein's nuclear program. But I got A's and the three courses were mid-morning. It worked out well."

"What did you talk about?"

"Middle Eastern history and culture to start; then the Qur'an, *Sunnah* , *Ahadith*, and the *Sira,* or Mohammed's biography. We finished it with *Shar'ia* as the final course."

"I assume he did it with a positive spin -- you know about kitman and *taqiyya,* yes? *Taqiyya* is 'Approved lying to advance the Cause of Allah' and kitman is the concealment of Islam's true agenda from the ignorant, " she said, "I hope you didn't take much of what he said at face value."

"Well, I did back then. But I've been doing independent research since they killed my brother," he said.

She turned slightly in the direction of the flower beds, bending to get a closer look.

His pager buzzed. He checked the warning, noting that he would have to increase the index tablespaces for one of the main application accounts when they returned to the office, but it wasn't an emergency at that point.

Conquest

"You know you're right about *shar'ia.* It hems the people in, choking off any hope for progress or improvement in their condition," she continued nosing the florets, speaking into them as if into a large pink microphone, "they continue to live in deplorable conditions. Sadly, their hate allows them to live on very little. But the resentment of the west and the hatred continues to flourish. I don't know what the solution would be, but I know democracy isn't in the list. Democracy won't elevate people by itself. It is the set of individual rights and a sound judicial system that does it. Votes don't fix problems. Case in point: Hitler was voted in democratically."

"That's true – but you know Dafna, over time that system will lose. It is losing already. The world will become even smaller and more connected. Any culture or belief system that keeps people in a box and restricts their lives will fail eventually. You can't keep people in a box so easily anymore and Technology, Progress and History will ensure that. They are the Pandora's box for tyrants and mullahs."

"The whole system is doomed to failure," she said, "you can't set a tent pole in the ground and say 'nothing beyond this time is valid'. Like one of your sayings: 'Time and tide wait for no man.'"

"Well, I agree with you, but unfortunately 1.2 billion people don't. That is the problem. I wish we could wait for Islamic culture to fix itself, but we don't have the luxury of time We're at a point in history where a small number of people can kill vast numbers of people. This hasn't been possible in the past. We're at a truly dangerous crossroads – where seventh century hate meets twenty-first century weapons," Ben said.

"I have to guess that many Muslims feel this or know it on some level. Islamic culture fails by any rational measure. People living in it see the inadequacy on a daily basis. They try to compensate by aggression and domination like school yard bullies. Or blaming others. They have too. Criticizing the system will get your killed. They're trapped. They can't change the system or the ideas behind it. It is all infallible, immutable and eternal – that is how they are taught. As Muslims say '*Talabe ilm ba'd az wossule ma'loom mazmoom* - The search of knowledge after gaining it is unnecessary'. How are they going to break out of that mind control?" she said.

She moved away from him to the next hydrangea bush, blooming in a mix of blues and pinks. She reached for one that seemed to be a mix – almost purplish.

Ben thought about what she said. He had been reading the Qur'an and commentary. He had researched the *Sunnah* – the words and deeds of Mohammed. What he found repulsed him. He realized no one around him knew it and how dangerous this ignorance would be. He had decided to make a stand against it. That was the main reason he hijacked the website, that and the fact that those same words had guided the terrorists who had guided the planes into his brother's building on September 11, 2001.

"I've been researching this since my brother died," he said, "People in the U.S. don't realize we're at war with a culture – not a state or a terrorist network. This is different from the wars our young country has fought up to now. But Western Civilization should remember its past. Fighting Islamic aggression isn't a new thing in the world. Not enough Western people realize this yet and the leadership isn't being forthright about it." He continued: "When you're at war, cultural or otherwise, the main goal is destroying the enemy's foundation, right? That means his factories, bridges, fighting forces and, most importantly, his reason for fighting in the first place. Islam itself is the foundation of the culture we're fighting. It gives the enemy reasons to fight and the justification to do so. The creator of the cult-ure, Mohammed, ordered his followers to use his life and words as *uswa hadana* 'a model for all time.' Allah told followers that Mohammed was *al-insan al-kamil* 'the best of men to be emulated by all Muslims.' If Mohammed practiced his example today he would be in prison. By any definition he was a pedophile, for God's sake, as well as rapist, a war criminal, a slave trader and a murderer to name of few of his crimes. He saw the Arabs as the 'best of peoples' and was as bad as any white supremacist you care to mention, including Hitler. In fact, Mohammed killed a higher percentage of your people within his grasp than Hitler did."

"I know," Dafna said quietly. Her eyes welled up and she jerked her head in another direction.

" I'm not making any of this up, as you know. It's all there in the canonical texts of Islam – in the *Sira*, the biography of the prophet and in the *Ahadith* – the reports of the sayings and doings of Mohammed. And his followers set this immoral, criminal example up on a pedestal to be emulated for all times and in all places -- like the words of his god, Allah, in the Qur'an. This belief system is far more dangerous than any terrorist or the entire worldwide network of terrorists. After all, al-Qaeda means 'the base.' Mohammed's example and the Qur'an are the basis for all the killing and hatred and fighting coming from the Islamic *cult*-ure for the last 1,400 years. It's this base which needs to be discredited and destroyed – way more than al-Qaeda the terrorist network. Words and ideas are far more dangerous and longer lasting than the latest group of religious thugs. Osama bin Laden is nothing special: he had the money to put a network together and did his time in Afghanistan as a mujahedeen. He pulls justification from the Qur'an and from the words and deeds of Mohammed. He's a regressor with money – a reactionary with money - not a great thinker or hero of the people. He's just the latest implementer of the Example of the Prophet, that's all. When he's dead other men will continue to rise up with the Will To Power provided in the Qur'an and by Mohammed's example, until this 'base' – the true and eternal 'al-Qaeda' – is not longer seen as valid or desirable. "

"They say Allah has ninety-nine names. But you-know-what is not one of them."

"Right. It can't be. The god of the Qur'an and the god of the Bible cannot be the same. All you have to do is compare them – you don't have to believe in either one. They are not the same entity. They can't be because they contradict each other. Anything calling itself a religion and elevating murder and suicide to 'holy' acts can't be worshipping the same god as the Jews and Christians."

They stopped in front of the last mass of blooming fury. He reached for a large, pink head of florets on the fullest Hydrangea, leaning over to take in more of its faintly musk-sweet scent. She did too. Ben spoke first.

"I think it's best to compare Islam to other totalitarian systems. It is a self-reflexive body of religious, political and legal ideas that rejects all others. And it's intentionally static. It hasn't changed for eleven hundred years. You can't change it to suit the times. Innovation is a sin in the law and the religion. But it's not really a 'religion' after all. It's a political movement bent on world domination which wraps itself in the cloak of religion. I've studied it. It's a jumble of contradictions with no context and is a third rate attempt at plagiarism. A lot of the religious material in the Qur'an is from pre-Talmudic Jewish sources, not even the old testament. And it's garbled in many cases. The Christian ideas come from heretical, apocalyptic gospels like Thomas – uninspired and rejected for the Church's canon. Most of the rituals come from a jumble of old pagan practices. They are designed to condition followers into submission and yes, this is another clue for us. The word 'Islam 'comes from the Arabic word for 'submission' -- not 'peace' as the spin doctors would have you believe. The word 'Salaam' means peace and that greeting is good from Muslim to Muslim only – it is never supposed to be given to an unbeliever. To most of us the word Peace means 'living cooperatively or harmoniously'. To the True Believer of Submission, Peace means 'When All Religion is for Allah', in other words, when Muslims dominate the world and no other religion can be practiced. Same word – but funny how the meaning differs. Tolerant western people project their concept of Peace onto the Islamic culture. Another fun fact – oppression to a Muslim means 'Open Disbelief Against Islam.' Allah and the prophet both told the faithful 'oppression is worse than killing.' So – leaving the religion or speaking out against it is a worse crime than manslaughter. Look at Saudi Arabia if you need living examples of this."

"Okay – I've had enough," she insisted, making slashing motions with her arms, "Let's not spoil the rest of the day trying to solve the world's problems. Do you think we're the first people to realize this?"

" I agree, this is one of the best days of the year. The problems will still be there tomorrow, unfortunately."

"You know, I was surprised by how green this country is when I first came over. I think I will miss that the most when I return home." She looked pensive now and the pink in her cheeks, which had matched the hydrangeas, faded away.

"Why not stay here as long as you can? Fighting and constant trouble is all Israel has to offer now."

"I'd like to have a family someday, you know." She said, beginning to walk again. They had to get back to the shop now. Her coal-black hair shined as they passed through patches of sunlight. She gathered it up, her hands adjusting the tortoise-shell clip at the back of her head. Her lithe movements intrigued him, down to the way she straightened her hair.

"You don't have to go home to find someone, you know. I'm sure many single men would be interested in someone as beautiful as you." He meant it.

She stopped, tried to suppress a smile and thanked him by flailing at him with playful slaps.

"Shut up," she beamed, "now I know you're bullshitting me. Can't you be serious for once?" Like she wanted him to stop. She didn't. "Besides, fighting and trouble are everywhere now, not just at home."

"Ain't that the truth..." he trailed, looking off in the distance. His expression grew darker and more distant. He thought about his brother.

"I'm sorry, Ben, I didn't mean to remind you," she said understanding what she had done, "I know what it means to lose someone you love."

"That's a cold comfort," he said.

They walked on a little further in an extended silence.

"Things will never change," he said, "every spring these flowers come up and the earth keeps turning and people keep hating and killing. We never learn. We never get past the same tribal aggression we've shown since the first monkey man picked up a sharp stick. Is this the best we'll ever get? Our weapons keep getting more destructive and efficient but we never improve," he said, his voice becoming raspier as he spoke. His jaw and fists clenched. He stared at some point on the horizon, past the buildings in front of them.

"Ben, all we can do is keep living and try to make a difference." She tried soothing him with the tone of her voice.

"What can any of us do to change the way other people think? Meaningful change comes from the heart. It's personal and individual. No amount of rational argument or concession changes a fanatic's belief. Meanwhile innocent people like my brother and your Nir die."

"What can I do? I want to make a difference. But what can any of us do to reverse fourteen hundred years of history? I'm just a computer dork from Saint Louis. I've never amounted to much anyway. At best I inconvenience the fanatic bastards. I can't change the way they think and feel. The day my brother died in those towers, Dafna, I knew he was in there. And I kept working that whole day. Then I went home and all I could do was sit and watch those towers crumble over and over."

She stepped in front of him, facing him. She put a hand on each shoulder.

"You have a good heart and a clear mind, Ben -- two things most men lack. You are so much like my Nir, you know it? And both you and him have that same stupid, crooked smile," she said, touching his lips. She had a good heart too, with a hole in it to match his. She knew how it was. "You and him are very much alike..." her voice fading off like a minor key at the end of some sad, silly love song.

Conquest

Ye are the best of peoples, evolved for mankind,
enjoining what is right, forbidding what is wrong,
and believing in Allah.
If only the People of the Book [Jews and Christians]
had faith, it were best for them: among them
are some who have faith,
but most of them are perverted transgressors.
Allah – Qur'an 3:110

Chapter 11

It took only two blocks to convince Abdullah bin Malak al Zalam to lighten his load. He felt the roll of money in his front pocket and thought about hiring a cab. He rejected the idea because he would have to get close enough for the driver to have a good look at him with all of his bags would attract attention. Instead, he struggled up the broken sidewalk in the neglected commercial area. Every so often trucks passed by, splashing muddy water onto his work clothes as their tires bounced through the potholes. He needed to get out of the costume as soon as possible since it linked him to the shipyard. Pepito's men could easily pick him out of a crowd as he looked.

Fatigue began to slow his pace and he knew his limp would get worse the longer he had to carry the load. This could slow him down enough to jeopardize things. Breathing hard, he sat for a moment, a steel case on each side. He felt the blood returning to his forearms, which had already began to cramp and lose their strength. He rested up against the metal building, cursing as he checked to see the oxidized paint working into the streak of sweat running along his back.

He grasped for a way to improve the situation. He scanned the area, looking for anything that might help him carry his things. Just then, he heard a metallic crashing sound. It came from behind him, a short distance off. He lowered his head, turning it enough for a peripheral glance. He put his hand on the Glock 17 Pepito had thrown to him on the boat. He squeezed the trigger enough to prime it. Then, he shifted his eyes as far as he could without turning his head. He saw a lone figure tottering along. Thinking it safe, he looked directly at his target. It was an old beggar, pushing a steel shopping cart over the shards of sidewalk. Abdullah hit on an idea.

He put a cigarette in his mouth. He ambled down the broken path, clutching at his shirt and coughing. He couldn't tell how old the greasy bum was but he could see the fellow wouldn't put up much of a fight, obviously in poor condition from drugs and alcohol. He got close enough to get hit by the wall-smell of fermenting piss and the rank, medicinal smell welling up from the beggar's breath.

"Could I get a light?" Abdullah asked slowly in his clearest English.

"Yeaas." The bum did his best to focus his jaundiced eyes at him. His hands tremmored as he lifted them off the cart handle, fumbling through what remained of pockets on his jacket, which from the look of it, never left his soiled body.

When both hands found pockets, Abdullah wheeled his arm as hard as possible, striking the length of his gun squarely across the miscreant's right temple. His eyes rolled completely yellow and he collapsed like a pile of shit-streaked rags. Abdullah looked around, seeing no one. Satisfied, he rummaged through the cart, tearing a piece of two-ply plastic sheeting from the tangled mess in the cart. He wrapped it around the bum's wrist. He had never touched pigs or dogs in his life and he didn't intend to start now. If he touched a kuffar he would be ritually unclean later and the prayers he needed most would not be accepted from him. He needed valid prayers now.

He drug the body, bloated from years of abuse, but surprisingly light for its size, into the breezeway between the two closest warehouses. The thought of taking some of the clothes crossed his mind, but he rejected the idea, they being *najis* like the thing that wore them. He would rather risk being spotted than put any of them on himself. He snarled in disgust at the heap under him. He spat on the infidel as he stepped over his belly, missing his face but landing on the putrefied jacket he had considered wearing.

He began sorting through the items in the cart, stacking the two trash bags full of aluminum cans at the entrance to the breezeway. He threw the filthy blanket over the two bags. He piled the rest of the unrecognizable things in the gaps between the bags and the walls of the buildings. This would hide the body, giving him more time to put distance between him and this place. Whether the damned fool lived or died mattered not. It wasn't really living anyway.

He kept an old collared shirt from the cart and the plastic sheeting as a protection for his things, which were stacked against the chalky blue building. He loaded the cart and began to push it, wheels bouncing wildly along the uneven sidewalk.

Conquest

He made decent progress pushing the cart along Louisiana Avenue despite the standing water, the fallen tree limbs and the condition of the streets and sidewalks. No one had given him so much as a look as far as he could tell. The storm that had caused him so much worry last night as he boarded the coffee ship had been a strong one. Its wind had blown down tree limbs and scattered trash all over the sidewalks. The rain had not drained away in this area; instead it filled the sidewalk holes and softened the earth to the point where the narrow, plastic wheels of his cart failed to move with ease. He had to use most of his weight to plow through the muddy spots. This delay concerned him. He tried to minimize his conspicuousness by mussing his hair, streaking it and his face with mud. He washed the beggar's shirt in the muddy water of the street to rid it of its rancid smell and clean it. He thought it telling that gutter water was preferable to its previous stench.

Everything along the way indicated rampant corruption and weakness. The street ran North/South and from what he could see offered nothing but rot; it being a collection of abandoned buildings separated by either trash-filled lots or the occasional slum house. Along its length, many buildings had partially burned, having large flame-shaped dark streaks rising upward from each of the boarded-up windows and doorways. The sidewalk had heaved up in jagged slivers at the base of the live oak trees. The trees themselves grew wildly, without purpose. The storm broke many of them, putting large branches in his path and forcing him out into the road. He passed abandoned storefronts faced in crumbling brick and also small, three- room shotgun shacks, with bad roofs and raw cypress clapboards. Some of these looked inhabited, based on the brightly colored plastic toys strewn around behind sagging chain link fences in front of the shacks.

He had passed two corner markets, with bars on the windows and doors and the many garish neon signs promoting alcohol. The customers all seemed either young and stupid, babbling and carrying on like idiots or were broken, weakened, disgusting cousins of the thing he had left for dead two kilometers back. *This place will collapse on its own*, he thought. *We'll just be helping it along, just speeding things up a bit. The people are weakened by lack of purpose and already diseased by this way of living. We have nothing to fear from them.*

He pushed his cart along, frequently repositioning his hands to avoid blistering. He had the hands of a programmer, soft from lack of manual labor. Getting to the safe house would have been much easier according to the original plan. Pepito had made that impossible, but Abdullah decided he should arrange for the second heroin delivery in spite of the trouble Pepito had caused. It didn't matter to him how these pathetic losers died, whether by his hand or by their own. Let them kill themselves with alcohol, drugs and senseless violence - fighting among themselves. They condemn themselves by their own actions. He would enjoy helping them along; this was his duty in fact.

He broke out of his thoughts, encouraged to see he had reached Magnolia Street. The safe house would be down to the right just a few blocks away. *Almost there.* Strengthened, he pushed along with a purpose uncharacteristic of the bum he played. His relief prevented him from realizing he had to pass through the belly of the beast.

Abdullah noticed all the buildings began to look the same -- the dung brown tinge, the foot-worn lots and groups of people idling about. At some of doors, he saw small brown and black children pressing grimy hands and faces against storm doors. Shopworn women, their heads wrapped in plastic caps or curlers, laconically surveyed the desolation. He had a hard time telling which of the buildings were occupied. Nothing of any value could be found on the grounds. Neglected cars and aged oil spots lined the curbs.

Now he realized he would have to walk past a group males shouting and making ape-like gestures at the next corner. He kept his head low, fixing his gaze at the moving spot three meters ahead. He kept gripping the handle with both hands, but mentally practiced how he would pull the gun out from underneath the shirt and estimated how much time he would need, calculating the distance he needed to keep from them to pull it off. He had only made it through a quarter of the C.J. Peete housing project, known to its residents as The Magnolia, as it used to be called and for the road which sliced through its middle. In the city center, it had grown over the years to 1,400 badly-tended units, less than half filled by this time. Its residents called themselves 'soldiers' having earned the title by surviving the day to day, black on black cycle of violence, drug use and squalor. They didn't take kindly to strangers as a matter of policy. Young punks in the neighborhood harassed and beat up bums like the one Abdullah claimed to be as a matter of course.

Conquest

He could see they had spotted him. Their demeanor changed. The body language more conspiratorial. They shifted their attention to his progress. Three of them talked among themselves while approaching him, looking at him with a mix of world-weary disinterest and malevolence. Abdullah rehearsed drawing the gun in his mind. He would avoid a confrontation if he could. He worked to keep from showing the anger welling up inside.

They walked up on him with hollow swaggers, their shoulders back. They looked down their broad, dark noses at him. Abdullah continued to play the fool for the time being, acting as if unaware of their approach.

The middle one, draped in a coordinated acid-green Phat Farm ensemble, spoke first. He seemed to be the leader.

"What up, muthafukker? Where y'all going in such a hurry?" He smiled, his grille showing more gold than a Bedouin wedding. He thrust his hands in the oversized jacket, out of place on a steamy New Orleans afternoon.

Abdullah didn't say anything. He looked up at Phat Farm, but keep his attention peripherally on the other two.

The one to the left wore a pair of ragged overalls, with only one of the straps in working order. He had a navy do-rag tied around his head and a brand new pair of Nikes on his feet. He kept shifting his attention from Abdullah's face to the poorly hidden baggage under the plastic. Even with the grime and use, the transparent sheeting still allowed a good look at the cases. They reflected too much light to be inconspicuous.

"My nigga axed you a question. You deaf, boy?" the one in overalls said.

Abdullah considered several options in the short space of time. He didn't want attention, even here. He didn't want to kill anyone in so public a place. If he had no choice, he would but it would ruin his plans. The safe house being a mere two or three blocks away would be at risk if the authorities got involved.

"I'm going nowheres," Abdullah said in the best raspy mumble he could manage. His throat was tightened and dry from the adrenaline. He moved his right hand off the handle, bringing it up in fist to cover his pseudo-cough. He didn't think Overalls had a weapon, but he guessed that Phat Farm did. The fellow acted like he could back it up without a doubt.

Phat Farm grew angry.

"I didn't hear you muthafukker. What you doin' in Magnolia? We don't 'llow no trash here. You bring down property values." He laughed, throwing back his head.

The third one, to the right, looped his thumbs into his back pockets, which hung way down the cheeks of his rear end. His ill-fitting denim pants hang too low, showing a good measure of his tightie whitie underwear. He wore no shirt and had a large hair pick coming out of side of his nappy hair, 70's style. He wore a cross as gaudy as Pepito's, and another comically oversized silver plated slave chain necklace, this one with a kilo's worth of scrap silver hanging from it in the shape of the dollar sign. He joined in.

"What you got under there, boy? Let's have a look-see."

Phat Farm stopped the cart's progress with his foot. Abdullah took his other hand off the cart, stopped and looked directly at Phat. *I'll shoot him first,* he thought, *then the other two if they don't run away.*

The one in overalls tried to remove the plastic. Abdullah reached out and grabbed his wrist. He pulled it back, cursing. The situation grew worse. He wouldn't have much time to stow the cases in a safe place if it he had to kill one of them. He would have to run with the cases and leave everything else behind.

"What's in your cart, boy? You don't look like any 'Nawlins street trash to me. What you got in those bags?" Phat Farm said, grabbing the cart with one hand and tearing at the plastic with the other. He was still brazen, but the other two started showing the feral caution of jackals. They smelled no fear from him.

"Get away from me. Walk away from here now. Just let me pass." His detached deliberateness spooked Overalls and Tightie-Whities even more now.

Phat retorted flashed a menacing golden smile. "You don't talk like no local trash neither. What you playin' at?"

Abdullah wiped his mouth, coughing again. He scratched his muddy cheek, keeping his hand close to the opening of his shirt. Anxiety had left him with the rush action provides. He would pull the gun when the leader started speaking again.

"Hand your shit ov--" Phat stopped as he looked into the empty, blank eye of the Glock's muzzle.

"Do you want to die today, brothers? Make your choice now." Abdullah leveled his piece at the green 't' written across Phat's jacket.

"Now look here, you crazy fucker, we just playin'," Overalls said.

"Jus' hold on now. Hold on!" said Phat, raising his hands up to jaw level, "What the fuck you doin'? It's all in fun, now, get real." He stepped back, stumbling a little as the plastic caught his heels. He didn't fall though.

Abdullah snarled at them. He considered killing them regardless for wasting his time, pathetic as they turned out to be. Put any of them in harm's way and they crumble. He squinted his eyes, his body tensing for the fight.

Phat pulled out a beaten-up, stubby revolver. He extended it sideways, like a gangsta in a Hollywood flick. His expression was resolute, but with the end of the pistol visibly shaking.

"I let you live if you let me leave. Fair enough?"

The threat seemed to diminish them. The two followers showed the unmistakable look of fear in their eyes, which darted back and forth between the two guns.

"Aw right, you crazy sumbitch, you right. We're on our way. Simpson, let's get the fuck outta here. This shithead got nuthin'. Put that nine away. I'm outta here, dawg." he shouted out of the side of his mouth, not taking his eyes off Abdullah.

"Now. Go!" Abdullah said, knowing he had the upper hand.

Phat chucked the pistol into the muddy patch between the sidewalk and the street.

Abdullah turned the gun slightly in the direction of Overalls and began waving it at him to chase him off, but they hadn't had enough yet. Tightie -Whities wind milled his left hand out from his back pocket. He gripped a do-rag tied up around a roll of quarters. It struck Abdullah's gun hand on the wrist with a wooden thud. Abdullah cried out in Arabic reflexively grabbing at his wrist with his left hand. In pain, nevertheless he regained composure and dropped to his knees, behind the protection of the cart and over the top of his gun. He picked it up with the left hand, just as the Phat kicked the front of the cart, crashing it up against Abdullah's cheek bone. He saw stars and struck his head against the ground. He pushed himself back to a sitting position to see the three of them reach the corner, carrying his two personal bags which had been on top of the stack. He sighted the one with the laptop bag over the barrel of the pistol as he scurried off towards the row houses. He loosened his finger when he realized he still had the stainless steel cases. They are the only things which matter, he told himself. Let them have the rest. I will still be able to carry out the plan without them, he thought. He pulled himself up by his good hand, staggering slightly from the blow to the head. He shook his head to clear it. He decided he should leave immediately, seeing several watchers from the houses recede back into the darkness of their open doorways when he looked at them. He doubted any of the frightened creatures would be so bold as to call the police and even if they were, the police might not be quick to come anyway.

He straightened himself, gathered the plastic sheeting in a heap and dumped it into the cart. He winced as pain shot up his arm from the wrist, now swelling and working up a multi-colored bruise. He leaned into a push to get the cart started. He appraised himself. He could finish the walk. It wasn't far. But he had to be sure no prying eyes followed him to the mosque. The cart rattled louder with the lighter load. He looked around in a 270-degree sweep and saw no one in the doorways. The children, being day-to-day soldiers, had had enough sense to make themselves scarce at the first sign of trouble. He lifted the front wheels over the broken edge of gutter and set off down Magnolia again, with about four blocks of brickbrown slum barracks to go. He pushed on, ignoring his pain and keeping constant vigil for spies and onlookers.

Conquest

"A man came to Allah's Apostle and said,
"Instruct me as to such a deed as equals Jihad (in reward)."
He replied, "I do not find such a deed."
Hadith Sahih Bukhari, V4B52N44

Chapter 12

He woke up with a start, not sure exactly where he was. He heard the muffled noises of water falling through pipes and then he remembered. He had spent the night in the lower level of the mosque. The *iman*, a pudgy and rather dull-witted man had been forewarned of his coming through contacts and had put together a semblance of comfort for him. Anything – even a musty pallet and scratchy blanket – seemed an improvement after living in the wretched rat hole of the last months, with its fumes and its threat of fevers and accumulated filth. He had disembarked two days earlier than planned and three days before the rendezvous. He needed to send al-Warraq a message as soon as possible. He laid still, trying to gather some intelligence on the house and trying to make a plan. The idiots he had almost killed yesterday had stolen his laptop. He needed to find a public computer someplace. He could find one in libraries, schools or internet cafés. He just needed to send a short note to speed up the timetable.

He walked up Magnolia Street at a deliberate but unhurried pace. The distance was a little more than a kilometer from the mosque to the Rosa Keller branch. The imam had given him a change of clothes. Not that it would arouse attention, but the shirt hung limply over his frame, at least a size too large. It was a standard blue oxford. The *imam* donated a pair of pants which Abdullah cinched up around his waist with an old black belt he had punched several new holes in. He wondered if he could truly trust him. The old fool wouldn't deliberately work against him, but a slip of the tongue was all it took. He had been in one situation already. Abdullah cursed the thieves again for good measure. He thanked God for having gotten him out of the situation with noting more than a knot on his head and a stolen computer and bag of clothes. He still had his two traveling companions.

He casually scanned everything along the route. Nothing alarmed him. He came within sight of the library. A mother with a child at each arm walked through the double doors, which automatically opened for them. He could see inside now. The mother struggled a bit to get both children through the detectors, having to pull them together to pass through. Abdullah hesitated a moment. He wouldn't be able to walk through a metal detector with the knife and gun he carried. He studied the device for a moment, comparing it to some of the detectors they had worked with in training. It didn't resemble any he could remember, so he decided to risk walking through. He didn't want to be unarmed at any time now.

He walked up to the reference desk and took one of the computer cards. The sign said :

"Internet use limited to 30 min. if others are waiting. Thank You!"

He would need less time than that. They didn't require proof of identification and one didn't have to sign a log sheet. The *imam* had given good advice.

Abdullah sat at the end of the rectangular table so no other users could see his screen. He opened a browser window and typed in the URL www.almuminum.org, looking around him before clicking 'Go'. Aside from him, only two other people were working from the table. An older, grizzled man with metal-frame glasses taped at the nose and a pasty, plain looking woman with short-cropped hair which needed combing. He calmly looked to either side looking for any potential trouble. Satisfied, he brought up the site he had created and worked on the last couple of years. It looked good, he thought. It was his best work after all – the sum total output of his professional life. He got the commission to build and maintain almuminum.org from one of his Saudi supporters, may peace and blessings be upon him, before he had taken up the jihad in Afghanistan. His benefactor had continued to send him money through the many Taliban coming and going the next year and a half. He had been glad to get the work and took pride in the site, since it became well known and well used by the brothers. He felt satisfaction in making an important contribution. He had returned to Saudi after his injury, and mulled about the empty shopping malls and coffee houses with the rest of them, having no purposeful work. He had made the sacrifice to go abroad for a technical degree, but he became angry and frustrated, seeing his life a waste. No one in his country needed his technical expertise aside from sites like almuminum.org and living in the West would have been untenable.

He went back through the listings, searching for the thread with the key. He couldn't find it. It should be on the site by now. A sense of dread sprouted at the pit of his stomach, rising and grabbing hold of his heart. Abdullah took a deep breath and tried to calm himself. He clicked around the site quickly, looking for any indication of what may have happened.

He changed his view of website into the source HTML. He searched for his account name, ArRad13 in the jumble of characters. He found nothing. How could this be? He owned the site. He opened a telnet session and banging desperately on the keyboard, he tried to connect to the host server's IP, which he had memorized. He connected. He sighed, burrowing down through the directories to get to the text pages. They weren't there. He went up a couple of levels and did a listing of files. Nothing. He let out a low involuntary groan. He rested his elbows on the edge of the desk and his hands, trembling with rage, rubbed the permanent bruise on his forehead – a sign of honor on one who prays intensely five times a day. Then he tried by IP number and port. Rejected. He connected to the site by name and it worked. *May they suffer an ignominious death, one and all*, he cursed. He felt The Others staring, labeling him, looking at him as if he were a worthless animal. He wanted to beat the old man sitting closest to him, the one who stared at him, slack-jawed like an ass, senseless. His anger came out in a flash an for a moment he lost control of himself, cursing loudly in Arabic. But then a quiet voice welled up from the inside, telling him not all was lost. Not yet. He had to remain calm for a time. He would have his day, God willing. He connected to the almuminum.org site as a regular user. *May Allah's curse be on the thief, he muttered under his breath.* He saw most the site intact but the key information had been removed. Nothing mattered on the site but the key information. Somehow the thief knew this. He feared the Jews had found the Uzbeki and erased the keys. Or was it one of these? He looked around. *You can't outwit God* , *you fools*, he thought. *Allah ta'alla knows best. And you certainly won't outwit me either.*

He began to log the same entry in capital letters at the bottom of each thread:

THIS SITE HAS BEEN TAKEN OVER BY AN INFIDEL, AN UNBELIVER. YOU ARE BEING DECEIVED BROTHERS. LEAVE THIS SITE NOW: IT IS BEING MONITORED BY THE YOUR ENEMIES.

His labored breathing returned to normal as he systematically exposed the evil deed. He didn't realize that the banging of the keyboard, punctuated by guttural noises, his muttering and cursing along with his wheezing had attracted the reference desk librarian. Patrons in the stacks a good ten meters away had frightened looks on their faces. The librarian, a slender man of thirty approached him, his gangly arms and legs tenuously swinging from a stiff torso. He stopped a little farther than an arm's reach away.

"Sir," he said, "um, if you continue to make a scene I'm going to have to ask you to leave."

"I apologize, I am overcome with emotion. I just learned my brother has fallen ill back in my homeland." He had minimized the al-mu'minum window, leaving only the NetMail account visible."

"I'm sorry for your loss sir, but I *will* have to ask you to leave if you continue," he bleated. His face had a look of concern while he shifted his weight back and forth on his heels as a young boy does when he needs to piss. Abdullah could see that confrontation made the book boy uncomfortable.

"I will, forgive me. I will be leaving shortly anyway." He concentrated on his delivery and dropped his pitch by an octave. " May I have another five or ten minutes? I need to write a letter to my mother, may God bless her. My brother will die soon and I need to send her instructions. In my country it is the men who take care of such things, do you understand?"

"That's fine sir, you have my sympathy." The bookish man turned and ambled over to his guard shack, looking back nervously at Abdullah once he sat down.

Abdullah knew he didn't have much time. Navigating as efficiently as he could, he accessed the other account and brought up a blank email. He didn't have the time to go through protocol by sending a coded message. He looked over at the book clerk, who glanced at him and then looked at his watch. He couldn't afford to make a scene. Too many had noticed him already. He felt the weight of the Earth on his shoulders. The mission had been preempted unless he could get help from al-Warraq. He couldn't fix this by himself now that he had no laptop, that was certain. He typed this note and left it in the Drafts folder, according to the practice.

> ArAzahad,
>
> The website has been compromised and I can't find my keys. I need your help immediately. My hajj will be finished it we do not find them. It will all be over.
>
> I can't search myself right now. I am not safe here. See what you can find out. May God help you in this.
>
> ArRad13

He imagined the worst of all scenes: his brothers, cousins and father all gathered in the closed circle around the dipping dish, their white *thobes* and checkered *gutras* fluttering in the warm western desert wind. They all smiled and nodded, waiting for the exquisite details of his glorious exploits. He would have to say the words. He had been tricked by the Jews and the unbelievers. He had failed God and them all. His failure impugned the honor of his family. They would spit on him and strike him on the head for it. He would be dirtier than dung, lower than a hateful Jew -- if that were possible.

He shook himself from the nightmare's grip and blinked hard. He logged himself out of NetMail and removed his web site history from the browser, as well as any temporary files and cookies he collected. He stood, returned the queue card back to the reference desk. He studied the librarian. He saw no deliberateness to him. He didn't think it would be necessary to return later and kill him. As he walked out, his mind rested solely on the terrible position he and his life's mission found themselves in. He walked as quickly as he could without being obvious. He had much to do and needed the imam to point the way to a less public computer he could use to hunt down his enemy and recover the keys. When he did, either he or Hassan al-Warraq would make certain the fool paid for his mischief a thousand times over.

Chapter 13

While on the train home, Ben Adams decided what to do with the blog gaps on almuminum.org. He would update the postings with the last few weeks' entries except for the thread with the strange numbers, which he planned to investigate further.

On the way home he picked up a sack of tacos and burritos for dinner. He parked in the garage for a change and went in through the back door. He had turned up the thermostat to save on air-conditioning and the air felt dampish and too warm, but since he would be downstairs most of the evening he didn't change the settings.

He pressed the button on the answering machine and the artificial voice warbled "No messages." It was an older model AT&T 1717, but Ben saw no reason to replace it. He had great fun with its 'room monitor' feature sometimes when he listened remotely to the goings on of Kristen and Sarah. He'd ask them about something they had done or said later when he came home. They thought he had magic "Daddy ears", like an eavesdropping Santa Claus.

He gathered up his food, the laptop and a couple of cold beers and went down to his office. He opened one of the French Doors and the smell of Dutch Rubbing compound from the oak trim wafted out toward him. Ben had used some of Nick's estate money to finish the basement. His office had oak veneer wainscoting with real trim and an inset bookcase, pushed back into the storage area at an interesting angle. One wall had an oversized gas fireplace in it for those cold mornings in winter, when Ben would need to take the chill out of the air as he worked from home one or two days a week. The salsa-colored walls added to the warm glow of the oak trim. He felt a calming stimulation from being in the room and knew it had been money well spent.

He sat the bag of burritos down next to his work laptop, which he opened and fired up, along with his wife's laptop and the custom PC Ike had put together for him. He connected the work PC to his five-way 100 Meg network switch. He pulled the web page over to the desktop PC and updated the logs and pushed them up to the web site. He double checked himself by hitting the site through a non-privileged account. He didn't see any discernible gap in the posting dates now.

He opened one of the burritos and generously shook cayenne pepper sauce all of the entrails of his first burrito. He folded it back up and took a healthy bite. He held it in one hand while scrolling the mouse wheel with the other.

He needed to figure out more about the guy who posted the numbers. an-Nasr had used cyzchk235@netmail.com. Ben logged into NetMail through his wife's laptop and created a new account with bogus information. He opened a piece of spam from his working NetMail account, copied the contents and subject and sent it to the cyzchk235 account to verify. In a few minutes he'd receive notice back if the mailer daemon couldn't deliver it.

He logged into the almuminum.org site as an administrator. He pulled down a copy of the traffic log. He began searching it, using the timestamps from the thread to narrow the search. He stopped at March 24th 2:47 AM – the time for the first entry. He cut and pasted the IP address into a notepad window. He changed the search to the next timestamp in the log and then the next, each time saving a copy of the IP addresses until he had them up to the entry with the fake Qur'an passages. He started with the last one first, putting the command 'tracert' in front of the address. Various IP addresses came back with the number of milliseconds it took for each hop. He hoped the command would take him back through all the servers the blog entry had traveled through to see where it had come from.

The screen began to fill with lines of server names and access times. He could see it pass through four servers in the U.S., then it made a couple of hops in Germany, then one in the Russian republic. It added another server name with the suffix 'uz' for Uzbekistan. It stopped.

stlkeipu1024-17.123.250.23 reports: destination net unreachable

Unreachable. It couldn't get through the firewall. He tried again with the same result. Hands still on the keyboard, he looked up at the ceiling tiles, searching his mind for a workaround. He didn't know much yet but he did know the post came from somewhere in Uzbekistan…

Chapter 14

By the bottom of the fifth they had made a mess of it. Mounds of empty peanut hulls littered the stadium concrete all around them, cracking under their feet. The Cardinals had also been making a mess of it, trailing by at least two runs the entire game. Ben and Ike gradually shifted their focus from the field to the beer. They had each stacked four empty 20-ounce cups as they took in the scene from the right field bleachers and had downed another three during batting practice. It was the eve of the vernal equinox, the longest day of the year, and the sun stubbornly sat at the edge of the Busch stadium cornice, which cast arch-shaped shadows onto the edge of right field. It was one of the best evenings of the year and Ben and Ike were enjoying it without reservation. They had been in the park since 5 p.m., finishing each overflowing cup of beer before it had a chance to grow warm. They had pretty much crossed the line into the wasteland at the bottom of the third inning.

The whites and reds in the uniforms of the hometown boys of summer popped against the deep greens of the outfield grass, still looking healthy as the wilting humid heat began in for the summer in the city. For the moment everything seemed fresh and bright and the dog days weren't yet on the calendar horizon. One of the best evenings to be at the ballpark. Ben leaned forward in the hard red plastic seat, stretching for a view of the right fielder, taking warm-up throws before the bottom of the seventh. He propped his wobbly head on his right arm, supporting it on his leg.

"It looks like the Cubs are gonna choke again."

"Yeah, thank God for the Cubs," Ike said into his cup.

"You got that right," Ben said. He straightened up a little and said, "Hey man, I need you to help me out with something,"

Ike belched in the form of a question and looked over at Ben.

"Will you help me crack some NetMail accounts?"

Ike jumped a little, this time spilling a shot onto his jersey. He slyly looked around. Everyone was either busy getting drunk or was preoccupied by the game.

"What did you say? I don't think I heard you right." He lowered his voice to just above a whisper. It cracked from overuse and the dryness of all the beer. "Did you say you want to crack some accounts?"

Ben leaned in as far as he could with beer breath. "Yeah, I want to get into a couple of accounts. You're a veteran, right? You could help me out with that, right?"

"Didn't your mother ever tell you cracking is illegal?"

"My mother died ten years ago. Email wasn't exactly a household term back then."

"Dewd, what's so important that you want to risk jail time?" he had an incredulous look on his face, "Here's a little brotherly advice – don't mess with it. The Feds are gettin' serious these days."

"I don't have a brother anymore to give advice, remember? My brother came down in pieces on September 11th. I was one of the 'lucky' ones. The found enough of him for a positive ID. All along, we'd been praying and hoping that maybe he'd been somewhere else that day. After a few days with no word we'd hoped that maybe he survived , but had a head injury or was in a coma or something. You know, something like that was better than the alternative. But we got the call a couple of months later. They found his hand with his Phi Beta Kappa ring still attached, remember?"

"Look man, I'm just trying to be a friend here. I know about all that – you told me. I'm just trying to keep you from doing something stupid."

"Stupid? Wanting to punish these asswipes is hardly stupid. They deserve all the trouble we can give them. I took over a website that's full of that fundamentalist tripe and that ultimately killed my brother. Someone posting on the blog is up to something -- I can tell. Can you help me or not?" He turned his shoulders toward Ike, challenging him.

"What're you going to do if you find what you're looking for?" Ike asked, looking at the bottom of his cup as he tipped it up again.

"Somebody will be interested in what I find, I'm sure. What about the Feds? I'll take it to them and lay it all out."

"Look, knowing them what they'd do is prosecute your ass and put your evidence in the circular file. Don't risk it man; haven't you lost enough already? Just get on with your life. You've got a good one. You're my hero, you know that? You've got it all. You've got on of those vacuums... what do you call them?"

"You mean the central vac?" Ben said.

"Yeah – you've got your central vac and the cute wife and kids and the house in the suburbs with the white picket fence. Why do you want to start some shit? Let your brother rest and get on with the good life. You've already got a damned good one. The way I see it, you need to get your shit together and do some long range planning and take care of the people who are counting on you – your wife and kids. You can't bring your brother back and you can't change the world. It's fucked up. It always has been and it always will be. Just focus on what you've got; your life is better than most, don't you see that? Look at me -- nobody's waiting to hug me when I come home. Nobody asks me how my day went. And my idea of long range planning is deciding what I'm going to do on Friday night. Do you want that?" Ike said, shuffling his feet in the mound of peanut shells under their seats.

"I hear what you're saying but some of my 'good life' comes from my brother's estate. He put a lot away as a single guy trading bonds those last years. He had no time to spend it. The market bubble kept him too busy making it. But I've got all the time in the world. My good life comes at the cost of my brother's life. I owe him big time, for that and for being around after my father died. I was messed up for a long time after that and he was the only one who gave a shit besides my mother. Now they're all dead. I don't have any family left," Ben said, adding, "And paybacks are a bitch."

Ike looked at him for a few moments, then took another long draw from his cup. He wiped the suds from his ill-trimmed beard with his forearm. He sat there, a wild-looking man, more a Moses in the Red Sea of Cardinals shirts than an Isaiah.

"What about Grace and your kids? They need you. You're talking crazy, dude."

Ben didn't say anything. He appeared to be deliberating.

"Are you sure you want to do this? You could be putting yourself into the eye of the hurricane if the F.B.I. finds out."

"Yeah, I've thought about it – just show me how to get into the accounts – that's all." Ben sat on the edge of the seat, elbows on knees and looked towards Home.

"NetMail... that should be easy enough. When do you want to start?"

"After the game. Why don't you just come on over?" Ben leaned forward, satisfied for the moment. He took off his cap, wiped his brow and then stood up and made his way down the row for his last bathroom break. Ike watched him with a mix of annoyance and apprehension.

"Well, what do you think now that you've seen it?" Ben asked, after having shown Ike the blog messages between ArRad and ArAzhad and the note with the misnumbered Qur'an quotes.

"Something's definitely F.U.B.A.R., but I doubt anybody's going to give it a second thought. Especially the suits at the F.B.I."

They sat next to each other behind the mission-style desk in the womb-like security of Ben's home office. Ike sat in the driver's seat typing away rapidly on the keyboard of the custom PC he had put together. Ben had his laptops and Ike's connected up for a total of four on the network.

"Some things never change. Bureaucracies don't want to change. The F.B.I. may change, but it's going against its own culture and if it does change it's going to happen on a geologic time scale," Ike said.

Ben opened his beer and took a little swig as we walked over to the French doors. He opened them both. In about ten minutes the room would have been a hothouse with all the PC fans running.

"I think you're wrong," Ben said, "We see dangers in the world better than before 9/11. And the F.B.I. should be trying to make up for lost time. It knows it looked ineffectual in the aftermath. It had tips about some of those guys but didn't do much to keep tabs on them. How sad for all of us." Ben had began to realize he and most of the people in the U.S. were ignorant of how the rest of the world saw things. His brother's death had changed that. He knew firsthand the world was full of toxic people and hateful violence and this began to bring out the worst in him.

"What makes you an expert on dealing with the F.B.I.? You're complaining like you work for them," Ben said, walking back over to sit and watch The Master. Ike laughed and connected to one of his NetMail accounts. He had three other windows up; one to UNICEF, another, something Brazilian by the Portuguese on the screen and a third server somewhere in the United States.

"Why are you connecting to charities?" Ben asked.

"Non-profits have little money for security and that makes it easier to break in. I keep accounts on these and many other servers, " he said, "I keep a little progie out here for purposes such as ours."

"Yes, master," Ben said, aping homage.

Ike brought the cracking tool down from the Brazilian server into the two-cpu hotrod that was Ben's desktop, which functioned very well as a website with its fixed IP address. It could handle a surprising amount of traffic.

"NetMail can be compromised without knowing an account's password. You simply have to know the account name and have to have enough patience and CPU to brute the individual message tag numbers," he explained, while typing, "We're gonna get a valid URL from my account and then change it to suit the target account. Which one do you want to try first?"

"Let's try ArRad13 first. It seems to be the focal point for everything."

"Okay, we cut and paste the URL from my account into a new browser window like so." Ike clicked the buttons on his mouse, moving the legitimate address into place. "Step two: we alter the message tag to some other nine-digit number. Next, we change the part of the string with my account name to the target account name." He highlighted that part of the address, deleted it and then typed in 'ArRad13'. "Finally, we change this part of the string," he removed another number and typed in '59'. I think this part is a number from zero to fifty-nine. Something the NetMail boys use to keep track of things."

With the changes in place, Ike clicked on the browser's 'Go' button. The page refreshed itself, but didn't show anything useful.

"We're going to have to try a bunch of combinations, aren't we?" Ben said. The failure didn't surprise him.

"Of course. Getting the valid message numbers is total guesswork, but that's where Daddy's little helper comes in." He looked over at Ben and grinned. He fired up the cracking tool, updated the target account name and brought it up. It worked in tandem with the legitimate account, generating the long URL strings and putting them in the address box and then automatically trying to connect. The page started blinking rapidly.

"Now this will be slow going. It will only be able to try about three combinations a second."

"But, we can parallelize this right?"

"Yes, we have four PCs here. We'll get a session going on each." We can also use the three servers and start multiple sessions on each of them. I'll set their displays back to the big boy here and then it's just a matter of time."

"How many sessions can we start on the other servers without being noticed?"

"I wouldn't do more than ten per server. That puts us at forty – and that's 120 attempts a second." He brought up a calculator and found at that scale they'd get 432,000 attempts an hour. *Impressive,* thought Ben.

"What's going to happen if we get a hit?"

"That window will stop on the message. You can only read the messages. The button links on the page won't work. If you click on them it'll bounce you back to the account you're working out of."

"That's some heavy stuff, dude," Ben said.

Conquest

Ben looked at the clock. It was already past one a.m. but they didn't have to show up for work later, being early Saturday morning. The NetMail windows kept blinking and the clicking sound coming from each attempt because a steady humming nuisance. Hot air spilled out of each PC as the work forced the fans on.

"Look man, I appreciate this immensely. Thanks again. It's getting late, you know, if you want to crash here tonight – no problem. We keep the bed in the spare room made up."

"Yeah thanks bro, I wasn't looking forward to the drive home," Ike said as they shuffled out towards the stairs.

A Plague on Both Houses

"If you gain mastery over them in battle,
inflict such a defeat as would terrorize them,
so that they would learn a lesson and be warned."
Allah – Qur'an 8:57

"Little do you remember My warning. How many towns have We destroyed as a raid by night? Our punishment took them suddenly while they slept for their afternoon rest. Our terror came to them; Our punishment overtook them."
Allah – Qur'an 7:3

Chapter 15

The steady hum of the midrange servers enveloped Hassan al-Warraq as he sat behind the cluttered old desk, pushed to the far corner of the Data Center. He had worked many nights in the dingy old university building and he echoed its threadbare decorum in his non-descript tee shirt and tattered blue jeans. His face, unnaturally sallow in the dingy florescent lighting, had a sour look that matched his stomach as he scraped the greasy litter from his meal into the old trash can. The trash hit the bottom of the can hard and reverberated across the room from the drum-like elevated floor. No one heard it but him. He worked alone most nights and this suited his purpose. He looked around, sniffing like a marsupial at the zone wafting from the server racks --a night hunter in his nocturnal niche.

He closed up his financial textbook and placed it on top of his backpack. He'd registered for two difficult classes in the shortened summer session had the load began to weigh on his mind. He wondered why he bothered, after all, he would be leaving this place altogether in just a matter of days. *I should be resting*, he thought, *I would be a fool to walk into this operation half-asleep*. He needed his wits about him if he were to come out of it successful and unscathed.

Now he began his real work.

At two-thirty a.m. only he and the machines were awake. He brought up a browser and logged into the NetMail site they used. Connected, he opened the new message, surprised to see it in clear English. The idiot had broken protocol. Reflexively, al-Warraq looked toward the door to make sure no one could approach while he read the note. Satisfied, he began to read it. He would have to leave in a few hours if Abdullah had sent the word.

His jaw slackened underneath the ill-kept scrub that passed for a beard. "This can't be true," he cried out in Arabic. His movements spasmodic, he put his head in his hands and stared at the screen. His mind raced ahead to the inevitable conclusion. The whole effort would be lost now. For a moment, he had the selfish thought that it would be for the best. He wouldn't have to risk his future for this plan, with its dubious outcome. But he had committed to it by an oath of fealty to the sheik and his loyalty, once decided, couldn't be changed. He thought about the danger the virus-like spread of Western corruption posed to his way of life. The *ummah*, the Islamic world, was hurting from the onslaught of this Western culture and had none of the economic growth that supposedly made the influx of filth palatable. Nothing to compensate for images of scandalous women and such trash flowing into the street shops and markets and on television. The people still had no jobs and no future. Only al-Qaeda and the Brothers stood in the way. They and the *imam* back home railed against it. Hassan joined the fight when he saw the struggle framed in its real terms -- the peoples of the East could not work out an agreement with the West. But it went beyond the world of men. No compromise can be worked out among men when Allah has been offended. Allah's slaves and warriors cannot and should not bargain over His will.

Several years ago, Hassan had put aside worldly ambitions and left for training as a Taliban with the *imam's* blessing and the encouragement of his family and village. He had prayed up in front, beside the imam on the day he'd left to join the Brothers in Afghanistan. After training, he set out for the United States, coming in on a student visa in 2000. He had learned more on the night shift with all the power at his disposal. He needed to use that now. The martyrdom operation depended on him alone. He paused for a moment, formulating a plan. He took a couple of deep breaths to try and calm himself. Stretching his neck from side to side, he began systematically search through all the known domain registry sites.

Al Warraq had been working non-stop to identify the hacker. He was hunched over the desk by six a.m., his eyes and hands the only animated features in an otherwise haggard state of mind. It had gone quickly at first. After 20 minutes of searching, he had found the hacker's registry service. al Warraq had not been surprised to find that the hacker used an Israeli registry service for the almuminum domain. He kicked himself for not looking there first. Of course he used one the Jew sites. To his surprise some idiot had left most of the account registration data visible to the world. Al Warraq could see the credit card number the thief used and the expiration date. He thanked Allah for the help. Having the number would make the hunt much easier. In fact, with it only one obstacle remained in his path. He needed to match the number to a billing name and address. He kept looking through records on the servers he had cracked over the last two years at Northwestern, trying to find a match on the credit card number.

He broke into the network for one of the major charities and began sniffing around. He had UNIX accounts on many servers by now. He'd be collecting them during his time in the Data Center, preparing for a situation like this for a long time, having cracked accounts in the networks of many corporations, U.S. and otherwise. He had points of entry into the insurance and charitable industries as well some telecoms and other assorted industries.

He went to the servers with test databases first – since the security was more lax and since they used subsets of production data most of the time. He had been trying this approach for hours now. Test systems were easier to get into... He checked the binary set and to his delight they were running Oracle a version 8. He knew that in cases like these some of the default accounts had dba level privileges and at the same time had simple passwords. Most Database Administrators wouldn't bother to remove the accounts or change the passwords in a development database. He checked it out, typing:

```
sqlplus dbsnmp@oradev358
```

He put in the default password when it prompted him. The first thing he did was use the dba-level privilege to create a superuser account – like 'oracle'. He switched himself over and now he could do anything he wanted. He first did a query to see if auditing had been turned on.

No auditing. Good.

He queried the data dictionary for links, cutting and pasting them into a text document. He then checked them against the tnsnames.ora file, the server's listing of known databases, and found an entry for a production database. Good. He would be able to use this link to access the production database if he couldn't find the data he was looking for.

Conquest

The rush of another success boosted his morale and straightened his back.

He scanned the entire development database, but didn't find a hit. He would have to access the real dataset now. He picked the link to production which he guessed would be the primary account and then connected to one of the tables using the link from the development server.

It worked.

He queried the data dictionary to get the DDL, the description of the table and column structure for objects in the main application account schema. He found 'Cred_Card_No' in the Donations and Donor_Main tables. He sent another piece of SQL over the link to extract any rows matching the credit card number from the Domain Registry. He didn't know how to narrow the search by date, so he did a full table scan. After what seemed like minutes, a single row came back to him.

donation_id	date	cc_no	exp_date	amount	donor_id
2341234709	11/09/2001 17:35:02	4555121200530032	02/2005	1000.00	76349335535

He rose out of the seat, throwing his arms skyward in exaltation and shouting for joy. He had him and it had taken him less than a night! Hassan al Warraq had saved the mission. He and he alone. He congratulated himself and laughed triumphantly. He thought himself unstoppable. Then a fountain of guilt flowed over him. Give Allah the praise! He had shown him the way. He had sustained Hassan through the long night – it always came down to His will after all. *Inshallah.*

Hassan's mind extruded an orgasmic wave of endorphins and the night's tension left him. He slumped back into the chair and dropped his limbs like so much dead weight onto the torn armrests, dingy at the pressure points from the body oils of many before him.

He ran another query against the Donor_Main table, using the donor_id as the key.

```
select /*+ parallel(donor_main, 8) */ donor_id
,substr(lastname,1,25)
,firstname
,addr1
```

```
,city,st,zip
,ccardno
,to_char(expdt,'MM/YYYY')
,don,btype
,phoneno
,donations_since
from Donor_Main where donor_id = 76349335535
```

He put a hint into the query to get the database engine to run eight parallel processes on the server to speed up performance. In less than twelve seconds he got a hit:

donor_id	Lastname	Firstname	Addr1	City	ST	ZIP
76349335535	Adams	Benjamin	6052 Waterman	Saint Louis	MO	63112

CCardNo	ExpDt	Don	BType	PhoneNo	donations_since
4555121200530032	02/2005	25	APos	636-555-1212	2001

He sent query results off to the printer, exited the servers and closed out all incriminating windows. He needed rest. He checked the time, noting six hours had passed and congratulating himself. He would sleep and dream after taking care of two last things.

As he worked out the coded message he thought, Blood type *A positive, eh? All the type A positive in the world will do nothing to help you once we pay our visit.* He finished the message, logged into the NetMail account they held in common and copied his message into the Drafts folder. Logging out, he closed all incriminating windows as he thought . *You are counted among the tormented of hell and I'm going to send you there post haste.*

He no longer felt tired. He decided to hack the almuminum website instead. At least until the next student showed up. On a Saturday, it was hard to say when that would be.

Chapter 16

Ben got out of bed easier than usual. He had slept lightly, waking up every couple of hours and wondering whether the cracking program had hit on anything. At six-thirty he finally decided to get out of bed. He took a shower, got dressed and put a pot of coffee on. He didn't hear any stirrings upstairs. He had no idea how long Ike would sleep in, but it didn't matter on a Saturday anyway. He planned to spend most of the day doing some house cleaning - tearing down the tangled web of hate and stepping on the cockroaches. Just like the old days, when he and his roommates would come home from the bars and turn on the kitchen lights, exposing the cockroaches and squashing them as they scattered back to their dank holes and cracks.

He bounded down the stairs and pushed open the study doors with anticipation. A blast of greenhouse air rushed out to greet him. The fans from all the machines were still blowing hot air off the motherboards. The excitement had him fully awake now, unusual this early in the morning. He swiveled around in his chair and grasped a mouse in each hand, moving them to bring a couple PCs out of screensaver mode. He adjusted his weight forward in the seat, leaning closer to the monitors. He saw a couple of opened email messages and the quick success encouraged him. The header on the first one read From: ArAzhad33 - To: ArRad13! He smiled and chuckled to himself. This was going to be easier than he'd thought.

He opened four more windows and pointed the parameters at the other account, ArAzhad33. They started running like before, blinking at a furious rate. Even so, brute force still took a long time to guess a valid string. He wanted to open up more windows, but deferred to Ike's experience. After all, Ike had been a hacker of some reputation out in California, going by the handle Cap'nSafT in reference to his time as a junior high crossing guard. He told Ben he had promoted himself to Captain in cyberworld since he'd taken so much shit from the kids at school. He had started his career as a Phreaker, riding the PacBell network. At the advent of the personal computer, he had cajoled his parents into getting a Trash80, the Tandy TRS80, one of the first commercial PC clones on the market. He told Ben behind the Trash80 he'd felt like he had come home for the first time in his life – that he'd found his place in the world.

After that, Ike had plunged deeper and deeper into the ether, lurking on bulletin boards and swapping boasts, lies and tips with the ever-growing subculture of kiddie hackers bent on world domination. But for some reason that he never mentioned, Ike had walked away from the love of his life. Ben didn't press for an explanation it didn't really matter. Ben guessed that he had gotten into some serious trouble and left it at that. In fact Ben had had misgivings when he decided to ask Ike for help. But Ben knew Ike could help him and would do so because of their friendship.

Ben was hungry. He climbed the stairs to get some breakfast and let the machines do their work.

Ben was sitting at the oval-shaped kitchen table finishing his second bowl of Lucky Charms when Ike shuffled into sight. By his body language, he was fighting a raging hangover, worse than Ben had. He slumped down into the Windsor chair opposite Ben and laid his head and all the ponderous prematurely gray hair on the table. He let out a groan and scratched himself.

"How'd you sleep?" Ben asked.

"Like the dead."

"Like *The* Dead, the Grateful Dead?"

"Funny dude. Believe me, there's nothing to be grateful about."

"How do you feel?" a sly smile pulled at his mouth.

"Like the dead," he mumbled, working his grizzled jaw against the cool, hard surface of the table.

"What do you want for breakfast?"

"Nothing... I don't think I'll be eating for a while, man."

"Draft beer can wreak havoc on a man," Ben said, "but you know, I don't feel too bad this morning. You know what? We got four hits on the ArRad account already."

"Yeah. Great." Ike said, trying to sound enthusiastic.

"You look like a train wreck – you want some coffee?"

"I think I can manage that, yeah." Ike said, not moving. Ben got up and walked past the breakfast bar counter, with its tan and black speckled granite top. They had redone the kitchen after Nick died, putting in custom cabinetry and a center island with a flush cook top on one side. A large verdigris metal rack hanging over the island suspended copper pots and pans of various shapes and sizes along cooking tools and implements of destruction, like the meat cleaver, dangling over the coffee pot. Ben looked up at it. He moved it to another hook away from the coffee pot. He didn't know why Grace kept putting it there, threatening him like the sword of Damocles every time he found it there. Was she out to get him? He laughed. He liked to tell people he had no life insurance to make sure he was worth more alive than dead.

Conquest

The kitchen looked really expensive, but it wasn't for show. Grace took cooking seriously and she never failed to come up with something imaginative and delicious. She had never disappointed Ben with her cooking, even when they had been first married. She could get away with anything in those honeymoon days – a box of macaroni was top shelf as long as she boiled it before serving. She had grown light years from then and continued to push her frontiers to Ben's gastronomic delight.

Ben poured a tall cup of black coffee for Ike and refreshed his own. He walked with measured deliberateness to avoid leaving stains on the Italian tile work. He was trying minimize the clean up he would need to do before Grace and the kids came back.

"Here you go. Hey, do you want to do down and have a look at the notes?" Ben said, "And I still haven't showed you my site. Do you think we can parallelize the search some more since we have three accounts to target?"

Ike grunted affirmatively into his cup, so Ben went down to the office and brought up all of the monitors. No new hits this time. Good things take time and patience. He opened up a window and connected to almuminum.org. He heard Ike flushing in the powder room upstairs, and then the heavy treads of Ike's bare feet and the creaking of the handrail as Ike lowered himself into the basement. Ben picked one of the newest threads and started looking through it.

"It's over," Ben said in a mix of shock and disappointment.

"What's over, dude?" Ike said, still not fully coherent.

"They've found me out," Ben said, a twitch of panic in his voice, "Look at this!"

Ike blinked a few times at the screen, bringing his eyes into focus:

THIS SITE HAS BEEN TAKEN OVER BY AN INFIDEL. AN UNBELIVER. YOU ARE BEING DECEIVED BROTHERS. LEAVE THIS SITE NOW: IT IS BEING MONITORED BY YOUR ENEMIES.

"It's ArRad13 again," Ben said, "This sucks!" He pounded his fist on the desk and the loudness of it caused Ike's stressed nervous system to involuntarily jump.

"You can still have fun with them anyway," Ike said, pulling up the home page in its native HTML source code. He typed up a couple of lines which would display "Hacked, Tracked and Hijacked by the good people of the U.S.A." in 48-point type and alternating red and blue letters. He worked fast. "You got any gifs or jpegs of the flag? I think we need to plant the flag on this foreign soil." Ben showed him to the directory and Ike put in the text which would bring up a four inch animated flag in dead center of home page.

"Let's do a round robin redirect for some of the hits."

"What do you have in mind?" asked Ike, still typing away rapidly. He seemed to be coming out of the lethargy.

"Let's put every third or fourth visitor on the Pork Producer Council's site mix in some porn sites too. Let's put 'em on every offensive site we can think of. You know any good religious art sites? That ought to drive them apeshit." Ben laughed, "Crucifixion scenes -- how about the page for the Vatican collection? And the 700 club and any other television evangelist we can find." He grinned his crooked grin out of mischievous glee.

"It'll take a while for the rest of them to figure it out."

They spent the next fifteen minutes setting it up. After updating the source code, they logged into five times, once getting almuminum.org, the next time going to the Pork Producers' Council home page, next they had a face-to-face with Billy Graham and finally they hooked up with barely-legal co-eds for intimate encounters. The site redirected like a charm. Ben made sure it still logged the originating IP addresses.

They had a good belly laugh and Ben took both cups upstairs to get refills. The premature exposure didn't bother him much at this point. He had some sweet revenge anyway. The site would cause a lot of frustration – at least for a week or two. He still had both the original logs and had work to do with the coded messages. That would keep him busy for a while. And Ike seemed interested enough in the challenge to help him out some more.

He could hear Ike pounding away at the keyboard as he approached the study's double doors. He looked up as Ben entered the room.

"Didn't you say this ArRad guy posted from the Mediterranean?" he asked, without slowing the pace of his typing.

"The last updates came from Morocco." Ben sat the larger cup down on a coaster at Ike's right hand. It sent steaming wisps straight up in the still air.

"Well, our boy has been busy. I did a traceroute on that warning he posted. He ain't in Europe or Africa anymore. He's coming out of the nutrias.com domain now and that's right here in the U.S. according to the DNS server."

"Have you resolved that yet -- where is it? What is it?" Ben's tone of voice grew more concerned by degrees.

"I just did a 'whois nutrias.org.' Take a look."

Ben sat down in the side chair and braced himself. It said:

Domain ID:D19600802-LROR
Domain Name:NUTRIAS.ORG
Created On:10-Feb-2000 21:16:31 UTC
Last Updated On:23-Jan-2002 15:24:57 UTC
Expiration Date:10-Feb-2007 21:16:31 UTC
Sponsoring Registrar:R63-LROR
Status:OK
Registrant ID:20103029-NSI
Registrant Organization:New Orleans Public Library
Registrant Street1:219 Loyola Ave.
Registrant City:New Orleans
Registrant State/Province:LA
Registrant Postal Code:70112-2044

"... he's here. In the States."

"Damned straight dude. And based on what you've told me so far, I don't think he's here to apply for an H1B visa or for the grand tour of the South."

They connected to www.nutrias.org to double check. A page on New Orleans' library system came up to greet them

"Can we be sure his session actually originated from there?" Ben asked, "What if he's only using it as a gateway to cover his tracks?"

"I don't know if we can verify that, but he didn't do that in Turkey or Morocco," Ike reminded him solemnly, "I think it's legit. He's in-country now."

Just then, the mouse cursor on the almuminum.org page began moving under its own volition. They watched as another page of HTML came up. A command line panel came up and it filled with the blur of commands and the listing of contents.

"Someone's taken control of the PC! I'm being hacked!" Ben shouted.

"Let me try to head them off," Ike said, bringing up the System Manager to see what processes the attack had spawned.

"We don't have time for that. He's looking for the old postings. Kill his session!" Ben shouted.

"I can't get control; he's got us locked up!"

Ike tried to work the mouse, but it didn't respond. He tried to bypass it, using the Alt keys at top of the keyboard, but the hacker kept closing the panels they tried to bring up. They couldn't stop it. They were searching for something he had. They needed something from the original pages.

He jumped to his feet in a panic, knocking his chair against the wall. He reached for the phone line which carried his DSL and grasping it, yanked it out of the wall, physically breaking the hacker's connection but also breaking the telephone jack in the process.

He had stopped the attack, but whether he prevented them from getting what they needed was anybody's guess.

Ike shouted, "Holy shit, dude, this is serious. What the hell is going on?"

Conquest

During the pre-Islamic period of ignorance
I saw a she-monkey surrounded by a number of monkeys.
They were all stoning it, because it had committed
illegal sexual intercourse. I too, stoned it along with them.
Mohammed – Hadith Sahih Bukhari V5B58N188

Chapter 17

Ike entered the new River's Edge area at the Saint Louis Zoo from the wrong way, passing through the artificial Bat cave at the end of the exhibit. He wove through groupings of young families, with their strollers, balloons and babbling children heading out to the rest of the park. He had business on his mind but tried to keep the fact from showing on his face. No one paid him much attention, except for the occasional soccer mom who had to adjust her course as he disrupted the stream of people flowing past the Asian elephant exhibit. Ike saw his contact standing by the faux-bamboo fence near the reticulated python display. His contact looked stiff and overdressed for a day at the Zoo in a starched blue oxford shirt, the pressed khakis and the Cole-Hahn tasseled loafers. He held a megaphone of popcorn in his hand and looked at the watch on his arm.

"What's so important that I had to meet you on my day off?" he asked. *No attempt at any courtesy at all*, thought Ike.

"You're always giving me grief for not having something, and you give me this bullshit when I do," Ike retorted.

"An even exchange. So far that's all we've got from you," his contact said, "You see that over there," he gestured with the popcorn, spilling a handful onto the concrete. The walkway had been crafted to look like riverbank mud. It had impressions of leaves, wheat and animal tracks in between the cracks, made to resemble dried mud. He pointed again. "You see that enormous pile of elephant shit, pardon my French? That's what I've come to expect from you, Ike. We've had you on the payroll for almost a year now and what I've gotten from you amounts to the value of that dung heap."

"We're talking about professionals here, Chief," not caring to hide the disdain in his voice, "do you expect them to leave it out on the desk when they go home for the night? Do you expect them to hold meetings with the door open? You know who we're dealing with, for Christ's sake. They're world class." Ike leaned up on the railing and pretended to watch the young male elephant, Raja, whose antics with a stack of old tires captivated the crowd at the railing. People began filling up the empty spaces so Ike and the Chief moved to the other side of the walkway, trying to get out of earshot if possible.

"During the Civil War the troops had a term for it. 'Seeing the elephant' they called it. Getting into the thick of things. With you I 'smell the elephant.' All you have to show for six months of opportunity and $3000 of informant money is a heap of elephant dung. I'm getting tired of your lack of results. You're a two-time loser, you know that?"

Ike took a justifiable offense to the insult. "I don't want to work with you either, okay man? So just lay off. I have to follow the terms of my plea bargain. Another six months and this'll be over."

Raja trumpeted for the crowd and the little kids squealed and chattered and pointed excitedly. The Chief didn't register any of it. Ike rubbed his back against the concrete wall, fashioned to resemble a tall river bank of crumbling clay. It had fake roots coming out of it a various spot and holes gouged in it like the entrances of small rodent dens.

"Okay - what golden nuggets are so important that you drug me out here? You'd better have something decent this time," the Chief said staring at him with arrogant contempt. Ike wanted to punch him right between his beady eyes.

"I think you and the boys know this already, but I've got a friend at work, named Ben Adams, who's stumbled onto something I think could be serious. I think a group of terrorists plan another hit in the U.S."

"The FBI needs intel on what games the Mossad's running out of your office, not what some techno-geek surfer is looking at when the porn sites are down. Do you realize I could have your agreement extended? You want to work for me for the next five years? Give me something I can work with here; not something about the dork in the next cubbyhole." He took another handful of popcorn and shoved it at his pie hole, dropping at least a quarter of it on the ground. *They used to call guys like him 'pigs' back in the sixties*, Ike thought, *I can see why.*

"Let me be as clear as I can with you, Chief," he said, "my bud took over one of the fundamentalist websites four days ago. He's got some encoded logs from it. One of the bloggers has been traveling Westward from Turkey and we can see that this same guy is in the U.S. now. We traced him back to the New Orleans public library system. That same guy or someone else hacked my friend's server yesterday. We think they want something from the original logs before he took over the site. There's a coded message in those logs."

"How many people does this involve?" asked the Chief.

"The guy in New Orleans has at least two contacts. We don't know how many others are involved."

"Involved in what? Some high jinx on a website? Listen Ike – you forget about this Red Herring and focus your vast espionage skills at the eight registered agents we watch coming and going from your office. Get off you ass and get something for us to work with. We've got three man-years in on this one already."

"That reminds me, you'd better watch what you doing over in the Brown building. The same 'dork' made one of you by a window the other day. If he can do it, I bet some of the professionals already have."

Ignoring him, the Chief changed the subject. "What about the new guy?" He casually looked around and adjusted his sunglasses, stopping to look at the rounded ass of a young woman bending over to point out some of the tracks in the walkway.

"His name's Ofer. He's set up shop next to Eitan. He isn't doing anything I can see, but he's only been in-country for a couple of weeks. I'm watching him. He's definitely from the Institute."

"I could have guess as much – without getting paid. The cleaning lady gives me better stuff than you do. Maybe what I should do is take away your stipend until you bring us something worthwhile. How'd you like that, hacker boy?" he sneered.

"You're all about 'by-the-book' and 'SOP' and 'send it up through the channels'," Ike said, his voice rising, "You won't get the drop on them if you put in another three man years because you're nothing but a stooge. You can't see through your boss' shadow and you can't see around the fucking rule book you carry around. Don't you see, these guys don't have rules and neither do the terrorists I'm telling you about. When something big happens, I'm going to report you up your precious channel for the mindless prick you are and I'll have this meeting to back me up. How'd *you* like to sit at home with a reprimand and a missing paycheck? How'd you like that Chiefy old boy? You stiff-necked suit."

"You got nothing. Your friend and what he's doing are insignificant, like everything else you've produced so far. Don't call me until you have something real on our Israeli friends – that's who this is all about."

Ike watched him spin on his leather soles and walk toward the exit. He joined the kids with their balloons and sing-song voices and watched their mothers and fathers fawn all over them and hold them up to see the elephants. As he looked at them he wondered how many children would have to die because of Chief's deaf ear. He needed to cover his tracks ASAP.

Ben had been working his boxes all day and night but he realized he might be on the downward slope of diminishing returns. In addition to the original four notes, he'd only found two more – only one from the ArAzahad33 account and another from ArRad13. Neither seemed to be related to the website or to suspicious activity.

He made two new URL strings, one to look into the Sent folder and the other to look in Drafts. He put five of the bots on each and let them run.

Ben washed the garden dirt off his forearms in the garage sink. He felt tired and hot but satisfied. He had finally finished building all of his planned flower beds. It was too late into the year to do anything with some of them, but the soil was ready. In the short term, he had moved some of his annuals into the beds to add some color. He poured cool water on the back of his neck and forehead and then did the same thing to his legs. He dried himself off and went downstairs to check if he had anymore hits. He had one on the ArRad13 account.

It was in the drafts folder addressed to no one:

jk92q3rzlwe

He Googled the string and found nothing.

He worked with them for another three hours, trying to figure out what they meant. Then he had an idea. He composed a test email, like he had with the cyzchk235 account from Uzbekistan and addressed it to jk92q3rzlwe@NetMail.com. He made copies of the note for every free email service he could think of as well. He also sent copies to every domain that he found in the blog threads where ArRad13 and ArAzahad33 had posted as well as every other free web-based email service he could find. He went upstairs to take a shower after he had sent them off.

He came back downstairs and waded through the mailer daemon notes. They had all been rejected except jk92q3rzlwe@NetMail.com. He closed all windows and put a new set of ten on that account alone. He focused half on the InBox and half on the Drafts folder set them off and went upstairs to fix dinner.

He came back down again around nine-thirty. He had a hit. Drafts folder.

His smile changed to a look of confusion as he scanned the note. He couldn't make heads or tails of it. The body of the message consisted wholly of numbers strung together:

8:15:7:8:13:20:1:1:2:2:126:10:10:30:8:2:151:37:109:1:2
88:20:2:77:30:9:18:81:10:19:109:3:7:4:25
103:1:5:99:6:1:1:4:4:12:43:12:12:46:23:81:4:4
12:69:32:22:15:9:37:7
21:80:7:20:107:10:20:98:7:42:20:5:34:13:17:3:91:35:17:78:4
38:23:8:7:142:24:[3,1,14,1,12]:96:11:8

His mind raced, trying to frame the note in some meaningful context. He couldn't come up with any. It was dated only two days ago. In code. It might take months to crack something like this, if he could at all. He bounced his legs to release some of his aggravation. *I'm back to square one,* he thought, *no, worse than square one.*

Chapter 18

Ben took a seat on the Metrolink train as it accelerated out from the North Hanley platform. He never felt good going into work on Mondays but this morning weighed exceptionally heavy on his mind. He wore blue jeans, faded to their half life. His outfit wasn't up to the AirWarez dress code, but he hadn't felt up to ironing a pair of khakis that morning and hadn't had time the night before. He had been up to midnight banging his head against the coded message with no results. He had tried replacing the numbers with the Latin alphabet and for Arabic characters. Neither had worked. Some of numbers were too large for the substitution. Latin substitution for the bracketed piece [3,1,14,1,12] gave him [c,a,n,a,l] but that wasn't enough to go on and the rest didn't work out that way.

He looked out at the scenery from of last night's thunderstorm wreckage. It had rained hard around three in the morning. Trees lay on the ground, their root balls uplifted, leaving large muddy scars in the green undergrowth. Thunderstorms unsettled him. They always reminded him of the night at Dad's office.

He returned to problem at hand, looking at a copy of the encrypted note. He knew he was on to something. He wouldn't be able to break it fast enough, if ever.

The train continued on its course, picking up speed between the two graveyards. Ben returned to his thoughts, but found he could only settle on the same dead ends. He needed help and more resources. He resolved to pay a visit to the FBI Office on Market Street. A pang of apprehension stabbed at his gut. He remembered what Ike had said about breaking into the accounts. He had to cover his tracks. He would say he found them in the blog entries. He wouldn't go into any detail and they wouldn't be able to disprove him anyway. He and Ike had changed the website yesterday, wiping the old threads. The old 'Scorched Earth' policy - but he had burned two discs before wiping the old files from his drive. He hung one copy by monofilament fishing line in the corner of his drop ceiling in the study, hiding it among a dozen junk disks in a makeshift mobile. He took the other copy to the Perpetual Adoration chapel at Saint Roch's Church, sliding it under the back of the tabernacle base in an unmarked envelope.

They were aware of him now. The attack Sunday morning scared Ben, but he needed to see this through as far as possible. He had a score to settle. He needed revenge. But it wasn't just for his brother, although this drove him on. He wanted to settle the score against all of the injustice of his life.

His brother had helped him when no one else had. He could always count on his brother. On the worst night of his life, his brother had been the one to see him through.

His father had been a tax attorney in a four man shop on High Street in Jefferson City. His firm did some tax work for the state government and the work came doubly heavy in the springtime. Dad put in seventy-hour weeks for several months until the wave passed. He worked out of a cluttered office on the fourth floor of an old brick building, vaguely Germanic in style, without a security guard but with three-times weekly janitorial service and an ancient elevator. It was back in the days when the stores lined High Street and the mall hadn't been built yet.

Ben and his brother had been messing around in the lobby that night, watching the lightning show and listening for the thunder, close and strong enough to rattle the old panes of glass in their frames. But kids have short attention spans and eventually they turned their attention to the janitor's closet, arming themselves for a sword fight. Ben had the plunger and Nick had the mop handle when their father came down in the elevator to check on them. They had made a mess of the floor, leaving splashes of dirty pail water all over the lobby floor. His father, already stressed from his workload deadlines and his smoking, lost it.

"Boys, what do you think you're doing!" he snapped, "I've got a mountain of files to wade through and you're creating more work for me. Both of them stood frozen in mid-swing, rudely shocked out of their fantasy world of pirates and plunder. Dad grabbed Ben by the ear and pulled him toward the elevator, shouting back over his shoulder, "Nick, get a mop head on that stick and get to work. I want this floor spotless. Then get back up to my office."

Nick was the oldest and should have known better. He always knew better.

Nick didn't say anything, standing at attention in his patched Toughskin blue jeans with half his buffalo plaid flannel shirt tail hanging out. He didn't argue or say anything. It wouldn't have mattered if he had. They had picked the wrong night to ask for trouble and they both knew it.

"I'm giving you ten minutes and if you're not finished and in my office you're in deep trouble," Dad yelled, "Make sure it's done right the first time." Ben winced, rubbing his ear and watching the sight of his brother narrow between the closing elevator doors. The doors clapped together and the car began to rise. Then it happened.

The storm had been strong enough to uproot trees and had succeeded in driving one of them into the electrical wires, breaking them and knocking the power out in Dad's office. The elevator went dead and dark.

"Oh, isn't this the topper," dad said, muttering something under his breath. Then he realized the situation might affect Ben.

"Son, are you all right?"

"Y-yes Dad."

"Don't worry, Ben, this won't last too long. He felt his father's hand stroking his head in the black stillness and this reassured him. His father was strict but was affectionate. He just had high expectations for his two boys; that's what he had always told them when they complained or tried to give up on something. He would never allow quitting.

"Dad, are we trapped in here?" Ben asked, the fear rising up, constricting his throat.

"We're going to be okay son, the power will probably come back on in a minute or two. Why don't we sit down and take a load off?" He listened to the rustling of his dad's shirt and tie as he sat down. He tried to form an image of how Dad was sitting so that he wouldn't trip and fall when he tried to find a place right next to him. Ben took his Dad's hand, noticing the cold sweat covering it. His father always had hot hands.

"Are you okay, Dad?" Ben asked. His voice echoed in the dark.

"I'm feeling kind of dizzy actually. I'm pretty tired too, you know, with all of the work mounting up." Ben heard his father's breathing get faster and more shallow. Dad wheezed a little bit. He smoked too much, Mom said. Dad let out a little groan, short and spastic, like he got hurt and was trying to fight it. Ben had an image of his father clutching his chest, as circle of blood growing larger and larger around his hand, claw like in painful tension.

"Ben, get your brother. I need help. I need to get off of the ele—," Dad gasped, struggling to speak in a regular tone of voice, "I need to get out of here."

Ben crawled to where he thought the doors would be. He groped for them, feeling the cold metal and finding the crack. They were as cold and lifeless as his father's hand.

"Nick! Help! Something's wrong with Dad. He's hurt. Help!" Ben banged against the metal with his seven-year-old fist. He strained his ear against the crack. He panicked and began heaving sobs. He heard the sharp smack of the wooden pole bouncing against the lobby floor. He heard running footsteps, then the loud vibrating thud of his brother against the outer doors.

"What's going on in there?" Nick's muffled voice said.

"Dad's hurt. Can you get us out of here? Help!"

He heard Nick struggling with the doors. Nothing.

"I can't open them. Hold on –"

"Help," Ben shouted.

He heard his brother running to the other side of the lobby. He could hear his brother trying to use the phone. He heard his brother shouting, 'my dad's sick, we need help!' into the phone, then he couldn't make the rest out. He whined and sobbed and pawed at the doors futilely trying to work his fingers into the crack to force it open. Then he heard a sharp bang and the sound of the bell echoing from the impact. The phone isn't working either, he thought, what are we going to do?

His father thrashed around, accidentally kicking him in the small of his back with the point of his wingtip shoe. Ben's useless eyes registered a shower of sparks and he winced in pain. He crawled back over to his dad's side, stroking him; trying to reassure him as Dad would do for him. It had no effect on him. Ben began to sob again.

"Daddy, are you okay, are you okay? Are you okay?" he kept repeating, as if saying the words would make things all right again.

"Benny, I called the police. They're sending some help. Is Dad okay?" came Nick's voice from outside the doors.

"No, I'm not okay, " Dad managed to say, but his words weren't strong enough to reach Nick through the doors.

"What? Ben, what's happening?"

"I don't know, I can't help him, Nick." Ben cried uncontrollably now. He felt the hot streams of tears covering his face. His nose ran thick with snot. He felt insignificant and powerless to help his father, now dying in the elevator halfway between the first and second floors. Ben screamed out in helpless desperation.

"Ben, Ben! Stop crying for God's sake. Help is on the way. Try to help Dad. It's okay. Do you hear me? Try to help Dad, okay. Help him." He kept repeating, "Help is coming Ben. Hang in there." Ben crawled back to his father's side. He felt him -- His shirt, wet in spots from sweat… He was cold. He didn't say anything.

Ben put his hand on his father's face, feeling it. Nothing. He shook his father's head with both hands, "Daddy, Daddy, NO!" he cried. Nothing. His head offered no resistance, no will of its own.

Ben stayed by his father's body for the next twenty minutes. Nick stayed by the doors, talking to him, trying to keep him tethered to reality while they waited out the eternity between the call and the arrival of the fire trucks. Nick stayed with him when the firefighters pried the door open and extracted them from the car. Nick hugged him and tried his best to soothe him, wrapped in a Red Cross blanket while paramedics strapped Dad into the gurney and hauled him to the Coroner's office.

Nick had done his best then and in the years afterward. They shared many things, but the trauma of their father's death had placed something between them that few brothers, no matter how close, shared. At some level they had been made closer than twins because of the shared trauma. Ben would never forget how good his brother had been to him. But now he was gone too. He was a just a nameless 'Other' to them. But Ben knew him and he would never forget that their sins caused his brother's suffering and death.

The dinging of the bells brought him back to the Metrolink train again. He looked out the window to get his bearings. He had missed his stop. He gathered up his pushed them into his laptop bag. He stood up and walked to the doors. He would be ten minutes late to work, as he backtracked the five blocks from the Convention Center stop to his office. So he'd be late. Big Deal. It didn't matter anyway, no one watched him that closely at work anyway, he told himself as he stepped out into the underground platform and made his way towards the stairs.

Chapter 19

The Saint Louis FBI field office sat in a patch of bluegrass behind a high iron fence a couple of blocks West of Union Station. Just five years old, it resembled a green, glass shoebox cut into thirds by two metal slabs. He took one of the free trains between the downtown stops at lunchtime.

The walk over to the FBI building took less than ten minutes. A guard sat on the left side, shifting his attention between Ben and the closed-circuit television monitors resting on the lower desk. The receptionist had a minimalist telephone headset worked carefully into her magenta-tinged hair, the victim of a bad dye job. She had also tweezed her eyebrows too thin, giving her a permanent expression of surprise.

"Good afternoon. Please sign into the visitor's log."

She reached for the binder and nudged it toward Ben. He picked up the pen and put his name down. He checked the time on his pager and then wrote '11:36a' in the next column.

"Whom should I bring up to the desk for you?"

"Uhmm, I don't have an appointment. But I would like to speak with an agent, if I could," he said. Her eyebrows distracted him. She pointed her chin at a grouping of chairs in the middle of the lobby. He sat in the chair next to the commercial-duty Bunn coffee maker. He drew himself a cup and sat down. He sipped his cup of coffee and played eye tag for the next eight minutes with a lady who was also waiting, until some FBI guy in summer-weight , navy wool pants and French Blue dress shirt came over and took her to the back offices.

Ben turned his attention to the three guys manning desks in the lobby. They looked like bank clerks. Two of them talked on the phone, while the third ate his lunch. One of them hung up, shuffled some items around on his desk and went over to the visitors' log that Ben had signed twelve minutes before.

"Mr. Adams'?" he asked, turning his attention to Ben. Ben acknowledged and stood up to meet him." He had a firm but friendly grip and shook Ben's hand in a steady, practiced sort of way. "Pleased to meet you Mr. Adams-- my name is J. Daniels. What can I do for you?" He spoke enthusiastically and smiled in a pleasant sort of way which showed off his perfect, brilliantly white teeth. He handed Ben a card with a four-color FBI logo on the left side, along with 'J. Daniels' and the title 'Agent' in oversized golden letters. His contact filled up the other half.

"Pleased to meet you," Ben said, "This is going to sound kind of weird," he laughed, " but I need help from the FBI with something I've found on the Internet. I think some people need to be investigated." He looked around, not being sure if a guy in the front office could really give him the kind of help he needed. He had pictured working with a thick-necked flattop, named Frank, who spoke with an honest throaty gruffness and had worked his way up to Special Agent over the last fifteen years. Instead he got a young guy, fresh out of some state college who probably whitened his teeth and flexed his abs in the mirror after taking showers.

J. Daniels offered Ben a stiff-looking visitor's chair alongside his desk. He swiveled towards Ben and folded his hands together, placing them on his crisply pleated gray wool trousers. Ben noticed that 'J' dressed a couple of degrees nicer than the other two agents working out of the lobby.

"Okay, so you say you're trying to track some people down? Have you filed a Missing Persons' report with the Saint Louis police?"

"No, this isn't about a missing person. It's about terrorists here in the United States." He tried to be as matter-of-fact as he could, although he began to regret the whole thing.

"What do you mean, Mr. Adams?"

Ben had his interest.

"I took control of one of the main Islamic websites that are suspected terrorist bulletin boards. For five days now I've had a fake web site put up in its place. But they spotted it for a fake yesterday and aren't leaving any more messages any longer."

"Islamic terrorists..." his doubt dripping out of the words, "So why do you think terrorists are using this site to communicate, Mr. Adams?" Ben detected the slick insincerity of a used car salesman. He never trusted people who overused his name.

"When I took over the site, I set up some cgi tracking on the page to log the page they jumped from to get onto my fake site," he translated, "I kept the list of sites and links where users originated from as they logged on to my site. I've also been keeping copies of all the messages that users are posting to the site. I have all the email accounts, IP addresses and a big list of other sites we could use to widen the search. Based on what I've seen in some of the threads, things aren't what they seem. I believe they may be talking in code – about what I don't know. And if that's not bad enough, I've traced the movement of one of those guys from Turkey, across the Mediterranean to New Orleans. He's in the United States now and I think they're going to hit the U.S. again."

Agent Daniels blinked at him. Maybe he would believe him after all. "Why do you think one of them is in New Orleans?"

"I logged a connection from the nutrias.org domain."

"Nutrias – Isn't that the public library system?"

"Yes, it is as a matter of fact. How do you know that?"

"I'm from New Orleans originally. Most of my family still lives there."

"Well, you're right, it's a library network. Someone's come halfway around the world to send coded emails from a New Orleans library. If I had to guess, I'd say his intentions aren't good."

"Are you sure about this? Can you prove it?"

"Of course, I have a record of everything. Would you like me to talk with one of your tech guys? I don't know what the FBI does about cryptography, but you're going to need some of those resources too. That's why I've come to ask for help. We need to figure out what's in the notes before something serious happens. Can you help me?"

"It definitely sounds like something we want to pursue. Did you bring the data with you?"

Ben shook his head. "Like I said earlier, they figured out the site was bogus. They hacked my server. I made a copy of it and wiped it from my disk. I don't carry it around and the only way to access it is to read the CD."

He definitely seemed interested after all. "I'm going to have to talk to my boss. Can I call you back in a day or two?" Agent Daniels said.

"A day or two? I think that would be a mistake. That might be all they need." He tried to keep his voice low -- tried hard to see if from the agent's perspective. How would he react if he sat in the other chair? Probably the same way. But it didn't help settle him down much.

"I have to go through the proper channels on something like this. I do have other work, you know. I'm not sitting here waiting for the next big case to come strolling in. We need to check some things out first and I need to talk to my boss and get the ball rolling."

Ben began to see him as just another clerk; a bureaucrat first and foremost. He felt like he had played his hand too soon. "You mean check me out, right? You'll spend the next week looking through my trash and laundry hamper while the bad guys stroll in and kill another three thousand people. Maybe this time they get really lucky and get ten thousand while you're checking my dental records. What about the focus on this kind of thing with Homeland Security and the new, improved FBI? Didn't you guys learn a lesson in the last year?"

He took offense to this, pulling at his shirt cuffs with a sour look on his face. "I *am* concerned, okay? Something like this has to done properly. I can't just cowboy it into my schedule, understand? Why don't you just write down your contact information and I'll get back to you as soon as I can."

Ben shook his head but wrote his home and pager numbers on the back of a card. He nonchalantly flicked it in Agent Daniels' general direction, as it skimmed the top of the desk like a stone across water. "You want my social security number, my bank account numbers and my voter's registration card too? It might save us some time. How about my old speeding tickets?"

"I think I have enough on the situation already," he said.

"Call me as soon as you can."

Ben walked out the doors, pissed off and recalled the dull throb in his head that night, sitting in front of the TV at home, watching the latest death toll roll up in front of the smoking debris from the twin towers. In his day-mare all he could do was sit and watch the carnage. This time he had been forewarned and could have done something about it. It ate at him. He had lost.

Agent Daniels pressed his badge up against the magnetic lock to open it. He stepped through the heavy steel door and walked down the hallway dividing the back offices. He stopped at his boss' door and gathered his thoughts for a moment. He knocked and then opened it after hearing what sounded like a 'come in'.

"Chief, I just had a walk-in and I think it's worth discussing."

Special Agent William Preston, a.k.a. 'Chief', sat behind the faux rosewood desk, his feet propped up on the corner with a telephone headset hanging precipitously to the side his head. He was eating a sandwich while listening to his conference call, but seemed to be tired of it and beckoned Daniels to come in. Daniels took his seat, adjusting his jacket to give himself the good shoulder lines. He looked out the window and spotted Ben Adams walking briskly toward Union Station. He framed his thoughts and rehearsed them, trying to prune them of embellishment. The Chief liked things brief.

Chief rolled his eyes and expelled some stale air. He pressed on the headset controls, muting the microphone. He took his feet off the desk and looked at Daniels. "What is it Jack?" he asked.

"Sir, I just finished with a walk-in and I think it's worth mentioning," Jack said.

The Chief deliberated for a moment. Fixing his gaze on the ceiling, mentally deciding which of the two he would blow off – Jack or the call. "Okay, what is it?" he repeated.

"A guy came in and told me he pirated a fundamentalist site – Islamic fundamentalists -- and he suspects the site is being used to send messages between groups of terrorists. He's found what he believes to be coded messages and he thinks he can place one of them on a route into the U.S."

"And what does our citizen soldier want from us?"

"He says he wants to turn over the logs and data so that we can crack this code and stop them."

The Chief affected a slight double-take, which surprised Jack. Chief usually expressed only variations of irritation or anger.

"In other words, he wants to work with us? What does he look like? Does he have long, stringy prematurely gray hair and beard and a beer gut? Does he dress in concert t-shirts and looks like he hasn't bathed in a couple of days?" the Chief said, his voice dripping sarcasm.

"No, he's about six foot, dressed business casual with pressed khakis. Looks presentable. A real all-American boy."

The Chief whistled and slapped his leg hard enough to fill the room with the sound. "Let me guess, name's Ben Adams."

"Yes…" Daniels said, his jaw slack.

"That's the second time in as many days I've heard Ben Adams: citizen, patriot, spy. He's building a reputation for himself." He pantomimed a laugh, then adjusted the headset, checking to see if he'd missed anything important.

"Sir, have you talked to Adams about this already?"

"Ike told me about this at the zoo yesterday."

"Ike, your informant in AirWarez?"

"The very same," Chief said, trying to make it sound dramatic. He swirled his tongue around on his teeth to remove the vestiges of the turkey sandwich. "Ike spoke highly of him – said he worked with the guy and thought he'd come across some terrorist plot. Suggested we should throw some people at it."

"You don't think much of the idea?" Jack said.

"I don't think much of Ike. He's a slacker and a lousy informant."

Jack decided to take a chance, he had a feeling about this. He wanted to move his desk into the back office. He'd been out in the lobby for three years, ever since he'd graduated. It was time he did something about it.

"You know, Chief, I could do a cursory check into this. It wouldn't take much."

"You're damn right it won't. Check it out if you like, but do it after hours. I need you on the crew over in the Paul Brown building. We've already got three man years in and we've got zilch to show for it."

Jack shrugged it off. So he'd run the leads while he sat in the musty chill during the evening shift. Nothing much happened at night. The Mossad agents mostly went home at night, posing as software salesman. Nothing much happened after hours. No big deal; he'd multitask.

Conquest

"Allah's Apostle said, 'I have been made victorious with terror.'"
Hadith Sahih Bukhari:V4B52N220

Chapter 20

Abdullah bin Malak al Zalam jumped in his seat when he decoded the message. Al-Warraq had managed to find the saboteur in a matter of days! He and the other brothers would take the keys from him along with his life as they came to the rendezvous in a few short days. They hadn't even fallen behind in the timetable, God be praised, the Benevolent and Ever Merciful.

Abdullah left al-Warraq an acknowledgment. He had underestimated him. Now firmly back in his self-confidence, he composed a new note and addressed it to the alphanumeric pager as he had agreed to do with Pepito on the boat that night. He typed in the coordinates and clicked on the Send button. The crisis had passed. He closed out everything, erased the history from the internet browser and walked toward the counter to surrender his computer card.

As he walked out the library doors his mind rested on feelings of good will and invincibility. The wind had always been at his back, even on the day he was born. His father liked to remind him of that. For he came into the world on 17 Safar 1399 (16 January 1979) the day the godless apostate, Shah Mohammed Reza Pahleri, fled Persia. Thought they didn't celebrate birthdays in his homeland, his good father always mentioned this date and the fact that Abdullah had been born under auspicious circumstances. An omen, if you will. He smiled, remembering his father patting him on the head saying, 'Abdullah, you will do great things for our people and our faith, I am sure of it. You are a harbinger of things to come, for you were born at the cusp of a great turn in world history.' Although his father, like all the right-minded people in his town, thought the Shi'a to be heretics and only a step above the *kuffar*, the Islamic nation they created would be the start of a turn in events, the constant, constant expansion in the House of Islam and perpetual, diminishing erosion for the House of War for all times until the day when all nations fell under Islamic law and the unbelievers found themselves utterly subdued. Abdullah walked with a lilt, even forgetting his injury, his heart overflowing with joy – the harbinger of great things to come.

As he stepped along the uneven sidewalks he stubbed the toes of his ill-fitting shoes. A sudden pang of recognition jolted him out of his good humor. He noticed movement turning the corner, coming up the other side of the street. Abdullah recognized him and thought it too coincidental that someone had the same route and schedule as he, especially in the middle of the day. He continued down the street, watching his shadow in the reflections of the unused and dusty storefront windows and in the windshields of the cars along the block. Whoever he was, he paced himself the same. He found it hard to get a good look in the distorted panes of glass. So, for show, he play-acted a stumble and fell, sprawling and rolling so as to get a look. His tail looked and acted like a small-time criminal. But the motive couldn't be robbery; wearing worn, baggy pants, a faded t-shirt, baseball cap and ill-fitting shoes Abdullah hardly suggested easy money. His tracker pretended to be searching for an address, stopping to look at two of houses along the street and then looking at a piece of folded paper he carried. The young punk stole a glance in his direction but continued to act as though he were merely lost on an errand. An errand boy, no doubt, but for whom? He looked Latino, not Anglo. Pepito's boy. *Damn him to the furnace of Hell,* Abdullah cursed. Involving this scum had been a serious mistake.

Abdullah began walking at a regular rate, then began increasing his pace every ten meters or so. As soon as he turned the next corner, Abdullah ran to mid-block, then resumed his pace. He looked over his shoulder to see the young Latino screeching to a halt back at the other corner. Yes, definitely now. And he knew he had been spotted. The punk trotted along towards him, cell phone in hand urgently shouting Spanish into it and locking eyes with Abdullah for the first time. He meant business. Abdullah quickly reached the speed limit of his oversized shoes. He had to lose him as soon as possible. He turned and ran up between two shotgun-style houses and crawled under the one with missing skirt boards. He strained to hear his pursuer over his own panting and wriggled away from the hole and the light streaming in from it. His blood roared in his ears. He got the gun ready.

His eyes adjusted to the dimness in the crawlspace.

Footfalls on the sidewalk… the sounds of agitated Spanish.

He heard the rustling of denim. Close.

He pointed the gun at the bright light streaming in.

Someone went by.

He lay on the damp earth, frozen, trying not to breathe. After a few moments, the voices came from farther away.

Conquest

He moved towards the opening after a few minutes. Abdullah scraped along the damp moldering humus in the crawl space until he could place one eye close enough to a wide gap in the boards, sighting the street like a gun. Some older sedan with fancy chrome wheels passed through his restricted range of vision. A car came up the street, cruising very slowly, out of place in this nation of rush-rush. He stayed another fifteen minutes to satisfy himself, and then he crawled out through the hole again and made his way back toward the library. He decided to swing in a wide southerly arc on the way back to the safety of the mosque boiler room. He congratulated himself on his cunning but failed to see another group of watchers pick up his progress halfway back.

A Plague on Both Houses

Now, when I was just a little boy,
Standin' to my daddy's knee,
My papa said, son, don't let the man get you
and do what he done to me.
'cause he'll get you,
'cause he'll get you now.
John Fogerty – Born on the Bayou

Chapter 21

Jack reached the surveillance station after the six-flight walk up which taxed even him, a man still in his mid-twenties. Only minimal electrical service had been set up, which included the phone lines and enough juice to power the two workstations. They were manned by one of the morning crew out in the hallway, which was coated in a decade of dust and smelled of musty pigeon droppings. Jack nodded a hello to relieve his fellow agent and looked sideways through the door opening into a room full of cameras, microphones and assorted electronic gear. Chief stood in the center of the room staring down at the Griesedieck Brothers' fifth floor through the disjointed blinds slats. Daniels didn't try to get the Chief's attention, choosing to commiserate with his peer and sniff at the air instead. He took a few moments to think about the meeting with Ben Adams, replaying it in his mind as he had several times already.

Chief came out into the hallway, in his standard blue oxford, sleeves rolled up for variety. He had on the ubiquitous khakis. Billowing dust hid the shine of the trusty American style loafers the Chief always wore. The Chief pulled at a cigarette and the smoke from it hung in the heavy, still air. Jack looked up and saw him standing in a murky half-silhouette, the bluish smoke wafting all around him, causing the line 'like a fiend in a cloud' from Blake's *Mad Song* to echo in his mind.

"You're gonna kill us both with that, you know?" Jack said, waving his hand to chase the smoke away.

"You think this is bad," Chief said, contemplating the burning end, "we're more at risk breathing in all of this lead-dust coming off the walls. Another three months of this and we'll both have brain damage." He took another big pull. The cherry glowed hot- orange.

"In more ways than one, Chief. We'll be dead from boredom before the paint gets us. Do we have anything for the six months we've been working this?"

"No," the Chief said in his usual candor. *He's such a talker I bet he keeps his wife up all night sometimes – a real talker, Chief,* Jack thought.

"Sir, look, I've been thinking about this Adams guy. Why don't we check into his story. We'll be remiss in our duties if we don't. He could have something, you know."

"We'll be remiss in our duties if we *do* check him out, Daniels," Chief said, "We have a job to do here and I won't be distracted by some wannabe hacker. We've got three man-years in already. That's already way too much time sweating this one out. We're understaffed as it is for something this big. We can't afford to waste resources on some pie-in-the-sky theory a local computer nerd created while waiting for his porn site to refresh. We'll pursue the terrorists out there -- don't worry -- when we have briefings and real leads coming in to us." He tossed the butt down and twisted his loafer on it, driving up a puff of dust on each side of his foot. It billowed and rolled in the light. Jack turned, dissatisfied, pulling at the tails of his Cardinals' jersey to free it from the seat. He had a red undershirt on, baggy denim pants, laceless running shoes and the fitted wool cap with a Redbird on a bat, the cap the team would wear on Sundays. He looked like any of ten thousand hip-hop posers in and around Saint Louis.

He logged in the workstation and checked the notes from the last two shifts. He saw nothing of interest.

"We're not getting anywhere," addressing the wall in front of him, "we're not making any progress here."

"Investigations like this take time." Chief's voice bounced off the bare walls and found its way out to the hall. They had taken the door off its hinges and it lay on its side at the dark end of the hallway, like a wounded soldier, damaged and forsaken.

Jack raised his voice but kept looking at the monitors. "Our boy on the inside hasn't gotten any closer to the action?"

"Not yet. Hey, come here and have a look at the new guy."

Jack scraped the legs of the creaking wooden chair against the floorboards and went into the old office, which for many years had been used by a small family jeweler who catered to wealthy Ladue families. The old glass counters still took up a large rectangular space in the center of the room. Chief stood a few feet from one of the windows, looking down into the Romanesque, fifth floor windows across the street.

"Get some snaps with the camera," he barked, looking

through a pair of binoculars and blindly pointing towards the camera.

Jack positioned himself behind the 400mm lens and the Nikon F4, screwed down on a tripod. He swung it to the right slightly and focused.

"The guy in the aisle near our boy? With the eyebrows?"

"Yeah, the new guy, name's Ofer something. Ike says he's been in-country about two weeks. I bet he's the real thing, baby." Chief adjusted his focus a little.

The camera motor whirred and warbled in pitch as it pulled against the film. Jack got three frames before his subject turned to the other cube and looked in, obscuring his face. *Not good enough for a profile shot*, thought Jack. He fiddled with the barrel of the lens until he had Ofer's ear tack-sharp again. The blurred face of the cube resident came into frame so he shifted focus, bringing Ben Adams' face into view, with its open, middle-American good looks. He smiled at Ofer and asked him something.

"You see who he's talking to?"

"Yeah. So what?"

"That's Ben Adams," said Jack.

"The web site hijacker and prognosticator of all things terror?" the Chief said, sarcastically. He adjusted his eyepieces. "Him? He doesn't look like he could talk down the price of a new Minivan."

"That's him, all right. And our freshly imported Mossad agent is cozying up."

They watched closely for a minute, looking for new bits of intel. They watched as he and Ben wrapped up the conversation with Ofer gesturing toward the offices at the core of the building and a sour look on Adams' face. Adams rose from his chair and said something over the wall to Ike, who had been eavesdropping the whole time. They walked out of sight with Ofer in the lead.

"What do you think?" Jack asked.

"I think we need to keep doing what we're doing. I'm going to drop the hammer on our corporate spy over there. He's had enough time already. We need results."

"What about Adams?"

"He's a sideshow," Chief dismissed, " Listen, I want you to get those images off to Washington ASAP. We need to see what our new partners in Langley have on the new man. Ike ought to be able to find out where he lives. He's good for at least that much anyway."

Jack rewound the film and took it out to the hallway. He phoned in for pick-up and arranged the details with one of the support crew back in the office. He grew tired always working out the details. It occurred to him he would still be doing this five years out. It had been three already and he hadn't progressed. He decided he would have to promote himself and he saw Adams as a means to do it.

Chapter 22

Ben immediately felt uncomfortable from the vibe in Eitan's office. A ponderous desk dominated the room and Ben wondered how the movers had been able to get it through the door in the first place. *It must be bolted together in pieces*, he thought. He felt trapped in one of the stiff side chairs, pushed against the wall so that two people could fit in the narrow space. Nothing but blank, dirty vanilla on the walls. Ben looked at the stacks of papers and binders on the desk. None of them had the company letterhead and all were in Hebrew. No pictures on the desk or anywhere else, he noted. The only other things of interest in the room were the squat black boxes but from stale air he knew they weren't fans or ionizers. The close quarters started up his all-too-familiar claustrophobic response. It sat his teeth on edge. He hoped to conclude the meeting quickly, before he had to insist that the door be opened. He didn't want to show a sign of weakness if he could avoid it. Negotiation was the key to working with the Israelis and he didn't want to bargain from an inferior position no matter what this happened to be about.

The new guy, Ofer, sat in the chair next to him, his bare arm rubbing up against Ben's, squeezing his personal space even more. He folded his hands, placing them in his lap to give himself a little room.

Eitan came in, opening the door in a rush. Ben breathed in the sweeter-smelling air as it washed over them. He stood behind the behemoth for a moment, then dropped into his chair.

"Good morning, Ben. I am pleased to meet you," Eitan said, extending a broad, stubby hand and shaking it vigorously past the point of American decorum. He stood about five foot seven and had the small paunch of a middle aged-man man moderate in his habits. He wore squarish wire rim glasses. The lenses magnified his darting eyes, giving them a misleadingly comical exaggeration. He sat down separated from them by an expanse of desk. "I have heard good things about your work here."

Ben waited. He couldn't read the direction the meeting would take nor the emotional tone. Neither gave it away. He felt the urge to shift in his chair, but avoided doing so.

"Ben, we have a need for a technical man of your caliber on a new project I'm directing. It will be a small, exploratory R&D effort. You will be working with me and Ofer Buzaglo here for a couple of months. Have you been introduced?" He affected a warm and diplomatic tone, but did it poorly. He looked at Ofer and swiveled his chair so that he faced away from both of them. His eyes rested on one of the black boxes, reassuring himself about some hidden thought.

The younger Israeli guardedly extended his hand. He and Ben had to twist slightly apart to get a proper handshake angle. Ben noticed Ofer gave away as nothing in his handshake and expression

"Sir, I don't think this is a good time for me start anything new," Ben said, "I 'm currently working on three projects; two of which are in system test. A change at this point could jeopardize the timelines for each of them."

"Take this as a compliment, would you please, Ben? Any of the other DBAs can finish your work. I have been appraised of the situation already. You are beyond the difficult phase now. If you're concerned about your colleagues' abilities, have two of them take over for you. We need you -- starting today. This is an intensive effort and we may have to ask you to stay after hours quite a bit. We need to present a proof-of-concept to our superiors in Tel Aviv 25 August at latest." Eitan swiveled slightly back and forth, aiming his clasped hands first and Ben then at Ofer.

"Okay, sir. I'm Gumby, sir. I'll try to do my best."

Mentally he began trying to translate this into how much off-hours work he might have to do. This could put an extended cramp in his plans.

"Gumby? What is Gumby?" Eitan asked. He looked at Ofer, who had a mix of disdain and boredom on his face.

"Gumby is a little rubber character that children play with and bend into all kinds of positions," Ben explained, "Forgive me, it's an

American anachronism. I'm trying to say I will be as flexible as possible, but I think you're unrealistic if you expect me to hand everything off in a day."

"Have the other DBAs worked with you on the Telesis and Dynacom accounts?"

"Yes, to a degree. But I don't think one of them would be ready to take a whole project on by himself. He's only been at it for six months."

"We hire top-quality people. Remember all the tests? That's part of our screening process. I think we will do fine. Under my direction this development center has produced under budget and ahead of schedule time and time again. I have good judgment in these matters, believe it or not," he said, with a trace of indignation in his voice. "We will make our dates, of that I am sure." He threw a dour look over his shoulder. He played the part of an accountant, everyone's quiet and respectable Uncle Leonard, but the undertow of his presence set off a jarring sensation in the nerves of Ben's teeth. Something did not quite add up.

"Do you want me to offload my projects today?" Ben asked.

"Yes, right away. You and Ofer will begin work immediately. Stop what you're doing now. Ofer will help you with the others if there's a scheduling conflict. He can get them reassigned."

"We're starting this afternoon?" Ben looked blankly at Ofer, who still looked as bored and annoyed as he had the entire time.

"Yes, you may have to stay late," Ofer said with a twinge of irritation, "We have some binary installations to do and I would like to orient you so that we may begin tomorrow."

"I'm afraid I won't be able to stay long tonight," Ben said, "I'm having some people over after work for dinner and drinks."

"Fine... I will come over and we can discuss some of the details at your party," Ofer stated in declarative Israeli fashion. At work, many questions and requests were phrased in the form of a statement. *The hard sell*, thought Ben, but it no longer had the edge it had when he'd first come to work at AirWarez. He expected the approach as a matter of course. Besides, he didn't see any harm in having 'The UniBrow' over tonight if it smoothed things out down the road.

"Sure, I'll give you directions before we're finished today." he said, nodding at Ofer, "Eitan, would you like to come as well?"

"No," he said abruptly, adding the requisite American, "thank you" after a pregnant pause. The Israelis were honest, direct and impolite.

"We're finished now, but tomorrow morning I want both of you to update me on where we stand," he said, looking at Ofer. Ofer raised and lowered his eyebrow – a singular overabundance which gave him a passing resemblance to Bert from Sesame Street – with the pointy head to match. Ben didn't like him already. He didn't like anyone butting in on his personal time.

Ben stood up and pulled at his pant legs, which had ridden up in the confines of the chair. Ofer stood and opened the door, moving out of the way. "I'll be over in about ten minutes," he said, thrusting his chin at Ben as he walked by. *What a prick*, thought Ben, *working with this guy will take all the air out of my summer.* He walked on down the hall, glad to be out of that coffin of an office.

Ofer waited until Ben turned into his aisle, then closed the door and sat down again. He picked at his nails and gave Eitan an 'I told you so' look.

"What do you have in mind?" he asked.

"I don't care. Work with one of the project managers and get something to load on his machine -- whatever seems reasonable. Make something up; you're used to that, am I right?" He spoke rapidly, with annoyance.

"Fine. But once we set him up, what then? He'll be able to see the farce."

"Let him sit there for a couple of weeks. He will put the time to his own use. His personality profile tells me he will become bored in a matter of days. He'll work on his personal project and we'll be able to follow the progress. He needs to feel 'well used' and he'll make the most of the time we're going to give him. Are we ready?"

"We have his phone routed and the microphones installed," Ofer said.

"Are the sniffers in place? I want all his packets intercepted, both in-coming and out-going. I want all his activity logged. The sixth floor desk needs to put an analyst on this."

"I'll double check. That should be done. We're also logging all of his keystrokes."

"Make sure it's well hidden. He'll notice a drag on his system, more likely than not. Make sure they've done it right. I want to know every move he makes, every site he visits, ever word he says. We don't have much time on this. If we give him the opportunity he will lead us to..." Eitan leaned over the laminated expanse, into the center of interference, "...Abdullah and the cells."

"What if he becomes a liability? I'm sure a cautious career man like yourself has contingencies laid out," Ofer snidely remarked, crossing his arms.

"I'm still alive and will retire from all of this. I didn't get here from a lack of contingency planning. You would do well to learn," Eitan said. "If he doesn't produce we will brush him aside, but we will find what we're looking for, one way or the other. We won't stop until we do."

Ofer said nothing, got up and opened the door. Eitan's eyes shot darts into his back as he left.

He had seen many like Ofer die through the years, but all that time Eitan had played his own hand well. He had made it across the minefield of thirty five years and he was nearly free and clear. This one task remained. After that he would retire to his cozy place by the sea, with its lemon trees in the courtyard and his long-suffering wife. He would try to make it up to her. He would be able to share himself fully with her, that is, if she would have him in these last years together. He wondered if that were still possible. So much of his life had been a degree removed – hidden from her on the other side of his inner wall. There was no other way it could have been done. But it didn't have to be that way soon. He had nearly paid his price in full. He could feel the wind at his back now, much like a marathon runner when he sees the finish line in the distance.

Chapter 23

Agent Jack Daniels sat at his desk in the lobby of the FBI field office on Market Street, where he was putting the finishing touches on his late lunch. He brought forkfuls of Jambalaya to his mouth while reading the tail end of his report on Adams. He noted the dry pastiness of the rice and thought about some of the really good beans and rice he used to eat back in the day, when he and his brother and father would drive out of the city along Highway 90, prospecting for crawfish with their little nets and would stop to buy a meal at some little gumbo stand, eating off the rusting trunk of Papa's Oldsmobile 98 in the early spring heat of a Louisiana March. Those were the good old days to be sure. They had nothing but everything back then. Good companionship and an uncluttered mind worked wonders for the soul. He knew that now because he'd lost both.

His intuition kept calling him back to Adams. He went over the report again, realizing the Chief had been right on the surface. It didn't have enough substance to warrant an investigation, but something in the back of his mind kept cajoling him about the whole thing. He tried to dismiss his state of mind owing to the fact that Adams traced the traffic back to New Orleans, to his home town. The suggestion that his family might suffer from his oversight, his inaction, continued to gnaw at him. He envisioned his brother's idle ship, moored to the wharf and empty of crew in a sort of Neutron-Bomb –Meets- Pearl- Harbor scenario. Other images of his father, now frail and tottering, suffering from some act of violence under a cloud, dark with poison spreading over the city prevented him from moving on to other, more salient issues. Like the current surveillance of the Israeli software company for instance.

He agreed with Chief in principle – that project had tangible targets. But he couldn't dismiss the feeling which constricted his diaphragm and made the ersatz ettoufé on his desk even more unpalatable.

He looked around the lobby as he wrestled with his decision. All the desks in a row -- set up for bank clerks. The past three years he had grown accustomed to this, but now he saw it for what it was. He had served well and done what was expected of him. That was commendable. But doing this would never take him to where he wanted to go. He would continue to be a lackey, an underling for Chief or Chief's replacement for another five years. He would have to do something to break out of this lobby situation. Things moved at a glacial pace in the bureau. He had ambitions, after all. He wanted to make his father proud. His father, who had scrimped for him, even with the whiskey he loved so much. He thought back to those times on the bayou again, picturing his father in the aluminum lawn chair with the green and white webbing and its missing strands and how his father had to position himself carefully so that he wouldn't break the rest of them or fall over. His father sitting there, sipping at the cheap whiskey and directing the boys this way and that, using his experience to put them over a depression filled with the crawfish they liked to eat so much. His father had given up most everything for them. When they all got together at the old house once or twice a year, dad puffed out his chest and strutted as best he could while talking up how well his sons had done. Johnny was a Lieutenant and commanded a Coast Guard cutter out of the Port of New Orleans. He had risen quickly, Dad said, and Johnny wasn't finished yet, no sir, he still had a ways to go. Jack was doing good things for the country in the FBI and would rise just as high, he would tell to the collection of cousins, aunts and uncles or whoever would pretend to listen to the bragging again. Jack and Johnny were modest about all of this, but relished the golden sunshine of their father's pride. Jack now weighed this adulation against the reality of his station in life - being a glorified go-fer, a grunt, no – more like a convict doing three-to-five in the lobby. He would make his father proud, he decided. His father needed new stories to tell. Jack needed to take himself to the next level. He committed himself to it right then. He cleared his desk of the Styrofoam cups, the greasy paper napkins and the plastic utensils.

He decided right then that he'd recruit Adams on the side and take this thing as far as he could. If nothing came of it, so be it. The Chief wouldn't have to know. If something did come of it, he would find a way to make it happen. He took out a scrap of paper and wrote down the contact information. He understood he would have to make it happen or he'd wake up some day, years from then, with the two-percent annual raise, a little bigger pension and the same old bank clerk desk in the lobby.

A Plague on Both Houses

Fight them, and Allah will punish them by your hands,
cover them with shame, help you (to victory) over them,
heal the breasts of Believers,
And still the indignation of their hearts.
For Allah will turn (in mercy) to whom He will;
and Allah is All-Knowing, All-Wise.
Allah – Qur'an 9:14-15

Chapter 24

They were chewing up the miles on I-55, running southbound in the old Plymouth minivan. Al-Warraq sat in the passenger seat and looked over at one of his traveling companions, guiding the car along the highway, just past Normal, Illinois. He had a heavy foot and was exceeding the posted speed limit by more than 15 kilometers per hour.

"Slow down. Stay just above 110 or we'll be stopped, " he sniped.

The Egyptian grunted negatively and slowed his pace. Al-Warraq was in charge – the de facto leader of this five-man cell, but none of the others had any admiration for him.

"How is it that these kuffar are blessed many times over with all of this water?" someone else said. Hassan al-Warraq had always heard 'Allah never listened to unbelievers, for he had sealed their hearts and had consigned them to hell. ' Why would he do anything good for them in this life?

Al-Warraq could see him wrestling with the inconsistency.

"The things of this Earth have been given to them by God, but they do not appreciate that fact. They continue in their unbelief and use the gifts in treacherous ways. They use all of this to oppose the *ummah*. Don't forget that they will pay a grievous penalty in the next life," al-Warraq said.

The thick-chested thug sitting on the rear bench continued to play around with the weapons, clicking pieces of metal together and working the slides at various angles.

"Keep that down, you idiot!" al-Warraq roared over the rush of air, "Don't you all realize that we could be stopped along the way? We still have many hours of travel remaining. Watch what you're doing. Do you see all of these *kuffar* jabbering like monkeys into their cell phones? What if they see your weapons and make a call to the authorities? Do you want to be stopped before we can strike and spend the rest of your miserable lives rotting in an American prison?

Think about the mission and what you're doing for once!" he spat. The pressure al-Warraq felt rushed up into his face, causing veins in his temples to protrude. He turned and looked at the road. He rested his shaking hands against his temples trying to calm himself. He wondered why he had to suffer from such willful incompetence. This was the best they could do?

"How much longer, Hassan?" the driver said.

"Several hours," al-Warraq said.

"We will make it before nightfall then, but we can't approach the house in the light," the driver said.

"I know that – it is not my intention to do that." al-Warraq said. He began fiddling with his laptop, plugging it into the lighter hole on the dashboard. He wanted full battery power for the note he would send to Abdullah.

"What do you intend? Why don't you let us know the plan now, before we get there? You do have a plan, yes?" The Egyptian checked his speed again, and then looked over as if questioning his ability to lead. Al-Warraq grew tired of these petty challenges. Not one of them could lead the group as well as he did. He thought maybe his smaller frame and lack of physical strength prompted all of this second guessing. The fools couldn't see the mission needed his mental strength more than the physical bulk they contributed.

"Just shut up and drive. I will tell you what to do and when to do it. Do NOT question me again. We will stop in the town of Saint Louis and we'll find this piece of filth named Adams. We will get the key from him. Then we will get rid of him and be on our way. Do not question me or my abilities. Don't ask me anymore questions either."

Chapter 25

Jack sat in his car, next to the pedestrian entrance for the parking lot closest to AireWarez and the Greisedieck Brothers building, watching people file past at the end of their work day. He was looking for a great beer belly and the bushy, prematurely gray mane of Ike Henderson. When he spotted his man, Daniels scanned the lot and the street in both directions, trying to spot any familiar faces which might be watching Ike. Satisfied that the coast was clear, he stepped out of his car and tailed him a short distance, waiting until the darker reaches of the covered lot concealed them both. He wanted to be as discreet as possible.

"*Henderson;* hey, *Ike*, I need to talk to you," he rasped.

Ike calmly looked over his shoulder, and then jumped when he realized who had been following him.

"What the fuck are you doing? Do you want to get me tagged? What are you trying to pull here?" he repeated, obviously disturbed.

"I need to talk to you about your friend Ben Adams. I know what he's doing with the website," Jack responded.

"Website? What are you talking about?" Ike said, trying to feign ignorance.

"The al-mu'minum site your friend hijacked. He came to me the other day. He said he wants to work with me." Jack looked around as he said this. They continued walking along, although at a slower pace and a few steps apart. Jack checked out the rest of the people he could see in the garage and continued on. "I want to work with Adams on this. We need to check it out."

"Leave him alone," Ike said forcefully, "he doesn't have anything you want. He's just playin' okay? He doesn't need to be involved in all of this. He's got kids, for Chrissake." Ike looked over at Jack with real anger in his eyes.

"Look, I'm sorry to have to approach you like this, but I don't see an alternative. Chief thinks this is bullshit, but I have a feeling about this. I need your help. I need to find out what you know about it and if you think it's legit. You're a hacker – what do you think? Is this for real?"

"Hacking got me into this mess. You say it's illegal and I'm being punished for it by having to work with you assholes, but then you try to wring every drop of knowledge out of me you can. You're using me and now you want to use him. He's like a brother to me. The Chief leads me around by the balls and now you want to get in on the act. You ain't gonna use my friend like you use me. No way." Ike stopped in his tracks, adjusted the sling of his laptop bag and looked squarely at Jack. Jack stopped and dropped his keys, putting on an act for anyone watching.

"Look, Adams came to me. He wanted to work with me – not the other way around. I've been going over what he told me and I think it's worth pursuing. He came to me first, you understand what

I'm saying?" Jack protested.

"Ben's got too much to lose. And if your boss findsout and he'll put you in the bureaucratic shit can. You lose too. Forget about it, okay?"

Ike started walking, picking up the pace and trying to ignore Jack. Jack bolted and matched his pace again.

"Just answer me this – do you think he's got something there? Yes or No?" Jack insisted. He looked at him so he could read the answer.

"No. Now get out of here before you get me killed." Ike said, never looking back. Jack stopped and turned. He had his answer.

Chapter 26

Ben had been getting more hits on the NetMail.com account. They all used the encryption scheme so far. He had three messages but no idea about their purpose. They all came out of the Drafts folder, so he concentrated six crackers on that folder alone. For the two other accounts he put one process each on the Draft and Sent folders and ran them non-stop. He took to using dial-up Internet service, so that his IP would be random, assigned at log-in. This slowed him down, but mattered little once he had the windows up in parallel and running off of other servers. They refreshed the monitors with a strobe-light effect.

His eyes grew tired of looking at the disjointed output after a few seconds and he shifted his attention to the one monitor with a hit. It came from the ArRad13 account. It was dated yesterday – very fresh. Unlike all the other notes, it consisted of a single line of clear text. He grew more interested and adjusted himself forward in his chair, his hand gripping the mouse tighter. He looked at it again.

27/06 23:15 24.5555-85.245

He tried to wrap his mind around the puzzle. The first part seemed obvious. Tomorrow at 11:15 pm, he thought, but what Time Zone. Times are usually local – but where? MIME header information told him it came out of Nutrias.org again so for the moment he assumed Central Daylight Time.

The recipient address, 55212346909@brasitbp.com, looked like a pager number. He checked the registry on the domain and confirmed the recipient to be Brazilian, international in range and with a Rio de Janeiro area code. But what about the other numbers: 24.5555 -85.245? He stared at them, putting them into the hollow spot in his mind. He began talking to himself, letting his eyes dart about the room, crossing over the salsa red of the walls and resting on his collection of Budweiser holiday steins lining the top shelf above the gas log fireplace. What does this look like? What would I send to someone on a pager? "120 characters or less", he said, resting his eyes on a picture of the kids.

It took him back to that perfect afternoon on their little desert island in the middle of the Lake. It was last June, a day much like this one, with the puffy clouds embossed on a deep blue sky. He remembered the water lapping against the bow and the rustling of the scrub bushes in the wind. They had been the only sounds on that island, in that time. He realized he missed them and hadn't called them in a couple of days. but he'd have to wait until tomorrow, because of the party.

His mind came back to the numbers. The pager message. The numbers. What information would he send? They had sent the day and the time... *time, date and place – when and where* --it must be a place, he thought. The place. ArRad13 reaches the U.S. and wants to rendezvous. Two numbers, as in GPS coordinates.

With a rush of excitement, he hopped on to a site to check up on his theory. He navigated through the links until he came to the spot where he could put the numbers in. He did it and clicked. The web page froze for what seemed too long, and then returned the results. He stared at them, disappointed.

He checked the numbers and tried again, thinking he had made a mistake. It came back the same, pinpointing a spot in the Gulf of Mexico, out in the middle of nowhere. He copied the results into a folder with the rest of the data to burn on a CD. He thought of giving up the whole thing. He risked prosecution for breaking into these accounts and had only produced gobbledygook and frustration for the effort. Maybe Ike was right for a change.

Chapter 27

The simple pleasures from beer, barbeque and friends promised a good evening. A few puffy cumulus clouds dotted the horizon, perfecting the tableau and the sun, still far above the horizon, cast the long, golden rays of evening through the gently swaying trees lining his back yard. *Heaven on Earth*, he thought.

Ben methodically passed along the ranks of the hundreds of Gladiolus lining the walkway to the backyard, fenced in with waist-high white vinyl pickets. The flowers stood at attention with the single-minded purpose of reaching up toward the warmth and the sunlight on one of the longest days of the year: June 24th. He pruned an armful of the tallest soldiers, picking among peak bloomers for their mix of color.

Most guys wouldn't give a rat's ass about displaying live flowers in the house, but Ben did. Gladiolus possessed a perfect combination of traits for Ben; they were showy, elegant flowers and didn't require much work on his part. He enjoyed the warm feeling he got from a house full of fresh-cut flowers. He also arranged them carefully, accounting for things such as a balance of color, and symmetry. He always put some thought into how best to position vases around the house for maximum effect. He liked to have a full vase in at least two if not three rooms at a time during the height of the season.

Finishing his selection, he fired up the gas grill and adjusted the flame to get the heat up quick. He wanted to be ready in case people came early. Someone was always coming early. He double-checked the cooler's ice and was lugging it out the sliding door when the doorbell rang. He sat it down and hurried to the front door, looking out the left sidelight through one of the larger pieces of leaded glass. His suspicions were correct -- it was Ike of course. That was fine, since Ike had been to the house enough times to make himself useful. He opened the door and noticed his guest swayed in the breeze, like the shade trees out back.

"Wassup dewd? You know what, with the little white fence and all the flowers and trees and shit, your house looks like something out of 'Leave It to Beaver'. Has anyone ever told you that?" Ike slurred. He looked preoccupied.

"Yes. You have. At least three times -- dude, are you wasted?" Ben looked at him disapprovingly.

"Well, not wasted. I did smoke a doob on the way over, though. It's some good shit." He hacked a dry cough a few times to emphasize his point. "Look: some people see the glass half empty;

some see it half full. I don't see the glass at all, since I drank all the booze in it, understan'?"

"Haven't you seen the commercials lately? Drug money supports terrorism. Every time you smoke some dope, you're helping some Columbian kill a judge or a cop," Ben said, not really joking.

Ike stepped up into the house and onto Persian rug that took up a third of the foyer floor. It matched the staircase runner, held against the oak-treads with polished brass rods.

"You're right, dude, I support terrorism with dope smoking. I'm just like soccer moms across America." He threw his arms up to emphasize his point.

"Soccer moms?"

"Yes, the soccer moms and all the rest of 'em in this great nation who drive those hulking S.U.V.s around town getting 10 miles to the gallon. All the poseurs who want to look cool in their shiny new ride. All sitting there in traffic, one poseur per S.U.V, burning it up at the rate of 10 miles a gallon. We wouldn't want to reduce our dependence on oil, now would we?"

They walked through the foyer, turned into the great room and walked into the kitchen, Ike still talking, "We wouldn't want to reduce the easy money al-Qaeda gets from the charities of the wives and daughters of the oil sheiks now would we? That would mean changing our habits. Why should we have to change our lifestyle? You know how hard it is to climb out of a Saturn when you want to go to that all-you-can-eat buffet? That's a serious sacrifice –" He stopped shouting and pounding on the kitchen table as Ben distracted him by opening the refrigerator door. He began to remove platters and bowls and placed them on the granite counter of the kitchen island. The metallic ringing of the bowls bounced off the cabinets with acoustic sharpness.

"Okay, let's not start some shit here," Ben said, picking up the pace. He continued talking as he rushed around the room from one side to the other in busy triangles. "I was just teasing. I don't want to ruin your vibe. Chill, all right? And about driving alone, don't worry, if you get too wasted I'll drive you home tonight. I'll pick you up for work tomorrow and then you can come over and get your car after work. It's all right, man, don't have an aneurism, okay?" Ben busied himself, moving selected trays out to the large, oval oak table and adjusted the two vases of Gladiolus, one with white flowers, the other with pale yellow. A larger and more elaborate vase of mixed colors sat on the wet bar, along with the blender and bottles of tequila. Ike paused as if considering the offer.

"Wait man…what time are you plannin' to go in tomorrow?"

"The usual time, I get in about 8:30."

"That's too early. I might have to stay here all night and drive in myself, sometime around 10." He was always such a joker. Sometimes he was even funny.

"Grace would love to hear that…" Ben said, adding, "I need some help getting ready. Will you cut up the celery and the carrots while I change?" Ben pointed at the empty tray and the cutting board over on the island.

"Appetizers? Celery? How long you been married dude? Are your balls still hanging in your sack or have they pulled back up into your body cavity? Celery? I don't need no stinkin' celery. Carnivores don't need no stinkin' celery," he grimaced and made growling noises while flexing his arms. Ike ambled into the kitchen and despite his protest, began to pull things out of the refrigerator. Ben could hear him opening cabinet doors as he walked into the master bedroom.

"Where's a knife?" he yelled from the kitchen

"Pull one out of that knife block to your left," he replied.

The tempered steel sang a little bit as it came out the oak block.

Chopping noises.

"Hey, do you mind if I put on some tunes?" He didn't wait for the answer.

The house filled up with reverberations. A blast from the past. Ike cranked up "The Four Horseman" by Aphrodite's Child to the point where the windows rattled. Ben listened to the jams as he changed into his dark green t-shirt with "Have Another Beer" spelled out in blurry letters, a pair of cut-offs and a pair of swimmer's sandals. He walked back into the Great Room, singing along to the atmospheric, Middle-Eastern intonations of "The Four Horsemen." Ike cranked it up.

"I haven't heard Aphrodite's Child since The Lost Years in college," Ben shouted over the guitars with a mix of nostalgia and disbelief. He walked outside to one of the coolers and fished around.

"Gotta love KSHE-95: Real Rock Radio. Hey, I've got an MP3 of this if you want it. Peer-to-Peer file sharing is a beautiful thing," Ike shouted.

"You can rip off an album as arcane as '666' out there?"

"It's called *sharing*," he yelled, "I had my pick of 196K or higher bit rates too. You can find just about anything out there, if you know how and where to look." Ike continued chopping and shouting over the music. "Audiogalaxy made it so easy too, until they had to shut the sharing down and start charging for it. That really sucks… "

"Can you burn me a copy of that? Hey... heads up!" he shouted, tossing a beer through the sliding glass door. Ben went back outside to check on the fire, then cut a few more flowers out of the beds.

He heard the sound of tires ripping a turn and looked up to see Dafna's car rounding the corner. He tipped his beer and drank a couple of swallows of ice-cold beer until the bubbles burned his throat.

She pulled up on the curb opposite his house in her late model silver Taurus. Dafna popped out vivaciously and waved over the top of the car. Ben pulled himself up from the flower bed until he stood completely erect and waved the bunch of Glads. He had clipped five different colors – white, yellow, a warm salmon, red and two dark purplish flowers.

She approached him with a charming, infectious enthusiasm. Her hair whipped back and forth in slow motion and shined coppery-golden in the dramatic side light of a late summer's eve. Her breasts bounced underneath a spaghetti-strap tank top the same color as the salmon blossoms he cradled in his arm. Her smooth, tanned legs contrasted nicely with the linen-colored shorts she had on. She was beautiful. She simply exuded it when she moved. She sort of twinkled at him as she latched onto his flower arm. Her hands caressed his forearm. She had warm and loving hands.

"Ben, how nice of you to think of us girls with the flowers." She smiled with her eyes. His eyes smiled back. Then remembered the other women.

"Us? Ya'el, Tzipi... I didn't think you'd be coming over tonight."

Conquest

With his attention on Miss Poetry In Motion he hadn't realized the two other ladies had come across the lawn as well. It's true that Ya'el means something like 'mountain goat' in Hebrew, but it was a misnomer. Ya'el was a fine-looking woman. She came across as a fun-loving person as well and had brains and talent. But she was overshadowed. It was her unfortunate circumstance to have roommate and friend who moved like Dafna did and who had a certain intangible quality which made men ignore all other women present. Dafna carried herself in a way which tapped into some deep longing inside of men. The man she fell in love again with would be the happiest and luckiest man in the world. She would show him a quality of love most men never know.

Men only want two things from a woman after all. They want sex. Lots of sex. Sex in energetic and imaginative ways. That's a matter of record. But men also want the undying love and devotion of their woman. That love comes from acceptance, appreciation and trust. It's a love that makes a man feel he's the best god-damned guy in the world despite all of his faults. Every guy knows he has faults. A rare creature like Dafna could look past those faults for the right man. Ignore them completely. Disregard them entirely. That made her radiant. That and the fact that she bounced when she was happy.

"Hi Ben. You grow beautiful flowers and in all the colors. What do you call those in English?" Ya'el asked.

"Thanks. They're Gladiolus. I think they came from South Africa originally, but don't hold me to that." He looked around the corner, towards the grill. "Would you please come around back? We're just getting ready."

"You and Ike, I suppose?" Dafna said. She was still holding on to his flower arm and gave him a flirtatious squeeze. Ben didn't fight the power, but he hadn't forgotten he was married. Yet.

"Ben you have a very nice house. I like the little white fence and all of the flowers, " Ya'el said.

"Have you and Ike been comparing notes?" he asked.

"I don't know what you mean."

"Never mind, I was only joking, " he said as he opened the latch and ushered the three fine Israeli women onto the back patio.

"Actually yes, I prefer a good Partagas if you're buying," Dafna said, passing over the smaller, blonde cigars for an after-dinner Dominican. *What could be sexier than a Mediterranean goddess sucking on a stogie,* Ben thought. He could come up with only one thing sexier and it still involved sucking…

"Dafna, can I watch you smoke that thing too? Something that good would probably cost me $50 on the East Side," Ike said with a dose of primal lust. *I know he's kidding, but you can almost see Ike's tongue hanging out at the thought, like a Pavlov dog salivating at the bell. What a horn-dog,* Ben thought, *but what am I saying? I'm just as bad.*

"I'll be back in a minute," Dafna said, the unlit cigar hanging from the side of her mouth. She coyly threw a backwards glance over her shoulder, catching both sets of eyes locked onto her sculpted ass. *Of course she catches us with our imaginary hands all over her fine kosher booty. Damn she's good! And I'll bet she is…*Ben thought, the beers helping to dampen any potential feelings of embarrassment he might have at being caught looking.

The deck had about twenty people on it, mostly people from work but with a few others Ben had invited over. Four of the American developers played a game of Washers on the lawn a few yards from the deck, punctuating their shouts and curses with clangs when the washers struck the metal cans in the center of the wooden boxes. Everyone seemed to be having a good time. The food was nearly gone and the beer supply was shrinking at a respectable rate. Music floated out into the still evening air and overpowered the drone of the occasional mosquito. Many Israelis had shown up, Ofer included. He hadn't pressed Ben about the new project but had insisted on a tour of the house. The four-piece crown molding around the top perimeter of the great room and foyer impressed him. He commented on the cost of such things back home and lingered on the balcony to look at its construction. He didn't want to talk shop and spoil the evening anyway, so he returned to the deck.

He heard Ike's voice booming out from the kitchen above the music and chatter. *Ike is really tying one on,* he thought, *something must be bothering him.*

Ben and one of the java developers were talking about the latest Cardinals' game when Dafna returned. She looked around with a lack of interest until their eyes met and hers brightened in her expression. She came back over and stood between them, turned slightly in Ben's direction. She locked her hands around the crook of his elbow again and broke into the conversation.

"You have a beautiful house, Ben. Your furnishings are so nice. And your lovely wife keeps the place in such order. You're a lucky man, do you know that?" The developer blushed a little at this fawning display of affection.

"Thank you very much Dafna" was all he said. It made Ben a little uneasy to have her attentions this way, so he tried to play it cool in front of the other guy. They resumed the baseball talk for a while longer, but Dafna stayed at his side, his evening escort, and eventually the developer went out to join the Washers game.

The phone rang. He excused himself and picked up the phone, at double pace, before it triggered the answering machine. They had an old digital machine, an ATT model 1717 which could have answered it well enough, but Ben thought it best to remove himself from Dafna's charms, which had been generating sexual fantasies in his mind's eye. Seeing the lake number in the CallerID window, he pressed the 'talk' button.

"Hello," he said, suddenly noting the loud mix of music and voices.

"Ben? This is Grace," her voice trailed off, sounding annoyed, "Are you having a party?"

Busted, he thought.

"Yes dear, I decided to have a few people over after work. How are things at the Lake?" he asked, trying to divert her attention.

"We're doing fine down here. We've had great weather. I've been trying to teach Kristen how to ski behind the WaveRunner. It sounds like you've been having a time, yourself," she said sarcastically, "with about fifty of your closest friends."

"No big deal, honey. Just a few people. It's pretty mellow here. We're barbequing and playing some Washers out back. No big thing."

"So you decide to have a little party while we're gone? I guess I shouldn't ask if you've missed us, you've probably been too busy to think about us, right? Ben, you're not in college anymore, you know, you've got a family now." The low roar of the party kept him from hearing if she was really pissed or not. He decided to play it safe.

"Honey, of course I miss you," he said sweetly, smiling into the mouthpiece, "I miss my other girls too. I'll be down Friday night – I can't wait to see you guys again." He took another hit off his bottle, the beer growing warm and light and in need of replacement. He looked out on the deck and saw Dafna watching him with a knowing expression on her face.

Just then Ike dropped the beer bottle he was shagging out of the cooler closest to the phone.

“Oh *SHIT* people," he yelled over the chat, "first drop of the night!” He punctuated the confession with one murderous blasting belch in the direction of the receiver.

“Ike’s there? Oh Jesus Ben, the house better still be standing when we get back. Standing and in one piece.” He heard her exhale into the phone.

“Honey you know how harmless Ike really is don’t you? He’s just all bluster and he gets loud and stupid when he’s been drinking. He probably sounds like three or four people over the phone.”

“How’s that different from when he’s sober?” she asked, her tone icy.

Grace never did like Ike.

He looked across the room just in time to see Ike miss his mouth with most of the tequila shooter he was throwing back.

“AW PEOPLE: I’ve got spillage. Wooo Dawwgie!!” he yelled.

"I'll call you back later when I put *your* kids to bed and *your* party dies down." Ben winced at the disagreeable click of a dead phone line.

He put the phone back in the cradle. He got himself that fresh beer and decided he'd better get Ike out onto the deck before it was too late. He didn’t want to spend the rest of the week patching holes in the walls and painting before driving down to the Lake.

Alone again, Ofer stopped playing the pinball machine and checked the stairs. Satisfied, he walked purposefully through the French Doors into the Adams' study. He took another device out of the side pocket of his American-style Cargo shorts and placed it behind a row of books on the top shelf of the bookcase. They would have no problem picking up any sound in the room from this location. He thoroughly surveyed the contents of the room, looking for any printed notes from the hacking work Adams had done. Most people were careless in their own spaces. Ofer had picked up much intel simply by walking in and taking scraps of paper off the tops of desks and file cabinets many times before. Unfortunately, he saw nothing of interest. Adams kept the place very neat. He shuffled through a pile of unlabeled CDs, looking at their tracks to see if he found one with a low volume of recorded data. Adams might burn off the website logs and a nearby CD would most likely be used. He took a couple of promising ones, putting them into his pocket with the two remaining bugs. He pictured the layout of the house in his mind, looking for any zones where a microphone would be necessary. The kitchen needed one.

After a couple of seconds, he pulled out the last of the miniature video cameras and placed it between the Collected works of Shakespeare and an old copy of Melville's Moby Dick, again in the built-in bookcase. It had the best viewing angle. He smiled and returned to his pinball game, the whole process taking about two minutes. He had the combination to the security system and the imprint for the key already. He would finish his game and then take care of the work in the kitchen. He had always loved American pinball games, even as a boy.

Ben said goodbye to the last of the software developers as they walked out the backyard gate. Only Ike, Dafna and her two girlfriends remained. Ya'el and Tzipi were sitting at the breakfast counter shaking their heads at Ike and his swaggering come-ons. Dafna came out onto the deck and joined Ben, gathering up the odd plates and plastic utensils left behind.

"Thank you for having us over tonight, Ben. I enjoyed being here with you." She looked up at him and the look she gave him stopped him in his tracks for a second. She had bedroom eyes and she didn't try to hide them.

"I'm glad you came, Dafna. It wouldn't be the same without you," he said, looking at her a little too long. He was glad they had a table between them.

"Would you like me to stay for a while?" she suggested, "I can help you clean up for a couple of hours. Ya'el can return for me later, if necessary." She said, putting the emphasis on 'if necessary'. Ben entertained the idea of keeping her at the house for a while. He couldn't allow that to happen. He could never do that to Grace.

"Thanks for the kind offer, but Ike and I can handle it," he said, his voice raspy. He felt it urgent to get her out of the house before he changed his mind. "We can take it from here," he said, looking at the roundness of her breasts as she leaned over to gather up the platters and the used dishes.

They stacked the dirty plates and emptied the cups into the sink the same time as Ben poured cold water on Ike's attempts to hook up with either of Dafna's friends. He got a look of relief from the girls and the opposite from Ike. They immediately picked up on his hint and readied themselves to leave, wasting no time well-wishing and thanking Ben for the evening and waving over their shoulders as they walked through the front door. Ben stood in the foyer, waving at them and waiting for Dafna. She came out of the bathroom her expression still warm, but muted by the abrupt send-off. She clutched the little handbag in from of her with both hands. She looked out the doorway and not seeing her friends in the line of sight, stopped directly in front of him, very close, and looked up, shaking her thick coppery-brown mane to fully expose her heart-shaped face.

"I'll stay if you want me to," she said, in a low, musical way, "you still need help cleaning up." Her features relaxed and her eyelids grew heavy as her lips slowly parted to reveal the tips of her teeth, separated by the pink wetness from the tip of her tongue. She waited for a response and not getting it, she wrapped her arm around his neck to the elbow, pressing herself against him and reaching into him with her tongue. He pulled away after a time and opened his eyes, becoming aware of his penis resting up against the flat of her belly. He couldn't feel the clothes between them. He felt her Mon Pubis rolling hard against his inner thigh. He drew a quick, sharp breath and shook his head to ground himself once again.

"Goodbye Ben," she said, releasing him and turning slowly, but giving him a look as she left to join her friends, now honking impatiently in the Taurus across the street. Ben stood there with a racing pulse and a mind in overdrive. She waved with the tips of her fingers, her bangles calling out a tune. A spaghetti strap fell and still looking over her shoulder, she mouthed "Goodbye Ben" and smiled. He wanted to run out to her, pick her up and throw her down on his bed, tear off her shorts and plow deeply into her. He imagined her warm and moist, drawing him in and throbbing in time with him.

Ike broke the bubble.

"Are you gonna help me out in the kitchen or not?" He complained, his arms dripping suds onto the polished oak planks. Ben turned his head and blinked a couple of times.

"Yeah, I'm coming," he said, absentmindedly shutting the door. He tried replaying his fantasy, but found it as ephemeral as those early-morning dreams that you can't get back to after waking up, no matter how long you lie in bed.

They cleaned pretty hard for a while working off their respective drunks. Ike had the worst of it, to the point of unsure feet. Dishes done, he went out onto the deck and took a smoke break. He leaned against the railing in the dark and watched Ben through the sliding screen. When he saw Ben winding down he lit another cigarette and spoke.

"We need to talk, man," he said, pinching the butt between his thumb and index finger.

Ben looked out in his direction. "All right, what about?"

"The hacking. Your website. I know you've been talking to the F.B.I."

"They weren't interested, really," Ben said, then after pausing: "How do you know that?"

"It's complicated – but look, I told you getting them involved would be a serious mistake. Why didn't you listen to me for once? You're getting into something that's not worth the trouble. After work today an agent approached me," he said in a low and measured tone, "his name is Jack Daniels. He wanted to know if I thought you were on to something. I told him to fuck off."

"You're a narc?" Ben asked incredulously. He could think of no other way Ike would be aware of his visit to the lobby the other day. "You work for the FBI?" Ben repeated.

"I don't have a choice. It's part of a plea bargain I made a few years ago out in California," he admitted.

Ben looked at him blankly, his jaw slack.

"You're playing with fire here, Ben. I'm asking you as a friend to reconsider this whole thing. Just drop it. You've got too much to lose and nothing to gain by messing around with these guys. They'll use you or they'll come after you and take away all of this," he said forcefully,"I've been their go-fer for almost three years now. I'll be marked the rest of my life. Don't make the same mistake."

Ben grew angry at the condescending tone. Ike had been a cracker for fun and profit. His motivation, on the other hand, had nothing to do with self interest. He wanted to protect his family and country. He crossed his arms and set his face hard.

" I'm trying to stop people bent on hurting all of us, you included. I want to stop them before they kill more good people like Nick," he said, his voice getting louder.

"You are doing this for yourself, dude. You're in it for the revenge. That's every bit as selfish as anything I ever did," Ike rebutted matter-of-factly.

"Bite me, asshole," Ben spat, "you haven't had anyone close to you killed in the prime of their life like I have."

"I want to stop you before I do."

The wave of anger in Ben subsided.

"Look," he said in a tone of conciliation, "I appreciate what you're saying. Thank you for caring enough to expose yourself. I understand you're taking a risk in talking about this. But it's all for nothing, really. They don't want to work with me anyway."

"You're wrong. Like I said, the one you talked to – Daniels -- approached me in the parking lot. He wanted to know what I thought of you. He wants to see what you've got. I think he's doing an end-run around his boss, too. That's bad about seven different ways, man. Chief is strictly by-the-book and this guy's going to drag you into the middle of something you don't want to be in. You won't see any results anyway dude. Your Boys From The Internet will come and go long before they can get their act together. I have first-hand experience with this, trust me," he said, trying to be reassuring.

"What are you doing for them anyway? Are you spying for them at work? What's going on?" Ben couldn't accept the idea that his friend, who looked like a roadie for a has-been classic rock band, was a narc. Ben didn't want to accept it, but how else would he know about the meeting with Daniels?

All this had ruined his buzz. Then his pager vibrated. He took it out of the cradle, pushing on the button to illuminate it. He'd set an alarm so he wouldn't miss his hour at the Perpetual Adoration chapel. He had ten minutes to get there.

"Look man, I've got to go up to church. I've got prayer hour now," he said, in a tired and defeated manner, "Are you going home now or what?" Ben stroked the top of his head, exhaling deeply.

Ike looked at him, concerned, with no traces of animosity in his face but darkened bags under his eyes made him look weary. "I'll stick around 'til you get back. I'll finish up in there, " he said, looking over Ben's shoulder toward the light.

Ben turned and they walked silently back to the deck. Ben went through the door first, put on his sandals and checked his pockets for keys. Ike rattled around in the cooler, got another beer and sat down. He looked up at the copper-rimmed kitchen clock, mounted on the wall next to the planning desk.

"It's five 'till ten," he said. He took a long pull off of his bottle. He set it down with a heavy thud and swallowed.

Ben walked out into the garage, closing and locking the service door behind him. Wrapped up in his thoughts, he failed to notice the beat-up minivan with Illinois plates slowly rolling by the front of his house.

Chapter 28

He entered the four-digit combination for the side door of Saint Roch's church. In the vestibule he noticed muddy tracks left by the visiting faithful during yesterday's rain. He turned and walked down the corridor to the Adoration chapel, passing the life-size portrait of Saint Roch, the patron of plague victims, himself a victim of that terrible affliction. In the painting his suffering eyes fixed on heaven as he raised a festering arm in supplication. A dog licked at the wounded, splitting flesh on the other arm. Ben walked on, listening to the trickling water of the Baptismal pool, the echoes of his footfalls and the ringing hiss of blood in his ears. A line of gothic lanterns cast dim pools of light along the chessboard hallway. He signed the Adorer's log and picked up a copy of the Bible as he scanned the never-ending petition list, scribbled in both male and female hands.

He entered the chapel respectfully, acknowledging the One before him with a nod and a raise of his brow. The old guy scheduled before him gathered up his paraphernalia, crossed himself and left. Ben sat for a moment, looking at the frayed ends of his cutoffs. The bells tolled a count of ten. He realized he still had on his 'have another beer' t-shirt. *What I wear to prayer doesn't matter,* he thought, *but my state of mind does.* He breathed to calm himself and to clear the static in his head: ground himself – that's right.

He still hadn't been able to clear his head completely after six months of this. Praying for an hour every week was a coping mechanism, like taking over the *al mu'minum* website. He had signed up to pray three months after his brother's death. He had hoped it would help him find closure and help him fight the intense hatred welling up from the center of his being. He realized that malignancy still ate at him, hollowing out his soul and could feel it draining the vivid colors out of his life, replacing them with muted shades of gray. He had made no progress.

He knelt and focused on the remonstrance containing the exposed Body of Christ. He crossed himself while saying his opening prayer. He swallowed hard, fidgeted and sighed deeply. The sounds echoed in the little room, hard and bare. He smelled the familiar faint odor of ecclesiastical oils and the scent of the church candles, burning in constant vigilance. He rose, pulled two CDs from his pocket and approached the tabernacle. He knelt, sliding them into the gap between the carved Gothic base and the cold tile floor. He had a total of four CDs stashed away now. Ever since he'd been attacked and his PC nearly compromised he'd been overly careful not to leave incriminating evidence in his house. He didn't know who had hacked him and why they had done it and the warning Ike had just given him in the back yard concerned him even more.

He returned to his seat, knelt again and began saying prayers for those in the book of petitions. His prayers, simple and of few words, amounted to an acknowledgement of those wishes rather than full thoughts. His mind rested briefly on the fragility of mankind. The impermanence of life. He reminded God of all those who needed help in some way, including himself. Especially himself, after all. He didn't say the formalized prayers very often for he knew 'The Church' was an ancient institution of men who sometimes imitated their Savior and sometimes not. He had already realized the difference between the institution of his birthright and a relationship with God. In his former life, before children, when he and Grace had swam in a warm sea of fresh, passionate honeymooners love they had made a grand tour of Europe together, hand in hand, with rucksacks stuffed to the breaking point and nothing but the future in front of them. They had spent twenty five days running from one Old World monument to another. When they'd been in Rome, under the awesome dome of St. Peter's Basilica, just above the entrance to the Popes' tombs, he had stopped to look at Bernini's undulating columns, part of the *balachino* over the high altar. As he looked up at the dome and marveled at the many patterns of precious marble throughout the enormous space he saw all of it, including the myriad

Renaissance masterworks filling the galleries and niches, for what it really was – a tribute to man's vanity and lust for territory and possessions. None of them, though beautiful and perfect in themselves, were the expressions of a God who chose to reveal himself as a poor young man in the backwater of the Roman empire. A Savior whose actions, teaching and lifestyle stood diametrically opposed to everything in front of Ben in that place and in that moment. Now he understood the difference between the institution that had built the awesome monument to Christian faith and the thing behind it all that had compelled its builders. Religion and relationship are two different things. That great building, in all of its majesty and richness, stood for the opposite of what had inspired it – the uncommon insights and teachings of an itinerant Jewish preacher about fifteen hundred years before. The building elicited awe in people but was far removed from the heart of the matter and far from the heart of The Master.

At that place he realized that the point of all the history, wisdom and words in the bible was relationship, not worship. It was all about the relationship of a soul to God. Man makes religions – not God. Religions are a means of unification and control for the ruling class. The word 'religion' never appears in the Old Testament and is never spoken by Jesus in the New Testament. Religion is a tool of obedience and ensures conformity in the people. It is a device suited for domination. It is an opiate of the people, as Marx had said. That was the one thing that he actually got right. Kings and rulers use the human institution of 'religion' to control people – to get the people to do what they want. Rulers ensure their people do as they wish by speaking in place of God.

We are all habitual creatures and most often substitute routine and ritual for real connection. Ben knew he was the same as everyone else in this respect. Muhammad used his alter ego, Allah, as a means of control just like the other rulers of this world. It was nothing new. Isn't that always the story? Isn't that what Jim Jones did with his followers in the Jungles of Guyana, and what Charles Manson did before him, and what David Koresh did after him in his Waco compound? Isn't that what Joseph Smith did for the Mormons? Isn't that what the Granddaddy of all these cult leaders, Mohammed, did as well? *Isn't it ALWAYS what cult leaders do*? he thought.

A Plague on Both Houses

The story usually goes: Since Allah/God/fill-in-the-blank is too distant and holy for the people, he/she/they/it sent down his/her/their/its instructions through the archangel Gabriel/a meteor/clear signs/fill-in-the-blank to guide the people. The people would do well to listen to Mohammed/Charles Manson/Adolph Hitler/Jim Jones/fill-in-the-blank since what he said and did were the 'perfect example for men in all times and places'. Mohammed knew the people would laugh at him if he said, "bow down in my direction five times a day and worship me." So he constructed a god in his own image, gave them 'The Complete Guide to Life' and ruled over the people by proxy, but set himself above the rules laid down for the rest of the people, *and Allah ta'alla knows best. Big Brother loves you. Ignorance is strength. War is Peace.*

Ben closed the book roughly, bouncing a sharp snapping sound off the aging plaster walls in the chapel. He began to assess himself with honest clarity. He had been at this adoration chapel for half a year now, with no discernible results. His heart still spewed the thick, green bile of hatred and his lust for revenge grew unabated. He had so much hatred for the Muslims who killed three thousand innocents on 9/11. He could bring up their faces his mind's eye; nineteen of them, the faces all young and fresh like his brother Nick's. Why is it that the young, with all of their potential and promise, most often carry out the dark, hateful plans of the old, treacherous and bitter? The young are either too stupid or too afraid to risk doing it a better way, he concluded.

Feeling the bitter gall rise to his throat, he apologized to God for dragging his hate in with him, soiling this place of reverence much worse than tracking mud in during a rain storm. Anyone could clean that up – it's not permanent, like the filth of hate and revenge in my heart. He began to fear for himself. *I sin by doing this*, he thought.

He squeezed his hands together, hard, until his fingers became white from the loss of blood. He strained his mind and posture, trying to force out his emptiness. He began reciting The Prayer of Saint Francis with a single-minded intensity:

> Lord, make me an instrument of Your peace,
> Where there is hatred, let me sow love,
> Where there is injury, your pardon Lord...

And then he stopped. He slumped back into the chair and let his head thud against the wall. He knew he wanted to be an Instrument of War, not Peace. He wanted to sow revenge; he wanted injury. He acknowledged the truth: he would remain far from God no matter how much he prayed.

Famine

Famine

Go and learn the meaning of the words, 'I desire mercy, not sacrifice'...
Jesus – Matthew 9:13

Blessed are the merciful, mercy shall be theirs.
Jesus – Matthew 5:7

Why do you only read the Qur'an verses of mercy
and do not read the verses of killing?
Qur'an says; kill, imprison!
Why are you only clinging to the part that talks about mercy?
Mercy is against God.
Ayatollah Khomeini -1981

Chapter 29

Ben pulled into the driveway, dreading the argument he and Ike would resume when he went inside. We walked around Ike's car and started up the path to the front door, tired from the emotional toll of prayer hour and the after effects of too many beers. It was past eleven o'clock now and he just wanted to go to bed. He didn't want to discuss the FBI or the website or the NetMail accounts any more. They could do that tomorrow. He needed rest.

He opened the front door and stepped into the foyer. It was dark in the house except for the kitchen. He hoped that Ike had crashed on the couch, strung out just like him. He kicked off his sandals, pushed them together at the side of the door and went in. He walked silently through the Great Room and then froze mid-step, just inside the kitchen.

Ike sat in one of the Windsor chairs surrounding the table, immobilized by yards of silver duct tape wound across his chest. He had a dishrag stuffed in his mouth. His eyes looked askance at Ben, bugged out to the whites, showing from the adrenaline of fear. He tried to cry out in muffled, throaty alarms.

An explosion of stars and streaks of light clouded Ben's eyes when someone struck him hard on the back of the head. He fell, banging his slack jaw against the rock-hard Italian porcelain floor of the breakfast room. He lay there, swimming in pain for what seemed like minutes until two set of hands lifted him by the arms and roughly pressed him against a chair. Vision blurred, he tried to focus on the strange hands, moving quickly to finish binding him. They had coarse, black hair and were dark in complexion. He shook his head from side to side, limply at first, in an effort to clear his senses. He noticed that he had a gag in his mouth as well.

He raised his head and squinted out into the darkened kitchen from underneath the singular glare of the light fixture, suspended over the oval table. He could see at least two people. He looked over at Ike sitting helpless, beads of sweat running down his face, reduced to grunting.

He could hear low, calm voices coming from the kitchen shadows. The language, incomprehensible at first, became clearer as the ringing in his ears subsided. They were speaking Arabic. He focused on it, trying to translate, but they stopped at that point and the two of them walked up to the edge of light. They looked at him, emotionless. Both of them dressed in the casual sloth of college students. They looked less than twenty-five. The taller one, thin and younger by several years, looked maybe nineteen at most. The shorter one began to speak in English.

"Ben Adams, *Ben Zona,* keeper of the *al mu' minum* website. The Nation of Islam owes you much for your efforts at *Da'wa.* You help bring the world to Islam," he sneered, his face growing darker by the second, "What did you think? That you could steal something important from us and not be noticed? Did you think we would be powerless to do something about it?" He stood about five foot six and weighed a hundred and thirty pounds soaking wet – that is, if he ever took a bath. It looked like he hadn't in a week. Dark bags puffed out under his eyes and a sweaty sheen covered his exposed skin. He looked like he'd been up for three days straight.

"I hope you came to accept Islam during your work on the web site; you know Islam means 'peace'.

"Peace? Who are you kidding? '*Salaam*' means peace. *Islam* means 'submission:' submission to a jumble of lies and the rants of the delusional. Peace? You get peace from justice, morality, fairness and equal treatment under the law. And the means to get these things are nowhere to be found in the Qur'an, nowhere in the words and deeds of its messenger and nowhere in the body of Islamic law - the *shar'ia.* You are delusional, just like your prophet."

The shorter terrorist began to visibly shake. "Shut up," he said, trying to keep himself under control, but Ben egged him on. Ben finally had his audience and he was going to give them both barrels no matter what.

"The old saying goes 'You shall know a false prophet by his fruits.' Your prophet's fruits are in a putrid, rotting pile. Why you insist on following the demented rants of a war criminal, pedophile, highway robber, and liar is beyond me. Haven't your read your own *Ahadith* or the *Sira*? These sources are accepted as scriptural by your religions leaders and the proof is all in there. Your own holy books condemn your prophet."

"The prophet was a man like you and me. He made mistakes, but the holy Qur'an contains all knowledge and prophecy. It has the words of life. For in his wisdom and mercy God marked its pages with the work of life for us, the true believers, and the words of death and judgment for the multitude like you. We use those words a guide to life and a key to our present operation. The Qur'an is an instruction from Allah for men past, present and future. It is a clear sign from God." Their leader looked satisfied with himself as he said this.

"Your Qur'an is clear all right - as clear as a handful of mud and about as useful as a guide for anything, except for being a terrorist. The Qur'an repeatedly contradicts itself, in fact it has to 'abrogate' or nullify earlier verses when it tries to explain itself. Even then it's not coherent – it has no context of time and place. You have to use the example of Mohammed's life to do the *salat*, to go on *hajj*, to pay the *zakat* -- to be a Muslim, in other words. Your 'clear guide' gives you no instruction on the basic tenets of your belief system. And even with abrogation the whole thing just doesn't make sense. Why would a god who created everything need the men he created to go around and kill and terrorize to enforce his dictates? He claimed to have 'destroyed and terrorized whole towns' in the past. Why wouldn't Allah just take care of business for himself? Because Allah really can't do it himself, that's why."

He kept going. Brent kept trying to stop him, but couldn't move much and muffled grunts couldn't drown out Ben as he condemned himself.

"You have over one hundred commands from Allah in the Qur'an to kill unbelievers. Mohammed said "If someone changes his [Islamic] religion, kill him." How can this be the Truth? Truth doesn't need mafia hitmen to defend itself. If a person leaves The True Religion, why would you need to kill him? If he's going to Hell anyway, what's the big hurry? Why coerce people to stay in the religion, setting the death penalty for apostates? Why does Islam need to prevent other religions from being practiced if it's the 'clear truth'? Mohammed set it up like this because he knew it couldn't stand up to questioning. You see, he knew it was a lie. Ethically, morally, logically and historically, the Qur'an is a joke. The Gospels and independent, pagan Roman sources attest to the crucifixion of Jesus, some of these sources being written down twenty to thirty years after the fact. We have independent corroboration that the person known as Jesus of Nazareth was crucified. It's a historical fact and is attested to better than most things from antiquity. This alone shows the Qur'an to be fundamentally in error. It cannot be the Truth and cannot be from God."

"Are you finished, you evil piece of dog shit?" the small one asked. They were all standing in the light now where he could see them, hardened and hateful looks in their faces.

"Your Qur'an isn't clear – but it is transparent. It's obvious Allah was made up by Mohammed to get himself the booty, power, women and respect he couldn't get any other way. Allah can't be God – he is a craven, unjust and unethical thing who throws half of creation to heaven and the other to hell, 'caring not'. That alone makes Allah unworthy of worship or even respect, for that matter. That's plain creepy and sociopathic but it's by no means the end. Allah constantly threatens eternal physical torture for unbelievers and those who reject him. He spends more time in Hell than Paradise. Allah is never in Paradise with his killers and martyrs – it's always the perpetual virgins and young boys taking care of the killers and martyrs. Allah prefers to be in Hell over Heaven – think about it for just one second - who does that *really* sound like? Allah needs you to grovel in the dirt five times a day, singing his praises and brown-nosing him. No all-powerful entity needs his Ego constantly stroked. Your belief system is all about the ritual, not the relationship. Allah needs you more than you need him, don't you see? Allah is really AlterEgo. Allah is Mohammed."

The one closest to Ben punched him hard across the jaw. Ben's head bounced off his shoulder and he had trouble focusing his eyes again.

"…what if I'm right? Think…" Ben said.

"We don't *think* or *analyze* things like you do in the West. We *act* on the words of God instead," one of them said.

"Every word you say condemns you in this life and the next. Do you have any more insults before we kill you? " the short one said.

"You're all good Muslims... true believers…" He finished.

They laughed.

Famine

"You know why we're here. Where is it?" he shouted, glaring at Ben. "I'll give you a few moments to think about it. Be careful how you answer! You will suffer if you answer wrongly," he said, with emphatic flourish. One of men standing behind him came back into view. He had a thick torso and muscular neck and shoulders. He lifted a laptop satchel onto the table and the short terrorist took out a laptop and opened it. The young, thin face of the tall one showed fear and excitement as he walked around the room, looking at the pictures on the wall and half-heartedly poking through the bills and stacks of papers on the planning desk. After a few moments, he went into the cooking area and busied himself at the stove. He took a couple of chef's knives out of the block and laid their broad, flat metal across the burner. The gas flames licked at their edges.

Ben knew they wanted something from the original website. He wished he had made his case better with Agent Daniels. He'd been right about this after all. Then the weight of the situation rested on his mind. He was going to pay a huge price for the small satisfaction of being right.

He looked at Ike, trying to read his thoughts. He didn't know what to do. Should he give them what they wanted? He bounced his legs against the chair. They hadn't bound his or Ike's hands together. He tried to think of how to use that against them, but he couldn't see how.

The small one finished logging into his laptop. He pressed the button on the side of the case, popping the CD player open. Not moving his head, he raised his eyes upwards, locking onto Ben's.

"Where is it?" he demanded. Everyone fixed their eyes on Ben., who lowered his head. He struggled against the tape with no effect.

"You have taken something that's ours. Something valuable. That's thievery, " he started, "You seem to be a student of the Qur'an, although a most perverted one. You know what the Qur'an prescribes for thieves and for 'those who create mischief in the land'?"

Ben said nothing.

"You have forfeited your hand, thief," the short one said.

"Since when do people like you follow the Qur'an?" Ben replied, "The Qur'an prohibits the killing of innocents, like my brother. He died in one of those towers. He was innocent. Tell me what gives you the right to pick and choose?"

"Your brother, innocent?" the leader said. The two that understood English laughed in derision. "He deserved an ignoble death just as you do. All three thousand of them in the towers that day got what they deserved. No one in this country is 'innocent'. You are all guilty of many sins against God and the men of this world. Your country attempts to rule this world as an evil tyrant. You *kuffar* use your shiny planes to send messengers of corruption and idolatry into the very heart of our countries. Your television shows and their dangerous ideas are corruption and death to our way of life and your satellites which beam it into our homes are nothing more than open sewers. You make deals with the hypocrites and *kuffar* who rule places like Egypt and who jail the righteous and torture the just to keep their hold on power. So don't tell me anyone in this country is innocent. You all support this way of life," he said, with a smug satisfaction on his face, "you all grow fat from its milk."

They took offense at him, spitting on him. They cursed him in Arabic. The two behind him took to punching him in the head. He reeled from the blows and felt his eye puffing up in a bloody knot. His jaw pulsed with a broad dull pain and he took an inventory of loose teeth, running his tongue over each of them from the inside.

"We export oil through pipelines. The West exports filth through television cables. This must stop," the young one said. Even he had set his face like flint by now.

"Yes, filth," the short one agreed, "your Christendom wallowed in filth and vermin for a thousand years while our culture reached new heights in navigation, astronomy and poetry."

"No!" Ben interjected. "Don't you see? Don't any of you see?" he cried out, "All you have is a fantasy of the past. You can't return to those golden days by setting a stake in the ground and regressing. You can't hold the world at 900 A.D. Even if you could, it wouldn't be the same as you think it was. The world has moved on. People have innovated. The wheel of progress has a natural force like gravity or erosion – it can't be stopped. The Qur'an weakens you. We all know the sun doesn't rest in a muddy spring like your book says. It doesn't rest at all. It's plain wrong. If you read the book with a rational approach you see it's full of historical errors, inconsistencies and invectives of hate and intolerance for anyone who isn't a Muslim. It demands you kill unbelievers and people with enough sense to see through and reject its lies. I've studied it, I know."

Famine

"That's where you fail to see the truth!" their little leader shouted, spit flying from his cracked lips, "Islam is the religion of peace – your own president calls it 'noble' and a 'religion of peace'. You are wrong."

"Allah called Mohammed 'the best example of men.' The *shar'ia* is the final seal of law. The Qur'an is the literal word of Allah sent down from heaven. It is immutable – it cannot be changed. Innovation and 'progress' are sins in Islam. Your culture incessantly works to pull us away from Allah's unchanging word," their leader said in a chant-like rhythm.

He stood and paced along the side of the table, gesticulating as he spoke, "As our culture reached its highest expression, Allah, may He be praised, saw fit to use the common rat to kill more than thirteen million of your putrid swarm in the Black Death. By the rat He punished you unbelievers and now again you will be punished through a rat. A very large and friendly rat. This July 4th it is we who will be dancing. The streets of Islamabad, Baghdad and Cairo and all other places Muslim will celebrate this holiday for a hundred years." He raised his eyes toward the ceiling, speaking as if to a great, unseen crowd. "On that day you will wail in torment. For as it is written, 'Allah is just and merciful to believers and stern with the unbelievers.'" Satisfied with himself, he lowered his arms and pointed at Ben. "Now where is the key, thief?" He threw his head back, motioning with his eyes toward the kitchen. One of the thugs followed his lead, went in and began rummaging around.

The phone began to ring. Ben squinted, trying to read the CallerID, but couldn't. The little man stopped and watched it, letting it ring twice more, waiting for the answering machine to pick it up. Ben heard a click, more like the sound of static on a phone line than anything. He saw a red LED light up. He knew it was for the room monitor feature. Grace had called back to chew him out over the party. He pictured Grace on the other end, standing on the deck down at the lake, looking out at the stars and growing impatient in that nagging, wonderful effort to check up on her man. A rush of hope welled up in his chest.

"Why don't you let us go? I don't know what you're talking about," he said, as loudly and clearly as he could in the direction of the answering machine.

The muscle-bound Arab came back to the table. He carried a meat cleaver.

"What are you doing with that knife!" Ben shouted. His head began to reel, the situation became real now in his mind

"Bind his hand to the table," the leader said matter-of-factly. He showed no emotion.

The second thug came from behind and held Ben's hand to the table while the other began ripping and applying lengths of tape to fasten it down. Ben tried to struggle, but couldn't get any leverage. He strained against them, but they were too strong and the tape held. A feeling of terror gripped at his chest and throat. He breathed spasmodically. He could feel his heart trying to break out of his chest.

Separate his fingers in the middle," the short one said in Arabic. Ben understood enough.

"What are you doing? Oh God, You're going to chop my fingers off?" he shouted, his voice cracking . He began to hyperventilate. "Oh mother of God, Jesus, help me!"

"Shut up! You woman," the young one said. He laughed.

Ben stared at his hand. The index and middle finger were taped together and had been drawn apart from the other two, making an obtuse 'V'. The muscular Arab walked around him to get a better angle. He stood right next to Ben, cleaver in hand. Ben smelled days-old sweat in his clothes.

Ben looked over at the answering machine. "Grace, get help! They're going to kill me! Hel-," he managed to scream, before the elbow smashed into his jaw. His head snapped again with the force of it. His vision blurred as his head grew too heavy to support. He slumped as far to the left as the tape would allow.

"Get the other knives," the leader said to the young one. He retrieved the hot ones from the stove.

Ben tried to raise his head. He couldn't manage it for long.

"I'm asking one last time -- where is the data from the *al mu' minum* website? The data! Now!" he lowered his voice, speaking intimately into Ben's ea, "Tell me now and I'll let you keep your hand."

Ben said nothing. He knew they were going to kill him and Ike, hand or not. A strange clarity came over his mind. He said nothing. He looked at his hand. It looked alien to him as he tried to dissociate himself from what was about to happen.

"Do it," the leader said.

Famine

Ben closed his eyes, feeling the crushing blow on his two little fingers. He heard the sharp, rapping sound of the cleaver wedging itself into the table top. He heard Ike trying to scream repeatedly through his gag. Ben opened his eyes and saw Ike staring wide, every muscle in his head and neck contacted. He looked down at the table where Ike stared. His two fingers had flown off in the impact and landed on the table, directly in front of Ike, where a dinner plate should be. Small trickles of blood came from their ends

"Burn him," the leader said.

Ben noticed the young one on his left side now. It all seemed unreal to him, as if he was watching from behind a curtain, until the hot-steel burned his skin down to the knuckles. The searing flesh closed and the pool of blood stopped growing. The pain shot upwards from his hand and gripped his whole being, paralyzing him in white-hot agony. When the pain released its grip slightly he had enough room to scream, pulling half of the tape from the table as he writhed. The one holding the cleaver jammed his gag, spotted with his own blood, back into his mouth. His nostrils flared as took a breath, deeply drawing in the dense smell of his own burning flesh

They let him and Ike scream into their gags until the wave subsided. Then he spoke again.

"Where is the key? Tell me now and you may keep the other two," he said amicably, "you can still do your computer work at this point." He let that soak in as he walked out to the kitchen to fill a glass with tap water. When he came back, he took a long drink, then folded his arms and considered the situation in front of him.

'We will find it, you know. We will find it whether you're alive or dead. We've got all night."

He relented. He wasn't ready to die and he didn't want his girls to go through life as he had – bitter at his father's death and following the course of least resistance.

"I'll give you the disks," he managed to say.

They all brightened at this.

"Where are they?" the leader said, animated at the prospect.

"Downstairs – in my office. Hanging from the ceiling in the corner. Just get them all," he mumbled, broken and defeated.

He could hear the two behind him walking across the wooden floor. The basement door sweep squealed as it rubbed an arc across the boards. He looked at Ike. "I'm sorry," he said, "I'm sorry I got you into this."

Ike nodded and looked at him sadly, as if he thought the world was coming to an end. They both had the bent shapes of condemned men, sitting in silence, wondering if they would see the next day.

The two Egyptians wasted no time in Ben's office. The stockier one pulled down the CD mobile Ben had hung in the corner nearest his desk. The other, carrying a little bag of tools, began ripping the wires out from the back of the computer. He took out a battery-powered screwdriver and opened the case, throwing it across the room with abandon.

"Shout down to me when you find the key," the other one said, as he walked out with the stack of disks, adding, "Do you need my help with the rest of it?"

"No, it will only take me five minutes once I find the gas line," he said, as he carefully laid his tools, the incendiary trigger and the timer down on the desk.

Presently, the one who had removed Ben's fingers came up the stairs clutching a handful of CDs. He stacked them on the table and the leader began to feed them into his laptop to read them, his eyes darting back and forth and up and down, searching for the prize while clicking and typing rapidly. He found it on the fifth disk. His demeanor rose. He smiled broadly and raised his arms in jubilation.

He shouted the Fear Prayer in Arabic, "*Allahu Akbar*! Allah is Greater!" He looked extremely satisfied at this. "He has delivered our enemies into our hands! He has guided us well. We have the keys!"

The other two repeated in Arabic, " *Allahu Akbar! Allahu Akbar! Allahu Akbar*!" in a rousing chant. They gathered around the monitor in a semi-circle to see the wonder for themselves.

Ben squinted at them through the glare of the kitchen light, enmity replacing fear in his heart. The scene reminded him of the celebrations in Pakistan and in Palestine and other Muslim areas the day his brother died. It sickened him to the bone to think that he had taken something so important from them, only to give it back at the cost of his fingers and probably his life. He had done nothing worth dying for and hadn't even slowed them down. *Now surely more of us will die*, he thought.

At that moment a loud knocking came from the front door. They all froze in position, looking in the direction of the sound. Ben turned his head, wincing at the pain. The knocking came again. The leader pulled a thick, boxy semiautomatic from his bag while the other two produced them from underneath the tails of their shirts. They held them high, close to their young faces; filled with emotions ranging from confusion to apprehensive determination. The young one tiptoed to the sliding door and leaned just enough to scan the backyard. He shook his head slightly at their leader, who seemed to be deciding how to respond. The knocking came again, longer and louder this time.

"Free him," he said jerking his head toward Ben. He closed the laptop.

The other two grabbed the chopping knives, still cooling on the table. They tore through the duct tape with hacking and sawing motions. He wobbled with a lack of balance from his concussion. Leaning over the pool of his blood, he rested against the table. He thought he would vomit.

The leader grabbed him by the throat, pulling him up. "Listen to me, you piece of shit, you answer the door and send them away. Understand?" He pointed his gun at Ike's head. "Hide your hand, now." he hissed at half-volume. Ben nodded and stepped away from the table.

Ben turned the corner to the foyer, wrapping his hand a couple of times in his shirt. He could see a broken silhouette in the many pieces of leaded glass, backlit from the street light. Someone was still out there on the porch.

The Egyptian pushed him to the side, jumping lithely towards the master bedroom double doors. He closed one of them, hiding behind it. He gave a threatening look at Ben and put a long, bony finger to the side of his nose, tapping it.

Ben stood in front of the door now. He had to reach across his body with his left hand to open it. He only opened it as wide as himself, blocking the terrorist behind him from getting a good view.

A patrolman stood at the edge of the porch, about three or four feet from the door. He had a serious look on his face and gripped his pistol, resting without a strap, in his holster. His eyes showed alarm.

"Good evening sir." He spoke quickly and gave Ben the

once-over, lingering at the hand wrapped in the shirt for a moment. "We have a reported assault and robbery at this address. Is everything all right? Are you all right?" he asked, watching Ben for any nuances or lies.

"No officer. Nothing like that's going on here," he said hoarsely, but he raised and lowered his eyebrows rapidly and exaggerated his eye movements back toward the dark interior of the foyer.

"We need to investigate any report like this, sir. I need your permission to have a look around – is anyone else at home tonight?, " he said, stepping back and looking at both corners of the house. Ben mouthed the words "help me", then said, "I don't think that's necessary officer, it must be a prank. Nothing's wrong, believe me." His delivery, cracked and hoarse, contradicted the story line.

At that point a second patrol car rounded the corner, stopping in a lurch at an odd angle in the middle of the street. Its lights flashed silently. Without a moment's hesitation, the driver threw open his door, the car still running at an odd angle in the street. He left it that way, speaking rapidly into the radio mike strapped to his epaulet and running to join his fellow cop.

"Bill," he said, "what's up?" He nodded at Ben, squinting through the shadows to study Ben's bruised face. He unfastened the strap on his holster found the grip of his gun.

"Look officers, no need to worry. Nothing's happening, believe me," Ben said, affecting a casual annoyance in his tone. He showed the four fingers on his good hand. He slowly pulled his hand from his shirt as they kept insisting on checking the place out. He held it up at the base of his sternum, modeling it for them in the dim, yellowish light coming from the sodium arc lamp. They got a good look at his two bloody stumps. Shock and revulsion swept across their faces simultaneously. They drew their weapons on cue. The second one reached for his radio set and called in for backup. The first one shouted, "Sir, open the door and step out here, now!" He held his gun at the ready, with both hands and at eye-level, like the terrorists.

"Do it now!" the second one shouted, sinking into a half-crouch.

Ben threw the door open wide and jumped out onto the porch. He flattened himself against the brick wall, shouting, "Guns. The door on the right." He heard the bedroom door dragging across the carpet as he watched the first cop aim, bending slightly at one knee.

"You in the house! Come out where we can see you, now!"

The second cop separated, angling over to the right for a better line of sight. Ben fell to the porch as the first cop pointed his weapon, shouting "Drop your weapon, now!" He rolled away, bumping into a column on the porch. He looked into the gaping blackness and for an instant, saw a face illuminated by muzzle flashes.

The first cop flew back more than five feet, landing on top of a creeping juniper bush. He laid motionless, his eyes and mouth still open. The other cop squeezed off several rounds at the flashpoint, the bullets streaking over Ben. His ears rang but he could hear the clattering of a gun as it struck the wood floor, followed immediately by the thudding echo of a body as it hit the floor. The second cop jumped the low-lying shrubbery in front of the porch and stepped over Ben. He thrust his gun into the doorway, moving it back and forth. He pulled himself back out of the doorway and leaned up against the brick wall, breathing hard. He took another look at his fellow officer, who still hadn't moved, and then looked at Ben.

"Are you okay?" he said. Ben had a hard time hearing him over the ringing static in his ears.

"Yes, my friend's in there...three more. They all have guns," he said.

A single shot rang out inside the house, then another.

The second cop went through the doorway, the barrel of his weapon moving in tandem with his eyes. Ben pulled himself up to sitting, then pushed himself up to stand, using his good hand. He went over to the dead one, who had started blinking at this point. His vest had saved him from taking a bullet squarely in the chest. He had been knocked unconscious - eyes wide open. He groaned and fluttered his eyes as they rolled back in his head. Ben picked up his pistol. It was heavy and cold in his hand. He stood up and let his sense of balance gather itself while he decided what to do. He had to help the other cop.

He knew they'd try to escape out the back. He managed something like a run around the side of the house, pulled by the desire to make them suffer.

Make Them Pay.

More shots as the terrorists and the patrolmen traded shots.

He slowed his approach at the gate. They could run right up on him. Be careful. Get ready.

He fingered the trigger, ready to squeeze off a round at first sight. But he saw no one. He heard something along the fence line at the back of the yard. He peered towards the sound, hard, as if the effort alone would allow him to see through the foliage. He raised the gun and tensed on the trigger, but couldn't fire. He couldn't see anything. He turned back to the house.

He stopped at the point where he could see Ike's body, head slumped on a shoulder. He collapsed onto the grass, convulsing in waves of heaving sobs. He cried wretchedly, just as he had that night in the elevator, next to his father.

The patrolman found him out there and helped him up. The officer called in for support and an ambulance to take Ike's body to the morgue. Ben felt compelled to look at Ike even thought it caused him to heave violently. Between the concussion and the enormous weight of guilt pressing down on his mind, he puked until it nothing came up but a frothy bile, the color of spring daffodils.

By this time the crime scene technicians were doing their thing. Ben stood off to the side, with hollowness in his pale blue eyes and watched as two thick-armed EMTs arrived with a gurney. They began to work on Ben. One of them was going back out to the ambulance to get supplies when he stopped by the basement door. He opened it and stuck his head in.

"Oh my God, there's a gas leak down there," he managed to say, before the rush of scent pervaded the room.

"Get everyone out of here now!" the EMT shouted, "Everyone out of the house! Gas leak! Get out!" he repeated, closing the door.

Ben ran to the front door, being closer to it. He just crossed the threshold when the house exploded.

The force blew them all into the yard. Ben landed on the grass, cushioning his blow. He rolled a couple of times afterward, coming to a stop at the edge of the flower bed lining the front walkway. Parts of the house came raining down on them. A few seconds later, when he no longer felt anything falling on him, he lowered his arm and looked back through the tangled mess at the shell of his house. Pieces of jagged framing lumber, glass fragments and chunks of pink fiberglass insulation covered everything. He could feel the intense heat coming from the flames, changing what remained standing into thick, black smoke.

A Plague on Both Houses

"We ask Muslims to . . . bleed the enemies of Allah anywhere by any means.
You can't do it by nuclear weapon,
you have to do it by kitchen knife, no other solution.
You can't do it by chemical weapons,
you have to do it by mice poison."
Abdullah Hamza al-Masri –
former imam of Finsbury Park mosque, London

Chapter 30

Ben laid back on the cold, sterile stainless steel of the emergency room table. The fact that he noticed how cold it was surprised him, given the pain from his bruised head, eye, the flash burns and of course, his hand.

He looked up at the face of the emergency room clock, shining like moon-cheese in the sickly pallor of the lights. He breathed vapors from the astringents the orderlies used to try and mask the other odors. It wasn't doing the job. The place still smelled like dead tissue, sweat and old, congealed blood, with several dashes of urine mixed in. His head started spinning as he fidgeted, trying to find a spot where sitting didn't hurt. Off balance from the concussion, he had difficulty sitting up straight and the sling on his arm didn't help matters.

The medical people had worked on him for a couple of hours. They couldn't do anything about the fingers. They were lost in the fire and besides, like the attending doc told him, the cauterization ruled out any hope of reattachment. He would go through the rest of his life with half a hand. He looked over at his reflection in the glass door of a cabinet. His head and upper body looked like a patchwork quilt in the colors of flesh and gauze and dark, dried blood.

They had left him alone to stew in his rage. He found it relieved his pains more than the drugs they had given him. The rage gripped him as he sat gazing at his spilled blood, drying in splotches on the floor.

He wanted to see them suffer and die, slowly, from wounds *he* inflicted. He imagined himself, standing over them, gloating, embracing the dark emptiness, laughing, relishing the sweet rush of adrenaline and the finality of it all. He would see them die, he promised himself. It wasn't over until he did.

Reality broke through again. He had a thought: Should he call Grace now? He looked up. The clock showed ten minutes after three. He decided against it. What did he need to tell here now that couldn't wait? The house would still be a pile of smoldering splinters in the morning. Ike would still be dead. He decided to wait.

He didn't hear them as they came in behind the curtain. Ben had been gazing in the direction of the floor, in the center of the blood splotches beneath his dangling feet. His peripheral vision picked up motion and he raised his head, thinking an attendant needed something. He blinked a couple of times, trying to focus himself. They were FBI – one was Daniels, the agent he talked to, but he'd never seen the other guy – older, balding guy with shiny tasseled loafers. *He must be Chief – the one Ike worked for,* he thought.

"Agent Daniels" he said, trying to nod, "and you're Chief, right?" he asked.

"That's right," Chief said, his prominent, bald forehead reflecting the same shade of light as the clock.

"Ike's dead… I suppose you know that, right?" he looked down at his bloodstains again, "You won't be able to squeeze anymore blood from that turnip, will you Chief?" Ben said with a sneer in his voice. He looked up at them sideways from his slump.

"We need to know what you know," Daniels said, with a touch of empathy in his voice, "Can you help us? We need to stop them, and shut this thing down before more people die."

"Sure I can help. I came to you. I *wanted* to help you. Remember? Two days ago, before all this happened. I came to *YOU*!" he screamed, jerking his head upwards and staring directly at agent Daniels. The cords of his neck stood out as he bared his lower teeth, "I came to you! What's changed, huh? Nothing's changed for you and the Chief here and all the other boy-scouts who do their time, fill out their reports and go home to a nice, warm bed. My bed's a pile of ashes and my friend's a pile of dead meat." He looked right at them, breathing hard, disgust on his face, teeth bared.

Agent Daniels spoke first, "We're on your side, Ben. Try to see that. He mattered to us, too, believe it or not. We've lost an important informer and it's going to damage the case we've been building for almost a year. He mattered to us, don't you see? And we know you've lost a great deal." He spoke softly and turned his palms up in a conciliatory gesture.

It didn't ring true for Ben.

"We're running the prints from the dead terrorist. When Interpol and the CIA confirm what we already know we'll be able to ramp up on this one," Chief said with all the emotion of a mortician.

"In a day or two it won't matter what your sources confirm. They'll still be out there, anonymous, in our country and on their merry way. You move too slow; Ike told me you guys can't get shit done. Never have."

"You need to come down to Market Street with us," Chief said, looking at his watch, "Jesus Christ, it's three a.m. already! We need to debrief you," he said, reaching out to take Ben by his good elbow.

"I'm not going anywhere with you."

"We can't do it here. Anyway ...you don't have a choice, sir," Daniels explained, "you're involved in a terrorist act on American soil and you witnessed an informant's death. You don't have a choice in the matter –"

"The Patriot Act gives us discretion in these situations," the Chief said, "and when we get the confirmation – *tonight*" he stressed, "you *will* help us. You're in our hands now whether you like it or not." A nasty, twitching smile came across his face.

"I'm in *your* hands now? That's good Chief. I'm going to need some good hands now," he said, "I don't have good hands now," he shouted, jerking his arm out of the sling.

"You see what I mean?" Ben said as he jabbed his oozing, bandaged club of a hand up under Chief's nose.

They put him in a 15x12 interview room with the requisite one-way mirror and worn table and chairs. He guessed that he'd been there for at least two hours and imagined the sun would be coming up soon, but he couldn't tell for sure without a window or clock. His pager had been destroyed in the fire too.

He wasn't sure about his car, but it had looked intact when he'd looked at it for the last time in the ambulance. Daniels and Chief had been in earlier, asking him about the details Ike had told him and about things he might have seen or heard at work. They hadn't asked a single question about the terrorists and what had happened at his house a few hours ago.

He sniffed at his shirt, pieces of duct tape still stuck to it, and noticed it smelled like ashes. Daniels had brought him a vending machine pastry and some bitter coffee to drink. They had gone out for a break or something. It was so late now it must be early morning, but he knew that he couldn't leave until they were satisfied. Where would he go anyway? Downtown, without a car and no place to hole up in for some needed sleep. He didn't want to call Grace from this place. The CallerID would probably show her "FBI" and he didn't want to upset her with that. He laughed a lung-rattling cough. Worrying over the CallerIDd incident struck him as irony. He'd have to confess he'd destroyed her house sooner or later. That wasn't the worst of it. He'd gotten his friend killed over a game of Cat and Mouse. That made him guilty of manslaughter or something very close to it. That was worse than the house. In the scheme of things the permanent damage to his hand seemed like a minor detail.

He heard the metallic snap of the magnetic lock and they both came back in, looking dour. Chief took up the seat directly in front of him. Daniels filled in the moments adjusting the microphone on the table, pointing it at Ben once again. Chief had a sheaf of papers with him this time and he collated them like some middle-aged newscaster.

"Okay, Ben, we know who the dead Arab is," Chief started. Ben looked up, eyes narrowing. "His name is Tariq Fahmy. Egyptian; twenty-four and from a middle-class Cairo neighborhood, mostly populated by tradesmen and small-time merchants. He had a record in Egypt – he was a member of the Islamic Brotherhood and was jailed and probably tortured, or at least beaten, along the rest of them. After a big release of this group, he left the country, joining the Taliban back in 1999 following the path many of them took. We think he left there soon afterward and went west to Uzbekistan or Chechnya to support forces aligned with al-Qaeda. That's where the trail stopped. We don't know what he did from the fall of 2000 up until now. "

He put on reading glasses, taking them from his standard issue, blue oxford shirt pocket.

"He's been in Chicago, " Ben offered.

"Why do you say that?" Jack Daniels asked, leaning forward in a genuine candor.

"The website, remember? I had control of it long enough to figure out that some of them worked out of Northwestern. I traced their IP addresses as they posted to my site. That's how I know that someone else came into New Orleans recently from the Mediterranean. Agent Daniels, you remember the other day? I explained it to you when I came in the first time," Ben said.

“Yeah,” Daniels nodded his head and frowned, clasping his hands together on the table, “Just call me Jack, okay?”

"We don't know how he made it to Chicago. He should have been on the radar at that point if he'd used his Egyptian passport. We're running the Customs records again, but we haven't found him yet." Chief explained.

"He didn't enter the country by plane. He came in on a ship; probably some Mediterranean freighter, just like his friend in New Orleans. You should check the Port of Chicago," Ben said.

"What else can you give us?" He gave Ben respectful acknowledgement for once.

"I know the date. They're planning the strike on the Fourth. The leader said that last night. He said, 'the Muslim world would celebrate this for a hundred years to come. It’s all coming in by sea from what I gather.” Ben sat for a moment, replaying it in his head. He had another thought. “ I know something's happening tomorrow night – Thursday the 27th was the date in one of the notes."

"That’s today. It's Thursday now," Chief said, looking at his watch, "It's 8:30 on Thursday now."

Ben continued, "I’ve been able to see several notes the New Orleans guy sent out. I traced the receiving account to a Brazilian paging service. He sent one line to an alphanumeric pager – the time, the date and two numbers."

"Telephone numbers?" Agent Daniels suggested.

"No - coordinates would be my guess, but they put you in the middle of the Gulf. That didn’t seem to make any sense before, but if they're doing it everything by sea…"

Ben leaned back in his chair, rubbing his forehead and eyes, "Look, I need to get out of here. I've got a lot of shit to do.”

“We’re well aware of that,” Chief said.

“Are you going to arrest me or something? 'Cause I need to get some sleep now and at this point it doesn’t matter to me if it’s in prison or some hotel. I just need to get out of here."

"We need to follow your leads as far as possible,” Daniels said, “Do you have the coordinates written down? "

Chief busied himself scribbling notes in the margins of his papers.

He shook his head.

"Do you remember them?"

"If I can give you that, will you let me out of here?"

"Yes, we've done enough for one night," the Chief relented.

Ben paused, trying to recall the note. He tried to picture it in his mind. He thought he could, having stared at it for some time while trying to decipher it. He could see it in his mind. The date: 27/06. The time, easy enough: 23:15

"The date is tomorrow. It was backwards, day first, then month. Like the Europeans do it. It read '27' slash '06. The time was 23:15. I assume that's local time if it's a rendezvous. That's our time, either Central or Eastern Daylight Time, I'm not sure – didn't check to see which zone the spot is in. The coordinates...well..." he said, his voice trailing off at the end, "the two whole numbers were 24 and 85."

"So we've got 24 by 85," Daniels repeated.

"Yes. 24 degrees longitude and negative 85 degrees latitude," he said, closing his eyes. His fatigue tried to pull his mind into twilight. He dozed for a few seconds, but fought it off. He thought maybe some good would come from this after all, if he could just remember. He hadn't written it down. After half a minute he opened his eyes.

"Let me have a pen and some paper."

Chief shoved them in his direction.

Ben wrote down the entire line as best he could:

27/06 23:15 24.5555-85.

"I know they both had at least four positions after the decimal. I think the second one had five, I can't remember, " he said, frustrated. He looked at it again, then completed the second number.

"I remember the second one was all twos and threes."

"What about the first? Any pattern to that?" Daniels said.

"Like a full house," he whispered to himself. He penciled in more numbers:

27/06 23:15 24.5555-85.22333

"I think that's it, " he said, pushing the paper back at Chief. He slumped over the table and rested his head on it. "Now I want out of here."

Chief relented, "Okay, fine -- leave. But you let us know where you are. We're not finished here. I want you to call us as soon as you get up and let us know where you're staying."

"Can I drive you to a motel or something?" Daniels asked.

"I have no idea what I'm going to do," Ben answered.

After Ben had shuffled out the door and down Market Street, Daniels returned to his lobby desk, trying to put some things in order. Chief came out of the back office doors and approached him, papers in hand.

"Daniels, I want you to work this up; find out if these coordinates are reasonable. Also work with the boys in Washington to see whether a ship route overlays the point. Find out everything you can about the ship or ships that do, understand?" he said, holding out the file.

Daniels felt a rush of excitement which washed away the all-nighter fatigue. Point man! Finally it had come to him. He prayed that this would turn out as high profile as he hoped so that he could distinguish himself.

"You're the point man on this – and don't fuck it up, pardon my French."

"I'll get right on it Chief," he said, enthusiastically.

"We've got fourteen hours to figure this out. And the Fourth is seven days away. I'm going to assemble a team if this rendezvous checks out. I want you to do the tactical on it, understand? Use my office for now," Chief said, "we need to keep this under wraps." I'm going home for a few hours' sleep. I want your report by lunchtime, understand? You've got two and a half hours. We have no time if this is real. And Daniels?"

“Yes sir?”

“Don’t mention this to anyone. Around here, especially. And tell me everything you do *before* you do it. I don’t want anything to go wrong here, capiche?”

“Right,” Daniels said.

Chief took off.

Jack went to work out in the lobby. People were coming in fresh for the new day.

Agent Jack Daniels, the one with the joke name and the lobby desk. Well not for long, you can be sure of that, he thought, as he scanned his ID and walked into the back office. He thought for a moment about how Chief wanted to keep everything hush-hush. It seemed weird, but Jack was too busy to give it much thought.

Chapter 31

"He's here. In the lobby, " Eitan said, incredulously. He spoke rapidly to Ofer, standing on the other side of the huge desk.

"Tel Aviv should be getting back to us soon on the IDs from the party last night," he offered, "What do you think we should do with Adams?"

"Let him come to us," Eitan suggested, "he may drop it in our laps. Why else would he be here?"

"Are you going to try to recruit him, now?"

"You have a better time in mind? After what he's just been through? You saw the tape, didn't you? What more opportune time would you suggest?" Eitan asked sarcastically, "Get the hell downstairs and make sure he signs in. Bring him up here immediately."

“Ben, what in God's name happened to you?" Dafna shouted from across the lobby. She ran over to him, instinctively trying to comfort him by stroking his cheek with her hand. She avoided the swollen side and its bulbous black eye. She looked up into his good eye, shocked at his condition. She began to weep silently, tears running down her cheeks in two tracks. "What happened?" she repeated, as she held him and ran her hand across his face. It was all she could manage to say at the moment.

"I don't want to talk about it now," he replied flatly.

"Why are you here? Shouldn't you be home now?"

"My house is gone, I can’t go back there. I had a gas explosion last night after the party broke up. Ike died," he said, beginning to choke at the name. Then straightened himself out once again.

"Do you need a place to stay? You're badly hurt, I'm surprised a hospital would release you under such conditions," She said, her anger flaring up at the thought, "What's wrong with the doctors in this country? Is it all about the insurance money? In Israel they would never do such a thing." She looked as if she wanted to keep complaining, but Ben cut her off.

"Look – I decided to leave. They did all they could for me."

"What are you doing here?" she asked, stroking the back of his neck. She stopped and her expression changed. "Forget this place. I will take care of you. Give me a few minutes. I'm going to take off the rest of the week. I will take you to my apartment. You need rest, Ben. Come, sit over there," she said, pointing at the sofa to one side of the lobby, "rest over there while I get my things and bring the car around. Are you a fool? Why do you come here?" She chided him, a faint smile on face all the while.

She escorted Ben towards the sofa and almost had him sitting when Ofer intercepted them.

"Ben, what happened to you? Are you all right?" he asked, feigning concern.

"My house exploded last night after the party. I had a gas leak. It killed Ike Henderson."

"The fellow who sat opposite you? I'm sorry to hear that."

A moment of silence passed and they all just looked at each other.

"Surely you're not here to work today, right?" Ofer asked.

"I don't know why I showed up. I'm messed up. I don't have a place to go. I've been up all night."

"You're coming home with me, I've already told you that!" Dafna said emphatically, almost shouting.

"Before you go, could you come up and talk with Eitan and me for a moment? So that we can figure out how to proceed with the new project?" Ofer said diplomatically, furrowing his single eyebrow in mock concern.

"Is work all you idiots think of? *Ya man manyak!* [you asshole]" she cursed at Ofer in Hebrew, "Let him be. Can't you see he's on the verge of collapse? What's the point of discussing work during a time like this?" she began to mutter at him in Hebrew again, a poisoned look on her face.

"Dafna, call off your dogs. It'll take ten or fifteen minutes. I'll meet you right here in fifteen, okay?" Ben said.

"All men are idiots! *Tembel!* Every last one of you! And this world you've made reflects your idiocy. Whatever ….go and have your bullshit talk. I will be waiting out front, *Ma nirat lech bamoch*?" she fumed. Turning, she stomped toward the brass revolving door, shooting knives over her shoulder at the Israeli agent taking Ben towards the stairwell.

Famine

The air in the little office made Ben uncomfortable as always. He felt trapped again, as he always did during the meetings with Eitan. He imagined his burns oozing lymph because of the stifling heat in the box of a room.

He sat in one of the chairs, leaning to one side to avoid jolting his throbbing hand. He regretted having agreed to come up for a talk, even just fifteen minutes. He needed to lay down somewhere; the impulse to sleep growing more insistent every moment.

Eitan shook his head and made 'tsk, tsk' noises. He seemed to almost be mocking Ben. Ofer stood at attention, his arms clasped behind him. He waited for Eitan to speak.

"Ben, Ben, what has become of you. You're the picture of disaster," he said, trying to suppress a smile.

"As I was telling Ofer, my house exploded in a gas leak last night. Everything has been destroyed. Ike Henderson died. Have you heard yet?" His rage returned as he gritted his teeth and recalled their faces. The terrorists. He adjusted himself in the seat, trying to quell the knotting in his stomach. He would excuse himself from working the rest of the week and then he'd get out of this little cage, he assured himself. It was beginning to bother him again.

"I am very sorry to hear of this tragedy. I know you and Ike were good friends. My condolences to you."

"Thank you," he said, preoccupied.

"Do you want help seeking revenge for your loss?" Eitan asked.

"What did you say?" Ben said, shocked. He looked at both of their impassive faces, furtively trying to eke some clue out of them.

"He said, do you wish to avenge your friend's death?" Ofer said.

Ben's mind reeled, wrapping itself around the question. *How did they know?*

Being a man of disciplined habit, as he was, Eitan paused for a bit, letting the drama of the moment sink in. Nonchalantly he swiveled his chair from point to point in the little cell, visually confirming that the devices in the black boxes were set properly. Ben now guessed they had to do with either monitoring the room or preventing it from being monitored.

"You know what happened to us last night? You bugged my house, didn't you? Who the hell are you people?" he cried, even though he knew now that Ike had told him the truth. *They are Mossad,* he thought.

"We are in a position to help you along..."

"-- an enemy of my enemy is my sometime friend," Ofer added, completing Eitan's thought.

"Not all things that call themselves a religion are well intentioned and benign in this world." Eitan said.

"I know that," Ben said, "and Islam is one of them. It makes suicide and killing holy acts, sanctioned by the commands of Allah himself for all time in the Qur'an. We in the West don't really have a word for this – it isn't racism in the same way as the Nazis, but it is the same in spirit – it divides the world on belief instead of race. That's the only substantial difference."

"And now, with petrodollars from Saudi and a huge baby boom from all the Islamic countries, the old beast is trying to define the world as believer versus infidel once again," Ofer added.

"After 'all religion is for Allah', of course, we'll have peace then," Ben said, "and only then if we do nothing about this. It must be stopped. The machine needs to be shut down and dismantled."

They both looked at him, but said nothing. Ben knew where this was going.

"Of course I want to see the sons of bitches die. They've taken everything from me. Their brothers took my brother's life. And now they've killed my friend. I think I understand part of what your people have been up against since 1948. Even before then, really. I look at it, realizing that the Nazis and the Muslims are the two most virulent anti-Semitic groups in history.

"I have often asked myself: Why do you think these groups have such inordinate hatred towards us, a statistically insignificant group? Think about it. Jews have never been more than one percent of the world's population, but they are the focus of the most eternal and virulent hatred from both of those belief systems. Why is that? Why would the tribes of Israel and now their tiny nation be the focus of such a huge amount of hatred?" Eitan said.

Ben finished for him, "It's because Hitler and Mohammed , prophets and leaders, or *fuehrers* for both groups, served the same dark spirit."

"We agree with you. This evil must be stopped here and now," Eitan said, "Tell us what you know. Besides the website postings. We know about them already. We watched *al-mu'minum* for at least a year before you hijacked it. What do you make of the coded messages? Any luck with them, eh?" Eitan said with a little twinkle in the beads of his coal-black eyes.

"I don't want to get into that now. I don't have a clue. Look, I need some rest. I'm falling apart here. The rendezvous isn't until tomorrow anyway, let's talk about this tomorrow," Ben said.

"If you hesitate, tomorrow never comes," Ofer said, "Just ask your good friend about tomorrow."

"One of my best friends just died and I'm responsible for that! Do you know how that feels, you son of a bitch?"

"Yes... I do know how that feels," Ofer answered.

Ben looked at him for a moment, surprised.

"Of course we can wait until you're better rested. We can talk tomorrow. Will you help us find these people then? I promise that if you do it will turn out to your liking." Eitan smiled pleasantly and folded his hands as if discussing a holiday bonus.

"I'll help you find them. I want them dead and I want to see the pictures," he added. Ofer gave him a double-take.

"You're a twisted *Ben Zona*," he commented.

"Yeah, I'm *the* Ben Zona, all right. They're going to pay seven times over," he said. The visible parts of his face grew beet red. "Okay - I've got to get out of this room. It's killing me." He stood up and walked into the hallway. "I'll call you tomorrow. We have unfinished business. Their big day approaches on the Fourth. But you know everything I can tell you already, don't you?"

"Of course, " said Eitan.

"What about the codes?" Ben asked, breathing in the fresher, cooler air of the cube farm.

"No luck yet. We'll talk about it tomorrow."

Ben limped down the hallway, saying a few words to one of the developers, who let him through the magnetic door. Ofer watched him leave, then returned to Eitan's stuffy office, closing the door behind him.

"Do you think he means it or is he just playing along?" Eitan asked.

"I think he means it. He wants revenge like most. I can see it in his eye."

"He has more data than we're aware of. He mentioned 'the rendezvous'. What is that? You found nothing on a rendezvous the other night, did you? Have you heard of this before," Eitan asked.

"No, nothing. Nothing on the disks I took either."

"Re-read the transcript from last night. Confirm that no mention of 'rendezvous' came up while they tortured them."

"He must have other sources of information," Ofer agreed.

Chapter 32

She opened the door to her apartment and pushed him along, like a mother hen shooing her chicks. He stopped after a few steps, dazed, while she opened the blinds in front of the sliding door, which led out to the small, cedar balcony. The breeze, cool because of the recent rainy spell, filled the room with welcome scents from late spring. Her collection of wind chimes softly jingled, hanging above the half-wall partition between the kitchen and the living room. She turned and looked at him, putting her hands on her well-proportioned hips.

"You're a mess," she said.

He simply grunted in affirmation. He couldn't think anymore.

"Let me get you cleaned up – you'll rest much better that way." She motioned toward the upholstered chair which matched her couch. Unable to do much else, he collapsed into it, stretching his legs out and slumping forward as far as his aches would allow. She knelt before him, pulling the shoes from his feet. Her kindness relaxed him. Once she had his socks off, she rose to her feet and walked toward the back rooms.

"Let me get the shower ready," she said. Her voice echoed off the tiles in the bathroom.

"I'm too tired. So tired. Just leave me here," he said, his voice diminishing as he fell into a doze. He could hear her moving things around in the other room, the sounds becoming more ephemeral as his mind tried to close down.

"Come with me, Ben, let's get you clean," she spoke into his ear. Her body was close, but her voice sounded like music off in the distance, from across the water.

He opened his unswollen eye. She stood in front of him, in

an nightshirt that almost reached to her mid-thigh. He could see her lovely, curvaceous form backlight in the light from the sliding door. She leaned forward to help him up, breasts bouncing naturally, free from any constraints. Her nipples poked through the thin cotton of the tee shirt and he could see their dark outlines easily.

She pulled him up, pressing her body against his as she locked her arms around his waist.

"Come on now... I will do the work. All you have to do is stand and I will do the rest," she said in a reassuring voice.

He staggered into the bathroom. She helped him lift his arm from the sling and took it from him, placing it on the lid of the toilet tank. He unbuttoned his cut-offs and she slid them off, as she dropped to a squat. He stepped out of them and she threw them in the direction of the doorway. Reaching up, she gently pulled down his boxers and discarded them the same way as before. She looked up at him, with her face close enough that he could feel the swirl of her warm breath .

She stood up and gently placed her hands on the sides of his bare chest. She ran her finger along the side of the four-inch gash along his torso, bandaged last night in the Emergency Room. She tugged at the wrapping carefully, lifting it out of his skin. She did this with the other two on his torso and leg, but left the bandages on his head alone.

She helped him into the tub, guiding and steadying his feet. She already had the water adjusted for temperature and the shower head in her hand.

Ben held onto the walls of the shower as she moved it over his body, washing the dirt, sweat, ash and grime off of him. She laid the shower head in the tub, letting the warm water run over his feet as she squirted liquid soap into her hands. She rubbed this all over his body, lovingly spreading it from his neck down to his belly button, working it into all the corners of his flesh. She rinsed this off, looking up at his face every so often and smiling. Neither of them said anything. Ben smiled back in appreciation.

She laid the shower head down again. She began soaping him from the feet up this time, taking care to rinse them so he wouldn't slip. She worked her way up each leg, stopping before his groin. After this, she rinsed him once again and then took another handful of soap.

“Dafna,” he said.

"Yes?"

"I'd better get the rest."

He leaned up against the wall and held out his good hand. She scraped the soap off into it. She had a cloudy expression on her face – hard to read.

"Thanks for all the help. Really. You're going above and beyond and I don't know what I would've done without your help."

"You are a good friend." She said, stopping there. She stood up and went over to the linen closet while he soaped up his groin area. She came back with a couple of towels and bent low, handing him the shower head so that he could finish the job.

He closed his eyes and she helped him out of the shower, toweling him off. She led him to her bed and laid him in the middle of it. After she started his load of laundry she returned to the bedroom and joined him on his good side, the least injured left side, stretching the front of her body up against him as he slept.

Chapter 33

Eitan shuffled the papers on his desk reminiscent of a bureaucratic *Three Card Monte.* Another day nearly over. It had been one of the more eventful in his Saint Louis tenure. He looked forward to the evening when he could sit on his patio, ringed with his plantings and listen to some of the Brandenburg concertos. A drink, the flowers, the golden calm of the evening and some Bach; he imagined the day when he'd be back home, no cares in the world, doing the same. Then the phone rang.

"Yes," he said, irritated with the abrupt ending of his daydream. He knew it was his handler before he picked up.

"Well, what do you think?" the American asked. Always to the point. He would be at home in Israel.

"Considering the options, he's the best way into the heart of the matter."

"I don't like it. He's unpredictable. We don't know enough about him."

"We did a profile on him when we hired him. Nothing to be concerned about." Then Eitan added, "he's just as neurotic as the rest of us, nothing more."

"He hasn't gotten anywhere with the Bureau."

"We'll cultivate him," Eitan said, looking around at his plants. "He is more than willing to help. He doesn't see any other way to exact his revenge. He might have stumbled into it by sheer chance, but he's got something they want."

"That's obvious."

"Let me finish -- he's got something they want. They called it 'The Key'. We'll get it from him shortly. We think he'll lead us to them. As long as he doesn't have any other option he'll do as we like. He has a strong need for revenge."

"I'll make sure he's frustrated. Keep in touch."

"Of course. You know it," Eitan said, disconnecting the scrambled line.

Adams will be easy to handle, he thought. *Like a mustard seed – small and insignificant to start but growing into the largest of bushes. And if something goes awry, I can have him cut down with few complications.*

Chapter 34

He struggled to open his eyes, trying to focus them on the strange ceiling. His mouth still tasted of ash and resinous smoke. He didn't know where he lay until he heard the wind chimes and began to remember. When he turned, the pain from his arm and hand brought the rest of it back. He began breathing deeply, noticing a woman's scent on the bedclothes even through his nose full of soot. His mind stuttered through images of Ike, the rubble of his house, the hospital and the long walk downtown. Then he heard her outside the doorway.

She brought him a glass of juice and a bagel with cream cheese, putting it on the nightstand. She still had on the thin, cotton t-shirt from earlier that morning -- if it was still morning. He couldn't tell from the light in the room. He glanced over at the nightstand, trying to find a clock.

"What time is it?"

"Twelve-thirty."

"Twelve-thirty Thursday?"

"Yes. How do you feel?"

He took a quick inventory. "I'll live, I think. I'd like to say 'I've had worse' but that would be a lie."

She tried to smile. She put her hand on his calf and gently squeezed it.

He made an attempt to sit up against the headboard, wincing at the pain from his arm. On the second try he did better, using his left side as much as possible. He coughed, tasting the smoke from his house again. His chest began to heave as the enormity of it all pressed down on him.

"Ben, I'm very sorry about everything. I want to help you any way I can. Please let me." He turned his head away from her as she said this, part of him glad she cared enough, but the other part of him still angry that he had been reduced to this.

"You should eat something," she said, stretching toward the nightstand.

"Food is the last thing I want."

"You need to heal. Food will help."

He said nothing, grinding his teeth. He stared out to some distant point, beyond her bedroom walls.

She turned her head and looked at him but her eyes were hollow this time.

After a few seconds he asked, "Do you have any coffee?"

She rose and took a couple of steps. "I can make some Turkish." She left him alone again.

He sat there trying to collect himself as she rummaged around in the kitchenette. He listened to her. He kept replaying the sight of Ike's body at his kitchen table and, after a few times, mixed in his familiar images of salvage workers finding a piece of his brother's arm. The same imaginings he had dwelt on months ago. He looked at his own hand, wrapped in gauze, which had darkened to a rust black punctuated with fresher blood and lymph in streaks. He settled on these images – Ike, his hand, the scraps of his brother in the rubble -- repeating them until the sounds of Dafna pouring coffee brought him out of it. He slid over to the edge of her bed and straightened himself up, standing for a moment until he felt stable enough to walk out to the other rooms.

Dafna looked up at him in surprise as walked past the partition and sat at the little round table. Her look changed into one of disapproval as she stared at him.

"What do you think you're doing?" She took one of the smallish cups off the tray and put it in front of him.

"I'm going to drink some coffee. Then I need to call Grace. She doesn't know if I'm alive or dead." He took too much of the hot coffee and had to spit it back into the cup. It burned his mouth.

She handed him the phone. He dialed the number and took another sip, carefully this time.

"Hello?" Her voice wavered.

"Grace?"

"Ohmigod, are you all right Ben? What happened? I've been worried sick. I tried calling over and over but the phone's off the hook or something." she said, in staccato.

"Grace... Grace..." was all he managed to say.

When she stopped rambling he began.

"They killed Ike, Grace."

"Who? Who killed Ike? The people at the house last night? Are you all right? What happened?"

"Terrorists."

He stared at the point where the wall met the ceiling and noticed the cobwebs. Grace would never allow cobwebs in the breakfast room… He came back and cut her off. "Somehow they found me. They wanted something from the website, a couple of strings of numbers. I don't know what they mean. Grace, they killed Ike last night. Shot him in the head."

"No," she paused, "What about you?"

"They messed me up really bad, but I'm going to live."

"What about the police? I called 911. Did the police get them? What happened?"

"They cut the gas line and destroyed our house. It's gone," he said, flatly. The words all seemed distant and unreal to him. Then he remembered he had Grace's laptop in the trunk of his car. It was out in the driveway. He would need that.

"Goddamit Ben! I told you to stay out of this. I told you it was nothing but trouble to start that website bullshit! I'm coming up there and –"

"—stay where you are," he said, the anger welling up from the pit of his stomach.

"I'm coming up there –"

"Listen to me! I don't know where these people are and I don't know if they're finished yet. The last thing I need is for you and the girls to get in harm's way. Stay where you are! I'll call you or come for you when it's safe again."

That seemed to stop her for a moment. They had silence on the line for a second or two while she considered the alternatives.

"Where are you? In the hospital? Are you all right?"

"They released me last night."

"What do the police have to say about this?"

He looked over at Dafna taking it all in. He didn't want to say anything about the FBI taking jurisdiction.

"I'll call you later. Just stay where you're at. You're safe there. I'll call you when I know more."

"Goddamit Ben, you son of a bitch! You get yourself out of this ASAP. I don't want to bury you!" She started weeping and gasping. She was out of control.

"Goodbye Grace," he said in monotone.

"Goddamit you son of a –" he cut her off then.

He looked over at Dafna. Tears were streaming down her cheeks.

Dafna's under-inflated front tires squealed as they rounded the corner. He had a clear angle on the rubble now. Only part of the garage walls still stood. The rest amounted to charcoal, bits of pink fiberglass insulation and parts of recognizable things, like the corner of a window frame or the front door with the leaded glass they'd bought just last Fall for $2,200.

He pulled his set of keys from his pocket, looking at the one for the front door. He would never use it again. But his car had managed to come through in spite of all of the missiles and falling debris. He got out and walked around it, finding no serious damage. He opened the trunk, checking on his work satchel and Grace's laptop case. He slammed the trunk closed and walked up to the crime scene barrier, running irregularly around the perimeter of the house. *Total destruction – total loss.*

He started walking around it in a clockwise direction, running the crime scene tape through his hand and shaking his head. A mournful howl emanated from his insides. He stopped at the back corner of the house, where the vinyl picket fence had melted into puddles the color of dirty snow. His roses stood untouched in their garden just a few feet away. He laughed at this but it did little to comfort him. He walked back to Dafna and spoke to her through the open window.

"I'm taking my car back to your place, okay?"

"I'll wait to see if you can drive it," she said. He didn't ask her if she was talking about him or the car.

He started it right up and followed her out of the neighborhood. It dawned on him that the Feds wouldn't want him to move the car, but it had been outside the cordon of tape. It didn't matter anyway. He would have driven through the tape regardless. The house was gone. *They had insurance. That would cover it*, he reassured himself.

He followed Dafna's Taurus until the entrance to Saint Roch's parking lot. He turned in and drove to the side nearest the Adoration Chapel. He went into the Narthex, crossing himself with his left hand, remembering how the nuns had admonished him for doing this back in elementary school. He had no choice in the matter now. He approached the doorway to the chapel, wondering who would be taking their turn for Adoration. Looking in he saw an older lady that he didn't recognize sitting in the front row, reading a devotional pamphlet. He entered the chapel respectfully and got a long stare from her. He realized he looked a mess. He knelt slowly, painfully with the care of a rheumatoid sufferer. He crossed himself and bowed in prayer.

"*Lord, you are merciful and forgiving. I know what you want me to do now, but I can',*" he began, *"Please forgive me even though I can't forgive them. You said we'd be judged by our words and actions."*

> Stop judging, that you may not be judged.
> For as you judge, so will you be judged,
> for the measure with which you measure
> will be measured out to you.

He turned to Matthew Chapter 6, verse 14 were it said:

> If you forgive others their transgressions,
> your heavenly Father will forgive you.
>
> But if you do not forgive others,
> neither will your Father forgive your
> transgressions.

He prayed, *I can't live up to that right now. It's too hard. I want them to suffer, Lord, and I can't get past that. Please forgive me for what I'm about to do.* He reminded himself, *'Those who live by the sword, will die by the sword.'*

He used his good arm to push himself up to standing and walked right up to the Tabernacle. He genuflected, grabbing onto its column to steady himself.

"What are you doing? Stop that," the old lady commanded.

Ben paid her no mind. He pulled a ball point pen out of his pocket and swept it under the edge of the Tabernacle base, brushing the disks out from underneath. He gathered them up, turned and looked at her.

"Pray for me," he said, "pray that what I'm about to do won't send me to Hell."

She gasped and crossed herself, muttering unintelligibly in her fear.

He walked out into the light of day, his face set against them like stone. He didn't have much time.

War

Those who know nothing of Islam pretend that Islam counsels against wars. Those [who say this] are witless. Islam says: Kill all the unbelievers just as they would kill you all! Does this mean that Muslims should sit back until are devoured by [the unbelievers]? Islam says: Kill them [the non-Muslims], put them to the sword and scatter [their armies]. Does this mean sitting back until [non-Muslims] overcome us? Islam says: Kill in the service of Allah those who may want to kill you! Does this mean that we should surrender [to the enemy]? Islam says: Whatever good there is exists thanks to the sword and in the shadow of the sword! People cannot be made obedient except with the sword! The sword is the key to paradise, which can be opened only for holy warriors!

There are hundreds of other [Koranic] psalms and hadiths urging Muslims to value war and to fight. Does all that mean that Islam is a religion that prevents men from waging war? I spit upon those foolish souls who make such a claim.

Ayatollah Khomeini - Islam is not a religion of Pacifists (1942)

War

Chapter 35

He set up shop in Dafna's living room, taking up all the space on the desk she had put in the corner. He had the laptop hooked up to her network and had it busy running the cracker program that Ike gave him. It kept picking away at the ArRad13 account, looking for new messages, while he opened up the logs from the almuminun.org site. *They called it 'The Key'. The key to what?* he asked himself. He looked through the data he'd kept off the site. He thought he'd know once he saw it. Something named 'The Key' should jump off the screen. It did. He remembered reading it on the train one morning:

AnNasr110 – June 18th, 2004 3:25AM

Brothers, a good word to you. I have some readings that will be the key to your success on this Hajj.

2:289,9:54,5:77,43:29,6:18,61:128,140:21 for your right hand

17:33,16:88,58:247,29:89,36:126,44:92 for the other.

Looking at it again, he remembered checking the numbers. They hadn't been what they appeared to be. They weren't passages from the Qur'an. The first one referred to a chapter with fewer than 289 verses; the sixth one, 61:128, had no match either. *Surah* 61 had only fourteen verses. Topping it off , the Qur'an only had 114 *surahs* – the last entry didn't even exist. *These numbers are the keys they wanted,* he told himself, *but the keys to what? Some sort of combination lock? Numbered Bank Accounts? A website passcode?* He didn't have enough to go on. They could be used for anything.

He copied the passage off to a notepad page and moved on through the posts, looking for more numbers. ArRad13 had sent notes to ArAzhad33 entirely in numbers:

8:15:7:8:13:20:1:1:2:2:126:10:10:30:8:2:151:37:109:1:2
88:20:2:77:30:9:18:81:10:19:109:3:7:4:25
103:1:5:99:6:1:1:4:4:12:43:12:12:46:23:81:4:4
12:69:32:22:15:9:37:7
21:80:7:20:107:10:20:98:7:42:20:5:34:13:17:3:91:35:17:78:4
38:23:8:7:142:24:[3,1,14,1,12]:96:11:8

Ben compared this to the website. The NetMail messages had numbers only, in groups of threes. The website post had pairs of numbers in two strings. *They couldn't be the same thing*, he thought. He put his elbow on the desk and rubbed his head, taking care to avoid his wounds. He exhaled deeply but still felt the tension building in the back of his neck. The creeping feeling of urgency – time urgency --- magnified the frustration. He knew they planned to do something soon – that evening in fact. He had no time to lose.

He pushed the old, wooden chair away from the desk and stood for a moment, letting his circulation change a bit. He began pacing back and forth, checking the microwave clock, blinking 12:00 at him each time he looked. *Didn't Dafna say she'd be coming back soon? Where was she?* He sat down again. His laptop had 2:20 pm. He looked at the numbers again.

8:15:7:8:13:20:1:1:2:2:126:10:10:30:8:2:151:37:109:1:2
88:20:2:77:30:9:18:81:10:19:109:3:7:4:25
103:1:5:99:6:1:1:4:4:12:43:12:12:46:23:81:4:4
12:69:32:22:15:9:37:7
21:80:7:20:107:10:20:98:7:42:20:5:34:13:17:3:91:35:17:78:4
38:23:8:7:142:24:[3,1,14,1,12]:96:11:8

They could be anything but they meant nothing. Modern, computer generated codes could take weeks or months to break, even with unlimited CPU. Breaking something sophisticated would take him months or years with just the two laptops available in the apartment. His mind wandered a bit. He listened to the sound of the wind chimes out on the balcony. He slid the door open and walked out into the afternoon breeze in his boxers. He leaned against the railing, wearied. He couldn't do it alone – no way. He considered his options. He could take it to the Israelis. They would run with it, no doubt. They would have the equipment to crack it, no doubt. But didn't that amount to treason? It came close if it didn't. Helping the Mossad would put his world in a permanent state of F.U.B.A.R. But what other choice did he have? He doubted the FBI could put something together fast enough to make a difference. The CIA? Forget about it. This would be passed off as a domestic issue, even after the Patriot Act. Shaking his head, he decided the FBI would be the best route. His future wouldn't be ruined working with them. So he decided to meet with the agent named Jack Daniels again and bring him a copy of what he had so far. He didn't feel good about the decision, but it was the least hazardous of the available options. He had his future to consider.

He walked back inside and fished his wallet out of his pants, hanging on the back of a chair. He pulled Daniels' card out and began dialing the number, stopping halfway through. *They knew about the website. They watched it all last night, too. They probably have this place covered too*, he realized, disconnecting the phone. *The Mossad was watching him already.*

He began to search for the nearest payphone in his mind, while he disconnected Grace's laptop and burned a CD. He didn't want them to see what he was doing through the network. He couldn't do anything while they watched. He needed to get out of the apartment before Dafna came back and started asking questions. As he pulled up his shorts he wondered if she was Mossad or not.

Chapter 36

"You are Israeli first and a friend second -- like the rest of us," Ofer told Dafna. He blocked the exit to Eitan's office. She wouldn't be able to leave the stuffy little box unless she climbed over him or went through him.

"Israeli? Jew? You offer those words up like they mean something good. Tell me what good they have has brought us? They say 'we are a chosen people.' Then tell me why the rest of the world has tried to kill us off the last three thousand years! Being Israeli has brought me nothing but a curse," Dafna said, her eyes watering.

"You don't mean what you say," Eitan suggested.

"I mean it all too well. I have lived it. So have both of you. You, me -- him," she cast a glance toward the dark bulk in the doorway, "we've all seen loved ones killed. I'm finished with this stupidity. I'm not going to help you kill my friend."

"He brought this on himself," said Ofer.

"Your mother made a mistake when she named you after a baby deer, *'Ofer'*," Dafna taunted, "she would have been right to name you *Faltzan Misken.*" [the unlucky fool who talks out his ass]

"*Tistom et a-pe, lechi lidfok be-ats-mech*," he said. He tried to keep his voice even and low, but the effort turned his face reddish purple.

"Ofer... Dafna... please, let's keep this civil. Stop the name calling. We are all Israelis. We all know what that means." He fixed his gaze on her. "Dafna, we just want you to keep an eye on him and let us know what's going on, that's all. Just watch him and talk to us, all right?"

"I wouldn't put money on that," she said.

"Your father and I worked together many years –"

"Leave my father out of this!"

"Your service record in the *Shin Bet*-- exemplary," he said, shuffling her papers together,

"Compulsory service for military intelligence. I did what we all have to do. Nothing more."

"We're not asking for a permanent commitment from you," he managed a smile, "We just need you to keep an eye on him – just keep him out of harm's way." He looked over his desk at her, tilting his head innocuously. "We need you again as a *Bat Leveyha* for a short time. You've helped us in the past..."

"He's an amateur. He made a serious mistake getting involved in your games. Don't make him pay any more than he has already."

"Look: he's involved no matter what we say or do," Ofer said, "Do you think he'll be able to walk away from this now?" He folded his arms and looked down his nose at her. "I doubt it. Not the way he talked this morning. He said wants them dead."

She shut her eyes at this, bending forward in pain.

"Can we count on you?"

"I'm not making any promises. Now get out of my way," she said, pushing her way past Ofer. He watched her until she stormed out the security doors.

He continued speaking in Hebrew. They had broken the English-Only rule since the door had been open the whole time.

"What do you make of that?" Eitan asked.

War

And I can remember the Fourth of July,
Runnin' through the backwood, bare.
And I can still hear my old hound dog barkin',
Chasin' down a hoodoo there.
Chasin' down a hoodoo there.
Born on the bayou;
Born on the bayou;
Born on the bayou.
John Fogerty – Born on the Bayou

Chapter 37

He walked up the broad, collegiate sidewalk that used to be West Olive Boulevard in the last century, but was now part of Saint Louis University's pedestrian campus. He passed bunches of students, dressed in sandals and cutoffs, carrying light loads of books on their backs and fewer worries about life in general. They were as bright and fresh as the June afternoon -- in the early Summer of their lives. He thought back to his time, suddenly feeling his age. Then it occurred to him he had many more years to become truly old but with the way things were going he wondered if he would see those days.

He pressed on up the hill, fixing his sight on the massive pile of Colorado sandstone looming up to meet him like a bad memory. The Cupples House sat in the middle of campus, a monument in Richardson Romanesque and to the city's Golden Age. It's exterior had been executed by English stone masons brought over especially for the purpose. Figures of men and beasts watched him approach from their nooks in the rough-hewn stone.

Gothic gloom most apropos for the task at hand.

He looked up at the copper-clad turret jutting out over the granite columns at the entrance. Someone was moving around in the shadows up there, changing positions in the turret windows. *Agent Daniels? Must be. Hopefully.* Who else around here would be wearing a shirt and tie? Ben couldn't see his face, but it had to be him.

He pulled against the heavy oaken door, the ornate hammered hinge work still allowing it to swing easily after all this time. He paid his three dollars to the student in the hallway and sauntered toward the carved balustrades on the stairway at the other end of the great hall. The ornate interior of the house outdid all of the exterior work. In each room rare woods had been carved in Celtic and medieval motifs. It had cost a half million in 1886 dollars to put it all together. Ben had chosen this place to meet because it was public, unconventional and because he knew its floor plan well. He had come here many times and his children liked to roam the halls as much as he did. It was familiar ground to him, but off the beaten path.

He walked up to the second story and nodded towards the schoolboy at his post on the *casapanca* to discourage furniture damage – the house being a museum of sorts after all. Ben took a leisurely tack across the hand-woven Portuguese rug covering hallway, toward the South East sitting room where Daniels waited for him. Satisfied his student shadow would let him be, he passed through the English Oak door way into the room where the builder, Samuel Cupples, had died in the care of his personal physician.

He could see Daniels' silhouette leaning out against one of the windows in the turret, making a semi-circular bay window in the corner of the room. Ben's footfalls brought Daniels upright. He turned and smiled in a mix of vinyl-siding-salesman smoothness and genuine anticipation. He took a few steps to close the gap and extended a French-cuffed shirtsleeve, but then pulled it back reminded of the condition of Ben's right hand.

"Mr. Adams." He broadened his smile. "I'm surprised that you called again so soon. Are you all right? How are you?" He grasped his hand with animation. He enjoyed this too much, thought Ben.

"Like I said before, 'I'll live'. "

"Have you thought of something else to help with the investigation? Why did you want to meet me here? It's like something out of an old whodunit. A good place for a murder."

"Look, " Ben said, "I can't do this alone. I need help."

"Help with what?" he said, "What do you have?"

"I've got the data from the website. And some emails from an account they used. Communications between them – all that sort of thing."

"Why didn't you say something about this earlier this morning?" his tone turning darker.

Ben looked around the room. He felt the emotional fatigue returning.

"Did you really expect me to tell you everything I knew after what happened last night? In the condition that I was in? Still am in?"

Daniels paused a moment, "No. No I don't. Please go on, tell me how I can help. You are the key to this."

"That's what they said they were looking for – the keys."

"The keys?" he echoed.

"That's what they tracked me down for and that's why they killed Ike. The website..." he stopped for a moment, his eyes settled on a rendering of St. Francis of Assisi. His mind wandered back to Adoration the night before. Just last night... It seemed an age ago. Every thing had changed since then.

"Go on Mr. Adams," he said.

"Just call me Ben, okay?" he said with irritation, "I don't have time for this over-polite formality. In fact, none of us have any time at all." His voice had began to rise and the pressure of it all caused the swollen parts of his head to pound. "When I put up my pages on the site, I made a partial copy of what had been posted before. I left out some of the earlier stuff. One of those messages had two strings of numbers. I think that's what they were after."

"What do you think numbers meant?" Daniels furrowed his brow.

The student-guard ambled by the doorway, looking in curiously. They both stole glances at him, pausing for a moment. Ben spoke again when he thought the guy was out of earshot.

"I have no idea, but it's important enough to kill for," he half-whispered.

"That's not saying much when you're talking about terrorists."

"But it is," Ben insisted, "it had to be something they needed. They wouldn't risk exposing themselves for something trivial, now would they?"

Daniels thought about this for a moment, then nodded.

"I don't think it's a set of coordinates or anything like that – there are too many numbers. Besides, I already gave you that message. When they talked about this at my house they used the term 'key'. Now to me that sounds like a combination or pass code. These numbers get them into something. Or decode something, maybe."

"An encryption scheme?"

"That's why I'm here, I don't have the resources, the computing power, to try to make sense of it. It would take me years with what I've got, if I could ever break it. You've got the full computing power of the government behind you. I'm giving you a copy of the disks." He reached into his back pocket and pulled out the CDs. "Get these to your cryptographers."

"That's NSA or CIA work you're talking about," Daniels said, "the Bureau hasn't been set up for this kind of thing."

"Aren't you supposed to be working hand-in-hand these days?" he looked Daniels up and down with a trace of disgust, "Or is the press full of bullshit on that as well? Look, you're the only chance I've got. We've got to figure this out by the third of July, that's it! Don't you get it? They have the key now. They'll be able to use it and do whatever they've planned on July 4th."

Daniels exhaled and slumped his shoulders. "I'll do what I can. But these things take time. You and I know this is the real thing, but getting this done in the next couple of days will be as easy as filling a hole in the ocean, man. It just ain't going to happen."

"Make it happen. Otherwise a lot of people are going to die. Do you want to live with that? It's time to make a difference. I'm in the middle of a hurricane-sized shitstorm myself. I'm taking a risk coming to meet you, you know, they're watching me."

"Who? The terrorists?"

"No, the people I work for. The Mossad – Israeli Foreign Intelligence? Some of them are working in Saint Louis and they know all about this. They tell me they've been monitoring the almuminum.org site for over a year. They're trying to recruit me, for God's sake! If we don't find these sons of bitches, they will."

Daniels rubbed the back of his neck, shaking his head to and fro. The watchman was back. Ben walked around the Eastlake-style center table and took a seat in the turret, in one of the Spanish-style leather side chairs. He leaned over and rested his elbows on his knees. Daniels took up the matching chair on the opposite side.

They leaned into the middle, conspiratorially.

Daniels clasped his hands together. His easy-going demeanor had left him. The student passed by the doorway again.

"Excuse me," Ben said, speaking loudly, "Could we have a few minutes without worrying about you out there?"

The student's face flushed and he turned and walked to the other side of the hallway. Daniels jiggled his knee a bit, bouncing his folded hands as he rested his eyes on the bright floral patterns in the Aubusson rug.

"Have you done anything with the first set of numbers I gave you?" Ben asked.

"We're looking into it. We agree with you. We think they're coordinates. We're checking shipping routes, but we haven't come up with anything so far. Nothing intersects."

"I don't think we'll be that lucky."

"The big problem is that we have no way to check it out. Our jurisdiction ends at the beach."

Ben grimaced, shaking his head.

"You'll find NetMail messages on the second disk. Some of it is in clear text; the other parts are the numbers again. But the pattern's not the same as the 'key' numbers. They tried to make the key numbers look like references in the Qur'an. I double-checked them – most are bogus."

"What do you think they mean – these other messages are they part of the key too?"

"No, that wouldn't make any sense. You'd have an extra number. The first would be the chapter, the second would be the verse and then you'd have an extra number..." he stopped for a moment, looking up at Daniels wide-eyed.

"I've got to go."

He stood up and walked out without saying another word. He remembered what they had said:

"We use those words a guide to life and a key to our present operation."

Chapter 38

He did have some luck left after all, arriving back at Dafna's apartment complex without a ticket after having broken seventeen traffic laws. His wounds unnoticed, he bounded up the stairs and let himself in. He went straight for the desk, not stopping to announce himself or even to check if she had returned. He sat down and reached across the table in a single motion. Heart pounding, he called up one of the NetMail notes in cipher. He remembered what the leader had said before they began torturing him.

We use those words as a guide to life and a key to this undertaking.

8:15:7:8:13:20:1:1:2:2:126:10:10:30:8:2:151:37:109:1:2
88:20:2:77:30:9:18:81:10:19:109:3:7:4:25
103:1:5:99:6:1:1:4:4:12:43:12:12:46:23:81:4:4
12:69:32:22:15:9:37:7
21:80:7:20:107:10:20:98:7:42:20:5:34:13:17:3:91:35:17:78:4
38:23:8:7:142:24:[3,1,14,1,12]:96:11:8

Splaying his left hand wide, he opened the book and turned to *Surah* VIII, fingered the page down to verse fifteen and then thumbed the seventh word.

The

Okay... well, not much… but he still thought maybe he was on to something. *It could be the start,* he thought, *but a word in itself says nothing.* Flipping the Koran over, he pulled down a piece of scratch paper and picked out a pencil from the jumble under the monitor. Doing this one-handed would be a pain. He needed a weight to hold the book in place. He stood up, looking around randomly when she entered the living room from the hallway.

"I was beginning to worry about you, " she said, wringing her hair in a towel, "where did you go with your car? I lost you on the way home." She smiled, then resumed her hair drying.

"Insurance Agency. I had to pay them a visit, you know, to get the claim rolling," he said, "do you have a paperweight or something I could use?"

"Paperweight?" she asked.

"Something heavy enough to hold the pages of a book without using hands," he explained.

"Ah, that," she said.

Not finding anything useful, he settled on a his the forearm attached to his damaged hand.

"What are you doing now? You should be resting. It hasn't been a day yet and moving around like that doesn't help wounds heal," she called out to him in the other room.

"This is exactly what I need to heal. Exactly."

She left him alone for a few minutes as he set himself up at the desk. He moved with a building intensity, flipping pages, poking the pencil at the targets and then writing them down.

War

He kept trying out the alternate translations… he knew he was on the right track, but just didn't have the one they used. He had been through several versions already – the Pickthall translation, the one by Abdal Hakim Murad, Mostafa al-Badawi, and Uthman Hutchinson and a couple of others. He pulled them down off the web. They seem to be close but the words didn't line up exactly. He needed to keep trying…

His expression had brightened, beaming at her as she checked in on him once again.

"Dafna, you know what I have here," he grinned at her, dangling the piece of scratch paper like a talisman.

"The numbers from the insurance people? What?"

"I have their balls in my hand. And this time it's me who's going to do the chopping." He let out a feral shout, wadding up the scratch paper as he clenched his fist, shaking it above his head. This startled the hell out of her; it was so unlike him.

"I can read their messages now." And he growl-laughed at the thought.

She brought him a plate of olives, hummus and falafel. Ben mumbled a 'thanks' and left it where it lay. He kept bringing up the coded messages and translating them. He put each of them on a separate piece of paper and moved from one to the next without interruption. It made sense to him that they would do something like this. They wouldn't want to rely on some machine-generated key. If something happened and they had no access to the decryption key they'd be dead in the water. It had to be something simpler, using something they all had access to and it had to be decidedly low tech. By using an English translation of the Qur'an they'd have the key with them at all times as long as they carried the same edition of the book. Their word of God as the source of all knowledge – earthly and heavenly. Just as they'd heard the imams say every Friday their entire lives. No one would see it as an encryption scheme. Hide the code in plain sight. Use the book translation easiest to find and buy in the target country. It would raise no suspicion being a common thing. They had used the Abdullah Yusuf Ali translation, favored by the Royal Saudi family for many years and common in the United States mosques. He had found an on-line copy of it on the first pass using Google. The number combinations turned into something that made sense now.

He rewarded himself with a break, stretching to the point where his wounds complained. He let his mind wander again. Thinking about the smoldering pile that used to be home, he picked up his cell phone and walked out onto the balcony, dialing his insurance agent and dodging the wind chimes. He surveyed the courtyard between the buildings while the phone rang, catching a glimpse of Ofer passing between two apartment buildings. Ben had mixed feelings about this. On one hand he'd love to tell him he could read the messages, but on the other his gut told him it would put him in world of hurt -- getting tangled up with that crew would cause damage that wouldn't heal. He wished he'd never spoke with them. He should have played the Ignorant American. Now they knew his number and wouldn't hesitate to use it.

His attention shifted to the earpiece. Someone picked up.

"Bill Westerling Agency – how may I help you?" said the cheery female voice on the other side.

"Hello, this is Ben Adams. I'm a client of Mr. Westerling's. May I speak to him?"

"Sure you can. Is this about a claim?"

"A new one."

She begged off and put him on hold. Ofer approached the entrance, sizing him up like a piece of meat hanging in a shop window. Ben listened to his gut for once but knew 'when you're in for a penny, you're in for a pound'. He'd have to take it all the way with them. He didn't want to -- he knew he was merely a means to an end for them.

The thing he had to decide at that moment was 'how important is this'?

He could lick his wounds, play stupid and it would be over for him. Or he could squeeze the killers in a vice – the Feds on one side and the Mossad on the other. Would it be worth it?

How important was this?

"Hello. Ben Adams? How're you doin'?" Westerling came on smooth, full of funeral-parlor concern.

"I'm fine, Bill, but my house is gone. I need to start filing the claim against it."

"I've already been out there, Ben. Saw it on the news."

War

"What do you think?"

"Total loss as far as I can see. They'll have to take it down to the foundation, if it's sound, that is. I've got someone going out to inspect it as soon as we get clearance from the FBI. They have the area cordoned off. They're still working the scene, as they say."

Ben didn't know what to think of that.

"Is that normal?" Ben heard the knock on the door. He glanced over his shoulder and watched Ofer come in.

"Well yes, it's not unheard of. I tell you what – can I have your cell number? I'll call you tomorrow and let you know how the inspection went. Then we can get this adjudicated right away and we'll cut you a check ASAP."

"Sounds good. Thanks for all the help," Ben said.

"How are you doing? Really? I heard you got the short end too, but I guess you're not seriously injured, after all, you're calling me the next day..."

Ben checked back inside, Ofer was coming in the door and walking over to the desk, talking to Dafna, but looking at the stack of decrypted messages.

"Yeah, like I keep saying, 'I'll live'. Look, I've got to go. Thanks for jumping in on this right away."

"That's what I'm here for... Well, I'll call you when I know more. Tomorrow, allright? Keep a record of your motel bills we'll need those when you file."

Ben turned the phone off and braced himself. Ofer knew already. Ben couldn't play the fool. He walked in.

"Ben, I came over to see if you were out of bed yet. I have underestimated you," his look of surprised admiration seemed genuine enough for once.

"What are you talking about?"

Now the familiar disdain came back. "Don't pretend to be stupid," he said, looking down at the sheaf of papers and brushing them with two fingers, "I can see you've managed to break their coding scheme. How did you do it?"

"I'm not going to say."

Silence.

Dafna kept shifting her eyes back and forth and furrowing her brow. She crossed her arms but said nothing.

"Just read it again," Ben said, "I could see you committing it to memory from the balcony." He picked up the paper, shoving it in Ofer's direction, "read them if you'd like."

Ofer ran over a couple of notes. He looked up. "They're meeting in New Orleans, no? The sixteenth of the month – Rabi II - that's 27 June on the Roman calendar. Today. We're out of time."

A quiet, measured knock came at the door. Dafna nudged the Israeli out of the way and looked out the peephole. She muttered something nasty in Hebrew and opened it so Eitan could join the party.

"Shalom," he said, nodding at one and all.

"Right," Dafna cleared her throat contemptuously and closed the door behind him, locking it. She came around to Ben's side, squaring off against the other two.

The old spook made a quick assessment. "You have some news, Ben?"

"He's managed to decipher the messages," Ofer said.

A thunder stoke of surprise flashed across Eitan's face, settling into a smile. He looked at Ofer, "So you have a sense of humor after all? You're joking?"

"No and Yes." Ofer said, handing it to him.

"Yes to what?" Eitan spoke into the paper.

"I can read the messages," Ben confirmed.

Eitan mouthed the words as he moved the paper to his point of focus, about a foot and a half from his face. "Well done," he said looking up, "how?"

"Like I told Ofer, I'm not saying."

Ofer turned to Eitan, speaking in Hebrew: "We have a day to set this up. We need to put them off, change their meeting place."

"Stop. Speak in English, " Ben insisted. They stopped and looked at him. "I want to hear everything that's said or I'm out of this."

Ofer frowned at him, switching to English.

"We need to divert them to a place where we have the advantage. We have the element of surprise but we should do this on our playing field – on our terms."

"No, we shouldn't change the place. It's off if they smell something wrong. Rats are survivors first and a plague second," said

Eitan, "we keep it in their place, where they feel in control." He returned to the notes. "Canal Street?"

"New Orleans. Tomorrow night. We have to move men and equipment, set up surveillance, get a *Kidon* team in place for the kill. We take them all out and make the world a better place. Weapon recovered: everyone happy," Ofer suggested.

"You don't know who you're gunning for. You've never seen them," Ben protested.

"We should have enough footage from your kitchen to make an educated guess," Eitan said.

Dafna kept shaking her head, "Typical."

Ben felt the decision building in him. It had to be now. They wouldn't get another chance like this. He had to commit.

"Look, they only had the one light on, over the kitchen table. Most of the time they stayed back from it, in the dark," Ben said, "are you really sure the Mossad face recognition database got you the match? How sure are you? Seventy, maybe eighty percent? That leaves a lot of reasonable doubt, doesn't it?" They looked at him, surprised. "It's not that big a deal, really. The Mossad face recognition mainframe computer is a matter of public record. It's in all the espionage novels too."

"Well, the faces don't match up at all. We're dealing some new ones here. Amateur *shahids* – martyrs - who want a guaranteed couch in the eternal whorehouse and their seventy-two virgins," Ofer said. Eitan shot him a look. "Do you want to find them or not?" he said, challenging the old man.

"You're going to need positive ids. You can't just go into a public place and start shooting. I know you wouldn't do that. It solves nothing and you know that as well as I do that walking into a place and just killing everyone blind isn't the answer. I'm surprised to hear 'professionals' talk this way," Ben said, "You disappoint me. Aren't you more subtle than that?"

"We don't have time for subtlety. Leave that to the movies," Ofer said. He turned to Eitan again -- "Look, we've got no time. We must leave immediately. We can't let them get to a position where they could actually deploy it."

"Deploy what?" Ben said, "You've known all along what they intend to do?"

They both paused, doing the calculus of risk.

Ofer spoke first, "I was on assignment in Uzbekistan before coming to Saint Louis. We know that the IMU, or Islamic Movement of Uzbekistan has aligned itself with al-Qaeda and other groups outside that country. They all fight for the same thing – a return to an Islamic society. A caliphate - a world government ruled by one man: a Muslim who must be Arab. All the groups are fighting for it: in Malaysia, Indonesia, Australia, the Kashmir – you pick a conflict. They all want to kill the resisting unbelievers, subdue the rest of us and put *shar'ia* law in place. Jihad or support of jihad is obligatory. Killing unbelievers and forcing survivors to adopt Muslim law is a type of jihad – the unofficial, sixth pillar of the Islamic credo." Ofer continued. "Our sources in the Uzbek group told us about a second agreement. A 'quid pro quo' as you might say."

"Something for something?"

"The Uzbeks under Muslim leaders Tohir Abdouhalilovitch Yuldeshev and Jumaboi Ahmadzhanovitch Khojaev got support and supplies through Afghanistan, as well as heroin to be sold to the West. In return, the Uzbeks worked their old Soviet connections to acquire what al-Qaeda wanted."

"Weapons."

"Not common weapons..." Ofer hesitated. "I think I've said enough."

"You have proof of this; are you sure?" Ben asked.

"As you say, it's a matter of public record that the Soviets had a massive biological warfare program working up through 1998. That's only four years ago. The program is still underway today – but in the 'nineties it was a juggernaut. The bureaucratic apparatus had been huge in scale, but very secret and compartmentalized. The agency was named Biopreparat.

The United States had been mostly ignorant of it all until a defector, Ken Alibek, disclosed what he knew. He had been of a rank sufficiently high to see the 'big picture' as you say. What he told them, for instance, is that production of weaponized agents had been made industrial. For instance, in the mid-nineties weaponized Bubonic Plague production had been around 1,500 metric tonnes a year and this had been going on for many years. Now what do you think happened to 10,000 tonnes of this material when the Soviet Union collapsed? Do you think it was all destroyed? Do you think it was all even accounted for?"

War

"So you think the terrorists have some of this stuff?"

"We don't know what they have. We only know it will be extremely lethal if they release it under the right conditions."

"How do you know it's still viable?" Ben asked.

"We don't know – but do you want to find out after the fact?" Eitan said.

"I'm not a scientist or technician in that sense, but I do know that they have put bacteriological agents into a dry form, using a desiccant named Trehalose. This is a sugar which dries out the bacteria and encases it – much like Anthrax spores. It would be very stable and probably viable for years. When you mix this with water in the lungs it comes back out of stasis and the bacteria goes about its business."

"We can't take a chance waiting around for it then. If it gets out into the environment and moves from person to person it will be like a wildfire – millions could die," Ben said.

"It will set off an uncontrollable chain of transmission," Ofer said.

"But why do you care? Why stop it here? The United States is set off on its own continent – it's isolated from your country."

"Air travel will render that buffer useless," Eitan said.

"Why do you care about this, though? Why would you help Americans?"

"What makes you think the U.S. is the only target? Israel is surrounded by hostile nations. Besides a weakened and distracted U.S. government is not in the best interests of the Israeli government or its people. We need strong allies, so our motives are selfish in this."

Ben turned to Ofer.

"How do you know they really have anything?"

"If you're asking if I saw it myself, the answer is 'no'". But I did follow them across half a continent. We got into a situation in Turkey. I'm 'hot' as they say –" he said, smiling.

Dafna rolled her eyes and feigned sickness when he bounced his one long eyebrow up and down "—but we kept watching the website for leads."

"That's why we had been giving it special attention," said Eitan.

Ben thought back to the posts on almuminum.org The messages had started in Turkey and ended in New Orleans.

"A rendezvous tomorrow doesn't give us enough time," Eitan said, adjusting his glasses. Ofer became rigid, as if steeling himself for a big push. Ben could see he was going to bluster and bully his way through an argument. If he won out and they charged down to New Orleans, they stood a sizable risk of botching it, scaring the terrorists into the woodwork and blowing the one good chance they had at stopping this before it happened. Whatever *it* was must be worse than he imagined.

Ofer began, "We don't have enough time to do this *right* --"

"—wait a minute; I think we can buy an extra day, " Ben said.

Eitan paused, shifting his weight from side to side," What do you suggest?"

"Let's send them notes. Each one gets a note from a different source. They all say they've ran into problems of one sort or another and they need an extra day to get to the meeting point. I've got the addresses. I know the code. I can spoof the notes using the mail command on port 25 through a Unix server. It will be convincing – the notes will look like they're coming from the other members. It isn't that hard to do. That will give us an extra day. The one thing that could be damaging is this: they've been putting the notes into an account – not sending them. I've been accessing the notes by hacking the NetMail account. They're all in the Drafts folder – meaning all the terrorists must log into the account and read the notes without sending them through the internet. That way, the message would never be transmitted and would be protected from packet-sniffing programs. It wouldn't be intercepted along the way."

"That is a problem." Eitan said, "if we break their protocol we give them a reason to run and hide."

"Well, I don't think we have an alternative. We have to send the notes instead. We don't know the password for the account."

"Give us the name. We'll have the password in less than a day most likely," Ofer said.

"We can't be sure of that – even if you through a supercomputer at it. Besides, we don't have a day. We have to get them to postpone *now* so we can have a day to prepare. We're out of time already!" Ben said.

"Spoofing the notes carries as much risk as hitting them without a plan, if not more. If they see the notes as forgeries, that will be the end of it. It's better to strike without warning, even if we're ill-prepared," Ofer said.

Eitan said nothing, as he stood between them and ruminated over the alternatives.

"We've carried out many successful operations with less lead time than this! If we send the notes, we'll be warning them that their operation has been comprised. They'll have a day to slither off and then they'll regroup. Think about it. We won't be able to find them again before they deploy!" Ofer shouted, droplets of his spit flew into the empty space at the center of the group.

"That's enough!" Eitan said, raising his voice as he spoke, "I am the desk chief here and I will make the determinations. Your 'plan' is a recipe for disaster. At best you'll expose us here. At worst we lose everything and thousands of people die," he said, pounding his fist into his palm for emphasis, " No, we need more time. We will send the messages. We need that extra day to get our people in place to do this right." He stared Ofer down.

"It's your show, clown master," Ofer said. He shrugged his shoulders, "You'd better not be wrong. Remember: Your pension depends on it." He stopped there and stared.

Eitan didn't return the favor. Instead, he looked over at the desk, picking up one of the notes. He glanced at it for a moment, then met Ben's eyes squarely.

"You need to send the notes right away. After that is done your part in the matter comes to an end. You will turn over all the data you have and give us the means to crack this code."

"No," Ben said.

"No, what?" Ofer said, taking a step toward him.

"No, I'm not giving you the solution to the code," Ben said, not budging an inch, "I'll send the notes and I'll give you everything I've got, but I'm not giving up the code. I want some insurance."

Eitan laughed, "Please yourself. Keep the code if you will – I don't care." He waved at the air loosely like an effeminate Frenchman.

"I want some assurances."

He laughed again. "You're in the wrong place for a-- how do you put it? A warm and furry."

"Fuzzy," Ben corrected, "Warm and Fuzzy. But I'm not looking for that. I want to come along for the show. You're going to need me to put the finger on them."

Ofer broke his stare off. "No – you would be a stone around our necks and if you come along you'll wind up just as dead as one."

Ben ignored the remark. "I want to make sure you get the right people. What if the place is crowded or dimly lit or some other thing? 'The fog of war'…you know. It's likely you won't be able to get a positive ID on them even with the extra day. Do you want to end up killing a bunch of people and not get them in the end? That's bad about seven ways to the Sabbath."

"Why would you put yourself at risk?" Eitan asked.

"You have to ask that question at this point? They destroyed my home, killed my friend and my only brother and mutilated my hand for God's sake," he said, thrusting the bandaged club up towards Eitan's face. "Do I need more than that? I think most people would agree the line's been crossed. If all that weren't enough, this doctrine of the Muslim as 'best of all men', has to be stopped. You negotiate with your equals – with your peers. You can't negotiate with a group of people who consider you 'the descendants of apes and pigs' and 'najis' – dirty. They interpret the actions of others through their cultural prism and in their culture, negotiation is weakness. It's only done for a 'timeout' to regroup, not a 'solution'. There is no peace treaty with a Muslim group, only a *hudna* – a truce to regroup. Besides, we won't be able to 'reason' with a people who have been given the absolute Truth and have been commanded by Allah to 'kill or subdue all unbelievers until such time as all religion on Earth is for Allah'. It's all or nothing: black and white: positive and negative. It's a matter of polar opposites until we can break them out of their mindset."

"Okay – so what?" said Ofer.

"So - someone has to do this. Someone has to stop them now. Someone has to get the word out. Unfortunately that seems to be up to us. My government still has the official line that 'Islam is a religion of peace.' All of us in this room know it's never been true. The people of the United States are lost until we understand the problem and define the enemy correctly. The belief system is the enemy. In other words *It's about the Qur'an, stupid.* It's a bloodthirsty construct – cobbled together with stories from uninspired, non-canonical Jewish and Christian writings and from pagan rock-worshipping practices from the seventh-century Arabian peninsula. Islam is just like other tribal religions from the past. Allah is vindictive and needs to be placated with blood. Consider the Mayas, the Incas, the Aztecs and other pagan belief systems. For the Aztecs, the god who needed the most blood was Huitzilopochtli, the war god. They thought that if he didn't receive the nourishment that he needed he wouldn't battle the forces of night. This would cause the sun to fail to rise the next morning. Think about some of the old Middle Eastern cults: Moloch of both the Canaanite and Phoenicians who required children of the believers as burnt offerings. We still have the same problem, but now it's not the few virgins or the just the children of the believers – it's the children of the Muslims as well as the children of non-believers – and all infidels for that matter. Muslim parents sacrifice their children when they approve of the bombs strapped to their bodies. You see, the only sure way to enter Paradise for a Muslim is by dying in The Cause of Allah. Nothing else is guaranteed. Hell, they don't know if Mohammed ended up in heaven. That's why they robotically say, "Peace Be Upon Him" every time they mention him. What kind of a belief system is that? You can't tell where someone ends up except if they 'slay or be slain' for The Cause? The god of the Qur'an is capricious, conspiratorial, vindictive and sadistic. He's always in Hell torturing souls, but never in the gardens of paradise – why is that? The spirit Muslims serve is more comfortable in Hell than in Heaven."

Eitan looked at him. "Okay - now tell us how you *really feel.*

They all laughed, surprisingly.

Eitan continued, "Fine. Have it your way. Who am I to argue about it. I won't stop you, but you must realize what you're about to do."

"One other thing. Don't give me any credit for this. I didn't help at all, okay? Nobody needs to know."

"I hope you have more life insurance than what AireWarez provides. That won't keep your family out of trouble for long." Dafna said, disturbed by the whole thing.

"Let me worry about my family," Ben said.

"Ben, think about this. You're not in any condition to do this anyway," Dafna said, pulling on his good arm.

He turned back fully towards Eitan. "You know I'm right about this. I'm the best card you have to play at this point. Trump them while we have the chance – we won't get another one ."

Eitan considered it for a moment, "I said 'have it your way.' Be my guest – you're on the next flight to New Orleans courtesy of AirWarez." He smiled and bowed his head.

"I'm going too. You're going to need me down there," Dafna begrudged, "I'm coming with you, you stubborn *ben zona.*"

He stood on the balcony and watched them leave. He checked the time.

18:30.

Was it past the point where he could do something about it? The group who had killed Ike would either still be on the road or close to arriving in New Orleans at this time. Would they even check the email accounts before the meeting?

He went back inside and began the slow work of finding each of the words in the text of the Qur'an. He needed to work smarter. He opened the Yusuf Ali edition and searched the text for the words he needed.

With his first note complete, he logged into one of the AirWarez servers. *Might as well use company resources now*, he thought. He switched to the root account and acquired all the privileges the 'superuser' of the machine would have. He checked to see if the box had reversed DNS and IP logging switched on. It did. He made the changes and restarted the box. Now the email headers wouldn't contain the true IP address of the originating box nor would it share its true name. He shuffled through his notes, trying to find the traceroutes he had done to track the group from Chicago. He would add their server lists to the spurious header information he would create, lending it some authenticity.

At the command prompt he typed,

```
HELO northwestern.edu

250 mail.stldevctr017.AireWarez.com

Hello stldevctr017.AireWarez.com [160.170.40.17], pleased to meet you
```

He was connected to port 25 – the one for Simple Mail Transfer Protocol (STMP). He typed:

```
MAIL FROM (get ArAzahad33@NetMail.com
250   (ArAzhahad33@NetMail.com... Sender ok
```

Now he would look like the terrorist from Chicago.

```
RCPT TO: ArRad13@NetMail.com
250  ArRad13@NetMail.com ... Recipient ok
```

He added the entries for two false 'hops' the note would have taken on its way out of Chicago. Then he put in the message itself:

```
DATA
1:5:3:8:83:31:8:84:7:7:34:18:7:38:7:10:7:9
10:27:47:129:8:2:267:33:3:284:1:4:20:10:39:24:13:41:36:5
55:29:5:55:39:14:84:6:18:52:16:5:52:30:15:5::37:11:8:24
.
```

Before sending it he decided to check Ike's cracker program. He had been running it against the ArRad13 and ArAzahad33 account, as well as the dead letter drop – the jk92q3rzlwe@NetMail.com account. The program's bots had hit on another note from ArRad13's Drafts folder:

```
n3w9deld89e
```

was all it said. He tried logging into the account, using this text as the password. It worked. He could use the dead letter account instead.

Chapter 39

He laid on her bed, just in his boxers , staring up at the crooks and crannies of her textured ceiling and finding all of his fears and regrets in their shadows. He knew he was out of his league. He had a feeling he'd end up dead. *Should he chase them down to New Orleans and put himself in harm's way?* He knew the answer. *Absolutely not.* In spite of the alarms going off in his head he simply couldn't let it go. They had to be stopped now and he had to be a part of it, regardless of the risk. One side of him knew how idiotic this would sound to other people – especially Grace, but he had to do it.

As if reading his thoughts she said, "It isn't too late to stop this," while coming back into the bedroom with an armful of clothes. She had began packing already. "Ben, no one would think you less of you if you just walked away. Leave it to the professionals – they get paid to take care of animals like this. They do it all the time. Just leave it alone."

"Dafna, I hear what you saying", he propped himself on a elbow to watch her, "I know you're right -- but there's always a time when a man has to say 'No more' and put it on the line." She looked at him askance but didn't slow her packing. "If you don't step up at that point, you lose your future self respect and your place in the world."

She walked over to him, wriggling her jeans over her hips. They fell compliantly to the floor. He leaned over the edge of the bed looking at them. She pushed him back on the bed and mounted him. She pressed his shoulders into the mattress with her hands and his groin with her hips. Her warmth and movement kept enticing him, making him fully erect. She began to breathe through her mouth and her eyelids got heavy as she looked down at him through the parted curtain of her shiny, dark hair.

"You'll keep your self-respect at the cost of your life, " she whispered, grinding herself into him, "Don't do it."

His breathing got faster. "Live to see your children grow old," she suggested as she rubbed herself against him.

"Goddamn it… stop! Stop now before I end up doing something else I'm going to regret…" he said, using his arm to wipe the corner of his mouth. He pushed her off, twisting away from her. She followed his movement, rolling with him to his side of the bed.

"I want you Ben – right now. While we still have a chance," she smiled and stroked his hair, "like they used to say here: 'Make Love Not War'. We could be dead tomorrow. We probably will be. Enjoy me one time at least."

"Don't think I don't want to: I do. But I can't, Dafna. Under different circumstances –"

"I don't want you to say anything, stupid man. Just shut up and fuck me!" She slapped him hard across the bruises on his face. "You're just like him. You're all alike. You all leave me with nothing."

She left him there, stomping out to the living room, where she sat down on the couch, drew her knees up and hugged them just like she had a few years before, when it had been the only comfort she could find.

War

She had been engaged to a fine soldier named Nir for about a month when his time had come and he'd gone off to the patrols in Gaza. That conflict had been drawn out for years, but some people like her had hope that the Knesset, the Israeli Parliament, and Ehud Barak, Prime Minister at the time, would disentangle the Israelis from that mess. If that could happen, she thought, then Nir could finish out his duty in a safer place and they would be reunited in the end.

She went to him for a few days that May when he had a pass. They spent the time at a little place along side the *Galei Kinnereth*, or the Sea of Galilee, not doing much except eating and drinking, and sailing in a four-man skiff when they weren't making love. She had felt complete and at peace during that brief holiday. They were the best days she'd ever see.

The morning of the last day they took the boat out again. Everything was perfect; the skies dotted with the puffy clouds she liked the most and the smells of the spring earth mixing with the warming waters swirled all around them, embracing them as they embraced each other. Out in the middle of the lake the only sounds were the waves lapping against the hull of the boat and the birds flying back and forth. No trace of day-to-day worries in any of it. They had the world to themselves and now that they were off shore far enough, he lashed the rudder and turned his attentions towards the one he loved.

"After I get discharged and we set up our house together, let's make sure we're near the water like this," he said, brushing her scented hair back behind her ears. He held her tight against the core of his lean body.

She felt this is where she should always be.

She could see him thinking of the boat and how it played on the water. "You're still thinking of the Olympics, aren't you?" For he was a competitive sailor and wanted to get a place on the Israeli team in 2000, but she knew his time in the Army had taken the edge away. He had said as much.

"Maybe in 2004 – I don't think I could qualify after spending this much time away from it."

"You will be busy in 2004: with the house, me and our children." She laughed and turned her face back to look up at him.

He gave her a squeeze, "You won't take up all my time," he suggested.

"Maybe not," she said coyly, "I'll agree if you plan on practicing between one and four in the morning," she poked him on the forehead with her index finger, "I have you for the rest of the day, make note of that."

He laughed and looked out toward the gulls gathering on the water. "I don't want this to end," he said distantly.

"It doesn't have to… " She pulled closer to him and they began to kiss.

A few minutes later, from the shore an observant person with field glasses may have seen that the boat began to rock harder than it should have in a breezy chop.

They were making love again in the bottom of that uncomfortable fiberglass boat, in front of God and the sea gulls. The fiberglass was almost too hot for bare skin, but they didn't notice.

"Promise me you'll come home soon," she said at the edge of her orgasm, "promise me."

"I'll come home to you. I promise. I love you Dafna," he said, as they both climaxed.

He was a man of his word, unfortunately. He came home four days later in the black bag the government always used. He lost his life to some unknown Muslim at a dirt crossroads with no name that belonged to no country. There; in Gaza. He had rotated into checkpoint duty as soon as their time together ended. A true believer terrorist had decided it was time to return to Allah and send as many Jews to Hell as he could along the way.

Nir came home to her one perfect May morning. She and his family buried him under a pile of stones, the color of ruined milk, along with her chance at happiness in this life.

He would no longer be her Nir, but from now on he would always be near her.

Chapter 40

Satisfied that he and Ofer were wrapped in his electronic cocoon, Etian closed his faux mahogany door and resumed his station behind the oversized desk. He folded his hands together and leaned forward over the tops of his knuckles. He cocked his head slightly in a show of mock curiosity.

"Are you going to say it? I can see it bubbling up inside you. You need to work on keeping that hidden. It could get you killed out there 'spy master'," he shot at Ofer.

"I don't need to…I'm among friends in a safe place, right?"

"I would never go that far. Even here."

"You don't think it's safe? We scanned the place and you've got your shields up Captain," Ofer asked, "what else do you need?"

"If I were you, I would never call me a 'friend'. I've killed several friends with these hands." He held them up, palms out, as if testifying in court.

"If you're trying to impress me, forget it. I know you're a good and faithful servant to The Office, a 'company man', if you will, but please don't tell me you're dangerous. You've spent more than half your career behind one desk or another and from the look of it, the size of the desk grows inversely to your importance in Office matters."

"How old are you Ofer?"

"Twenty-eight," he said firmly, trying to give it additional weight.

"If you want to see another twenty-eight, like I have, and still be breathing behind an old desk like this then you should listen to this: don't *ever* trust your boss and don't *ever* fucking *feel* anything on the job. Don't let *anything* you're thinking ever show." He swept his hand across the room. "We're in the middle of a back-alley street fight. Underestimating your opponent will put you face down fast. Never hesitate either."

"You're here because you never did anything remarkable after age thirty I suppose?" Ofer asked.

"Exactly. Never. And I've always erred on the side of caution. That doesn't mean I've moved slowly – I've been careful. Do you understand the difference?" He looked at him with what might be taken as concern.

"I would say we're breaking one of your rules with Ben *zona.* Not that I don't agree with our plan, but it's risky."

"Risky – how?"

"What if he actually survives his ordeal? He'll have seen enough to expose the considerable range of operations here. Something like that might set your pension back a few percentage points old man."

"Have some respect for a survivor, " he said off-handedly, adjusting the lapels of his coat.

"Well? Using this him as an asset is ill-advised in my estimation. He has no training; doesn't know the tradecraft; he's injured and emotional and your handler hates this whole setup.

"Well Dafna will be coming along. She's the daughter of another thirty-five-year survivor in whom I have the utmost respect. Also, she has the training and some experience. She served *Shin Bet* with distinction. Her file suggests it wasn't desk duty. Her father confirms it. I called him before setting all this in motion."

"He sent his daughter to die?"

Eitan looked at him as if he had farted loudly and stunk up the place. He didn't reply for a few moments. "They're not going to die. You know the plan --"

" -- And you know how often life follows The Plan. Listen, I've been through enough to know that already. Still - what if he survives? He's likely to expose all of this," Ofer said, making his own grand sweep.

"He won't." Eitan waved his hand at him, "I've been in this business longer than you've been alive. The only way you put in that much time is to plan for and meet all contingencies. We're covered on this. Now you have a plane to catch. When you get down there use caution…do you understand? We're among friends here in the U.S., but that doesn't mean we have the run of the house."

"Sure boss," Ofer said, standing and taking the manila folder from Eitan, "I just hope you run a better circus than my Uzbeki case officer. He was more a clown than a ringmaster.

"Don't let the package leave that building with anyone else," Eitan said emotionless, "Bring it to me. Kill them all if you have to. Make the plan work. We have too much time and blood spilled on this to stop short."

War

There may be moderate Muslims in Islam, but Islam itself is not moderate.
Author and Muslim Apostate Ibn Warraq

Chapter 41

Abdullah bin Malak al Zalam entered the Rosa Keller branch of the New Orleans Public Library for the third time – and with bad luck – as one of the librarians recognized him, looking at him as though she recalled something unpleasant. It was stupid of him to have made a scene the other time, but he dismissed it quickly. His time in the city would be over that evening. Still, he knew he needed to be discrete. He tried to carry himself as unobtrusively as possible to allay her suspicions. He picked up some scratch paper and the nub of a pencil as he walked over to the computers.

He sat at the terminal farthest from the other users at the opposite end of a long table. He opened a browser and logged into the drop site. He opened his English version of the Noble Qur'an and then began to read the note from al-Warraq. A fine brother and one of the true believers, to be sure. Abdullah owed him his life.

Hassan had been the one that saw the pin and lever fall from the grenade during the exercise. He had shouted out the warning. It hadn't been enough time to save the Egyptian, but, praise Allah, the call had given him enough time to protect most of himself behind a barricade. The explosion peppered the area around his left knee with shrapnel. The doctor had pulled him through, but couldn't do enough to keep him from having the permanent limp. Allah the beneficent and ever-merciful had allowed him to live. He took the fact as a confirmation that he would be allowed to do great things for Allah's Cause.

He used the numbers to look up the words and scratched them down in Arabic. Frustration well up in him again. He wanted to shout out loud. He felt the urge to break something, but mindful that he needed to keep the impulses under check this time, he gritted his teeth and clenched his fist and kept the rage from spilling out.

Al-Warraq had to put the meeting off by a day.

Troubles – whatever that meant.

Abdullah didn't like it at all. He knew al-Warraq had killed the hacker, that was as it should be, but it had caused them to be late a day somehow. Would this put the operation in jeopardy? He didn't think so – they still had enough time before 4 July. The note said they'd meet in the same place but a day later than planned. Abdullah didn't think this wise. Al-Warraq should have changed the meeting place as well.

The thought occurred to him that maybe this note was a ruse. Could that be? He carefully looked at the wording, thinking back to other notes to see if anything had changed. He verified the timestamps in the note headers. No problems there. The note followed their cipher as well. That alone should be enough to legitimize it. Hassan had come up with the code – a work of genius. Unbreakable, yet very simple.

He transcribed the other new note – seeing that the California group had received the message as well and confirmed. Again, he saw no reason to doubt the authenticity. Pushing the timetable back a day wouldn't jeopardize anything.

He logged off and shuffled off to the doors. He dropped pieces of the notes in several rubbish bins and kept parts of them to scatter in the wind as he walked back to his corner in the basement of the mosque on Magnolia Street.

He had walked a couple of blocks when he noticed someone following him again.

He stopped for a moment and rubbed his knee, pretending it bothered him. Glancing back he could see a man on the other side of the street, two blocks down but not the same one as before.

Chapter 42

Jack Daniels sat at his desk, mulling over the decision he had to make. Now he understood making decisions was a lot harder than criticizing them. He wadded up some reports, squeezing the balls of paper and tossing them back and forth between his hands. A janitor came up to his desk, bending over to pick up the trash can. Nate was his name. They'd been on speaking terms for some time since Jack often stayed late, trying to get that promotion and since he had no family to go home to.

Nate held out the can, encouraging Jack to take a shot.

Two points – nothing but net.

The janitor smiled – a grizzled old man with a gold tooth just like Jack's father.

"You played hoop in school?"

"Yeah, a little."

War

The old man nodded.

"I made varsity my freshman year. We went to state a couple of times and won it my Junior year; down in 'Nawlins. Played on a college scholarship down in Baton Rouge. We never won much, but it got me through school. Free ride."

The old man nodded in approval, "You still got it."

"You got that right."

Nate laughed a little and went on emptying cans in the same circuit he always took. Nate moved like Jack's father did. He supposed years of work did that to a man with little future and even less money in his pocket. But his father's way of carrying himself showed more pride. His father had always been proud of his two sons.

Agent Daniels thought back to the time when he came home with $200 dollars in his pocket. His brother had the same amount. They had been going down to Bourbon Street during the run up to Mardi Gras his freshman year of high school. They'd made pairs of tap shoes by fastening parts of spoons to the bottoms of their church shoes. They didn't know many steps, but carried on enthusiastically, clowning for the drunks and tourists. It was easy money and more than they'd ever had before. Flush with it, they saw this route as better than trying to get jobs down at the tavern where their father always went. He was a drinker. He liked his whiskey, for sure; that was the God's honest truth.

Their father always came home after work and sat in the easy chair opposite the TV in the front room of their shotgun-style bungalow. He didn't usually bother to change out of his janitor's uniform and always a tumbler of Jack Black on the rocks. He'd always liked his whiskey but by then he was drinking it all the time. The tumbler sat next to him in the evenings just like mama had before she died. That particular night his father had taken up his post and was watching The Tonight Show when Carson still hosted it. Jack and his brother came in, tap shoes tied together at the laces and dangling from their shoulders. They tried to hide the shoes as they walked past the hall door. It didn't work.

"Come over here boys. I want to see you. What you been up to? Why you tryin' to sneak on past that door?"

They didn't say anything – they just walked over to his chair. They hadn't had a chance to ditch the shoes. He sort of chuckled a bit, then the smile dropped off his face.

"Boys, you been tappin' down in the Quarter?" He sat his glass down on the worn armrest. "I told you not to go down there anymore. Nothin' good can come of it."

"Dad," Johnny said, "We both made two hundred dollars."

"We jus' tapped a little, dad," Jack added, "no harm in that."

"No harm in that... I'm your father and I say don't go down in the Quarter," he shook his head, "I don' want you fools to get the notion that money come easy, don't you see? Two hundred dollars don't amount to nuthin. You need to put your time in for school. Study. Then you get a real job with a future. After that, you make real money."

He took a sip of whiskey.

"But it's good money," Johnny protested. He dug in his pocket and showed him, holding a wad of bills in each hand.

"Put that away. You think that impress me? You likely to end face down in an alley. You think this here is the 'Big Easy' right? Tap a little, play the fool, get all kinds o' money. Easy. Well, you as likely to end up in the parish jail by the by. Ain't no easy money in the Quarter, let me tell you. Ain't no easy money: no how, no way. I been there. Look where I am now."

"What kinda life did you have in mind when you named us after yo' whiskey, Dad? You have some kind of big plans for us then? Jack Daniels and Johnny Walker Daniels... a coupla names for tap dancin' street fools, I'd say," Jack said, baiting him. He'd heard his Dad's high-minded speeches before, with the scent of whiskey all around it. Didn't smell right to him.

"Now you listen good, you pry those spoons off the bottoms of yo' shoes. If they busted you buy new ones with what money you have. You keep the rest, but don' eva' go down there again lookin' for the easy money. You work for your money, you hear? You study like I told you and get to college. You both got it in you. You *both* gonna end up amountin' to something', not some flunky janitor chump like me wit' two hundred dollars in your pocket. *You responsible now. You old enough to understand. You know.*"

Despite the teenage bluster, both boys listened to their father. Mr. Daniels had been successful in that one regard. He drank too much, but that was his only real vice. He made sure they stayed in school and did the work, even if he didn't understand it himself. They both grew up, went to college and had good jobs. Johnny had joined the Coast Guard as a means of getting through school and had risen to Lieutenant Junior Grade and was running one of the cutters out of the Port of New Orleans. Jack had played his hoop and had done his level best in school, worked hard at smoothing out his 'Nawlins accent and had gotten into the training program in Washington, D.C. He graduated in the ninetieth percentile of his class, full of promise, but he took a position in Saint Louis, thinking it would be best to start as a big fish in a little pond where he would be noticed quicker and would advance faster.

In the three years at station, he had done a mountain of paperwork, worked long and late, but hadn't had the opportunity distinguish himself. It's true, he was on the AireWarez case, but in a supporting role. It moved along at the speed of a glacier. He had been itching to find a short cut. Now he had it. But he hesitated. Was this really the way? Was it worth it? The case with Ben Adams could go south about ten different ways he could see or it would amount to nothing in the end. He looked around him, taking stock of where he was. Literally, he still worked in what could be considered the lobby, like a bank clerk. Taking a shot at it meant exposing himself to risk, but he saw no way around it.

He picked up the phone. The sound of the dial tone stopped him. He took a deep breath and looked over at Nate again.

Agent Daniels wanted to be somebody. So did his brother. It was 'sink or swim' time. He dialed the number.

No answer. His brother's cell phone went to voice mail. Daniels paged through his daily planner and dialed another number.

"U.S. Coast Guard, New Orleans," a female voice said. Good - they still had people in the office.

"I need you to put me through to Johnny Daniels. This is Jack, his brother."

"One moment please," the voice said. She back after ten or fifteen seconds. "I'm sorry, sir, I can't do that. He's aboard ship now."

Jack leaned back in his chair and exhaled. "I need you to get him on the ship-to-shore for me."

"Sir, that's not easy to do. And if it's not official business it's against regulations."

"Look – I know that. Just get him on, okay? I'm his brother. This is a family emergency."

A Plague on Both Houses

Lobotomy, Lobotomy
DDT did a job on me,
Now I am a real sickie,
Guess I'll have to break the news,
That I got no mind to loose.
All the girls are in love with me,
I'm a teenage lobotomy.
The Ramones – Teenage Lobotomy

Chapter 43

Abdullah bin Malak al Zalam couldn't tell if the spy following him belonged to Pepito or to some arm of the U.S. government. He guessed him to be one of Pepito's men by because of the unruly black shock of hair, the choice of punked-out sunglasses and the brutish, slouching way the infidel moved. Pepito had to be keeping an eye on him to either gain leverage in the next drugs-for-arms deal or for extortion when he found himself at a disadvantage. It didn't matter anyway. – regardless of who his tail worked for, Abdullah had to lose him. No problem. New Orleans always had crowds and he'd get lost in the middle of the next one he could find. He started to make his move. At the next block he turned left off of Loyola onto Perdido Street. He picked up his pace gradually. After three blocks, moving toward the river, he stopped at the corner and made a big show out of tying his shoe against the light post. He looked back, seeing the same man on foot, moving at a slow amble and looking at the second floor of a commercial building. He couldn't see anyone else and no car either.

He turned left on Baronne Street and walked as fast as he could, crossing the street in mid-block and turning right onto Common Street. He glanced sideways as he turned the corner. He saw a dark sedan down at the other end of the street. He began to walk quickly again once the buildings blocked their line of sight. He crossed the street again, trying to stay as close to the buildings and fences as possible with the idea that heavy shadow might make it harder to pick him up. It was about 7:30 p.m. and the sun continued to sink, casting deep shadows on his side.

He resolved to keep walking as long as it took. He would walk around the city until either the crowds or the darkness concealed him. He couldn't lead them back to the cases. He wondered if they already knew where he stayed.

Although he had taken pains to make sure no one in the mosque knew where he had hidden the weapons, he knew what a few men can do with guns and the will to use them. It amused him that he might have to kill some of them with their own boss' gun until he realized Pepito had killed at least one of them with it himself, emptying a clip from the Glock 17 into the Venezuelan, expending quadruple the rounds necessary. Wasteful and hardly impressive, Abdullah had thought.

He found himself hemmed in at that point. He had moved into a section consisting of a mish mash of old three and four story commercial buildings, some unused. The buildings stood very close together and the gaps between then had been boarded up or had iron gates secured with chains and padlocks. He walked as fast as he could to try and position himself better. He wouldn't be able to duck down an alley if necessary.

At the next block he turned left on Saint Charles Street, where it opened up a little. His mood lifted a bit as he walked more slowly towards the Old Quarter, but he knew he should continue with his plan and find a crowd to make certain he had lost them. His leg bothered him more than usual, but knew he could walk at least another five kilometers if necessary.

After another long block he reached Canal Street. He surveyed both directions for several blocks. They would meet on this street tomorrow -- at a *halal* butcher shop in the nine hundred block. He was very close to it, but even looking at it would be a bad idea at this point.

He crossed the streetcar tracks and entered the Old Quarter. He began to modulate his pace, walking fast, then slowing down to look at the shop windows, then fast again, weaving through the couples and groups of people on the tilting, slate flagstone sidewalks. By Conti Street he noticed another, new Hispanic had been keeping the same distance from him regardless of pace. Abdullah muttered to himself and thrust his hand into the gun pocket. He had cut out the lining so that he could easily reach the gun in the nylon holster, lashed to his leg with Velcro strips. The shops in the Quarter kept rubbish bins right on the walkways, making it harder to weave in and out of the thickening groups of people. Clouds, heavy and dark, raced up from the South to cover the skies now. Another storm had arrived. He couldn't believe how much water these *kuffar* had. They had more than they could handle. It didn't seem fair at first glance, but Allah *ta'alla* knows best. It had to make sense, somehow, for the unbelievers to have a better life in obvious ways, but he was not privy to the plan and did not question it. Allah's slaves do not question his wisdom nor do they critique his methods.

Abdullah ducked into the corner store at Saint Louis Street, pulled a 'New Orleans' t-shirt off the rack and grabbed a baseball cap lettered with *Lassiez les bon temps roulez* (Let the good times roll) from the top of the counter. He threw the cashier a twenty and walked out the other door onto Saint Louis Street. He changed as he walked, weaving in and out of the strollers and stuffing Jesús Cansadas' brown work shirt into the rotting plate scrapings in the first rubbish can he passed. The heavy gray sky began to drop its burden on them all, slowly at first, giving him the unfamiliar feeling of a growing, cool wetness soaking through the clothing and touching his skin.

Chapter 44

Agent Daniels looked at his watch: 19:35. The Coast Guard lady still hadn't put him through to Johnny. They had less than four hours before the time specified in the pager message. He had no idea where his brother was or if he could make it to the coordinates in time. He looked around the office nervously. Nate the janitor was gone. He was alone.

He heard a couple of clicks and then some static through the receiver. Then he heard his brother's voice, very tinny and in a higher-than-normal register.

"This is Johnny Daniels," he seemed to be in a noisy location and had to raise his voice over the ambient sound. He sounded stressed too.

"Johnny, this is Jack."

"Is Dad okay?"

"Yes, look, I'm sorry if I worried you. I had to say this is a family emergency to get through."

"This better be good, Jack. I'm out to sea. The Guard doesn't take calls like this lightly."

"I know. Listen - I'm working a case here in Saint Louis. I can't go into the details over the line, but I have a reliable source that says something big is going down out there in the Gulf tonight. It's a rendezvous of some sort. I've got the coordinates."

Johnny didn't say anything for a few moments. Jack could hear two or three voices in the background. They sounded as if they were resonating out of a small metal box along with mix of machine noises and the scraping of metal on metal. He imagined Johnny was on the bridge.

"Drugs? Rendezvous?" Johnny asked.

"We don't know. Look, I can't say much more than that, understand?"

"Okay, bro, let me get this straight. You want me to change the official course of this ship and check out some tip one of yo' informers gave you. In Saint Louis?" he said mockingly.

"That's right ---but"

"-- but nuttin. Have you lost yo' mind Jack?" He lowered his voice, rasping into the phone. "I can't be suggestin' crazy-ass shit like that, even if I have command. We're talking about my career here, okay? I got a good thing goin' now."

Jack thought about it. He didn't really have enough to conclusively say that Johnny would find something. He only had a date, a time and some coordinates. He knew he was asking too much.

"Look bro, I ain't playin' -- have I ever steered you wrong?" Jack said.

"Of course you have, you asinine muthafucker. Plenty a times. Brothers mess with brothers all the time. We always did. You know that. Are you drunk or somethin'? You got anything better than that or are we finished here? I'm on the bridge now – I'm on duty," he said, his voice returning to its previous volume.

"Listen Johnny, my career is on the hook here too, you know? I have reliable intelligence that a rendezvous will happen tonight at 23:15 and it may involve either drugs or terrorist activities or both. Now I know the commander of a ship has discretion. You're supposed to interdict. Just tell me if you can reach this set of coordinates by 23:15 Central Time. If you can't – no problem. I apologize for all of this if you can't reach it."

Johnny considered it for a moment.

"Are you sure about this? If we do this and it turns out to be a bunch of nothin' it ain't gonna to be pretty. The hammer's gonna drop on both of us."

"I know. I realize that."

"Are you sure about this?"

"Not absolutely sure. How can I be absolutely sure, Johnny?"

"You know you're going outside the normal chain of command too, don't you? On my side and yours."

Jack could hear his brother's exasperated breath in the receiver.

"What coordinates you got?" he asked.

"Twenty-four point five, five, five, five by negative Eighty-five point two four five."

Johnny read them back.

"Stay on the line. Let me check it out."

He left the mike open. Jack listened to the crew call back and forth to each other and heard the squawking sound of another radio in the distance. He heard a constant pattering noise behind it all. It resembled rain on the tin roof back home.

"Jack, you better not get me onto the list, you hear me?"

"You can reach it by 23:15?"

"You sure that's local time?"

"We think so, yeah. Is it raining there?"

"Yeah – a storm's coming up. That will make it harder to find your boat, by the way. I'm gonna change course to intercept. You always had good luck growing up, Jack. Hope it holds out tonight."

"Thanks. You're doing the right thing Johnny," Jack said, hanging up. He didn't know if he should stay in the office or go home.

He didn't know what to do next. Unlike his brother, he was in uncharted waters.

War

The following ten things are essentially najis [unclean]:
1. Urine
2. Faeces
3. Semen
4. Dead body
5. Blood
6. Dog
7. Pig
8. Kafir [An Unbeliever]
9. Alcoholic liquors
10. The sweat of an animal who persistently eats najasat [i.e., unclean things].
Grand Ayatolla al-Sistani of Iraq
www.sistani.org/html/eng/menu/3/inside/12.htm

Chapter 45

He pressed on, taking care not to give his two new companions any indication he was aware of them Darkness had come rather quickly because of the rain, which continued to fall in an unhurried, casual way. It wasn't strong enough to drive the gaggle of drunks and partiers from the street. He had to work harder at weaving in and out of them – even on the sidewalks they ignored his progress, too tied up with rendering themselves senseless with drink and lechery. So many of the women's nipples poked through their thinly-strapped cotton tops of various bright colors, clinging to them as the rain soaked them. Most of them wore tight, short pants which showed off their leg flesh. *The sinners and their sins are thick on this street,* he thought. *Worse than any whore in the back alleys of Karachi, or any Islamic city for that matter.* Gyrating and grinding their hips while holding alcohol in one hand and cigarettes in the other -- if indeed they weren't grabbing at men's asses. How truly corrupted these animals were. Filthy.

He stepped out over the rough-cut granite curb, taking care not to step in the filth lining the gutters. "Street broth" they called it. A soup of brown water, mixed with puke, grease and the dregs of a thousand whores' drinks. The street broth shimmered a rainbow of reflected evils under the neon signs and it smelled like the rot in their souls. Now Abdullah understood just how bad this nation really was. *Until you see it you can never imagine the depths of its depravity*, he told himself. He had imagined far less and had given them far too much credit.

He still had the evening prayer to do and he didn't think he would be able to ritually purify himself after this. He felt dirty. He tried not to touch any of them, especially the women as he still tried to shake off the two following him.

He looked askance to see if he'd gained any ground. Too many bodies got in the way to judge. He stepped over the rivulet of gutter filth on the other side of Bourbon Street and threaded his way along the sidewalk again. As he walked past the open doorways, blasts of cold, heavy air pushed against his side.

The place constantly assaulted his senses and sensibilities.

He began to shiver slightly when the stronger gusts of air conditioning hit him now. His shirt was nearly soaked through. The bars competed to see which could be the noisiest hive of confusion. People kept colliding with him – men with half-closed senseless looks turned to say 'Sorry buddy" and then resumed their inanities.

Senseless shouting. Sinners staggering around in circles. The crowd matching whatever beat currently registered in their intoxicated brains. He thanked Allah then and there that he had been chosen as an instrument of retribution. Allah is all-knowing and wise. He command his followers to punish vermin like this in the Qur'an. *Inshallah,* Abdullah would do that very thing in a matter of days. *He couldn't allow himself to fail in the midst of all of this. He feared for his place in heaven. Surely it would weigh against him on the last day if he couldn't overcome this test and …*

The rain began to pelt him on the face as he scanned the next corner. Two muscular policemen dispassionately surveyed the coming and going revelers. They had thick, shiny black leather belts with guns and other equipment hanging down over their dark, blue pants. Now he felt vulnerable, caught between police on one side and criminals on the other. He plucked a used plastic drink cup off one of the weather-beaten, wooden pens holding in a heap of trash. He mimicked how the drunks held their cups. He slowed his pace by degrees, trying to put a more random lilt into his walk. Fifteen meters from the police, he decided to enter the corner bar to avoid walking directly past them. The bar had another doorway on Saint Peter Street that he could use to get around them. He stepped up into the cool rush of smoky air, mixed with the scents of puke, stale beer and mothballs. A group of musicians played some rapid, dissonant mix of notes and a woman tried to shout above it in the peculiar bastard French spoken by the *kuffar* in that god-forsaken part of the world. *Allah reserved a special place in hell for women who sang in public for the prophet, may peace be upon him, said it was like seeing them naked. If that were true she must look hideous,* Abdullah thought.

The crowd pressed against him from all sides; some of them just trying to get out of the rain, others to lose themselves in the roar of the band. He positioned himself squarely in the middle of the seating area, his back to the band and his gaze outward through a sliver of the crowd, to the street. He waited through the next song. At that point one of his unwelcome companions passed through the narrow wedge of vision. It was the infidel from the library, still after him. He lowered his head, just to be careful.

Abdullah pushed his way over toward the Saint Peter's Street entrance. He sat his empty cup on the top of an overflowing rubbish bin and eased his way towards the side door. He'd walk toward the river, to the Moonwalk and then turn North on the other side of Canal Street…

He stepped out onto the bluish flagstones, shiny but mottled with the dark circles of old chewing gum. Hands in his pockets, he shrugged against the raindrops as he reassured himself the Glock was still in good order. He carried a folded hunting knife in the other pocket, along with a wad of American dollars and the Venezuelan passport. He doubted he could fool anyone for long with it.

The rain had become nuisance at that point, for it had collected on roofs and streamed over the leaning balconies and through the gaps in their boards where they needed repair. The balconies alternately spared him or showered him. As he walked along, he brushed up against crumbling stucco, soiling his new shirt with the mildew-slime growing on it. Even with a bath, the place reeked and a layer of grime or rust rubbed off every surface he touched.

Up ahead, a queue of tourists – about a dozen of them - blocked the sidewalk in front of an old, grey stucco single-story building, with a vaguely French façade.

Abdullah decided against crossing the street again to avoid giving away his position. Besides, it was open to car traffic, and the drivers seemed more impatient than usual, blaring horns when the drunks weren't crossing fast enough. He noticed a brightly-lit shop across the street advertising VooDoo supplies.

Idolatry – open pagan idolatry! For sale in the streets!

His father had always said that Christian *kuffar* ran this country. That was bad enough – they assigned partners to Allah.

The Trinity…an abomination...but this went far beyond that. Idol worship – openly bought and sold. Revulsion rose up in his throat. They would all pay allowing this worst of transgressions. They deserved worse than what he had brought for them. Far worse. All of them. They allowed this to happen in the light of day. They all deserved the ignoble death his cargo would bring to a mere hundred thousand. Now that wasn't enough for him. They should all be punished. Innocent? Not one.

He snapped out of it and looked back towards Bourbon street. He caught the face of the Latino at the corner. He had been spotted again. Abdullah had to do something fast.

He moved quickly, bumping past several people in the queue, which had dwindled to a mere handful. He looked down the street, calculating his odds. He decided to join the ranks, wedging himself between the remaining tourists and the grimy stucco to try and hide himself from the Latino, now moving cautiously but deliberately down the opposite side of Saint Peter Street.

Abdullah gave the man a twenty at the door and moved as quickly as possible down the hallway to the second doorway on the left. Worn wooden benches lined one side of the hallway, about three meters across, with two large double doors leading into the main room, which had a piano and drum kit set up on the street side. Folding chairs filled up the majority of the rest of the space. All seats were taken and more infidels stood three deep behind them.

He paused behind the doorway, considering whether he should pass through it and find an exit through the courtyard. He looked back to see if the doorman was preoccupied -- unfortunately not. Since he had no means to cover his movements, he turned and took a place about four people from the doorway in the last row next to the wall.

The air in the place tasted used. They stood close, almost shoulder to shoulder. The dread of touching someone before prayers crossed his mind again, but that couldn't take priority at the moment. He knew the Latino would be watching from the street at the very least. He considered the few options he had. First: he could walk out onto Saint Peter Street, concealing himself in the departing throng and go along with whatever direction they took. Not much of an option, he thought. Second: at the end of the performance he could slip out to the courtyard and find a way to get out, hopefully not by the street. While he searched for a third option, the band members filed in and took up their instruments. The sounds bounced off the walls, grating on his nerves. He scratched his ear and moved his feet as much as he could from side to side, the limited space constricting his movements. The band struck up a song and when the clarinet started wailing, the noise reminded him of the sound sack of cats would make when being whipped with a knotted cord.

Truly awful, this 'music' called Jazz. It had no structure, no seeming purpose, no message. Then, Abdullah saw the Latino's head and shoulders leaning in from the first door. He moved his head slowly, systematically scanning the rows of listeners. Abdullah lowered himself, trying to get fully behind the sweating rolls of an obese American woman who had been nattering on about having to stand during the show.

He cursed the Brothers' decision to use these *kuffar* in something that would have been holy and pure. They had polluted this jihad. Trading hundred of thousands of lives for mere thousands was unacceptable. Why hadn't the Brothers seen this? Why hadn't Allah guided them rightly? But he didn't doubt the mission or its righteousness. Some of The Brothers must be at fault. Their intentions weren't either pure enough or Allah, may his blessings be upon us, in His infinite mercy and wisdom, had decided to make this a test of sincerity. Abdullah took solace in the purity of his intent and his single-minded resolve. Allah knew this. Abdullah would overcome these *kuffar* and any others who came between him and the mission. He had no doubt of this.

But the present situation posed a serious obstacle to him. He had to get away somehow. He couldn't retrieve the two cases until then. Time ran short – he would rendezvous tomorrow.

Constantly adjusting himself to hide behind the odiferous, sweating flesh of the sow in front of him, he considered his options. His enemy knew he was in the room, but Abdullah surmised he didn't know exactly where. When the listeners began to file out he would use the confusion to make his way to the courtyard at the end of the entrance hall. The rain would prevent any of these people from lingering in the courtyard. There he would either find another way out or would wait to kill the Latino in the shadows.

Mercifully, may Allah be praised, the performance lasted less than thirty minutes. The mass of the infidels began to push toward the doorway, bleating like a bunch of stinking goats. Abdullah pushed harder than the rest, slinking along the wall in a crouch. He positioned his cap to block his profile as best he could, but kept his body at an angle where he could look down the hallway. He moved against the flow of the crowd and reached the entrance to the courtyard. He stepped over the chain barrier, darting sideways to put the wall between him and any watchful eyes. The only light source in the courtyard came from the second-story windows' light, reflecting off the sheen of the flagstones in the rain. Potted palms and other plants lined the walls of the courtyard. Abdullah positioned himself behind a potted palm along the wall, trying to give himself enough coverage, but it wasn't adequate for a hiding spot. His adversary would be able to anticipate since the palm was the only plant large enough to conceal him.

His eyes traced the perimeter, looking for an alternate exit. None of the doors seemed to be a way out to the street. He noticed a breezeway in the corner directly across from the palm. He hesitated a moment. To get to the breezeway he would have to show himself again and his leg would not allow him to outrun the Latino if it came down to a foot race.

He looked back to the hallway. The crowd cast a moving jumble of shadows out onto the old red bricks of the courtyard, stretching out until they almost reached the fountain at its center. Still, Abdullah saw no sign of the Latino. He unfolded his knife, pressing it against his left thigh to conceal it. He stepped away from the palm tree, taking his chances. He stayed as close to the wall he could and still have ease of movement. He skirted around to the point where they would be able to see him from the hallway.

He became conscious of his increasing heart rate and his rapid breathing.

He stepped into the line of sight and saw the silhouettes in the hallway. As he limped toward the gaping, empty rectangle of the breezeway, he recognized the blocky shape of the one who followed him. His dark shape turned toward him, moving the opposite direction of the others.

He had been spotted again. He quickened his pace and plunged into the breezeway darkness. Now he could see a dim light at the other end. He bumped into cardboard boxes and other things lining the alley sides as he careened towards safety. About fifteen meters into it he saw that an iron gate with a chain and lock would prevent his escape. He wheeled around and listened. Footsteps echoed into the spillway, rapidly getting louder and closer.

Trapped. He had to do something fast. He turned and moved back towards the Latino, diving behind some of the junk to hide in the pitch. He crouched down as low as he could. He adjusted his grip on the knife, holding the sharp side up.

The shape of the man stopped briefly at the courtyard entrance. He put his hands on both sides of the wall. The shape peered into the blackness, looked his shoulder, then plunged down the hallway. Just like Abdullah, the Latino couldn't yet see the chain and lock on the gate. He closed the distance to Abdullah's hiding spot in a few seconds, moving towards the light in the quick-slippery way of a night creature. When he came within a footstep Abdullah sprang at him, using the sidewall to leverage as much power as he could. He hit him hard from the side. He stabbed him deep in the thigh. The Latino bounced off the opposite wall as he fell, making a loud 'Huhhhhgggh' noise as he hit the floor squarely on his back, forcing the air out of his lungs. As he fell, Abdullah climbed up on him until he found the spot where his ribs ended. He stabbed him two or three times, punching the blade into his flesh as hard as he could and pulling it out with a twisting motion. The man writhed, but didn't make much noise without a full breath in his lungs. "Allah, give me the strength to defeat your enemies. Help me kill them -- *Allahu Akbar, Allahu Akbar*", Abdullah cried out in Arabic as he finished the unbeliever by grabbing his hair and slicing at his throat, severing his carotid artery. He twisted the head to the shoulder, trying to shield himself from the blood pulsing from the neck. He felt the lifewarmth on his hands but couldn't see it in the darkness.

He imagined he had much blood on him. At the edge of the courtyard, he could see it on his hands and arms. Since he had struck from an odd angle he didn't have much on his clothing, *Allah be praised.*

The hallway light spilling onto the courtyard had assumed the shape of a pale yellow rectangle, leaning to one side and shimmering as the drops of rain fell on to the bricks. No one remained in the doorway. He could hear the voices of lingerers at the other end of the hall, leading out to Saint Peter street. He plunged the knife and his arms into the fountain, rubbing himself vigorously in its stagnant, fishy stench. The blood came off easily. He did the same with his entire head and neck. He folded the knife and returned it to his left pocket. He assessed his condition: unhurt and still in possession of both the knife and pistol.

He pulled his shirt off, plunging it into the fountain, twice wrenching it like a rope to remove the blood. He did this a third time to remove as much water as possible and then put it back on. He took a couple of deep breaths to calm himself and walked into the hallway light. A handful of stragglers had the attention of the doorman, who didn't notice him until he had passed the first set of double doors to the music room.

He didn't look at any of them directly as stepped out onto the sidewalk, glancing around for the other Latino. Pulling his cap down, he hunched his shoulders against the rain and turned in the direction of the river. He muttered his evening prayers as he tried to conceal his limping gait the best he could. He asked Allah for harder rain and larger crowds to hide in. He doubted his prayer would be acceptable without the usual rituals and this made his pleading all the more earnest.

Chapter 46

Ben and Dafna disembarked the flight the same way all the other business travelers did. Routine. They each had a laptop, a cell phone and pager, along with a single piece of black nylon luggage. They looked like any of a thousand other travelers in the New Orleans airport, with the exception of Ben's hand, club shaped in all of the gauze and the sling. An Israeli employee of AirWarez would be waiting to drive them to a place for the night. Whether this person worked for Mossad directly or not, Ben didn't know. It didn't matter to him anyway. He assumed everyone from the company did, even the 'Americans.'

They walked purposefully half way down the concourse where Dafna excused herself. Ben picked a pay phone from the nearest cluster and placed a collect call to Grace's cell phone. He had no doubt they would be listening in on the lake house land line. He knew realistically that being the professionals they were, they'd leave nothing to chance. She had opened the cell phone account under the name G. Adams.

She answered on the first ring and accepted the charges. Her voice had a distorted warble to it.

"Ben, why haven't you called? I don't know what to do with myself down here. I'm going nuts!"

"Grace, good – stay down at the Lake, okay? You're safer there than up in Saint Louis. Just stay there until it's safe."

Just then another round of public announcements came over the airport intercom. An electric-powered passenger assistance cart whizzed by, blaring its warnings to the throng of preoccupied travelers.

"Ben – where are you?" Grace said. She didn't miss much.

"I'm in the New Orleans airport."

"What the hell –"

"Grace, stop. I don't have much time here. I'm not alone. In fact I don't know if someone's listening now. I need you to do something right now. Take down this number,"

"Go ahead," she said, her voice trembling in both fear and anger.

He gave her the number of the phone. "Read it back to me," he said.

She had the correct number. "Now listen. I want you to call another number." He rattled off Agent Daniel's cell phone number, "The guy's name is Daniels. Tell him that you're going to connect him to Ben Adams. Say it's urgent. He'll understand." He looked around the concourse for any telling expressions. He didn't see any. "Then three-way him into this number, okay? I don't have much time. Hurry -- I can't explain."

He hung up. He looked around as casually as possible, holding the phone switch down with his good hand. He play-acted one side of a friendly conversation while he sandwiched the receiver between his shoulder and ear. It seemed like a minute had passed and he still hadn't gotten the call back. Dafna hadn't come out of the restrooms yet, but he wouldn't have much time. He looked around to see if someone were listening to him but couldn't pick anyone out of the shifting crowd to confirm this. He shifted his weight back and forth from one foot to the other, babbling on while he tried to smile and keep his expression light. Then the phone rang. He let go of the switch.

"Daniels here."

"It's Ben Adams. Just listen, okay? I don't have much time." He blurted, "we're in New Orleans. I can read the emails now. I'm going to take the people from my office to meet them, understand? The meeting is tomorrow in the 900 block of Canal Street in butcher shop somewhere in the 900 block of Canal Street. Got that? One p.m."

"I'm going to have to clear it with the Chief. That doesn't give us much time."

"It's going to happen whether you're here or not – understand? It may be the last chance you have, you understand that, right? Do what you have to. I'm going to stop them with or without your help."

"Ben? Think about what you're saying. You've got a family," Grace said. She began to sob.

" I know I do," he replied, "I'm doing this for you, don't you see? We've got to stop this before a lot of people die. I can't just walk away and let all those people die."

"Don't try and con me, Ben, I know you too well," she retorted, "You're doing this to satisfy your own needs. Well, we need you more than that, don't you get it? You want revenge – Don't lie to yourself. This isn't about protecting us. You're willing to give up what's best for me and the kids – the people who love you for God's sake – so that you can have your vendetta."

"That's not true," Ben said.

"Don't call me again until you're ready to come home" she repeated.

"Ben, your wife is right. Don't do it. Don't go there tomorrow."

"If I don't point them out, they could get away. I have to."

At this point, Dafna walked out into the concourse. She hesitated briefly, until she found him, then worked her way over to him against traffic.

"I've got to go. Jack – listen - I called my insurance agent. Your people have screwed it up. My agent says they won't honor the policy since it's considered a terrorist act, which is an act of war. They're saying the damage isn't covered. I need you to do something about this or else I'm out three hundred thousand dollars…"

Grace began screaming into the phone.

Dafna was within earshot now.

He changed his tone. “I’ll be out of town on business for a few days. I’ll come by the office as soon as I get back home. I need you to expedite the process. Thank You.”

“Who were you talking to?” she asked, trying to be off-the-cuff.

“My insurance agent. I’m having trouble with my policy on the house.”

“They don’t want to pay? Imagine that…” she said.

“They’re calling it ‘an act of war’ since the FBI has labeled it a terrorist investigation. The weasels will do anything to refuse a claim.”

“Your own President calls it ‘the war on terrorism.’ Are you ready for your own little war of lawyers?”

“I have no other choice,” he said, “but I don’t think I can fight three wars at the same time. Something’s got to give.”

“Three wars?”

“Never mind,” he said. He picked up his bag and they joined the flow of travelers once again, following the signs to the main entrance. He kept thinking about what she had said; about choosing between the dead and the living. Couldn’t she see he cared more about the living? Unless he stepped up right here and now many more living would soon be dead. Didn’t that mean something? Why couldn’t she understand that – understand him? She said she understood him in the past; was that all just touchy-feely B.S. for convenience’s sake?

He and Dafna threaded their way through the crowd and past the security checkpoints. They reached the main entrance and walked along until they found their ride. He stood by the late model, dark Camry: about twenty-five and with a buzz cut, hard looking with the olive complexion and facial features not uncommon to Israelis at AirWarez. He opened the trunk for the bags. He spoke clear American English, but said very little. Dafna took shotgun and Ben slouched low in the back seat, replaying Grace’s ultimatum in his mind. He didn’t have enough time to convince her, but he did care more about the living – *she just doesn’t know enough about this situation to understand*, he said to himself.

Chapter 47

Johnny Walker Daniels played by the book.

A Plague on Both Houses

U.S.C.G - S.O.P

He had always followed protocol and the Guard's regulations and they had never let him down. He had his own ship, one of the newer eighty-seven foot Point class and had nine enlisted men under his command. It was true, as the officer he had some discretion, but now he had done something that could be questionable way up the chain of command. He had set Jack's course to intercept earlier and it would put the ship out in the deep – where his jurisdiction could be denied. He would be at the edge of what Cuba claimed for itself. If this thing went south, it could be the worst decision he had ever made or even more, the worse decision he would ever have the power to make. It could turn out that bad.

He still had time to change his mind. They would know in a few minutes, that is, if the radar held out. Conditions weren't the best. The drug runners had the weather on their side -- if they were really out there. The ten-foot sea slowed the cutter down and would make any interdiction more difficult by an order of magnitude. Lieutenant Daniels had radioed port when he changed course but that was all. He kept hoping he wouldn't pay too high a price for listening to his brother.

"Lieutenant, I've got two bogies on the screen. Confirming an intercept on our present heading."

Lieutenant Daniels looked over at McKenzie. His face had a sickly green pallor from the instrument panel. He didn't look so good because of the heavy sea, either.

"Sound the general alert. Williams…"

"Sir?"

"Have LeBeau check out the twin fifties. It's lock and load time. After that, get down to the armory and issue the rest of the men their weapons. McKenzie, what's the estimate?"

"At present speed and under the conditions, about an hour and a half, Sir."

"How close will we be to Cuban waters at that position?"

"Too close Sir, less than forty nautical miles."

Daniels turned to the helmsman. "Come up to three-quarters speed."

We're going to take a pounding, Lt. Daniels thought. He fidgeted with his cap, thinking, *but we can't let them slip behind that line. No way.*

War

Chapter 48

Abdullah bin Malak al Zalam, although a ruthless terrorist, would have inspired pity that evening in any but the hardest of hearts. His clothes, dirty and soaked through, clung to his thin frame at odd angles. His hair, stringy and mussed, hung down haphazardly and dripped water onto his face. His leg complained now, shooting pains all the way to his big toe. He couldn't hide his limp and gave up trying, instead trying to focus on a place to hide and wait out the storm.

He had weaved his way through the old Quarter, choosing side streets and those which only allowed bicycle and foot traffic on his way to the Moonwalk alongside the river. The streets had become more like rivers themselves and did not drain. To his surprise, the drains actually started blowing water up into the streets in a rhythmic fashion. This world was the inverse of everything he had known to be true and right. They lived here in every imaginable abomination and sin, with an overabundance of water and where the laws of gravity seemed unnatural. The drains as well as some of the manhole covers, worn down like old coins from a million feet, shot more water into the street from around their edges precisely at the time when their intended function was needed most. A strange place this, *Dar al Harb*, the House of War and Land of the Infidel. This place was a negative image of home. So wild, uninhibited, so individualistic and ignorant of shame – a place as deserving of the wrath of Allah as any than ever existed in space and time.

He thought he had rid himself of his unholy followers until he saw the second one again, about four blocks into his stroll on the Moonwalk.

He had taken been trying to hail a taxi, with much difficulty due to his condition, no doubt. Two of them passed by and he had been refused by another driver who had actually stopped. By the sound of his accent, the coward came from Lebanon, a refuge who had locked his doors and cursed at him in Arabic after getting a good look under the street lamps. No matter.

He walked towards the huge shipping cranes. He could see them arching over the water now, about half a kilometer ahead. He could no longer see the *kafir* behind him and this bothered him even though he'd been trying to elude him all this time. The scenery along the way had changed to things entirely industrial now at the edge of the wharves. *No prying eyes at this time of night,* he thought. *The*

Americans feared their own cities at night. He would use their fears and weaknesses against them then and on their Fourth of July. They would truly know fear in the days to come, inshallah.

After some time, he came to a portion of the docks where large, concrete sewer lines had been stacked for loading onto a ship. He went into one and stood at its center. No one would be able to see him until he was directly in front of the pipe. It immediately felt better to be out of the rain. *Water as a curse and an obstacle, how ironic*, he thought. For millennia his people had known the lack of water to be a curse, but for the lack of it. *What a strange place indeed.* He took his shirt and pants off and wrung them out as best he could. He began to shiver. He didn't have anything to block the wind or to dry himself any further. He put the clothes back on and felt no better for it. They clung to him and chilled his body. Unfortunately he would have to wait in this condition until first light. Tired as well, but he didn't dare sleep. He would lose everything if the Latinos came upon him unconscious and vulnerable. The idea of little sleep didn't bother him – in his present state he wouldn't be able to sleep anyway.

He sat down and let his mind wander. He thought back to desert times, when he and his father and some uncles and cousins would go out into the sands for a few days. They would pitch their tents and gather around the warmth of the fires, sitting in a closed circle, telling the old stories. He would listen to them, the awesome silence all around them, under the dome of the sky. He remembered looking up into the vastness of the seven heavens and tried to count the stars as his father or uncles recounted the glories of their forefathers. He had loved those times and his days of innocence. Now he realized he could never be in that place again. Now that he had been to the *Dar al Harb*, the House of War where the infidel ruled, the *Bilad al Kuffar,* he would never be able to look into the heavens as freely as he had those nights. That simplicity and innocence could never withstand the advance of this world.

The old ways will lose.

The Others looked at the same stars as he did, but he knew how differently they saw them. The Others didn't care at all about such things. The Others who would bring licentiousness and corruption to his people and deprive them of all the simple pleasures like those found in the desert. They would replace them with the rude incessant, babbling of bikini-clad women on the television. He saw it happening before he left for jihad, while he still lived in Saudi;

the images from the West, the unbelievers who worked the oil fields and their soldiers who propped up the *Dar al-Saud* – a tottering and corrupt monarchy. The Others intruded upon his homeland and threatened the old ways. This could be very dangerous, for Allah would see that people did nothing to stop it. All surely faced hellfire if he and The Brothers did nothing to stop this encroachment. They had to push the infidels back to evil places like New Orleans and this French Quarter. That's where they belonged. They needed to be put into submission once again, like the *kuffar* from the old stories Father used to tell those wonderful nights when the men of the family had roamed out under the stars.

He would see to it in the next few days.

Dar al Islam, the House of Submission to the will of Allah, would be a waxing moon; *Dar al Harb*, the House of War, would soon be waning.

Chapter 49

Lieutenant Daniels and the crew of the USCGC *Palmera* had been closing the gap the last half an hour. The ship's diesel engines hammered away at full speed now against the eight-to-ten foot sea, constantly rushing up to strike the bow as it pushed on toward the faster of the two ships detected earlier on radar. As they had come up on the two ships, the slower one took the most direct heading towards Cuba's claimed territorial waters. That line was a matter of dispute, but was also a matter for people at a higher station than Lieutenant Daniels to fight over. He didn't want to be the pawn of an international incident if he could avoid it.

The faster ship took a Southern bearing that would keep it in neutral waters for the present. Daniels surmised the pilot of that ship was thinking he could outrun the cutter. That would be true in a calmer sea, but the cutter could take the heavy water better in its length and his crew was seasoned and professional. The *Palmera* would be able to run up on her in the next half hour.

Daniels finally radioed in his position when the pursuit began. He reported both ships and their headings. They had come into visual range about an hour ago. The storm had diminished to the point where they would be able to see their target ship. It had been running without lights since they first tried to hail her. She hadn't responded at all, except to bring her speed up and take flight. But every wave fought against its progress. The captain of the ship had seriously miscalculated his best course. Now, if they changed course and made for Cuban waters, the *Palmera* would have a shorter distance to close and would reach her before she could cross the line.

One of the crew brought Lieutenant Daniels the night vision equipment. He could see her now as she capped the peaks of the waves. They were close – he could read her name off the stern.

Daniels called into the Port of New Orleans with the latest information.

"Ship of interest is the *El Cid* registered out of the Port of Caracas, Venezuela. Seems to be a new Viking, approximately fifty feet," the duty officer reported back.

"Roger that. Will advise when we have information"

Lt. Daniels switched to the ship system.

"Williams? Stand by on those guns."

"Sir."

"McKenzie, hail the *El Cid* again -- by name. Request permission to board. Give them the ultimatum."

McKenzie relayed the message on four frequencies.

No response. Daniels gave them a good five minutes. The Palmera had closed the distance to less than a nautical mile now and it became easy to see her with the naked eye. Even under the blackened sky she gleamed. Her crew had been too diligent keeping her clean.

"Williams?"

"Sir," he replied, over the intercom.

"Give her the last warning."

Williams opened up with the twin .50 caliber guns. He stayed well clear of her to the port side, but put the rounds close enough to create a disturbance.

Daniels, with the Starlight equipment, could see a couple of hands come up to the transom. The clambered around briefly, then one of them shouldered a Rocket Propelled Grenade and launched it. It exploded within fifty yards of the ship.

"Men, make sure your equipment is on you and secure!" Daniels shouted into the ship's intercom, "We are taking fire. Take all precautions."

He released the switch on the handset and took up the other one.

"Command; we are taking fire. Ship of interest unresponsive. At present estimate we will intercept in --"

" -- Lieutenant, they're changing course, they're headed for the line," McKenzie reported, "new heading takes them to Cuban waters."

"Match it."

The helmsman responded in turn.

Lieutenant Daniels kept the Starlight on them, adjusting his viewing angle. He saw two more hands bringing up RPGs and some armament cases from below decks. Two of them shouldered RPGs and fired, while another one pulled a shoulder-fired missile out it's case and prepped it for use.

"Williams, fire on them, now! Direct fire at the stern."

The ships had less than a quarter mile between them at this point. Williams' fire shredded the gunwale at the stern. He kept at it. Daniels could see them all go down, including the pilot up on the flying bridge. Three dead for sure. The ship slowed and veered off course to the starboard side.

"Cease fire! Hold your fire!" he shouted into the mike. "We're going to sink her," Daniels ordered. He took another look, then pressed the intercom switch again. "Boarding party – the first thing we need to do is disarm that missile. We may still have combatants – take every precaution." He dropped the microphone and breathed deeply. He turned to the helmsman. "Take her alongside."

Allah's Messenger said, 'Isa [Jesus], the son of Mariam,
will shortly descend amongst you Muslims
and will judge mankind by the law of the Qur'an.
He will break the cross and kill the swine [Jews]
and there will be no Jizyah tax [protection tax]
taken from non-Muslims.
Money will be so abundant no one will accept it.
So you may recite this Holy Verse:
"Isa was just a human being before his death.
On the Day of Resurrection he [Jesus]
will be a witness against the Christians."'
Mohammed – Hadith Sahih Bukhari:V4B55N657

Chapter 50

The amount of activity on the quay surprised Abdullah bin Malak al Zalam. Even in the early hours of the morning rows sodium arc lights illuminated the docks as well as the low-hanging clouds, the color of dim embers. The rain had stopped and the wind died down. The air still held heavy mist, making the sounds all around the port seem closer. He could hear a myriad of activity; metal scraping against metal, the occasional horn sounding and the engines of cranes and vehicles. People's voices rolled across the water from long distances. Several trucks and cars had passed his hiding spot, but had been on the way to other place so their occupants had failed to notice his shape in the darkness of the sewer pipe. He looked at his watch again – past midnight. He would have to bear another four or five hours of this. He shuddered and rocked himself in an attempt to warm himself. He didn't think it wise to begin his walk back to the mosque on Magnolia street; he feared being stopped by the police. He couldn't risk anything so close to the appointed time. He would meet the two groups of Brothers in a little over twelve hours. He would have to bide his time and suffer a little longer.

As he considered his options, he heard another vehicle approaching. This one sounded lower, slower. A van came into view, stopping in front of the pipe. He could see at least three men inside. The driver peered into opening, then shifted into Park. Abdullah put his hands in his pockets, gripping his pistol and readying it to fire. He didn't stand, but shifted his body slightly in their direction ready to shoot them if need be.

A tall, thin, balding man came around the front of the van from the passenger side, his head hung low with an inquisitive gaze.

He stopped at the edge of the pipe, leaning against it, straining to get a good look at Abdullah.

"You all right in there?" he asked. Abdullah detected no malice for the time being.

"Yes, now go away." He rested his head on his left arm, across his knees. He had a good line to draw down on the stranger now. He held the gun tight.

"You're gonna catch your death out here on a night like this."

Under different circumstances you would have caught Death already, he thought, but he said nothing.

"Looky here, we can help you. Down at The Good Fisherman mission. You can get some hot soup and a warm cot for the rest of the night, y'all understand? We want to help you. We don't charge nothin'."

Abdullah looked up at him. He felt strung out enough to consider the offer, even from the likes of this cross worshipper.

"What's your name, son?" the bible-thumping cross worshiper asked.

"Jesús Cansadas. I'm not your 'son', you son of bitch."

He spat in his direction.

"Jesús… I don't mean any disrespect. We want to help, you hear? No one has to live in these conditions. We're all His sons and daughters – that's all I meant by that. You're a child of the Lord just like ev'rybody else, you know what I mean? I don't mean no disrespect. Come on down to the shelter with us, all right? We'll get some hot food for y'all." He extended a hand into the shadows of the pipe. From his vantage point, Abdullah could see the stenciling on the faded bluish van now, "Good Fisherman Mission 1545 Lafayette St." Abdullah recognized the street name from his walks. It was no more than six blocks from Magnolia.

If he went with them, he could get a change of clothes and a hot meal. He would simply walk out of the place as soon as it was light. He stood up and walked toward them.

"Have you found the Lord, son?"

"I never lost him, señor," Abdullah said.

The disbeliever laughed.

"You believe in your namesake, the Lord Jesús, don't you brother?"

He didn't have to lie, " Si, Jesús was mighty prophet to the Jew and Christian both," he said.

"More than just a prophet," the tall, bald one said.

"No..." Abdullah meant to argue but he stopped himself there.

As he came out of the pipe into the yellow-orange light, the old man driving the van called out to him, "You look like you're hurt; are you well enough to walk?"

"Many year ago, missionary came to my village en Venezuela. He beat the young boys and me also - he do this to my leg. Force us to say we believe. No doctor come – so I walk this way. This make me see true Christian, no? He do the Christian work."

"Absolutely not," the bearded one protested. His beard, a wiry gray and white nest on fleshy face, prevented Abdullah from seeing the mouth move. The words came out from underneath as it quaked. "That man was evil – a wolf in sheep's clothing. He didn't do the works of God."

"God is love," said the tall one.

Abdullah flinched when he put his hand on his shoulder. "Don't be afraid of us, we're here to help. Trust us, we're true believers."

You are true believers in the lie of the Trinity, he thought. *You will be sent to the hell-fire with the rest of they who subscribe partners to Allah.* Shirk *is an unforgivable sin.*

Since he found himself at a disadvantage, he decided it would be better to use them and play the victim. In a few days all of these cross kissers would feel his strength. He could wait.

Sound and motion down the quay caught his attention. A marked New Orleans police car was coming towards them. *Looking for miscreants to harass and detain*, he thought. He had to get away quickly.

"I will come with you. I am tired," he said, feigning resignation.

They complied with his wishes most eagerly, nearly tripping themselves up to prove how good and kind they could be. The tall one gave him the front passenger seat. And they all looked at him with concern and mercy, even the bums. The Christians decided to stop searching at this point, taking him and the other lost souls directly to the mission on Lafayette Street. Abdullah said little more than 'yes' or 'no' after this, since the dogs had lapped up his lies about mistreatment and had helped him elude the police. Anything more wasn't necessary.

Chapter 51

The call came in to Jorge Arravanchía at 4 a.m., local time. One of the goons knocked tentatively on the cabin door, bookending his bad news with apologies. Jorge's yacht was a twin to the one Pepito had been cruising around in and would have been on course to meet up with it later that morning. The Arravanchía brothers had moved their day-to-day business offshore after a 'misunderstanding' broke out in their native Colombia about a year back. The heroin deal was the proof of concept phase of their new plan.

The offshore move had been easy, but had done nothing to moderate Jorge's life perspective. He still had a temper to match his stature – short. Most of all he did not like surprises and unanticipated setbacks ranked as the worst of all.

Jorge had let his brother talk him into doing the deal. Pepito had made a good case for it. They stood to gain near ten million with little effort and no resources up front. Pepito had downplayed the risk. It would be easy, he had said, but Jorge knew the Arabs better than Pepito. They were fine company to whore around with in the Mediterranean and had been good sources of arms in the past. They were all about the product and the cash. But this deal had been different from the start. At the root, this deal was about religion, not money. All his life, he had known priests and religious men were untrustworthy. Their crazy ideas about God and heaven clouded their thinking. You couldn't trust them to act in rational ways. They didn't always act in their self-interest and this made them inscrutable -- unpredictable.

Jorge had gone against his better judgment and agreed to deal with the terrorists. He already knew by the sound of the knocking that Pepito, his only brother, had paid with his life.

The goon outside the door resembled a piece of classic statuary caught in a moment of fight-or-flight, updated with the modern touch of an untraceable cell phone in his hand. No one in Jorge's entourage wanted to be holding the phone in times like this. The bodyguard hesitated a moment until Jorge roared from the other side of the door.

"I said 'come in', you *idiota.* You waiting for a written invitation?"

His delivery boy twisted the handle and handed off the phone quickly as he could. The old man pulled himself up, resting on the head board. The latest flavor of the month, laying next to him, turned away a little more and pulled the pillow over her head.

The goon shifted his weight from one foot to the other, rubbing his beard stubble several times during Jorge's conversation.

It was bad all right.

Veins popped out from the old man's temples and he began to curse more and more. At this point the goon could see Jorge's veins popping out in the middle of his forehead, running down between his eyebrows to the bridge of his nose.

"I don't care if he's Osama bin Laden's first-born," he shouted, "He caused it. Whether he meant to or not don't mean nothing!" he roared at the top of his lungs.

The delivery boy jumped in his deck shoes, his .45s rattled in their shoulder holsters.

"Find him…" he said, "get it out on the street. I want his greasy balls swinging from my flagpole TONIGHT!..." another brief pause. "…put a quarter million on his head… I don't give… NO excuses! My brother is dead and I've lost millions on this…and I want him to suffer, you got that? I want to see it. If they send me a tape they get double. Now go. He don't see the sun set tonight, understand?" He shouted a string of obscenities and punctuated it by hurling the phone against the opposite wall. He got out of bed: a round, rolling mass or hairy, naked flesh, chubby feet with hairy knuckles stamping the floor He threw his arms up, still cursing as he made his way to his private head. He slammed the door and the goon slinked out of the cabin, wincing as he heard *el Toro* taking apart the china closet in primal rage.

Chapter 52

He felt much better after a shower. They had shown him to his cot for the night, one of dozen in two rows, six to a side, in an under-lit, dingy room adjacent to the kitchen. The smell of cooking pork offended his sensibilities. Abdullah bin Malak al-Zalam swam in the pants they had given him. He kept adjusting the worn and baggy t-shirt to set it square on his shoulders. It must have been a deep red at one time, but had faded. The script on the front said "Jesus. The Real Thing." He had almost refused this "gift", but held himself back. The leaders of the true religion, in their inspired wisdom, had always said that lies in moments of vulnerability were acceptable as long as they advanced the Cause of Allah. The scholars could easily back this up with the *Ahadith* accounts of the prophet, peace be upon him, making truce in times when he had been vulnerable. And of course Allah had dissolved treaty obligations for the prophet, may peace be upon him, when the ummah was strong. That was time to break the treaties and press on in jihad - struggle in the Cause of Allah. He wore the *Isa* shirt because of his temporary disadvantage and because it served the greater cause of jihad. He had no guilt attached to it. Things considered evil by men but done for Allah would always be forgiven. *And Allah ta'alla knows best.* Wearing it built a rapport between him and his useful idiots. Abdullah would discard it when it suited him. The ends justified the means.

And wearing the shirt stamped with the Crusader name for the prophet *Isa had* helped him. Their cordial acceptance of him worked to his advantage when he needed a few moments alone to conceal his weapons.

He relaxed, feeling secure for the moment. Most of the others on the cots looked too old or used up to be a threat to him. Nonetheless, he kept a watchful eye on the bony one with the cowlick on the cot directly across the aisle. He caught this one sizing up his wristwatch a couple of times. He had the look of a drug addict – the darkened circles around the eyes, the disheveled appearance and the twitchy way he moved. His teeth had dark stains on them. The quickness and purpose in his eyes ruled out a mental condition. He was less than thirty years, too young to be one of these street people for any other reason but drugs. Abdullah rested on his left arm, swinging his legs up on the cot. He would relax and wait out the night.

The addict kept looking to and fro, touching his nose and sniffing. The lights stayed on, but at a low level. A couple of the guests hacked and honked deep from the lungs. The stench of slow death and phlegmatic lung hovered over the cots. It relieved Abdullah to think that he would only be staying a few more hours.

He mulled over his plan for the day, making a list of actions he would take. First he would free himself from this place. He'd walk back to the mosque, like he had when he first arrived a few days ago. It occurred to him that it seemed weeks since he'd arrived on the ship. This whole thing had been far more difficult than he'd imagined, but it would be much easier after the rendezvous, when he'd have the Brothers to help him. Things would happen much quicker then. They had spent two years setting this mission up and no doubt the Brothers coming to meet him would have things set up just so, *inshallah*.

He glanced around to see what The Others were doing. He caught the addict looking at his arm again. A disturbance with this dog was the last thing Abdullah needed. He stared at him.

"You want my watch?"

"What?" the addict said after a few moments. He tried to put up an air of disinterest, looking at the bare light hanging from the ceiling.

"I see you want my watch? You need to buy more drugs or something? Why don't you ask the Christians for money. Tell them a priest sexed you from behind when you were a boy. They'll fall over each other to give you pity money." Abdullah paused for a moment, letting that sink in. He spoke in a low rasp, now that he had the addict's attention. "They'll probably go as far as getting the drugs for you," he said, sneering at him, "better yet, why don't you go out and find one of the preachers? Go ask him for some more." Abdullah grinned at him with real hatred.

It scared the meth head something fierce. He'd been around some bad-ass muthafuckas before and knew one when he saw one.

"Why don't you shut the fuck up? I'm trying to sleep over here," the addict said belligerently. He made some motions on his cot as if he was trying to get more comfortable. His face glowered now.

"Oh, did I say the truth? Excuse me." Abdullah said, giving off a rumbling, nasty laugh. He laid a heavy finger on the side of his nose and winked.

"You're a head case, man," the addict said, turning onto his back, but looking in Abdullah's direction, "you're messed up, dude. Really. Messed up." The bony one stared at the bare bulb again.

Abdullah watched him for a couple of minutes. When the addict no longer challenged him he got up and walked over to him, bumping his cot with his shin.

"You don't want to work for your watch? It's better to steal it?"

No answer. The doper quickly looked up at him, afraid. Abdullah looked through the open doorway and seeing no one in charge, he reached into his pocket. The man cringed. He pulled a twenty out of the tangle of paper and released it over him with exaggerated grace, letting it float down unto the addict's sunken chest.

"Go buy yourself a watch. It will be better for you. If you try to take mine I'd have to chop your thieving hand, you understand?"

The man on the cot just looked at him with a mix of fear and surprise.

Feeling superior by putting the human trash in his place, Abdullah returned to his cot and stretched out casually on his back. Putting his hands behind his head, he hummed to himself as he went over the day's list a couple more times. Yesterday had been one long trial. He relaxed. A hard, dark sleep descended over his mind.

He woke with a jolt. Checking his watch, he realized he had been sleeping too long. He rose up and entered the room that doubled as a dining area and chapel. The fleshy one with the beard was cooking up breakfast in the kitchen, with his facial hair uncovered. Abdullah imagined anyone who ate his cooking would probably get some of that beard as well. Animals in the homeland had as much hygiene as the *kuffar* in this country. Truly dirty *najasat and haram*. He would ignore what his stomach told him. He did go over to the coffee urn, pouring himself a cup. The bearded one noticed him and said, "Jesús, would you like some bacon and eggs this morning?"

Bacon - pig flesh – a son of pigs cooking his own kind - cannibal pigs.

"No. Only coffee, I am -- how you say – my body don't like pig," he said, trying to hide his disgust.

"Allergic to pork?" the fat one offered.

"Sí." He didn't look at him, thinking his face would give him away. He stayed long enough to drink another cup, then made his way to the door. He met the tall, thin missionary from the van, descending the stairs and smiling at him with an open expression.

"Leaving so soon, Jesús?"

All the cross worshippers loved to say the name Jesús. Jesús, Jesús, Jesús. That infidel Pepito had some fun, the bastard.

"Sí. Leave now. Go to find work. No money."

"You don't have to feel ashamed to ask for help, you know. We want to help you. You deserve more than this; all God's children deserve dignity and a second chance."

Abdullah nodded and grunted in mock assent. He looked past him, to the door at the top of the stairs.

"Won't you stay a while longer? Give a few moments to the Lord. Have some food and listen to a short sermon. We don't ask anything for it. We can give you a few dollars to help, too."

Abdullah looked at the infidel with disdain. "I no want your religion, free or no free," he said. He started up the stairs. When he reached the top, Abdullah turned to see if he was still looking at him.

"We'll pray for you. We're not like the missionary who hurt you. That man wasn't a Christian. Try to find the forgiveness in your heart; it's there. Ask Jesus to help you brother."

Abdullah gave him a look as if he had stepped, ankle deep, into a pile of steaming dung. Then he turned and walked out into the bright, new day.

Chapter 53

"Jack, I'm telling you this is a major interdiction. The DEA puts the street value at five to ten million." Johnny Daniels told his brother.

"No way."

"Way – The preliminaries indicate it's Asian. Top shelf stuff. I'll call you again when I have the full report. Thanks for listening, man."

Johnny had called his brother early, as he was driving in to work. The news elevated Jack, thinking he could get used to starting off every Friday with great news like this. He was shining like a new penny as he entered the lobby -- everything pressed and he was dressed in his best. He still had the cell phone up to his ear. "All right bro, let me know all the details when you have them. I didn't get you into any trouble, did I?" he said, the irrepressible smile leaking into his voice.

"Let's say all was forgiven when we made the big score. We have the dope and some other valuable pieces of intel on the Arravanchía organization now. And the number two man – they're ID'ing one of the dead as one of the brothers himself. A co-founder."

"What about the ship?" Jack asked, using his magnetic card to open the front lobby doors.

"Well, it's a mess. We had to engage them. They fired on us and we had to tear it up pretty bad in the firefight. But Uncle Sam ought to be able to salvage it. It'll be worth at least seven hundred fifty thousand at auction."

"Nobody got hurt?"

"None of the good guys. Hey listen, I got to go. I'll call you later."

"All right; peace out," Jack said.

People in the hallway stopped to look at him as he passed by.

"Somebody got laid last night," one of the younger guys suggested.

Daniels looked back over his shoulder, "Better than that, my friend, if you can believe it." He smiled wide again, his brilliant whites eliciting a chorus of raised eyebrows and shakes of heads.

After he settled in, the excitement became too great and he passed through the secure doors at the back of the lobby to see the Chief. He pushed against Chief's half-opened door without knocking. He was still shining. Chief looked up at him, a little miffed, then looked back at the pile of paper directly in front of him as he signed off on a form and moved it to one of the smaller piles to his right. Then he repeated the process.

"Morning, Chief," Daniels said, beaming.

He grunted a hello and continued with his paperwork. "Looks like you've had your coffee already," Chief said into the stack.

"I just talked to my brother, Johnny, the one in the Coast Guard. I gave him those coordinates we got off of Ben Adams during the interrogation."

Now he had his attention.

"You're kidding," he said, looking blankly at Daniels' mouth.

"They got 'em, sir. Interdicted five to ten million in heroin and killed one of the Arravanchía brothers, you know, the ones ran out of Colombia last --"

"Yeah, I know…", he said, his voice trailing off, " Killed one of them…What are you grinning for like that? You think you did something good? I told you to run everything by me."

"Look, Chief," Daniels started, with irritation. Then he caught himself, "If I'd gone through the Bureau channels there's no way this would have went down."

"All you've done for me is create another ream like this, " he gestured to the paperwork on his desk.

"I think keeping fifty keys out of the country is more important than making sure we get home on time for the weekend -- C'mon Chief!?" he said exasperated.

Chief looked at him unchanged. "Look, what if that tip you passed off had turned out to be wrong? What if Adams had gotten something mixed up? Look, I know how Federal agencies work. Your brother could have been busted down to junior swabbie for a miscalculation like that."

Daniels just stood there, turning over explanations for this in his mind.

"From now on, no more of this cowboy mentality, you got it? We're coming up on two years in the AirWarez investigation and I don't want you to get distracted and do something stupid. I need your full attention on *our* big bust."

. Jack had expected beaucoup 'atta boys' and got a lecture instead. It didn't make sense.

"Our bust? They'll find a cure for cancer first," Daniels said, pissed.

"From now on I want you to tell me everything you're doing, understand? Like you were supposed to -- *remember*? We're on the line here and the accountants will have my ass. Follow the chain of command. Everything goes through me. That's an explicit order."

"What about the rest of what Adams has said? What about the Taliban reunion taking place today down on Canal Street? What are we going to do about that?"

"I have a crew from the office down there checking it out."

"A crew?"

"Okay, a couple of agents—"

"That's all we're going to do? After Adams gets his hand chopped and his house leveled… after his intel turns out to be worth ten million in heroin… is that all you're going to do? Send two guys?"

Jack cocked his head, stroking his cheek with his hand. He felt anger rising out of his center.

"I don't see the need for any more resources than that. Let's see."

Jack changed topic. He didn't see the possibility of further progress at the moment. "What do we have from the discs he gave us? Do we have any leads from that data?"

"So far, not much. I've got a call in to the cyber terror group in Washington. They should be getting back any time now." Chief drummed the desk with his pencil. "Haven't heard back yet."

"Sir, waiting around for a report might get people killed. This is serious. Why don't you agree? This threat is real. We need to get answers now!" he said, forcefully enough to send droplets of spittle towards Chief's desk.

He stared up at Jack, unmoved. "Let's review the facts, shall we? You are my subordinate. We will do this *my* way and in *my* time." He paused for effect.

Jack considered spinning around, going out to his desk and calling Chief's boss in Washington right there and then. He turned and opened the door, looking back spitefully. Chief could read his intentions.

"You go over my head with this and so help me, your desk will be out in the parking lot. I'll bury your ass in leftover paperwork until I can find the 'politically correct' way to get rid of you," he said.

Jack stopped and turned. This guy would never close the AirWarez case – he didn't have what it took. Chief was a classic Midwestern hoosier, a hog farmer in a Brooks Brothers suit who worried more about making the speeding ticket quota for the month than shutting down the meth labs along the street. The Israelis had nothing to worry about from him.

Jack held his tongue and left the room. He had overestimated Chief. But as he passed through the security door, he listened to the clicking of his hard soles on the lobby tiles and began wondering if Chief had turned. *Was Chief intentionally slowing the pace down? Was he working for them or maybe just looking the other way?* He remembered what Ike Henderson had said the other day in the parking lot: *is he that dense or is he playing me? Or both?* Jack sat at his lobby desk, staring at the phone. *Was it worth it? Should he go over Chief's head? Was what Adams had worth it?*

Chapter 54

– In the Magnolia

Bones weaved around the sidewalk gaps and puddles with firm purpose in his step. He wasted no time getting up to the Magnolia. Twenty dollars wouldn't buy much crank, but it was all he had. The money was safe in his pocket, but clenching it in his fist made him feel more at ease. He didn't want to lose it. He laughed under his breath, dismissing the crazy asshole who'd given it to him last night. He should have kicked his ass when he had the chance, but he had been really strung out and needed to crash. Fighting the psycho would have only gotten him thrown out onto the street without any money and the storm would have made it worse. Those missionary bastards never gave you money, just food and bible verses. He hadn't eaten in a few days, but he could live with that. What he really needed to do was hook up with Special K and party on his twenty. That would set him to rights.

Okay, the plan was he'd score his crystal and then go back to the Good Fisherman and get a change of clothes out of them. But business first. Bones figured the dopers and runners would be up by now. Special K had a woman in the Magnolia who had a place on the side nearest to him. He could see the edge of the projects now - the brown brick boxes curving off into the distance. Bones snorted and wiped his nose with his forearm. He needed to score before it got really hot.

He saw Special K up ahead, hands on his knees, leaning over to talk to someone in a nice ride. Looked like some kind of pimped-out Lexus coupe or something: silver colored with tinted windows and those rims that spun around. K seemed to be spazzing more than usual - bouncing up and down while he semi-squatted and pointing this way and that, like he was on Channel 2 describing the latest house fire. Bones kept walking toward him, more slowly now. It wasn't a good idea to walk up on a deal. Especially when something funky was goin' down, like his radar told him. K recognized him coming, now less than a block away. The look on his face didn't seem to signal trouble, so Bones changed his mind and just walked right up. K was still talking to two Latinos: they were in too good of shape to be Mexicans and didn't have that Indian look.

"I wish I could help y'all out, y'know, but I ain't seen any dude like that. I been axing around too."

They didn't say anything, ignoring K for the moment. Bones didn't like the way they were sizing him up. "This your friend?" The Lexus driver asked.

"We party now and then," Special K said, "he Bones."

The Driver just looked at him.

"What about him?" the passenger suggested flatly.

K straightened up, wincing as his back popped.

"Dude, these friends of mine need to find someone. Dark complected. Thin. About your height. How tall are you?"

"Five-ten."

"Yeah, thas about right." He glanced into the car, seeking their approval. "Dude walks with a limp; foreign looking."

They were looking for the psycho. Bones tried to keep it on the down low.

"You think he's been down by the docks or in the quarter for the last few days, right?"

The driver nodded.

"Talks with a strange accent. Mean son of a bitch. He ain't Latino is he?" Bones suggested, "he got a mark about here, right? A big bruise?" He pointed at his forehead, just above the eyes.

The driver raised his eyebrows. "Where is he?"

. "I want to help you boys out, right? But you got to help me first. I came up here with twenty dollars in my pocket and that won't get the party started. You know what I'm sayin'?"

"What you want?" the passenger asked.

"What you got?"

"We don't carry nothin', see," the driver said. He looked up at Special K, with only half a measure of disdain this time. "What you got, man?"

"I got about a quarter key of crank, two pounds of your dope and some coke."

The driver looked to Bones and said, "How about half the meth and a bag of weed?" He let go a malicious little smile. "That enough?"

Bones saw his opportunity. "I can give you the guy. Saw him this morning." He waited. But his mind reeled now. He didn't know if psycho would come back to the mission or not; didn't know where he'd gone, but he did see him arguing with one of the preachers at the door. He'd gone the same way as Bones had -- towards the Magnolia. The sorry-ass was probably around somewhere close. They hadn't upped the ante yet, so Bones took the initiative.

"I'll point the guy out for all the crank, one of the bags of dope and all the money in your pockets." They looked at each other, then back at him, blankly at first. "The *both* of you. All your pockets," he said. He enjoyed being in control, now that he was making the big score. He could party for a month on the shit he'd reel in. Special K gave him a slack-jawed look of disapproval. *Fuck him – what did he know?*

The Lexus dudes pulled out a couple of bank rolls. It looked like several thousand to him.

"Here…" the driver beckoned at the passenger. It didn't seem to bother him. Special K took a step back, surprised on how much it was worth to them. The driver took the roll from his friend and handed it out to Bones, who immediately put it in his pocket.

"K – go get the man his stuff. We'll be back 'round to settle."

K went off to his old lady's place to get the rest of it. The passenger opened the door and got out, saying, "Let's get the guy, *vamos,"* gesturing toward the back seat.

Bones looked both ways as he stepped off the curb. He did a double-take off toward the left. He smiled as he looked back at them.

"Just give me the money now," he said, chuckling to himself as he returned to the driver's window.

"Let's go, hey - *vamanos.* We don't wanna waste no time here," the driver said, full of urgency now they'd bought him.

"The money, man. The deal was half now, the other half when we find him. Well I found him already." After the driver handed his wad, Bones said, "You see that guy pushing the shopping cart a block down?"

"Yeah." The could see a thin, dark haired man limping along behind a shopping cart, filled with bags and assorted trash. He stopped for a minute at the corner, looking all around him in a casual, unhurried way. He couldn't believe how easy it was after all the shit he'd been through. Major score. He thrust the second roll of money into his pocket, keeping his fist around it as he had the twenty. He a lot more to hold onto now.

"That's your man – down on the next corner. Wears a 'Jesus' t-shirt and limps. A real nasty mother." Bones pointed with his chin. "Enjoy."

They forgot all about Bones after that. It was all about calling someone and not losing sight of Psycho now. They didn't care about losing all their money either. Funny. He stood next to the car for what seemed about a minute, until they rolled away slowly. Bones looked down the street, noticing Psycho was already at the next corner. He was making good time in spite of his leg. Now thanks to whatever that headcase had done, Bones would have a month's worth of fun. *Lassiez les bon temps roulez– let the good times roll, Nawlin's style, you gimpy-ass muthafucka.*

A Plague on Both Houses

As to those who reject faith [Islam], I will punish them
with terrible agony in this world
and in the Hereafter,
nor will they have anyone to help.
Allah – Qur'an 3.56

Chapter 55

-- Algiers, Louisiana Saturday, 10 am Central Time

Ben took the headset from Ofer and placed it in his ear. No bigger than a small hearing aid, it was tan in color and fit easily.

"Test it," Ofer called out to one of the others in an adjoining room.

"Test, test, test," came the voice, about two settings too loud. Ben reflexively put his good hand to his ear.

Ofer walked over to the table and took out two bundles of clothes from a cardboard box. "Put these on," he said, handing him the top half. The rest consisted of dark brown head covering and a sheath-robe, a *dishdash*, ankle length by the look of it. He laid it on the table and went into the other room to finish the preparations.

Ben looked at the clothes and then at his friend.

"Dafna, there's no reason for you to do this," he protested.

"No Ben, you're wrong," she said, "I have every reason to do this. They're the same kind who have been killing my family and my future since I was a little girl. And my people for millennia. I'm involved already."

"You've got your whole life ahead of you," he said, "What are you, twenty-five?"

"I've got a whole life? No, I've been dead to this world for two years now, since they took my Nir from me. Maybe I can start over if this works out." She looked at him honestly, speaking from the heart. "So far, moving to this country has kept me safe, but hasn't helped me live. I have no life to speak of. I'm helping you and myself." She smiled genuinely. "Besides, you and I will make a more convincing statement to them as the loving couple, don't you think? It may allay their suspicious minds long enough for this to work." She smiled again and picked up the clothes. He didn't say anything further. She took the bundle and went off to the bathroom to change. He sat down on the couch, wriggled out of his pants and changed into the faded olive twill replacements. He started to put on the old brown leather lace up shoes, but would need help getting them tied. He was still messed up pretty badly.

War

Dafna came back into the room, covered head to toe as a good *Muslimah* would. She looked like a nun, except younger and much better looking than any he'd ever seen. He couldn't help laughing a little.

"Could you help me with the shoes and shirt?"

She knelt down before him, putting his foot on her thigh as she laced the shoe. She looked up at him as she switched feet, the soft and rounded features of her face framed in the *hijab*.

"Now I can see why they force their women dress like this."

"Shut up, Ben," she said, feigning protest and slapping his calf. She tied the other one and helped him get the loose-fitting shirt on. Ofer came back in and decided they should leave his arm in the sling without changing anything.

"I can't wear these indoors, " he said, "they'll know something's up."

"I have an idea," Ofer said, "you'll be able to keep the glasses and be able to look around without any questions being asked." He left the room, speaking rapidly in Hebrew to Daniel, who left the apartment right away.

"Are the preparations in order?" Eitan asked. He was talking into the secure line through a speaker phone on his desk. His door was closed as always making thee room as stuffy as his demeanor again.

"We are as ready as we can be. This won't be easy or clean under the circumstances," Ofer said.

"What about Moshe's daughter?"

"She insists on helping the *goyim*. She's taking him in."

"Do what you can to keep her from harm. Her father has had enough loss for one man."

"I'll do what I can. Do we still need Adams?"

"We know it's an Arnold cipher now, but we haven't located the reference source yet. It would be best to keep him alive."

"It's in God's hands if the shooting starts, " Ofer said.

"Make sure it doesn't. As soon as you identify them and confirm the package, take them. I know we're short handed here. Two *kidon* will be on the inside, correct?"

"Yes, we'll have them, Adams and Dafna inside. Four total. We'll have two at each door and I'll be out in front, directing traffic. When we get the visual for the group and the package, we'll move the three groups at the doors. The standard approach. Once retrieved we'll go to the consulate."

"Are they ready?"

"Yes."

"Good luck," Eitan said, pressing the button to disconnect. He rubbed the top of his head and sighed. He had done this work for many years and experience told him this would be the only chance they'd get.

Ben squeezed his hands together, trying to keep them from trembling. His breathing accelerated and became shallow, the inverse of Dafna's ponderous pace for the butcher shop drive-by. The place had a green sign with the name 'The Crescent' done in white pseudo-middle eastern calligraphy. The double meaning of the name would be hidden to most persons in New Orleans, also called Crescent City, as would the duplicitous nature of the owners and most patrons inside.

It was in a two-story building midblock along Canal Street. Its left wall joined the building next to it and on the right a weathered, iron gate secured the narrow breezeway. As luck would have it, traffic forced Dafna to stop for a few moments directly in front. Ben tried to peer in from behind his sunglasses, but the dark interior didn't give up any of its secrets. The 9mm Berretta they'd given him kept rubbing against the interior of his bicep, as unnatural and out of place as a grapefruit-sized cyst. He sat up as straight as he could and breathed deeply. He closed his eyes to focus himself, exhaling loudly through his nose and taking notice of the ragged edges all along his peripheral nervous system; his inner eye registering a flurry of nerve endings, which were ringing out from every hair follicle and internal organ. He forced himself under control again. He was thinking about Grace and the girls when the earpiece went off.

"Who's breathing so loud? Adams, is that you?"

"You don't have to do this, you know. We're close enough. Let them handle it from here," Dafna said, looking at him from the rear view mirror with concern.

"I'm all right. I'll be all right," he said.

"Remember – you identify them only. No approach – nothing. Identify them. Call it in. Then leave. That's it for you."

"Yeah, I hear you," he said, wiping his sweating palms on his dishdash.

Dafna had turned off to a side street and found a spot at the end of the block. She turned the ignition off, then took a few moments to adjust the silenced Uzi machine pistol under her sack-dress, ugly and wasteful on her, given the beauty of her form, but good for concealing weapons. Ben tugged on his skull cap and pushed the earpiece in deeper. He stepped out of the car and pulled out his laptop bag and the long, white walking cane Daniel had given him to complete his ensemble. He put the laptop in the trunk and stepped up on to the sidewalk, trying to get himself into character. He extended the cane, sweeping it irregularly along the roughness of the sidewalk as she held him by the elbow of his injured arm.

"You're not doing that very well," she said.

"I haven't had much practice, you know, I haven't been blind long enough."

"Shut up. Speak only when necessary," Ofer said into their ears.

They slowed down at the alley and spotted the back door, closed and set in among a grease trap, some old oak pallets and a dumpster.

"The back door is closed," Dafna said.

"We know," Ofer said. Ben and Dafna looked around, but couldn't see anyone. Ofer began a radio check. They had six k*idon* outside: someone on the back, Ofer and another out front and a driver standing by. Two others were supposed to be inside already. They had come on short notice and from the vibe in Daniel's place that fact didn't sit very well with any of them.

According to the plan, Ben and Dafna would be the last into position and the first ones out. They would stay to confirm a positive id only, then leave it to the professionals. Dafna and Ben carried the heavy metal to allay fears – but it wasn't helping him much.

Ben knew this was for real. He wanted to see them dead, lusted after it in fact, but knew that if it came down to a shooting match inside a restaurant he would lose.

They didn't have much more time before they entered. Thirty paces out from the door it occurred to him that he should just walk on by. *You care more about the dead than the living,* Grace had accused. At that point he knew she was right. *Good Grace, she was always right about him. She knew him well. And she had decided to stick around anyway. What a lady.* He knew going into the butcher shop was the wrong way to repay her.

Ben kept swinging the cane in jerky motions. Dafna gripped him tighter at the elbow. He looked over at her and she managed a half smile.

They began final approach. He looked across the street at the row of commercial buildings lining the sunny side of Canal Street. It was very wide, with the streetcar tracks running north and south between four car lanes. Ben couldn't see Ofer anywhere. He felt an acute singularity and had a hint of what dying must feel. *For we all come into the world alone and leave it the same way.* He clamped down on his breathing once again.

They were at the door now.

She paused for a moment and looked at him.

"Rock and Roll," he said.

She opened it for him.

They went inside.

They left the brightness and heat of summer in New Orleans behind them, stepping into an antechamber with its swirling mix of street smells, air conditioning and spiced meat. They opened the second door entered the darkness of the interior. The patrons inside looked at the two of them coming in and saw a young Muslimah in *hijab* leading her blind uncle or older brother, rendered truly blind for a moment during the lighting change, stumbling slightly at the threshold while entering the shop. It was convincing enough for them, as they seemed to pay only fleeting attention. Ben's sight adjusted but he kept his head at odd angles and glanced around. The main dining area had maybe nine tables in the front, center section. The entry way ran along the right wall, which was lined by 12 x 12 mirrored squares, in fact all walls in the dining area had them. The windows were 3 x 5, coated with fuzzy dust and covered with dusty blinds the color of bleached bone. *No wonder he couldn't see in from the street,* he thought. He bobbed his head from side to side, but behind the shades his eyes moved in other directions, darting among all the faces.

He didn't recognize any of them. They were all men of various ages and stages, but none of them had been at his house.

The counter ran along the middle two thirds of the shop, wrapped in dented stainless steel. A single row of tables lined a section to the left of the kitchen area. He could see a door in the back, left corner; the one they had seen in the alley. He noted three men in the kitchen; the older one worked the counter, the other two younger ones did the cooking. The older one watched them cautiously as Dafna threaded him through the break in the half wall, stopping in front of a table right in the middle of the front section. She pulled at a chair and said, 'Sit here brother," in Arabic, just loud enough for the ears behind the counter. Ben did a bit of groping for the chair and edge of the table and then turned himself to get a viewing angle on the mirrored wall. She left him and went to the counter to order, rattling it off like it was second nature. His earpiece was silent for the moment. He looked askew at the reflections, trying to put the id on any of the young men sitting at the tables along the side of the kitchen, near its door. Two men sat in the first booth and three more in booth behind it. They were all between nineteen and twenty-five and by the dress, grooming, speech and mannerisms were all guests of the United States. *Tourists, no doubt.* They seemed to be agitated, but kept it on the down-low.

Slow burn. Just like me, he thought. He moved his head around some more, doing his best Stevie Wonder. An old man and his woman sat two tables over in his section. Beyond them, over the partition a couple more young men sat along the wall. They didn't seem bothered at all about this – in fact they began lively discussion which seemed to be on the edge of a shouting match. They spoke the Arabic too quickly for him, but he could pick out 'Gaza' and 'Askelon' as they argued over the Palestinian situation. But he knew it was a ruse – he could hear it in stereo – both in the room and through his earpiece. They were *kidon* – professional assassins. Pretty soon someone was going to die.

Dafna brought over a tray of hummus, cous cous and some spiced goat meat, along with a pot of tea. They sat there for another ten minutes as she fussed over him in Arabic. He either grunted in assent or spoke lowly in one word responses. They had told him not to speak if possible – they had evaluated his Arabic in the apartment and found his pronunciation wasn't worth the risk. Ofer whispered, 'more coming in' as Dafna continued to play it out. *She was good under fire,* he thought. *She seemed to be taking it all in stride – didn't seem to miss a beat.* He didn't fare as well. He kept his hands on his lap whenever possible to hide the tremors. He had to force his food down with exaggerated swallows. She took little bites, but was making a dent in the cous cous. He didn't know how she could eat with a sword dangling over her head, but he was glad she could.

Ben could see a young man, middle eastern, parking a shopping cart along the front window. He bent over the front of it, jerking his arms and back as he lifted a steel case out from under some scraps of plastic and rags. He put in on the ground and pulled out a second one. He dipped slightly in the dirty frame of the window, then pulled himself to standing, both shoulders drooping with the extra weight.

Ben heard a smattering of anticipation from the back tables rising over the clanging kitchen noises. He didn't look towards the door – Dafna did that. She didn't acknowledge it visually one way or the other. Ben heard dull thumps in the antechamber. Then the whoosh of the inner door and he came in. Ben used the opposite wall to get a look. He was thin. His face was shiny from lack of a bath or perspiration or both. Scraggly tufts of hair on the jaw. He looked like he'd been living on the street for a while. One of the cases thumped against his knee repeatedly He walked with a limp. Dafna glanced at Ben for a second. He said 'no' under his breath. A stranger – but he was one of them. Ben guessed him to be none other than ArRad13, the one who'd sent the notes and had come across two continents and an ocean to do his damage. He looked relieved as if his long, strange trip was nearly over.

Two of the fellows from the booths came out to meet him in front of the counter. They tried to take the load from him, but he refused and they walked back to their seats. The new terrorist took his place at the second table, closest to the kitchen door.

Their expressions changed; they grew lighter and smiled at him, nodding. ArRad13 looked the room over carefully but unemotionally. Then he turned his attention to the group. They tried to keep it inconspicuous, but they were all as excited as if they'd just ran into an long-lost childhood playmate.

Ben tried to get a good look at the baggage. He hadn't been able to see the suitcases as he'd come in, since he carried them low, under the edge of the partition which encircled the dining area. Ben could see the end of a case under the table. It looked heavy-duty. The terrorist had taken some pains to make the cases look insignificant and old. But they were more than the garden variety hardened aluminum travel cases.

The other terrorists brought him some tea and treated him deferentially. He didn't say much. They were still waiting for someone. Ben was certain he'd know someone in the next group of old school friends.

Ofer stood behind the people at the Canal Street streetcar stop nearest to the Crescent. He had to shift his stance from time to time to keep a good view of the butcher shop, but the tourists made good cover. He looked like one of them in his shorts and tee shirt, but wore a thin rain coat to conceal his weapon. His radio resembled a cellular headset, complete with the wire attached to the dummy phone. The team inside had gone quiet now and neither Dafna nor the American had given the sign. The courier had arrived just a few moments ago. Another member of the team got some clear shots of his face and was uploading the snaps to the satellite, to get a match on the likeness. They'd find out his identity in the next fifteen minutes – maybe thirty worst case – if the Institute had a history on him. But he had a little time to wonder. Ofer had gotten a good look at him as he had pushed the shopping cart across the tracks, but didn't recognize him.

At the moment everything seemed to be going well, but the waiting always wore him down. It was the uncertainty, the unknown that stretched the seconds out into hours. He had been in these situations plenty of times, but the waiting never got easier. He had the opportunity to doubt in these moments. He knew it could go either way but yet it seemed like the outcome still rested in his hands. He hated the stillness. Stillness was worse than failure.

Ofer looked for something to shake him out of the funk. He found it in a couple of dark suits, approaching the Crescent from opposite sides of the block. Federal agents, no doubt, and FBI by the anachronistic, blocky haircuts and the affected casualness in their gaits.

Now they had a problem.

"Another company is making a bid," he said into the mouthpiece, "can you confirm the order?" he asked.

"No," Adams said.

He weighed the options. He would expose the Office's role in this if he played out the hand. Eitan had warned him not to let that happen. It would be most embarrassing to politicians on both sides when the world learned that the Mossad operated inside United States real estate. But on the other hand, letting the terrorists complete the transaction was unacceptable. He assumed they'd split into smaller groups after this point; that seemed clear enough from the arrival of two containers. He stood a serious risk of losing one or both groups if he kept the *kidon* back and allowed them all to leave. He flipped the options over several times in his mind*: go ahead with it regardless and expose the operation, wait until a more discrete time and chance losing them or? Option Two? What? Take the FBI out as well?* He laughed. *That would be the end of his time for sure. But so would the first option if it lead to exposure and some Tel Aviv clownmaster had it in for him. What if he simply killed everyone, FBI included? Problem solved.* Explaining it back at the Office would be the only problem and that might not be as bad as he imagined. *At worst, they'd send him away with a numbered bank account and no forwarding address. At thirty-two he was young enough to enjoy life…*

Inside the butcher shop, Ben focused on his breathing again. The air began to get heavy; began to weigh down on him. He imagined the room smaller than it had been before. He had to fight against his anxiety, manifesting itself in the old, familiar feeling of entrapment that he'd suffered from ever since he'd been a child. He felt a panic attack coming on with the usual tightness in his chest building, but he forgot about it when the door swung inward and he got the first look at that little bastard from Chicago leading the last group of them into The Crescent. Chicago had just a couple of them following him today; the young one who had burned the stumps of his fingers to stop the bleeding and the one who'd done the chopping. Ben stiffened and forced his head downward towards the table. Dafna kept chatting him up in Arabic as he stole a glance. Ben nodded 'yes'.

Some of the others from the booths got up to greet them. As they were doing this, one of them shouted to the owner.

The owner then announced emphatically, "We close now. Everybody go. Go home now!"

Ben stood up, groping for the cane. He turned to the right to make his way toward the exit. The old man and woman blocked his view of the *kidon* as they shuffled toward the exit. All the terrorists where on alert, all were looking towards Ben and Dafna. Neither one of them had given the signal to them or Ofer. Several terrorists and one of the cooks had gathered round the old folks by then, shouting at them and trying to push them out the door.

Ben said, "It's them. I know the short one," into his wire, but they were creating a tremendous racket. He couldn't see if the *kidon* had received the message or not. They were literally surrounded and shooed out the door. They wouldn't have had a decent line of fire anyway. The *kidon* looked backwards towards Ben and Dafna, but left without giving themselves away.

Dafna followed their lead, turning to wait for Ben. She glanced back at them, then said, 'Come on brother, let's go home," in Arabic, sounding irritated.

Ben extended the cane and tapped it up against a couple of chairs, pretending to get his bearings as she took him by the elbow. They walked toward the door. In the mirror reflections, Ben could see Chicago intently looking at his arm. They had ten feet to go.

"You, blind one," Chicago said in Arabic. Then barking disrespectfully, in a guttural English: "Blind man!"

Dafna stopped. Ben turned a three-quarter profile to them. "What do you want?" he said in Arabic.

Chicago smiled. "Aaaah, you speak like a Midwesterner." He laughed a little, then said, " I live here for a while – I know this. You learn to speak the Arabic in Saint Louis?" The little man approached, drawing his weapon as he closed in on them. "I think I know you. What happened to your hand, good brother?" he said in Arabic.

"*Kalb – najis kalb.* A pack of unclean dogs attacked me, *najis kalb,*" said Ben, stressing the Arabic. He looked out over the top of the little man's head. The rest of the terrorists watched the scene play out, but ready to act if necessary.

"Look down here you lying pig," Chicago said. He leveled the gun at Ben's sternum and commanded, "take off those glasses."

When he did they could all see his blue eyes.

The young one and the Egyptian grabbed him as they had before, a few days ago and eight hundred miles to the north. Two of the new ones approached Dafna with their pistols up and hammers back. They took hold of her.

The Egyptian grabbed Ben by the injured hand, twisting it. Ben cried out in pain and fell to his knees. Chicago pistol whipped him two or three times, hitting him in the cheek and head. They did the same to Dafna. They searched them and found the weapons, using them to strike both of them on the head, neck and shoulders. Chicago tore off Ben's cap and grabbed him by the hair. "Now you pay the price," he said. He leveled his weapon, pressing it against the base of Ben's skull as his finger squeezed the trigger.

"Stop!" the owner said in Arabic, "Take them to the back. It will be easier to clean the mess up in the kitchen.

Chicago hesitated, lowered the pistol and shrugged his shoulders. A couple of thugs took each by the arm and dragged them toward the kitchen door. Others busied themselves by checking out the views in the alley and along Canal street, peering out between the blind slats.

When they had Ben and Dafna on the tile floor they resumed the execution.

"Stop."

This time it came from Abdullah bin Malak al Zalam.

"We take them with us; find out what they know, then kill them."

Chicago stood down once again, but grabbed a handful of Ben's hair and shook his head for good measure. As he did this, he noticed the earpiece.

"What's this?" he said, prying it out with his stubby fingers. He held it up for a moment, then dropped it on the floor, stomping it to pieces with his boot.

Abdullah spoke: "Put them in the freezer for a few minutes. Then we can be on our way."

One of the workers opened the freezer door; the other produced a roll of duct tape. The Egyptian bound Ben's arms together just below the wrists. Two of them raised him up to hang from a meat hook. They did the same with Dafna.

"Allah commanded that if a *kafir* denies him he will be punished with 'hooked iron rods' and here we have the proof," one of them said as they jeered at them, dangling by their wrists in the meat locker. They were bound but not gagged.

"That is just the beginning," another one of them said.

"The Holy Qur'an is a peace and a blessing on men," the first one said. The other one nodded and smiled.

"It's a piece all right," Ben said, between breaths.

They struck him on the face a couple times before putting a gag over his mouth while threatening and insulting him again.

"You're going to get what's coming to you, now and on the last day, you filthy son of a whore. If we didn't need to beat the knowledge out of you I'd cut your throat as you hang there now," the Egyptian said. The young one spit on him. The glob dangled from Ben's chin as it solidified in the whirl of freezing air.

Satisfied for the moment, they turned their attention to Dafna. The Egyptian admired the lower half of her body as she hung in front of him like a side of beef. They had ripped her robe off when they found the Uzi, leaving her in only a tee shirt and pair of panties.

"If we have enough time I'll be back for you," the Egyptian said, pulling her underwear to her knees. He roughly grabbed her crotch, putting a finger inside her. "Umm, how's that?" he said. She shouted a string of Arabic obscenities at him. He raised his hand to his nose and sniffed it. Dirt lined all of his nails.

"Jew woman. Good stuff. You know what?" he came close enough to whisper in her ear, "Now we're going have to have you before we kill you." He grinned and waved at her while he closed the door. The latch snapped into place and Ben and Dafna were alone in a cold, dark place.

Inside the meat locker, the noisy fan and the insulation of the cold, dark box made it impossible to hear what was going on outside. His weight pulled against the tape around his upper forearms, cutting off circulation and causing his injured hand to throb. The joints in his arms and shoulders were coming out of alignment. Dafna moaned muffled curses under her silver duct tape gag. Ben knew she was in as much pain as he, if not more but he couldn't see her in the absolute darkness. The locker must have been about eight feet square. He tried to swing himself, starting slowly at first, and building momentum. He brushed up against her legs. He kept swinging, trying to bump into something that he could lever against and get himself off the hook.

"Ben, I'm feeling dizzy," her voice said. This startled him. It sounded disembodied, echoing all around him. She had worked the gag off somehow. "I need help; help me," she said faintly over the sound of the freezer fan. Then she began to wheeze.

This triggered the memories in him, hanging still, suspended in body and time between two tragedies; he was at once in the elevator of his father's death and in the meat locker of his own. She sounded like the old man, as he remembered it just then. He had been dizzy too. The wheezing. The plaintive tone. It didn't matter that the voices differed in pitch or accent. It was the same voice.

"Help me get off this hook," she said, weakening.

It sounded like she'd given up hope. Ben felt the old familiar panic attack gathering strength, trying to put a death grip on him. He couldn't do anything to save his dad back then – couldn't even make it easier for the old man as he died on the dirty elevator floor. It had smelled of oil and moldering cheese. He remembered it distinctly.

He dangled on the hook, replaying the agony of helplessness in his mind. He couldn't do anything back then and he couldn't do anything in the now either. His hands were tied once again, literally this time, as Death overtook them in the cold, dark box the same size as the old elevator car.

He decided to try anyway. *Never Give Up. Never.*

He began to swing again. He knew they had no time left. They would be tortured and beaten. She would be raped and then they would get that bullet in the head, if they were lucky. Their bodies would end up in a nameless bayou, roadside, in the heat of Summer, swelling from gases and the maggots until someone found them.

Unless the alligators did first.

He kept at it, swinging hard. He knew it hurt his hand, because he was aware of the pain, but it registered as an abstraction. The pain didn't really sink in. He didn't have time to be hurt. He was going to do something about it this time. He was tired of being a victim – of reacting – of trying to avoid pain. He faced it, diminishing its power. He began to think. Even if he managed to come down off the hook, they wouldn't be able to escape. Still, he had the feeling that history wouldn't stop for him in the meat locker. He had a strange sense that history, *his-story* wasn't going to end there and then.

The feeling came from a place deeper than the fear. He knew he had more living to do. People depended on him: Grace, Kristen and Sarah. He had more softball games to go to, more life to live. He had to take them to Disneyworld in a few days. *Absurd*, he thought, *I'm hanging by a hook waiting to have my throat cut and I'm worried about getting to Disneyworld on schedule.* So he kept trying and he laughed behind his gag for a second. He kept trying to come down off the hook. His sweat began to crust up in the frigid air.

Ofer had a panic attack of his own among the sweating streetcar riders out on the Canal Street esplanade and in the brightness of a tropical day. He had heard Adams' mic go out and Dafna's didn't seem to be working either. Both of them were probably as dead as their earpieces. None of the spotters could tell him what was happening inside. And the two FBI agents were still lurking, but at least they hadn't run up on the place directly. That would have made it even worse. The street was too busy to force the issue. The *kidon* were asking what to do now and he didn't want to answer. The situation had gone to Hell.

Ofer told the driver to get ready. They could easily take out people in the alley from their firing positions on adjoining roofs. Most likely they would split into at least two groups, some leaving from the front, the rest out the back. *Should they kill them in the street or not?* He had to decide and he knew this would be the one that would affect the rest of his life. He turned it over mentally once again to see if the costs had changed in the last two seconds. They hadn't. One of the *kidon* reported he would be at the alley entrance in a matter of seconds.

Just then, he noticed a late model, silver Acura speeding up one of the side streets, ignoring the signals. It changed lanes as it crossed the tracks diagonally and swerved into Canal Street. Someone on the radio made a comment about it, but Ofer didn't think it belonged to the terrorists, noting it wouldn't be able to carry more than two or three at most, since it had already had two occupants.

The Acura came to an abrupt halt, blocking two lanes of traffic in the center of the street, farthest away from the storefront. The passenger got out, reached behind his seat and pulled out a dark green tube.

Ofer stared for a moment, then drew his pistol as he walked toward the action, picking up his pace the closer he came. The guy was ethnic, maybe South American. He shouldered the green tube. Ofer realized it was a grenade launcher, U.S. Army issue M-79.

"Incoming. Protect ..." was all Ofer could manage.

The South American fired into one of the plate glass windows, which then burst into millions of energetic glass missiles.

The explosion rocked the block.

People screamed and began running in every direction as they always did. Ofer ran along the tracks, taking up a position behind one of the planters in the esplanade between the tracks and Canal Street. Another dark sedan came up fast, threading itself through the traffic. It stopped at an odd angle and three got out, firing automatic rifles at the shop. Ofer could see one of the FBI agents returning fire behind a mail box on the corner. He couldn't see the second agent from his position, but didn't hear the report of a second pistol. *Probably dead.*

The force of the explosion racked the freezer.

It broke the metal rail securing the hooks to the ceiling. Ben wondered if the cases had prematurely detonated. He and Dafna had been lucky to be in the freezer after all. One minute it seemed like a large, metal coffin; in the next it had protected them from the full force of whatever had just exploded.

Ben swung himself some more, bending the metal railing downward until he cleared the hook and flew off, meeting the unforgiving hardness of the floor with his ribcage. He stood, breathing hard and full of adrenaline. He realized he could distinguish Dafna's outline. Light streamed in around the top edge of the door as well as the hinge side. He bent down and threaded his arms, still bound together, with Dafna's thighs. Squeezing, he lifted her off the point of her hook. They strained their eyes in the dimness, looking for something sharp enough to cut the tape. Dafna found a box knife on a stack of frozen goods and held it out for Ben to saw himself free. He cut her loose after that. They were both squatting low, instinctively, listening to the violent percussion just outside the door.

Gunfire – automatic.

Voices shouting in Arabic.

The sharp smacking from lead hitting the concrete walls.

Loud thudding when slugs hit the freezer walls.

Screams.

They scurried to the door and Ben peered out one of the gaps at the top. He could smell the acrid cordite and saw heavy, bluish smoke filling the room as if it contained a hundred burning cigars. He could see a couple of dead jihadis in the kitchen area, bleeding from more places than he could count. The blast had destroyed the kitchen, leaving black and gray streaks all over the walls. Two large blue jets shot upwards from the twisted metal where the stove had been. The gas lines were flaming. Ben couldn't see anyone in his restricted field of vision. He knew they were out there, some of them. He couldn't tell how many.

"Let's go out the back," Dafna said.

He peeked out again. The back door seemed to be unguarded and intact. It was still closed.

"I don't see anyone by it," he said.

"Let's open this door, then crawl to the back door and get out."

"Okay."

Dafna pushed the door knob inward. It slid about half the way it should have, then stopped without unlatching the door.

"I didn't feel it open," she said.

"Let me push against it." He tried and felt it give about a half inch. "I think it's unlocked. We push on three:"

They moved to face it directly.

"One, two, three…" They gave it a shove. The lower half scraped along the floor, off kilter.

"The bottom hinge is broken. Let's do it again."

They pushed harder. The outside corner of the door skidded along the tiles and after another push they finally had enough room to crawl out. They wormed their way towards the back door staying as low as they could due to bullets striking all the walls. *The place got chewed up in a hurry*, he thought. The noise level was deafening.

Ben crawled over the body of one of the bastards that had chopped his fingers off and had destroyed his home. He pried the chunky, squarish 9mm from its hand. He began to have second thoughts about leaving so soon. Dafna picked up on the hesitation.

"Let's go! What are you doing?" she implored.

He worked the slide, checking for a round in the chamber.

"Come on! Let's get out of here. NOW!"

"You go." He said, "I'm going to kill that son of a bitch."

"Goddamit, you idiot," she said. She crawled rapidly towards the door. He crawled towards the side door, leading out to the row of booths along the wall where they had all sat earlier. He could see both of their metal cases, unharmed, under the tables. He listened to the gunfire, trying to map out their positions. Between the shots, he didn't hear any voices or movement near the cases.

He felt a hand gripping him at his Achilles' tendon.

He twisted his torso, pointing the gun in the same movement, to fire on the offender.

Then he realized Dafna hadn't left. He relaxed his index finger.

"I almost shot," he rasped at her. He exhaled. "The cases." He waved towards the door with the Glock.

Dafna suddenly raised a pistol, firing over the top of Ben. He turned his head to see a man's head, shoulders and left arm bounce off the floor as he fell. He still moved.

Reacting, Ben gave him a *coup de grace*, which sprayed the cases with blood and tissue. Ben slithered over the to the doorway, peeking around the jamb. He saw no one else from that angle. He lifted himself up on all fours and reached across the body, grabbing the handle of the front case and still trying to stay low to the floor.

The firefight kept raging.

Ben tugged at the nearest case, from an awkward angle. It proved hard to handle and was heavy, weighing at least forty pounds. He dragged along the floor until the dead body blocked it. He jerked at the handle, tipping it over the dead terrorist's midsection and pulled it into the relative safety of the kitchen, where Dafna took it from him. He turned to get the other one. Chicago came into view, screaming in Arabic.

Ben's mind moved so fast it all looked like slow motion.

The muzzle of gun coming up to meet him, with its dark, dead eye.

The flash.

Ben screamed too, rolling on his side and picking up the Glock in one, fluid motion. He squeezed the trigger over and over as they exchanged point-blank fire. Chicago's gun flashed two or three more times at him, jerking with the force. The little psychopath fell backward against the edge of the trash bin, arms flailing, but still firing. Ben kept squeezing his finger until the burning became too much.

Chicago ran out of rounds. He had slumped himself up against the trash container and relaxed, resting the gun on his bleeding thigh. He was a mess – bleeding from several wounds He rolled his head and stared at Ben, emotionless.

Ben felt himself full of emotion and his gun wasn't empty.

The universe shrank to those two men, three feet apart. Ben could see or hear nothing else. Chicago's eyes began to roll. Then he recovered for a moment.

Ben saw the emptiness. They looked at each other. In the end, Chicago, a.k.a. Hassan al-Warraq, had no contrition. No remorse. Nothing but the vacuum of hate.

"I win. On the last day you'll be in Hell and you've sent me to Paradise, you son of a whore, " he managed to say, choking on blood and phlegm. He spit the mixture at Ben, but didn't have enough lung power to reach him.

At that moment the bloodlust would have allowed Ben to reach up under Chicago's sternum and pull his beating heart out if this had been the only way of killing him. The wave emanated from Ben's core, somewhere just above his diaphragm. Ben Adams visited a place beyond reason, beyond justice, beyond humanity. The same place that the serial killers and Hitlers and Mohammeds of the world know very well. The Empty Place.

He looked at Chicago over the top of his barrel, pointing it squarely at the bridge of his nose.

"*Allahu Akbar*!" Chicago cried out.

Ben put three rounds into Chicago's face.

Then the world and his senses came back.

He stopped firing when he realized Dafna was pulling on his leg.

They needed to leave.

The firing from the front room became sporadic. The voices were getting louder now, moving in his direction. He reached for the second case, but his arm wouldn't do what he wanted. He realized he'd been hit. He knew he wouldn't be able to get the second case. As quick as he could, he raised himself on three points and backed into the kitchen, sideways, like a beach crab.

Dafna was at the back door with the case. He scurried over, falling a couple of times, rolling, but always moving to the door. She pushed on the metal cross bar to open the back door. The bright light streamed in and the voices stopped for a moment then jumbled into chaos once again. Dafna held the door open as he tumbled into the alley. Shots began to splatter against the inside of the metal fire door. They got it closed. Dafna pried a loose plank from one of the heavy oak shipping pallets stacked against the wall. She levered it under the stainless steel handle of the door and kicked it into place. They began to pound against it.

Bending hard and thrusting her hips, she lifted the case with her leg muscles and clutched it tenuously at the handle, using both hands. They ran down the alley as best they could. He admired how tough and strong she was. Even with the heavy case, she moved down the alley faster than he could.

He looked at his shoulder, bleeding and hit in the meat just underneath the collar bone. His shoulder blade seemed to be intact, but he had trouble moving his arm. He felt a large patch of cool wetness on his back. He imagined a large hole in his back, blown out in shreds, but since he could still walk he put his mind on escaping. Neither of them said a word as they ran past a couple of dead men in the alley. *They must be with the crew that took the place apart*, Ben thought. Neither Ben nor Dafna made the effort to speak.

They made it to the side street.

A deserted sidewalk – good.

They could hear the sirens now. Sporadic gunfire. They hustled along the sidewalk. He began to feel weaker. He became very tired. And thirsty. He could see the car now and both managed to keep up the pace, still pumping on fear and adrenaline. They reached the car. The doors were locked, of course.

"The keys are in the robe," she said. She was still stripped down to her tee shirt and panties. Ben didn't have a second set of keys.

The cops were coming. Sirens everywhere.

"Help me lift this," she said, trying to lift the case over her head. He put the stump of his right hand underneath its edge and together they brought it up high enough. She pushed it down as hard as she could, managing to put it through the front passenger window. The alarm went off. Reaching through the hole, she opened the glove box and pulled out the other set of keys, killing the alarm with a button on the fob.

She unlocked the doors and opened the trunk, hefting the case into it. Ben fell into the back seat. He still had enough presence of mind to spread a plastic bag out on the seat to keep from soiling it.

Police cars, ambulances and fire trucks wailed and flashed down the street.

Dafna leaned over until they had passed, then sat up, started the car and slowly pulled away.

The rhythmic thumping brought him back to consciousness.

He didn't know how much time had passed.

Opening his eyes, he propped himself up enough to see they were somewhere out on the middle of the Lake Pontchartrain causeway. Nothing but the rough texture of a white-capped lake and the stream of traffic on the two bridges, leading off to the Northern and Southern horizons, and the reverberations of hundreds of tires against the expansion joints.

"Where--" he didn't have strength to say more.

"You're going to live. The *sayan* will see to it. Rest."

"What's *sayan?*"

"Helper. The helper will see to it."

He tried to keep himself awake but drifted off again as he watched the gusts of wind from the broken window tussle her hair. The thumping of the bridge joints lulled him into a twilight. His mind descended until it settled on the events of the day.

Revenge has a shape and a velocity, he thought. His mind rested on that for a while.

The shape is a sphere. And it pushes warm, solid things out of the heart and fills the empty space it with a cold, expanding hollow emptiness. Revenge leaves an abcess. He rolled in the clammy thickness of his blood spill, trying to take some of the pressure off of the wound.

He realized he didn't feel either satisfied or happy about killing Chicago. He tried to pass this off to his temporary state of mind and his wound and the loss of blood, but he knew better. He didn't want to acknowledge it.

'Nature abhors a vacuum', some dead scientist said long ago. Why hasn't a philosopher discovered the same about the human soul?

Chapter 56

Ofer finally got his chance less than an hour to the Texas border. He and one of the local *katsas*, Daniel, the driver from the

Crescent, had been following one of the groups since the shootout. Their group had at least one of the packages and as far as he could tell, he and Daniel were still undetected. It had not been easy to maintain a neutral distance and at the same time remain in the line of sight, but the flatness of the swamps had helped them. Now the terrain would be changing and Ofer needed to get a tracking device planted. If not, it was just a matter of time and circumstance before they lost them.

He hadn't discarded the brute force option, thinking it would be easier and cleaner to kill them all, as he had considered back at the streetcar station.

The terrorists were stopping for gas. Ofer and his new partner pulled in on the opposite side of the same pump. When the time was right – when they were all trying to get back into the car - Ofer would fire on them from one side and Daniel from the other. They could take out four men in a matter of seconds. Getting the case out of the trunk would take longer. Ofer didn't know if the car had a release latch in the cabin and if it didn't, they'd need extra time finding the keys. He weighed the odds.

He looked around. The terrorists had chosen a Shell station at the junction of Interstate 10 and the main road leading into Jennings, Louisiana. It sat behind a clump of scrubby trees far enough from the highway to be visually isolated. If Ofer decided to take them out the only witnesses would locals and a few unfortunates from the highway. But doing it here would only give them half the shipment. He had confirmed two cases at the Crescent but didn't know who had the other one. He assumed another group had the second case. Retrieving half was not a good solution. He had spent more than two years of his life on this and didn't really want his name stamped on a half-assed resolution. It would get him nothing in the long run. And if it went down wrong they might loose it all. Ofer frowned. The risk of losing both cases increased the longer they followed.

From the tinted shade inside the car Ofer could see two of them; one pumping and looking in all directions. *Nervous.* That would be a problem. The other fumbled around in the backseat for something. Young – looked shocked. Like he'd seen Reality. *It wasn't like they said in the Friday sermons, now was it boy? Ofer thought.* Probably had some of the Brothers' blood or worse splattered all over him during fight in the butcher shop. It had all finally come home to this young jihadi for the first time. *No, it wasn't like what the* imams *say in the sermons and the teachers repeat in the* madrassas. Not all things and people bow before the Allah of the Qur'an. In the middle of the noise and smoke and screaming and anguish and loss and stench and shock and pain and death The Truth will never be as certain as it is from the comfort of a prayer rug. The Truth will be always be trumped by THE TRUTH, of course. *These Muslims are taught to embrace Death and Hate,* Ofer thought, *I'd like nothing more than to give them all a martyr's death – the thing they covet most.* He would send the young terrorist home for his reward as soon as possible. *But first things first….*

Ofer checked the situation out while he washed his car windshield with a squeegee. Two of them were out of sight in the restroom; one pumped gas. The pumper was also the driver and seemed to be the sharpest. He had the keys in a pocket. The one with shell-shock ambled in the direction of the store. He wouldn't be a problem – wouldn't see it coming. Ofer continued to work on the windows, using one of the blue paper towels to remove a stubborn splotch of bug guts. He could see the others in the food section of the store now. Only the driver remained by the car. From the look of it he didn't intend on leaving until replaced by one of the others. Ofer patted his pocket to make sure he still had the device. He could attach to any kind of material, but needed a couple of seconds. It had to be done at this stop. He and Daniel would be recognized if they had to come this close again. It had to be done then.

Daniel circled around the rear of the pumps as he went into the store. The other driver kept him in his peripheral vision at all times. They exchanged glances. The driver didn't seem concerned about Daniel at all. Good. Ofer began checking the air pressure in the tires. He started on the far side. The driver finished pumping, returning the nozzle its holder. Ofer became concerned when one of the others came out of the store with an arm full of junk food and a cigarette carton. The driver spoke to him in Arabic.

"Pay for the gas. It's twenty-eight dollars."

The driver sounded like a Saudi.

"I don't think I have that much, " the other one said.

"You pay for it. You have all the money anyway." He sounded Egyptian even with food in his mouth.

The driver looked around another time, then walked across the limestone gravel separating the pumps from the store. The driver passed the Egyptian fifteen meters out from the car and started arguing. Ofer couldn't hear what they were saying. He came around to the front passenger tire, bending down to get out of sight. He kept listening as he pulled the device from his pocket. They were arguing a little, their voices rose. He could tell they were still both far enough away.

Ofer flattened himself out, reaching across the pump stand. He had to scurry about a meter to get close enough. The *wheel well might be too obvious.* He dirtied himself, rolling in an oil patch as he flattened himself on the stained concrete. He kept listening to them, gauging their distances as he reached for the undercarriage.

All steel under there - good.

They finished talking. Ofer bent his hand upward in between two pieces of metal. It would last longer if he could get it into a protected place. As he probed with his hand, he heard the sound of gravel crunching under feet.

The crunching came nearer.

Ofer was still partially under their car.

The crunching sound stopped. The feet were on the concrete pad now.

Only have a second or two left…

He let the magnet on the device find the metal. It clicked loudly into place. He hoped the other one hadn't heard the sound. From under the car Ofer could see feet getting way too close, coming back fast.

Ofer rolled, then pushed himself backwards over the pump island, scuttling along with his hands and toes until he got behind the pump. He picked up the tire gauge and reached for the tire valve, shifting his weight towards his car just before the driver came into view. The terrorist gave him a hard stare. Ofer glanced at him nonchalantly over his shoulder. He put the valve cap back on, stood up and went to check the last tire for good measure. Daniel came out of the store, followed by the one who had argued about paying for the gas. Then the other two finally returned. They took off .

"Well?" Daniel said.

"I got it on."

Daniel slid in and started the car. Ofer retrieved the locator from their trunk and turned it on as he climbed into the passenger seat. They had a good signal.

"Pull into one of those parking spaces," Ofer said, "I need to relieve myself."

Daniel looked at him with some doubt.

"You think this is a good idea?"

"As long as this is working, they won't be able to hide."

Chapter 57

"Our helper, the *satya,* says he's going to live; he'll recover fully," Dafna reported to Eitan over the encrypted cell phone. She looked over at the old physician, nearing retirement, as he stooped over Adams' wounds. She and the old man had wheeled Ben into the house and used the kitchen table as an operating theater due to the urgency and the blood pool from the car. But she could tell the Doctor thought the crisis had passed. Ben lay on his stomach, unmoving, mouth agape and with the dusty pallor of the anemic. His blood had made pooled up quite a bit in the plastic bags he had spread before passing out. He'd spared her of a good deal of clean-up work and she needed the extra time. Eitan kept asking questions.

"How did he perform?" Eitan asked.

"Ben? Or Remlevski?"

"The Doctor."

"Admirably," she said, "he has already sewn up the entry wound. It passed under his right clavicle and exited at the edge of his shoulder blade. It chipped the bone, but didn't break it. He is very lucky – no major arteries. Remlevski says he will be finished in about an hour."

"And I assume you are untouched?"

"Unharmed, but not untouched by the whole thing. We should be dead by now," she said, voice tightening. She rubbed the bruises on her face. The swelling hadn't gone down, but she didn't mention it.

"I want you to know that this will be the last time I do favors for you."

"I need you to do one more thing. A small matter – contingencies. You have done a great service for your people and for our nation – you know that, don't you?"

She didn't reply.

"I need you to go out to the supplies bag the team put in your trunk. Find the device that looks like a pacemaker. Do you know what I'm talking about?"

"I know what a pacemaker looks like. My sister is a nurse, you know."

"Have Remlevski put it in him before he sews him up. Then you are finished."

"No."

"We need this, Dafna. This isn't over yet. You have only one of two packages. We think we have sight of the other, but we need to cover all the contingencies and Adams is one of the biggest," he said, his voice growing louder and more coercive.

She pulled the phone away from her ear and brought the volume down by three bars. She cursed, took a deep breath then began listening again.

"I am not one of your *katsas.* I don't have to do this, understand? I'm doing you a favor out of respect for my father, but that has its limits. I don't have to betray someone I care about." Her voice wavered after she said 'betray'. She gripped the phone in pulses, feeling the urge to dash it against the wall. *It's a cell phone, I'll disconnect and then tell them my battery went dead,* she thought. She looked over to check Remlevski's progress. Still working – the wound still open.

"Dafna, your father and I go back many years. We came up together at the Institute just before the '67 war. Those were the best of times for us. Your father and I did many things, fought many battles and have killed many of the animals that would have slit your throat or my children's throats as you all played in the street. Sadly, the world hasn't improved since then; in all those years and after all the bloodshed. But the one thing that does get better is the trust and friendship that people like your father and I have together. We are brothers in arms. He and I are old men now. We need your help."

"Don't try to use my love for my father."

"Then what of your country, your people, not just your father, but your entire family? Isn't that any of that worth preserving?" he took a plaintive tone.

"My actions here won't decide the destiny of those things," she said.

"Don't be too sure. What you do will decide whether many live or die. Think of all the lives you can save by covering the contingencies."

"What about my life? I need to think about *my life*; that's surely worth a great deal, is it not?" her tempo increased, "What about my soul? When it comes down to it, I have to answer for my sins every Yom Kippur. I answer alone, as always – as we all do. Who will save me from those late nights, when I stare at the ceiling alone and unloved."

He didn't say anything for a moment.

"You love this man? Dafna, you know he is married. Don't make that mistake. Think about it. I know as well as you what your father would say."

She didn't give him a reply right away; a whole set of replies and alternative replies flashed in her mind's eye, like the sight of rushing concrete beneath the wheels of Nir's old motorcycle on those Summer evenings when they used to go out along the coast, making their own breeze to escape the Summer heat. She settled on that image for a moment, remembering how it felt to live with pleasure, connectedness and meaning in her life. It was happiness. Now she felt she would never have that again. And putting a piece of metal into him might as well just be a bullet…

"What is it? The device," she asked.

"A GPS locator and a listening device. Very slim – won't be the least bit uncomfortable," he added.

"Are you selling me lemons in the market?" she retorted.

"You've got to do this. Don't jeopardize your people and his, for that matter, for a man you can't have –"

She cut him off there. She turned the phone off so she wouldn't have to hear the incessant ringing. She gathered herself for a moment, then watched the old surgeon doing his charity work.

"Dr. Remlevski – is everything all right?"

"Yes dear," he said, looking over his shoulder at her. He looked more like a shoe cobbler with his reading glasses, tussled salt and pepper hair, and the old striped shirt, apron and baggy trousers. He looked more like Pinnochio's Geppetto than the third generation, upper middle-class grandson of immigrant Russian Jews. He spoke with the curious New Orleans accent. Native born, highly educated and anchored in the United States. Still, something had lead him to offer his services if they were ever needed.

"I can't repay you for what you've done. Thank you for saving my friend. But I must ask you: Why are you doing this," she asked, cradling her arms under her breasts.

"You mean helping you?" he kept stitching, not looking up from his work. "Because it is the right thing to do. I don't want or need to know the details, of course, but we are from the same place if you look back long enough."

"Couldn't you say that about all of us – not just *US*," she said, "I mean the story tells us that we all have the same mother if you go back far enough. Why pick the Hebrews over the Arabs? Why pick any tribe over any other?"

"The Arabs are not my brothers in mind, heart or soul. I am a student of history, you see. Whether you believe in God or not, you must conclude the Jewish people are a force for good in the world. Have you ever realized that the Jews have always been a tiny minority in terms of population, but have always played a much bigger role in things? The truly dark forces of the world have hated us and have tried to destroy us over and over again. Why is that? I know it's because our sense of morality predominates in a large part of the world. That has been our legacy. We have helped shape history in a good way. You are all part of that; part of my heritage. This perspective gives a life direction, a reference point to measure a man's progress or failure, you see." He stopped working for a moment and looked at her again. "Think of what the world would be like if people like you and I hadn't tried to protect it. People would be disoriented and would drift, like a rudderless ship in the fog. Despite what the relativists say these days, evil exists in the world. It would like nothing better than to destroy what progress we've made." He resumed his work, talking while working, as if talking to the unconscious man on the table. "I see our common heritage worth preserving. I don't know what you've done or why this man has been injured, but I do know it's worthy of my help. That's why I became one of the *satyamin.* I need to help. Besides, with Sophie gone these five years, I needed to find some way to get behind the Eight Ball again. I was always in trouble while she was alive." He winked at her. She laughed in spite of herself.

"Like I said, I'm a student of history. *Our history,*" he said.

She approached him and put her hand on his rounded shoulder. “I hope you’re right. More for my own sake than anything.”

He looked up at her compassionately and smiled again.

“I must ask you to do something.”

Now she had his attention. “I need you to place a device in him. No larger than a pacemaker.

A Plague on Both Houses

"Unless ye go forth [to fight in the Jihad]
He [Allah] will punish you with a grievous penalty
and put others in your place.
Allah – Qur'an 9:39

Chapter 58

The three of them kept moving. Abdullah had the driver stay off well-lit main streets and out of places where the police might get a good look into the car. They had stopped long enough to steal a set of Louisiana plates, replacing those they had. Two members of this cell had been killed during the firefight with the *kuffar* drug dealers and the American agents. As for the two survivors, the one driving seemed to be in good shape, like Abdullah, not harmed to any degree. The one laying across the back seat had been deafened in the blasts. Abdullah had known all along that involving the *kuffar* drug dealers would be a mistake, but never guessed it would be of this magnitude. Still all was not lost: yet. Abdullah had seen the California group make their escape with one of the metal cases.

The wounded one sobbed and groaned as he rolled from side to side on the backseat. They had had to stop twice so that he could vomit. Abdullah guessed he had a concussion as well. They kept the windows open to help him clear his head and to get the stench out of the cabin. Besides vomit, it reeked of smoke, cordite and the sourness of sweat laced with adrenaline. He thought back to his time on Bourbon street – similar in stench.

The driver spoke. "Do you think they'll make it, Abdullah," his speech warbling with fear and doubt.

"What's your name, brother?" He realized he'd forgotten it in the blur of the butcher shop.

"Abu. Abu Shakha Da."

"Abu, it does not matter if they reach the target site or not. They will release the weapon before they die. How many people die and what area will be hit are the only questions here." The thought of this comforted Abdullah. He had sacrificed much in the last two years.

"What about him?" the driver asked, glancing over the back of his seat.

"He has done a great service for the religion. Allah be praised. We have all done good works here. Did you know the martyrs well?"

"We were together in training and then one by one, we joined the cell earlier this year."

"So you knew them well. They will be in paradise with their *Houris*, the eternal virgins, after the Last Day. They will intercede on our behalf as they watch this unfold. The *kuffar* cannot stop it now. Even if we should fail because of the Zionist-Crusader alliance, the curse of Allah be on them, and the *naji* drug dealers who brought this turn of events on us. Even with this set back, we will be victorious. Many will die in spite of our success or failure."

Abu Shakha Da didn't respond. They were coming up to a red street light. Abdullah reassured his readiness by looking down at the pistol in his hand. A car pulled up parallel to them on Abdullah's side, waiting for the light. Abdullah rolled the window up. Neither of them looked over directly, but kept the other car in peripheral vision, checking to make sure they didn't suspect anything or get a good look at the injured one in the back seat. The light changed and the car sped away. They had been driving like this for hours.

Abdullah looked at the clock, noting it was past eleven p.m. They needed to find a place to hide for the night. He set the gun down and picked up the tracking device. No signal yet. He checked it again, wondering if he needed to adjust something.

"Do you think we'll be able to find them?" Shakha Da said.

"If they open the case, we'll know where they are."

"What if they're out of range? They could be hundreds of miles from here."

"al-Warraq shot one of them. They won't be able to go far."

"What if they don't open it? And if they do, they will probably take it to a fortified place with heavy guard. We won't be able to get at it."

"True; but you assume too much. The woman works for the Mossad. Has to. That makes the American a stooge for the Zionists. She won't take him to a hospital. We're still close to them, don't worry."

They came up on a stop sign. Shakha Da stopped completely, making a pregnant pause just to be sure. After all, they had no place to go until the device picked up the beacon. They began to roll again. Abdullah checked the one in the backseat. He had stopped moaning. He had a film of sweat coating his skin, which seemed to be turning gray in the pulse of the streetlights.

"We need to find a place to hide the car for the night." Abdullah made a pledge to Allah in front of Abu that he would not taste food again until he had retrieved the weapon or died trying.

"What if they don't open the case? We'll never find them."

"They will. al-Warraq had to stop in Saint Louis to retrieve the key from the American. He was the one that removed it from our website. You know he still has it. If you were him, wouldn't you look inside if you had the key? Just to see what this is all about. When he does they will all die, either by the contents of the case or by us shortly after, *inshallah*. We will know where to find him. Allah, may he alone be worshipped, has ninety-nine names and many more eyes."

Chapter 59

-- Quartzite, Arizona

Ofer and Daniel had been following them non-stop for a day and a half by then, pacing the drive to the beat of a monitor blip as the scenery changed from the flat green of East Texas, to the gradual build up of hills in the midsection of the state into the higher, and then through the dry mesquite scrub in the west. The pursuit continued through nightfall as they passed into the mesas and Piñon pines of New Mexico and then entered the desert. Ofer and Daniel stopped to refuel when their quarry stopped, at an unseen distance, usually between five and ten kilometers ahead. Ofer and Daniel traded driving and watching the monitor back and forth between cat naps.

Eventually, the land around them came to resemble the ridges and washes of home. The grinding, rumbling monotony of car noises and the familiarity of landscape kept them in the recollection of things past, both the good and the bad.

But a new day had been born and brightness of the sun, in its eternal course, had brought them back to the present and it pulled their minds upward and outward, as if connected to them by a thread, as it arched towards its place in the cloudless blanket of desert sky, deepening in tone towards electric blue. It would have been beautiful if not for the situation being played out beneath.

The blip on the monitor stopped three to five kilometers ahead.

War

They were close to the crest of the valley now. When the capped the ridge they could see the flashing lights two or three kilometers ahead.

Ofer's concern increased exponentially.

"Slow down, " he said.

Daniel reduced the speed to a shade under one hundred kilometers an hour. Ofer kept looking at the LCD ticking off its signal. He looked over at Daniel and shook his head. They would close on the patrol car in less time than it took to strangle the life out of a man.

Daniel continued to slow down gradually, glancing at Ofer every few seconds. He killed the lights and rolled into the mix of crumbling asphalt and loose rock on the shoulder. They had no one to worry about in the rear view mirror. Daniel hadn't seen another car for a long time. They closed in on the Arizona state trooper's sedan, its door wide open. The red and blue lights were flashing against a dark shape in the middle of the road.

"Roll down your window," Ofer said, as he did the same. He picked up the field glasses and stared down into the valley.

"What's going on?" Daniel said.

"They've killed him."

"The Patrolman?"

"Yes, I see a body in the road," he reported,

Daniel muttered curses under his breath.

After looking all around, Ofer said, "Approach it slowly but don't stop. Don't get the tires into the shoulder either."

He jumped out as Daniel continued to roll up on the scene, albeit slowly. The sounds of static and radio voices came from underneath the trooper, sprawled out and embracing the firmness and the rising heat of the highway.

Ofer bent into the cabin of the cruiser and, with his hand covered by his shirt tail, turned off the camera and computer system. The trooper's right hand gripped the butt of his pistol, still in the holster. His face, turned in their direction registered, surprise and pain. He had died young – less than thirty from the look of it.

Ofer synchronized himself with the movement of his car and hopped in.

"Had to do turn the camera off."

"The Arizona State Police will have their plate numbers now," Daniel noted, "Do you think they realized that?"

"If they have any training they'll realize they need to switch cars. Or at least the plates."

"Do you think they're that stupid?"

"Probably not. But our hand is forced now. We'll have to take the case from them as soon as we can. You and I – alone." Ofer looked intently at Daniel. He didn't know much about the man or his history. "Do you agree with that?"

"Yes. It's the safest way." Daniel didn't give much of a reading. That reassured Ofer somewhat.

"When we see the opportunity, here's what we'll do," Ofer began. They went over the scenarios as their car passed under the shadows of the valley wall. Daniel brought the distance between them to seven kilometers and maintained it for the time being. Ofer changed out the SIM card in his cellular phone and rang up Eitan to appraise him of this latest development.

Chapter 60

He heard the voices first.

A woman. Dafna's voice-- speaking to a man in Hebrew. Their voices had a harsh reverberation as if he was listening to the conversation outside a racquetball court. He listened to them so more. The other one seemed to be a man – old man. They didn't seem to be discussing anything serious – by the tone and tempo it sounded more like a recap of the day's events than a crisis. He heard no duress in it.

He could hear them coming down the hall as he rubbed his eyes. From what he could tell, he was on the kitchen table in some old vacation house. The place smelled of mothballs and moldy fabric. The air in the place had been in one place too long, like it always did at the lake house the first time they opened it up for the season each year.

He squinted to block the glare from the table light and looked out towards the doorway, where he could make out Dafna's familiar frame on the threshold. After her cam a blocky, stoop-shouldered shadow, which became an old man as he shuffled into the perimeter of light. He had big, dark drooping bags under his eyes, which held up a pair of unfashionable bifocals. He wore an old flannel shirt and brown trousers.

Dafna moved as she always had. She seemed unharmed for the most part. Her face, usually symmetrically oval, had swollen and deeply bruised on one side where they had beaten her. But she smiled as she looked at him, listing to his port side as he recovered from his initial light-headedness.

"Where are we?" he croaked. He spoke as if he had the mother of all hangovers.

"Ben, I'd like you to meet Doctor Remlevski." He nodded and tightened his lips as he acknowledged him. He came over and extended his hand. Ben shook it.

"No, take it," he said, "try to stand up."

Ben grabbed it as he extended his legs toward the checkered linoleum floor. Doctor Remlevski picked up the slack and Ben swayed back a forth, but stood.

"Good..." he said, "healthy young man... You'll heal pretty fast, I'd say." He looked him up and down superficially, then said, "try to walk around a little. We've got to get you out of here in a hurry --you know the insurance companies want you up and gone ASAP." He let out a rumbling laugh at his own joke, pleased at Ben's condition and no doubt a little proud that his own skill hadn't diminished.

Ben made a circuit around the table.

"That's enough for now," Remlevski said, "Dafna, help Ben onto the sofa in the other room." Remlevski ambled over to the counter and began pulling pill bottles onto the counter.

Dafna took Ben by the left arm, threading him through the kitchen. The warmth of her hand made him feel better.

"Are you hurt at all?"

"No, not really," she said, "You are really lucky, Ben, you know that? The bullet passed through nothing but muscle."

They crossed into sitting room where the natural light showed her bruises. She had really been beaten hard on the right side of her face. The outer part of the white of her eye had turned reddish black and he could see at least three distinct bruises. He thought of what had happened back at the butcher shop.

"Dafna, I'm sorry I got you into this. My god, you look bad."

"I'm going to be okay. If you think I look bad, you'd better not look into a mirror. You got the shit kicked out of you, mister." She laughed and gave his arm a tug. He didn't wince, but it hurt like hell when she did that.

She made a fuss of him, getting the pillows just so and guiding him down on them. His strength began to drain as his blood had earlier.

"Have you talked to Eitan yet? Where is the suitcase? How long have we been here?" He asked, not waiting for the answers. He wanted to be sure he got the questions out first.

"Yes, the case is out in the boathouse and it's Monday."

He thought for a moment.

"June 30th?"

"Yes, you slept all day yesterday. You bled a lot. You're probably still anemic, even with the two pints I gave you." She smiled. You're lucky, you know that? We found your donor card. You're A positive, I'm A positive. She smiled.

"Dafna," he paused, "thanks."

"You'd do the same for me, I know." Her expression changed as she said this. She began to weep. *She must be tired,* he thought. He drifted off.

War

Fighting is prescribed for you, and ye dislike it.
But it is possible that ye dislike a thing
which is good for you,
and that ye love a thing
which is bad for you.
But Allah knoweth, and ye know not.
Allah – Qur'an 2:216

Chapter 61

As the road into Blythe, California got busier and more built up along the sides, Ofer had Daniel close the gap. They had just crossed the border. He wanted to keep a closer watch over them and they stayed within sight distance. They had left the dead trooper in a long, desolate stretch of Arizona desert about two hours before. The terrorists hadn't done anything impulsive since, but Ofer didn't want to take chances. Putting himself in their shoes, he would want to change cars and his appearance if possible. They had left the record of the murder in the patrol car. If they realized this, they would want to make themselves invisible again. Changing the car would be the easiest step in that direction.

Daniel kept a discreet distance from them as they tooled along, just under the speed limit, their sedan flickering in the shadows of palm trees. The visual rhythm of rocks, ecru dust and trees lining the highway seemed just like home.

It took them less than the length of the song on the radio to make it to the far edge of Blythe. Their target slowed, hitting the brakes several times.

"Are you ready for this?" Ofer asked. He pulled out his Beretta, giving it the once-over.

"What do you have in mind? Where?" Daniel asked.

"We move on them when they stop," Ofer said, matter-of-factly, "If the situation is right, yes? You take the driver's side." He put a round into the chamber.

"Doing this on a busy street in daylight will be hard to justify," Daniel said, "What about Saint Louis? "

"The bureaucrat will have to deal with it," Ofer said, dismissing it with a pistol wave, "We'll loose our tracking ability if they make a switch and we won't get a second chance."

He looked over at Daniel.

" I don't like it anymore than you, but this situation dictates action. We're fortunate that they haven't been pulled over again," Ofer said.

"For them and us."

"It's over for them already." Ofer looked at him, hard, "We won't have any margin for error. I wish one of the *kidon* had gotten the car back there. I don't know about you," he said, thinking out loud. This angered the young man.

"I'm ready. Don't worry."

"Have you ever killed someone? Close enough to feel the blood spray? That's what's going to happen, understand? If you hesitate, you'll die. And you'll get me killed me too, worst case." He smiled like a boy who just slipped a spider into a girl's blouse.

Daniel didn't reply – instead he steadied the wheel with his left hand as he reached for his pistol. He began to evaluate it. Ofer took it from him.

"Just drive, hot rocks," he said, running through the checklist.

Their mark hesitated up ahead, then hung a sharp right into a parking lot. It was a narrow, two-row space wedged in between some older, one-story commercial buildings. On the left was the Blythe Pizza Stop. Ofer could see the empty delivery cars lined up against the building. At least one of them idled while the drivers picked up the orders. He could see exhaust coming from the old, blue metal flake Chevrolet Impala. The terrorists angled their car toward the closest empty space.

Daniel looked for a nod.

"Now. Hurry. Before they all get out. Hit them!"

Daniel sped up, still accelerating and screeching into the lot.

"Hit the car, NOW!"

They came in at angle over the curb, clipping their sedan on the rear corner. Throwing it into park as he opened his door, Daniel jumped out, gesturing, running up and shouting about the damage to his car, his gun stiffly held against the side of his left leg. He knew this would slow him down at shooting time, but he had practiced many times to shoot out of the left hand, as well the right. He hoped the element of surprise would compensate and it seemed it would.

The terrorists were taken off-guard for a moment, giving Ofer a couple of seconds to cover the longer distance to the passenger side. The driver started to get out, shouting. The one who had been dazed and confused back in Louisiana seemed to be back to normal now, peering out from the rear window. The other two were getting out of the car.

Ofer never stopped walking as he raised his pistol. He took the first one down with a tap to the chest. Then adjusted his sights and put two through the chest of the one riding shotgun.

The driver, screaming in Arabic, lunged at Daniel while he tried to bring his weapon up to sights. Just two steps away from him, Daniel put the first round through the bridge of his nose, then two to the chest. As he fell, the last one in the back seat pressed his palms against the glass. "Don't kill--" he shouted at them in English, pounding on the glass. Then Ofer's bullets came through his head, reshaping his face and pushing it though the hole in the shattered window. Ofer scanned for the suit case.

"Find the keys!" he screamed in Hebrew. Daniel saw them, still swinging in the steering column. He reached in and pulled them out. "Get the car ready," Ofer said. He spoke loudly, but evenly now, with all the emotion of someone reading a telephone registry. Daniel threw the keys to him, over the roof of the car. He turned and ran to their car.

Daniel looked all around, seeing people running to the door and windows of the Pizza Stop. Covering his face with his right hand, he leveled the pistol at them. They all hit the floor.

He glanced backwards. Ofer had the trunk open and was rifling the contents. He reached in, jerking his shoulder as he pulled the heavy case out from underneath a heap of gym bags and paper sacks. He left everything else as it was and trotted unevenly back to Daniel and their car. Daniel put it in gear as Ofer hefted the case into the back seat and slid in behind it. Daniel stomped on the accelerator, gunning the car backwards onto the highway. He switched gears and they took off, tires smoking. All told, it had taken less than a minute.

Chapter 62

Eitan was behind his desk as always. He should be out on his patio already, but duty called. It had always called. He was tired of this – he had had too much of it all these years without something he could point to and say 'well I worked hard and long into the nights, but it was worth it. I made a difference.' He supposed that the mere survival of his country should be enough, but it rang hollow. *He should be out in his chair after the good rain today. The flowers were always at their best*, he thought. He lingered on the little scene as he called his handler again. *If Tel Aviv wanted it to play out like this who was he to argue?* He rang his handler up. The familiar voice answered.

"Are we secure?" Eitan said out of habit.

"Yes, go ahead, I'm across the street, actually," the American said.

"We have both suitcases now. Both should be on the way back here."

"How long?"

"Two days for California – the other is still in New Orleans."

"In New Orleans…" the American repeated, "any complications? You're letting them drive it back in?"

"They were injured. They need to wait until they can travel. They'll be coming back up tomorrow."

"You're letting them drive it back in?"

"Do you have a better way of doing it? Other, faster ways of bringing it in have risks. I assume you don't want any authorities, besides yours, finding out about this. It would be out of our control then. Your press might be informed. Other, faster ways of transporting the weapons would have variables we can't control."

The handler cut him off. "Have it your way. Just make sure nothing fucks this up, pardon my French." He paused and changed direction. "Look Eitan, you're doing us a great service here. Really, we appreciate it immensely. But I have the feeling you're not being completely forthcoming. Suspecting friends is an old habit of the trade. I'm sure you can empathize with me, right?"

"You know what I know."

"Somehow I doubt that," the American said, "but let me know as soon as you have them. The souvenirs. I'll arrange for the pick up immediately."

Chapter 63

-- Madisonville, Louisiana. Evening.

Ben Adams blinked his eyes a few times to bring them into focus. He could see the fine, light green feathery leaves of the cypress trees in a low-angled, golden light framed by the rectangular window. It could have been a painting hanging on the wall, as beautiful as it was, but the leaves moved in the breeze. Blue sky. *It must be late in the evening now*, he thought.

He smelled cooking. Chicken. He could hear it frying in the pan. He noticed his ears weren't ringing anymore. He sat up on the edge of the old leather couch, drew his breath, then stood up. He felt better than before. He walked through the unlit hallway toward the yellowish, specular light coming from the kitchen. They were talking again in low voices.

He stepped onto the linoleum, probing at his shoulder to gauge his expectations for pain. He didn't want drugs unless he couldn't deal with it. He wanted to have his wits. He knew they were't out of the woods yet.

Dr. Remlevski bent his head around the table light to get a look. He smiled and threw his arms out wide.

"He lives!" he said, somewhat sarcastically, "I've still got the touch."

Ben mumbled in affirmation.

"Are you hungry?" She asked.

She stood over the frying pan, turning the meat with a metal spatula. She had on some old Oxford cloth button down shirt, three sizes too big. She was barefoot and wore nothing to cover her legs. She would have looked sexy, had it not been for the swelling on her face and the dark bruises under her eyes. She tried to look cheerful, but Ben knew better. She had trouble looking at him for any length of time, for some reason. Something had changed. He knew he should have insisted she stay out of all of this.

Still groggy, he sat down at the table. She brought him a few chunks of chicken on a plastic plate that had been through the dishwasher too many times. She sat down next to him, propping up her cheek with the palm of her hand. He could see the ligature marks on her wrists hadn't faded yet.

Remlevski was looking at her too. "You know, you'll make someone a good Jewish wife someday, like my Sophie," he said.

Nobody laughed.

"What day is it?" Ben asked.

"Monday," Remlevski said, "the thirtieth."

"This is where he worked on me, right?" he said, pointing his chin at the old man.

She nodded and put some food in front of him.

"We're going to eat on my operating table?" Ben said to no one in particular.

"It's cleaner than any other place in the house," Remlevski answered. Then he looked back over his shoulder. "I've been a bachelor for a while, you see. But don't worry."

Ben looked at Dafna as he chewed. He felt better already.

Remlevski came over to him with a large pill bottle.

"Take these," he said, offering the bottle.

Ben took it from him, spinning it around to look at the label.

Ciproflavoxin 100mg.

"Cipro is a high powered antibiotic," Remlevski said, "you need to take it three times a day. There's enough of it to take you through the entire period you'll be susceptible to infection from the wound. Don't worry, if you do that, you should do fine," he said, satisfaction in his voice. He went over the stove to fix up another plate of food.

Dafna had a curious look on her face. He didn't know how to read it, but thought it came from the trauma they had been through. They had killed people, point-blank. Ben started to feel sick again as he flashed through the scenes. They deserved it, no doubt. He wanted to feel glad about it but he just came off feeling hard inside. Compressed. Either hard or he felt a vacuousness that prevented him from feeling satisfied like he thought he would.

Dr. Remlevski sat down opposite them rested his forearms on the table as he shoveled in Dafna's cooking. She watched him them both with a newfound detachment that flashed warning lights at Ben.

"Are you all right?" he asked. He knew the answer, but wanted to draw it out.

"Yeah, sure," she said distantly. Remlevski nodded in agreement, chewing.

"You called them?"

"Yes, just before you woke up on this table, " she said, rapping it with her knuckles. He noticed she clenched her fist hard enough to whiten her knuckles.

"What'd they say?"

"Nothing. I told them what happened, how you were and that we had the case." Then she added. "That's all. I hung up on him."

"What now? What about Ofer? Are we supposed to meet them?"

Remlevski started to fidget, looking like he didn't want to eavesdrop any longer. He stood up with his plate. I'll finish this on the porch," he said.

They chewed some more in silence until the old man closed the weathered cypress wood door behind him.

"Let's open it," Ben said.

"The case?" she said, locking eyes with Ben, "I don't think that would be a good idea. Besides, have you seen the locking mechanism on it? It looks to be Soviet military. Digital."

"I think we can get past that pretty quickly," Ben said.

"From the looks of it, it would take a long sequence of digits. If we got it wrong twice, maybe even once, the thing might have a self-destruct mechanism." She eyed him hard for effect, "and God knows what's in there if we do get it open."

"Exactly," he said, "We need to know what's in there for sure. For leverage. Don't you want to know what's in it?"

She shrugged. "I don't care."

"I do. I care," he said, adding, "I would bet my house that the way into that case is the 'key' that I have stored on disk." He twisted his head and changed his expression to one of mock-surprise, "Oh wait a minute. I did lose my house on that bet already. And look at this, " he said, holding up his injured hand, "and I lost three of my fingers too."

She didn't say anything.

"Look, I've given up a lot to get to this point and I'll feel a little unfulfilled if I didn't know for sure what's in the cases before we turn them over to the FBI."

"Turn them over to the Mossad, don't you mean?"

"We need to talk about that too."

Dafna began to regret putting the device into the meat of Ben's shoulder.

Ben began gathering the things they'd need out in the boat house. He had placed his laptop and cell phone on the old telephone cable spool out in the shack, which was more of a pole barn than a shack - built on piles driven into the muddy flat at the edge of the Tcefuncta and into the river itself. The doctor had filled it with a collection of rusty farm implements, an old truck, cans of paint at various stages of neglect and a scarred-up work bench. Everything looked and smelled musty-old except for the shiny new Kawasaki Jet Ski, suspended by nylon slings over the slip built years ago. *Remlevski still wanted to have his fun,* Ben thought, *that's the way I want to be when I reach his age.* He opened the garage door fitted to the opening and let the fresh smells of earth and brackish water replace the mustiness and dust.

The slight breeze from the Pontchartrain felt good in his lungs, though he took care not to breathe too deeply because the hole in his side would complain. Remlevski's place was on an old rice farm at the edge of a little town situated on the Pontchartrain, in Saint Tammany Parish, directly north of New Orleans. City people used to leave the heat and grime of the city in Summer and boat across the thirty miles of brackish water to the little town of Madisonville. But it wasn't isolated like it must have been before the causeway. He could hear but the sounds of tires on pavement rolling up to the farm from across the flat expanse of water. The house must have been one of the early summer cottages. It had the large, overhanging roof that made a shady porch and had a couple of dormer windows in it. The touches were the neo-classical vernacular Southerners used so much in the past: neo-classical lites around the weathered cypress door, which needed painting, and floor-to-ceiling windows and the Dorian columns holding up the Creole roof. A picket fence separated the patch of grass around the house from the square of gravel that Dafna had parked on. The pickets were checkered with the texture of 'gator skin from a decade of neglect.

He opened the trunk and felt a twinge of pain again in both his hand and shoulder. He imagined what he must look like to other people. His right side was all messed up: the hand, the gunshot wounds in the shoulder, his cuts and bruises and the flash burns still had him reddish on the right side. *He had been in the wrong place at the wrong time,* he told himself. *More than once.* He had brought it all on himself. He got himself involved. And he hadn't walked away. But in spite of the huge price he had already paid, he had to see it through. Like Pandora, he had to know what was in the box. He couldn't stop himself.

Dafna came out to help as he pushed the shed's service door open with his hip. He didn't know how she really fit in to all of this or where she stood in it. For the time being she supported him, but he couldn't afford to think she'd do the right thing by him when the time came. And it was coming. Soon.

He lugged the case over to the old telephone cable spool by the workbench and tried to lift it himself. It weighed at least seventy-five pounds. He couldn't bring it up high enough in his condition. He set it down on the dusty concrete and waited.

The ambient light flickered and he turned to see her walking through the dusty shaft of light streaming in from the door. Even in her present condition, she moved with an elegance that had always attracted him. His eyes adjusted to her dimly backlit face. She tried to force a sternness on it, but it wasn't working out too well.

"I don't think we should be doing this," she said crossly, "we don't know for sure what's in there. We know it's extremely dangerous, whatever it is. We don't know for sure if your 'key' will open it. Look at it. With a locking mechanism like that, how do we know all it takes is the string of numbers? What if you have to do something else at the same time or have your hand on a certain place? The thing could be triggered with a fail-safe device to kill the likes of us."

"You mean, you think it's booby-trapped?"

"Who knows? Why take the chance?"

"I need to know what's in there."

"Who cares? What does it matter?"

"It matters," he said, "it could get me – us – out of serious trouble. Knowledge is power, you know. In the IT industry and here – everywhere for that matter. We need to know."

"It's too great a risk for a trump card at the negotiating table, if you ask me."

"Look Dafna, I'm up on charges of sedition or espionage if things go wrong for me. I don't know who I'll be dealing with."

She hesitated. He could see she didn't want to talk.

"What is it? Just say it," he said, "I've been honest with you all along." He took her hand and noticed it trembled. She squeezed it, let out a long breath and relaxed her jaw muscles.

"We have to give it to Eitan. We can't turn it in to the FBI as you say." She lowered her head, not wanting to look at him.

"I can't do that, Dafna. No way. I would be aiding a foreign government at the expense of my country. To the detriment of the United States. I'll be sent to prison the rest of my life if the Feds find out."

"They'll never be able to prove it," she said, "look -- I know Eitan will move it out of the country as quickly as he can. He's been with the Institute all of his adult life. He's a consummate professional."

"He's a Mossad agent and he's working against my people and my government. If I help him, I'm working against them too," Ben said, lifting her chin with a hooked index finger.

She looked at him and he knew she loved him for the first time. It made his heart contract because he understood the depth of it and knew he could never reciprocate, no matter if he wanted to or not. He had a wife and family he loved. They needed him. They needed him alive and outside the walls of Leavenworth Prison.

Still he loved her back.

"I'm going to open it," he said, letting his hand drop from her face.

He stepped backwards and turned to the laptop. He found the file that had been the cause of all of his loss and opened it.

2:289,9:54,5:77,43:29,6:18,63:128,140:21 for your right hand
17:33,16:88,58:247,29:89,36:126,44:92 for the other.

He looked at the case. It was top quality and built very strongly. Along the edge near the digital keypad he could see that stampings had been filed off. Probably Cyrillic lettering or the serial number of the case. *What if she was right? What if this was one of the missing Soviet suitcase nukes floating around out there?* If he got it wrong they would probably level New Orleans and the entire delta of the Mississippi from where they stood. They'd vaporize a large portion of the lake and send it skyward, creating a radioactive rain cloud that would contaminate a swath of the Southern States for decades. Thinking of the implications stopped him.

"How do we know which one this is?" He said.

"You mean, is it 'the right hand' or 'the other'? Which is it?"

She examined it minutely as did he. Someone had tried to make it look old by smearing it with oil and dirt and by scratching it, but it wasn't dented in the slightest. *It must be extremely hard,* he thought.

"How would you hold it?" She asked.

"What do you mean?"

"Which hand would you use to orient the keypad the correct way?"

He made the mental adjustment, then said, "The right. But that doesn't prove anything. Both cases are probably set up the same way and we have no way finding out."

It was laying on its side. They walked around the spool and looked at the bottom.

"Look at those scratches."

He looked. They looked like random swirls and lines at first. She pointed at a section.

"Does that look like anything to you?"

"Some scratches."

"Think in Arabic script."

He stared at if for a five or ten seconds. Then a word rose out of the field into the foreground. It said, "right" from what he remembered.

"Right. Do you agree?" He asked, pointing it out to her.

"Right is right," she said, now smiling at him.

He adjusted the angle of his laptop screen to remove the glare of the shed windows, opaque from the grime building over the years. He coughed lightly as he pulled the close enough to enter numbers on its red, digital keypad.

He looked at her for a moment. If they were this close to unshielded uranium-235 or plutonium they were already dead. He hadn't considered this before.

"Pandora couldn't help herself either," she said. She had a curious look on her face. He didn't know what to make of it. "Pandora had a box, too – a long time ago. Deep down inside she knew she shouldn't open it, but she just had to find out."

"What she released only corrupted people – it didn't kill anyone," Ben replied.

"Right – her box didn't kill anyone. Not immediately, anyway, like whatever you find in there," she said, pointing to the case, "but you could say Pandora caused this. She released Jealousy, Pride, Envy – all the traits these Islamics hold against the West. Their fear of losing is what's driving this, you know. They see the West and at some level deep down, nestled in their hearts along with Pandora's creatures, is the Fear of Losing. Their culture will never match the West in any measurable way and so we must pay the price for their failure."

"Isn't a letting a Genie out of a bottle a better analogy?" he said, "after all this hatred and failure is the product of Arab culture."

She didn't reply. She just watched him.

He put his hand on the pad. "The time to leave is now," he said.

The air inside the boathouse had gotten close. Swamp dust swirled in shafts of light and settled onto the sweat beading up all over his body.

He began pressing the keypad, albeit very slowly. He had a long string of digits to enter and didn't want to make a mistake. They didn't want to find out what happened if he fat fingered a '5' instead of a '4'.

228995457743296186312814021

With the last digit a clicking sound came from the locks. He breathed out, relaxing his shoulders. Dafna moved over next to him. He reached for the buttons on the locks. He jumped when he heard the sound, coming from the door.

He looked towards the door through the sunbeams and saw Remlevski's pear-shaped silhouette.

"Doctor, please, go on back outside, " Ben said, reassuringly. He didn't want to get the old man into it any deeper. No need for it.

Ben walked over to head him off.

"But I just wanted to see what you kids were doing, " he protested.

A gust of wind took the door out of Remlevski's hand. Ben shooed him out and closed the door. As it opening got smaller, the force of wind increased. Turning his back to the breeze, he saw Dafna opening the case. The air blew up the curving ends of her hair and she waved a hand in front of her face and coughed. A bit of dust billowed up into her face. Ben closed the door behind him, walked back over to the makeshift table.

Dafna had the lid propped open. He looked inside: a row of three metal cylinders on the bottom section, which was as deep as the case itself and a binder and some other papers in Arabic strapped to the other side, which was shallow. On each of the cylinders a label in red, yellow and black with the interlocking crescents that stand for a biohazard and some Russian writing. Dire warnings, no doubt.

"It's a bioweapon," he said, feeling the precise coldness of the machined steel.

"For some reason I was thinking it would be a nuclear device, even after the conversation we had with Eitan and Ofer, " Dafna said.

He took the digital camera out of his laptop bag and began snapping off pictures at various angles and distances.

"Something like this could actually be worse than a bomb. It could end up killing more people across a wider area, would definitely terrorize the entire country and would bring everything to a standstill. Way worse," Ben said.

"They got this in Uzbekistan? The markings are Cyrillic – Russian – probably Soviet," Dafna said. She coughed a little in the dust and moved away so that Ben could get a couple more shots.

"I did some 'net surfing on the way down, remember?"

"Yes?" Dafna said, in the form of a question.

"Yes, but why not buy something else?" Dafna said.

"It would be much easier to get some of this than a nuke. It couldn't be protected as well. And a virulent agent engineered to resist standard anti-biotics would be just as deadly as a nuke, if not more. I bet what's in these three canisters would kill far more people than a 20 kiloton suitcase nuke ever would."

"But the really insane thing about using this is once this Genie is let out of the bottle, they'll be no way to put it back in. It will kill infidels and Muslims without discrimination. Without conscience. This will be uncontrollable," Dafna said.

A Plague on Both Houses

Allah's Apostle said, "Know that Paradise lies under the shade of swords."
Hadith Sahih Bukhari V4B52N73

Chapter 64

"Abu: wake up!" Abdullah shouted. He prodded him with the pistol he'd been carrying from the very beginning. *It wasn't over yet, God willing*, he thought.

Abu Shakha Da stirred, bumped his head on the passenger side window, then opened his eyes, one after the other. They were bloodshot and looked like they were growing hair. He looked like shit and smelled worse. He rubbed one of the eyes with the back of his hand and muttered something unintelligible.

"Wake up: look!" Abdullah thrust the tracking device at him. It was too close to focus on.

"What do you see?"

"We have their position. At last. Praise be to Allah. He has made them open the case." Abdullah kept talking excitedly as he put the keys in the ignition and turned the Chevy's engine over. "When the case is opened a beacon transmits the location. This must be turned off manually. A fail safe, if you will. So they must have used the proper code sequence. If they hadn't the thing would have gone off and we would have had a different signal from the device." He shook the tracker toward Abu, to emphasize his point as he eased the car out from behind the dumpsters. They had stopped early that morning, somewhere in the mean streets north and west of the old Quarter.

"Wake up!" he shouted over his shoulder. The wounded one had been feverish earlier, tossing and turning and crying out. But he had grown quieter as he slept. "Wake him up," he said to Abu, who leaned back between the seats to poke at the other one. Abdullah never knew his name. As they came to the end of the alley, Abu sat upright. He had a blank look on his face.

Abdullah jumped to the conclusion like Men Of Action always do.

"Is he dead?"

"Yes."

Abdullah stopped the car. He switched gears, retracing their path back up the alley to the old lot with the dumpsters they'd been hiding between earlier. After he'd stopped the car and checked for witnesses, Abdullah put on his hat and a pair of sunglasses. Then he got out of the car. He casually looked around again, opening the trunk. He opened the lid to one of the dumpsters and threw a few token things in it, casually looking around again. Abu was busy wrapping the dead man in the sheet he had been laying on. Abdullah pulled the body on to the broken asphalt as Abu pushed, disgorging it from the back seat. Shakha Da then came around to the other side without hesitation, bending to grasp at the folds of sheet. Together they swung the weight a couple of times, then heaved their brother into his dumpster grave, beside the old tire and between the black plastic trash bags, greasy and slick with the stench of rot.

They got back into the car, taking off without ceremony.

"Did you know him?"

"I will know him when we walk together in Paradise with the other martyrs. Did you know him?" Abdullah asked.

"I am from the Florida group. He was from the California group. He just followed me out in the confusion of the battle after he was shot."

"He has fallen a martyr. He is one of the blessed, true believers. He is now guaranteed a place in the Garden, for Allah has promised us this in his blessed Qur'an. He is one of the lucky ones. I hope I am on that list as well, brother. You too, " Abdullah said, patting Abu's hand as they pulled out onto the street.

Abdullah checked the tracking device once more.

"Latitude 30.3804 by Longitude -90.1691. That's where we will find the weapon. It is close. No more than sixty kilometers from us." Abdullah took care not to go too fast.

Patience had always been his test. He would have to wait again. *Allah is wise, all-knowing.*

Chapter 65

They launched the old pirogue made from swamp cypress, a la Cajun style, and left Remlevski's boathouse, traveling down the Techefecte river. The old fifteen horsepower Evinrude mounted alongside its stern coughed and belched gunmetal smoke as they pushed along the river bank on Remlevski's side. Morning sunlight danced golden along the edges of the generous, wraparound porches surrounding the old houses along the way, but the jumble of worries in Ben's head pushed out any recognition of just how picturesque the moment really was.

He needed to talk to Dafna, about what they'd do next. He needed her support. He also needed to contact Agent Daniels to get some help. He had no way of knowing how all this would turn out and so far good luck sure hadn't been a factor.

They decided to have a look at the lighthouse situated at the mouth of the river on Little Island. It hadn't been used for years, probably even many years before the causeway had made the trip across the Ponchartrain inconsequential. They finally passed the marina at the mouth of the river and waved at some along the Madisonville side. The wind strengthened at the edge of the brackish lake, and this caused wavelets the color of café au liat to pat against the boat. They got nearer the lighthouse. It looked forsaken on the edge of the island. Neglected, it was smooth concrete, painted white with some large, black vertical stripes. The scrub trees and bushes were doing their best to hide it now. The lighthouse stood about thirty five or forty feet tall, a little taller the oldest trees behind it. It looked like no one had given it much attention in a quarter century. They trolled along the shoreline now, looking for a mooring. Remnants of a wooden pier were useless to tie off on.

Ben twisted the handle of the two-stroke engine, gunning it to run the pirogue aground. The shoreline had enough rock and concrete rubble to keep his feet from sinking into the muck as he waded in and pulled the bow ashore until satisfied it wouldn't float away. He retrieved his laptop bag. He had urgent work to do.

They walked over through the lighthouse doorway, black in trim with an oversized, rounded Italianate lintel. The interior turned out to be just as dark. They made their way, cautiously marking out each step on the neglected metal treads of the spiral staircase -- pausing a little with each step to hear if it rang true in pitch before giving it full weight. They made it to the top, circled the warning lamp and sat at the place with the best view of the lake.

"This old light stood for years protecting people from danger as they escaped the heat of a summer in New Orleans. Now it's forgotten," Dafna said.

Ben nodded, working on booting up his laptop and connecting his cellular phone to the modem.

"Lighthouses have a great deal of Romantic appeal to people, you know. I mean, they are symbolic of many things. Women seem to like them the most, don't you agree? The solitary protector…" Dafna suggested.

"And they look like erect penises. Don't underestimate that appeal," Ben said, checking his equipment. He couldn't tell how much juice his battery had and it bothered him.

"Ben," she said slowly, "let's make love." She crawled over to him, took his laptop and the phone, still tethered to it and set it down on the concrete. "Make love to me, now, while we still have a chance," her voice had a purity of tone that reverberated in him as she straddled him and wrapped her arms around his neck. She leaned back, pulling him down on her. He pressed against her, into the soft warmth of her touch. The heady atmosphere of her scent engulfed him. He smiled.

"I do love you Dafna," he admitted, "and I know you love me. I've felt it for a while."

"Yes," she whispered. She stoked him behind the ears and smiled back. Her eyes filled with light. "Let's make love. Then we will go away together. Forget all this trouble. I'll make you happy. You make me happy already."

"If circumstances were different, there'd be no doubt. But I can't do that, even if I want to. I love you, but it can't happen between us. I have a wife and another life. I can never leave that. I'm sorry, Dafna."

She didn't look sad or disappointed. Her face had no trace of negativity as he told her this.

"I know." She kissed him gently and traced circles delicately on his cheek, tickling the two-day growth of his beard, "Part of me knew you would say that. You are a good man. A good husband and father -- The kind I would marry. Make love to me anyway. We will never have another time together. This will be the end for us, you see, and I want my memories to have the depth of lovemaking so they last the rest of my life."

Then he pulled away in a single motion.

"Don't think about it – just do it," she urged.

"No. It can't happen, I'm sorry. It's against everything I've promised to Grace and the children. And I'd be doing you wrong too, " he was sitting up, elbows resting on his knees as he put his forehead in his hands.

"It's not wrong if I want it." She protested, while straightening her skirt.

But it was over before it began.

"It *is* wrong. For you and me both. For my family. For everyone involved. It would be a mistake to let it follow its course. Sometimes it comes down just the voice inside your head. Call it the conscience if you want. The thing that knows what you must do."

"No matter how much it hurts?" she retorted.

Now she was weeping in streams down the front of her cheeks.

"I do love you, Dafna. You know that. God, I wish I could, really. I want to. I want to make love to you, but I can't."

"That's what I see in you, Ben, your sense of what's good and right in the world. That's why I love you – I love you for the little voice in your head even if it gives me all this trouble."

She laugh-cried. He kissed her.

"What are we going to do now?" she mused.

They sat there and looked at each other for a moment.

"We need to decide what to do with the weapon, " he started, "I trust you too, Dafna. I know you've had my life in your hands on this trip and you haven't let me down yet. He grinned whimsically. "But you know I can't give the case to Eitan. Besides, what do you think Mossad and the Israeli government would do with? Why do they want it so bad? Your government probably has its own biological program anyway and might have even deadlier stuff than whatever's in those canisters. Why is the Mossad so interested in chasing this group of terrorists all around the world and through the United States? Why not just tell the CIA and FBI and be done with it? Wouldn't that be easier? What does Israel have to gain from this?"

She didn't say anything for a minute, looking out over the whitecaps that gave the lake a rough texture. Like the last day in the boat with Nir. The water looked the same.

"We'll go back to Saint Louis…" he started, "but we – I -- can't let it leave the United States." His expression turned serious, concerned. "I don't know what your arrangement is with the company or whether you *really* work for AirWarez or the Mossad but Dafna, come on, let's think about the implications of this. I can't help a foreign government track down a group of terrorist cells, then arrange the meeting time and place, then show up with a team of professionals and kill several of them while taking a weapon of mass destruction away from Islamic terrorists and then just go home and forget the whole thing. Think about it. I have."

"I don't work for the Mossad. I came along for personal reasons -- for you."

"Do you see why I need to turn this over to *my* government? The rest of my life depends on it."

She nodded somewhat grudgingly.

"I can see these last few days have set a course for a new direction in my life. I see it differently now. It amounts to this: God is not subject to my schedule and how and when I decide things should play out. God is outside time and I am a slave to time: time, place and season. I can't expect things to be done along my schedule. What I need to do the rest of the days I have on this Earth is: get up, wash my face, take care of what I'm responsible for in this world and the next and do a good day's work. I need to be around to help my kids up when they fall. And I need to support them when the world, in all of its pettiness and people, with their selfish interests, bear down on them. And I need to teach them to do what's good an right and to care about others to some degree – even The Others. This is what I'm meant to do.

I've known revenge isn't the answer, but I ignored that for a while. Getting killed while trying to get revenge won't help anyone. Revenge and violence only advance us to the next round of violence. It leads us around in a closed circle. If enough of us do what we're meant to do on this Earth and we do it long enough then maybe we'll reach that date in the Cosmological Calendar when the effort will add up and will make a difference. Maybe at some point people will put the tribalism and the petty self interest behind them. When that day comes is not for me to know. But if it is to come then I have to start playing my part. Killing people to avenge my brother is not part of my future. It will end up turning my wife and kids into a widow and orphans. I need to stick around and raise them right. This fight will last longer than our life spans combined. "

"What if people like them keep coming after you. What if they don't stop killing your brothers? Then what you do won't matter," she said.

"You're right. They can't be reasoned with. Negotiation only works with opponents and equals – not enemies and people who consider you worth less than themselves and on par with unclean animals. Cutting deals with the Islamic world will never work. They will interpret this as a weakness. Besides, their god commanded eternal war with the rest of the world 'until all religion is for Allah'.

"Then we must show Allah to be wrong," Dafna said.

"Exactly."

"Then you will fail. They will never change their minds."

"That's true for some of them, but not all. And its' not true for future generations. Okay - at present their mindset is limited. They remind me of the Saturday Night Live sketch where they parodied 'Behind the Music' when Blue Oyster Cult was recording 'Don't Fear the Reaper' and the producer, played by Christopher Walken, kept coming into the studio and insisting "more cowbell... I've got a fever and the prescription is: more cowbell." Absurdity is funny on TV, but deadly serious when applied to a billion people in the Muslim world. Their answer to everything is *more* Islam, *better* Islam – *Islam is the answer* – our country is destitute and the people suffer; well, they haven't been practicing enough and need to return to 'real' Islam. The terrorists score a kill – Allah be praised – Islam is victorious. Islam, Islam, Islam. If you only have a hammer everything looks like a nail. Islam is all they've got. We've got to supply them with the tools. They need to break out of their mindset. They lack the mental toolset and vocabulary to think their way out of it and the exceptional Muslims who could put their lives at risk.

The war of Ideas will be the most important part of World War IV – the war against worldwide Jihad. We're in it already, but most people don't realize it yet. This is another problem," Ben said.

"The Middle East will continue to be the armpit of the world until enough Middle Easterners realize that Islam is THE problem – not the solution. Mohammed was a tyrant. Islam encourages other tyrants. Islam demands mental submission and promotes the habit of inshallah-fatalism – in other words 'it's useless to try anything, since Allah decided everything at the beginning of time.' Islam itself is the main reason for their troubles, for their unresponsive political system, and for the rumors, nonsense, lies and stupidity that come so easily to Muslim societies. Skepticism has never been accepted as a way to view the world. Progress and innovation are sins. Until people have the freedom to think these problems will not go away," Dafna said.

"I know you're right. The Islamic world must be made to see Islam as the problem, not the solution," Ben said.

"How?"

"Well, we can't expect some contingent of 'moderate Muslims', or in other words, people hesitant to kill for Islam, to arise and take command of the agenda either. Moderate Muslims are what Mohammed referred to as hypocrites. He and his sock puppet, Allah, said hypocrites belonged to hellfire and should be killed by true, believing Muslims. Moderates will always loose the argument in Islam; the reason being that neither the Words and Deeds of Mohammed nor the words of Allah are moderate. Moderates have no leverage over extremists. Besides, we can't tell a 'moderate' from a True Believer. Out of common sense and self-preservation the *kuffar* world needs to assume all Muslims are either active jihadis or in remission, like dormant cancer cells. Muslims in remission can switch on at any time, when they begin to practice their religion again. We have many examples of this. In addition, Mohammed provided an example of extremism that cannot be questioned. Moderate thinkers will always loose in *Dar al-Islam*. Besides, They are not the answer and neither is 'reform'. The Qur'an is a recitation of the immutable, unchanging word of Allah. It can never be changed or compromised. To do this would be unthinkable and a great sin to believers. They have divided the world into the Muslim and the Unbeliever, the dark and the light, the negative and the positive. Change is not possible from within the system. So the solution must come from outside the system... from out in the lands of the infidels; from the 'House of War', the *Dar al-Harb*. The solution must come from the us, the *kuffar;* the unbelievers."

Dafna said nothing but kept looking at him as he continued.

"Okay - the West needs to get its head on straight and define Islam as it should be. It isn't a religion which is focused on spirituality and growth. It is focused on fascistic ritual and conquest and conversion of all unbelievers, by force if necessary. That is not a religion – it's a political movement. The kingdom of Mohammed is this world, not the next. Islam isn't a race of people in the genetic sense – it a cultic belief system -- a Ponzi scheme – and when it's in power it runs things like the Mafiosi. Christians and Jews may keep their creeds as 'protected peoples' if they pay exorbitant *jizya*, which translated means 'protection tax.' "

"It's just like it sounds - extortion," Dafna added.

"And the money doesn't guarantee the lives and property of the 'protected peoples' are safe anyway. Historically, it's all been subject to the whim of the local tyrant and the lynch mob – both behaving much like Allah who capriciously decides the believers who go to paradise and those who don't, according to whim. This explains why Muslims must bleat 'may peace be upon him' every time their prophet is mentioned. It's because they honestly don't know if he's in Heaven or Hell. And their belief system gives them no way of knowing. But Islam is a political system first and foremost, with bits of ripped-off religiosity and pagan rituals to conceal the fact. Western law needs to define this system in plain terms. Islam is not a race in the genetic sense, but a belief system. Any fool or child can be indoctrinated – regardless of the color of their eyes. Islam differs from all other religions in its focus on dominating the world. It recognizes no other authority than itself. Islam as it stands is incompatible with liberal, representative democracies. It is an alternative political system. It is a direct threat and an enemy to the foundations of western institutions and documents like the Magna Carta, the U.S. Constitution and all other constitutions as well as the United Nations Universal Declaration of Human Rights. Islam wants to destroy these principles. The Islamic belief system defines itself as being at constant and eternal war with all other belief systems and institutions. It is by definition, seditious if practiced by True Believers and is treasonous if practiced by citizens of the United States. Islam is the antithesis of Western governance and all other world-wide notions of spirituality, " Ben said.

Dafna nodded her head. She breathed a big sigh and looked out over the waters. Ben said nothing either. Then Dafna picked it up again.

"Today the Western nations are strong but blind – like Samson from the Old Testament."

"Tolerance of everything leads to blindness. Belief systems which threaten the very foundation of a society and which aim to overthrow their host societies need to be seen for the threat that they pose. It would be stupid to be tolerant of something that regards me and my children as second class or unclean based on beliefs," Ben said, "It is suicidal to be tolerant of something that calls for the destruction of everything good in this nation. Tolerance can't be applied to a thing which would destroy that tolerance."

"The German writer Thomas Mann said, 'Tolerance becomes a crime when applied to evil.'" Dafna quoted.

Ben looked at her and nodded. "Damned straight. I think you're on to something. You mentioned Samson. Okay, well, in my opinion the world needs a 'Project Samson.' Islam is said to be made of five pillars – with jihad as the unofficial and most important sixth. Western civilization, Samson in other words, needs use its strength to pull down the pillars of Temple Islam. It's not limited to the West, though. All non-Muslim people, four billion of us, need to focus our strength and join together to defeat the world-wide jihad. We need to target each of the six pillars: the Profession of Faith, Ritual Prayer, Fasting, Alms giving, the Hajj and Jihad. We need to focus on each one and pull it down.

"Sounds like a plan," Dafna said, "what do you have in mind?"

"Let's start with the first pillar: belief in Allah and Mohammed as his messenger. We can pull this one down by showing the Qur'an can't be from God and that Allah doesn't deserve to be worshipped and then we can illustrate the despicable, criminal way that Mohammed lived. Islam is a house built on lies and crimes. Why do you think they call Islam "The religion of truth". Insecurity. They know Islam is not "true". They know when rational, un-biased Muslims are given a choice, with all the facts presented, most would not stay Muslim. Islam as a belief system is only held together by force: Your are to be killed if you leave Islam, no other beliefs may be practiced in Saudi Arabia, no other beliefs may be preached in Islamic countries, no criticism of Islam or Mohammed anywhere in the world and Hellfire in the next if you questioning the Qur'an. It wins using the Appeal to Force and by having the monopoly of ideas wherever it can impose its will. Truth and Information are our weapons here. Like I said, the religion is as fragile as an eggshell. It claims, among other things, in *Surah* 3, verse 7 and in *surah* 5 verses 46 and 47 that Gospels are true and yet Jesus was not crucified and claimed to be a "prophet" of Allah. It also claims Mohammed brought the "final" revelation to something he didn't even know about: his religion that claims the Christian trinity is Mary, Son, and Father, which is an error in understanding. It claims Mary was the sister of Moses, which is an error of history. Its god thinks and behaves like a sociopath and spends more time punishing people in Hell than having a relationship with them in heaven. Allah is distant and creepy, not caring which 'half of men go to heaven and which half do not.' But yet Allah commands men to grovel in the dirt five times a day, covering in fear. Put those two things together and it shows a deity not worthy of respect, let alone worship. The religion exhorts followers to kill in the name of an all-powerful god who made all humans and tells young Muslims they will go straight to "paradise" for murdering infidels while committing suicide. Why would an all-powerful god need help in "punishing" so-called "infidels", particularly if "infidels" are headed to Hell anyway? It makes no sense when you start to look at it closely. Muslims must take it all on blind faith, despite every fact and every error. That drives the whole issue of Jihad: the whole world must be under the delusion of Islam so that nobody can speak the truth.

But the truth is the system's full of historical, scientific and logical errors. It's not consistent internally either. In fact, the contradictions are so obvious, even seventh century, illiterate, desert Bedouins could see through Mohammed. But Allah came to the rescue several times, explaining away the inconsistencies in *surah* 2, verse 106 and *surah* 16, verse 101 among others. Why didn't Allah say what we needed to know the first time? Why substitute one thing for another at all? The all-knowing god contradicts himself – how is that possible? Why do you think the *imams* have to repeat "And Allah Ta'alla Knows Best" after their rulings? It's because would-be 'Submitters' intuitively know the thing as a whole makes no rational sense. The imams have to tell people not to think about it. Mohammed himself got angry when people asked questions. He told them 'Allah hates you for asking too many questions' in the *Ahadith*. What kind of god would consign people to hell, but not help them figure out how to avoid it? Not a god who should be worshipped. Islam 'the system' is not consistent, like a framework of ethics would be. Islam knows no real 'right' or 'wrong'. The words tell you that… defining words like *halal* or *haram* which mean 'permitted' or 'forbidden', not 'right' or 'wrong'. Deeds are justified based on the situation, not by any real ethical standard. The meaning of words changes if they are applied to Believers instead of the Unbelievers.

Christianity is more or less an ethical system based on the Jewish moral code. This is different from Islam, which a rigid system of rules, regulations and punishments, and lists of that which is 'Permitted' and that which is 'Forbidden'. How is the Qur'an The Set of Instructions for All Time when a noticeable percentage has to do with the details of Muhammad's life? These things haven't been 'valid instructions' since Muhammad died. They mean nothing to us in the present. Sure, they bailed Muhammad out of problems with his followers and helped justify lies, murder and robbery when dealing with unbelievers and kept his stable of sex partners in line but they don't guide anyone today. There isn't anything approaching right or wrong or ethics in it at all.

The Islamic world is condemned to pain and suffering on Earth because it thinks it has to obey a set of rules and commands which make no consistent sense.

Western, liberal, representative governments didn't develop in spite of Judeo-Christian teaching; We enjoy these rights and freedoms today because the West followed the moral code of the Old Testament and the teachings of the New Testament. It hasn't been easy to get where we are and the progress has never been linear. But it's no accident that guaranteed rights and freedoms developed in the West alone. Just as it's no accident that people in the Islamic world are mostly uneducated, mostly poor and usually live a short and brutish life. Half of the Nation of Islam lives under the caprice of tyrants and imams and the other half lives under house arrest and wears a veil. The 'Nation of Islam' has no guarantee of anything except more Islam - more Submission – more of the same. Muslim are the first victims of Submission and have suffered the worst from it. We need to remember that as we destroy their belief system.

But according to Islam, whatever the prophet did is right, regardless of what he did. The words that the prophet insisted came from either the angel Gabriel or Allah himself are right, regardless of whether they make sense or not. And what Mohammed did, according to the accepted, canonical texts of Islam itself, turns the stomach. We need to use the scripture of Islam against Islam! It's just that simple. It's all there and cannot be denied. Mohammed was a terrorist by his own admission. He had sex with a nine-year-old girl at the age of 53. He robbed caravans for a living. He supported the assassination of Poet women who were nursing babies and blind, old men. He had them killed because they mocked him and opposed him. Mohamed broke treaties. He was a genocidal war criminal, beheading at least six hundred Jewish men and boys in one day after they fell under his power. He tortured and robbed people. He raped women the same day he had their fathers, brother and husbands beheaded. We don't have to make anything up. What the sociopath did is far worse than what we could come up with anyway. Truth is stranger than fiction.

We need to tell them Islam is morally bankrupt – and need to point out that it's irrational in that it has no system of ethics – no objective frame of reference to good and evil. Whatever worked in the Cause of Allah (or his messenger, Mohammed) was permitted. This is why things are either 'haram' and 'halal' for believers. Things aren't good or bad – they're either prohibited, haram, or permissible, halal. A system turns out to be very irrational when it's based on actions of a self-serving megalomaniac. He called his religion 'Submission.' I think we should propose it be renamed 'Expedience' since the sole proponent of the system sold out anything if it meant gaining treasure, power or more women. Evidence: the treaty of Hudaibiyah, which he signed when weak but broke as so as he thought his mob was strong enough. He couldn't be trusted at his word or by treaty. The convenient *surah* 66, which commanded him to forget about social taboos and steal his daughter-in-law from his adopted son. Monotheism wasn't even sacred enough to him. In the Quraysh Bargain he accepted offers of tribal power, money and women over principle and for them he recited the Satanic Verses, which accepted pagan goddesses and associated partners with Allah, which is a grave sin and destroys the core belief of Islam. It's in *surah* 53. We need to start hammering away at Islam from every angle so that someday we will get to the point where the 'bad' Muslims or the 'cultural' Muslims look at it all begin to ask themselves questions like, "Is this what I want to be? Do I want to be associated with this junk? Do I want my son to become this kind of thing? Do I want my daughters to live like this?"

"People who live in Muslim countries can't leave it, they will be killed, " Dafna said.

"That's true. Why do people cling to it? Ignorance and Fear. We need to have a whole system slamming against it – discredit it. Point out the errors, plagiarisms, syntactical mistakes, everything about how poorly its put together. Show how it fails as a guide to life. It's nowhere near complete. The people have been taught it's unchanging, complete perfect. Demonstrate the obvious. Show the Qur'an can't be from God. Show that Mohammed shouldn't be held up as 'The Perfect Man' to be emulated in all times. Point out that the *imams* say it the Qur'an must be read in medieval Arabic to be the True Word. Now why would an all-knowing god do this? If it's the guide for all men and for all times and places – why would it be in a form that no one understands? It's because the Qur'an doesn't come from God and hiding behind an anachronistic language keeps the idea alive and the power in the hands of the *imams*. We need to show them, over and over, that something so imperfect can not be from God. We must shine the spotlight on the imams and make them pay for the hate they stir up every Friday. Make sure it's all out in the open and translated. Find the mosque leaders that advocate the violence and deport them. Deport everyone that's not a citizen. Their terrorist behead their captives. Why don't we behead Islam? Cut the brains out of the operation - find the leaders and deport them or bring them up on charges for hate crimes or for sedition or inciting a crowd to violence. If that doesn't work, let the IRS go after them. Those sons of bitches get their man – they put Al Capone into Al-Catraz. We need to get smart and use all our resources.

Muslims are kept in line with fear – fear of eternal hellfire. Show them that the words of the Qur'an cannot be from a perfect source. Drag their idol – Muhammad down into the dirt. Show how he shouldn't be an example to emulate. Use their texts against them – shine some light on them, for God's sake. For humanities' sake! They won't be able to stand the scrutiny. and the doubtful will increase. Remove the fear of eternal punishment by showing the words and examples can't be from God. Never give the 'religion' any respect. We need to show how arbitrary *shar'ia* is – how it is built on inference and subjectivity. We need to show some of the asinine rulings which come out of it. We need to show complete insanity and injustice of it - temporary marriages, sexual contact with infants, et cetera… it's all there waiting to be used.

I think we can shake the people out of the mind control. It's like working with alcoholics or cult members. They must be deprogrammed. Islam is fragile – that's the good news. Shake it at the base, strike at the foundations. the building will come down. The enemy we fight is not limited to al-Qaeda and other groups. We do need to hunt them down and incapacitate them. the true enemy is much larger and older. Al-Qaeda means 'the base'. They are the enemy. The larger enemy is another base – the foundation of their thought and the justification for their actions. That base is the Qur'an. It's the base of all Islamic thought, behavior and culture. It needs to be fought. World War Four is a war of culture and belief. We must identify it as such and face the enemy. The Qur'an, the *Sunnah*, the *Sira* and the *Ahadith* are the source of all we fight against. We must show them for what they are and destroy the will of the ummah to be dominated by them."

"Okay, but what about the other pillars?" Dafna asked.

"Knock down the second pillar, the five daily prayers by bringing up the points? Why would God need you to grovel in the dirt five times a day? Why would the motions of the prayer be more important than what's in your heart? Tell them it's a form of control – that they are robots in a cult that tells them to wipe their asses with an odd number of stones, that tells them how to have sex, that, in fact, tries to control their every move and therefore every thought. They are slaves, indeed, but to a man, Mohammed, not God. Why would a real god need such control? A man would, however. Plant the seed of doubt. Introduce it for the Qur'an as well. The Muslims believe the version of the Qur'an we have today has never changed since before time. We need to describe to them how the book came out of two hundred years of darkness – how it was kept on jawbones and scraps of this and that – how it has versions – how it isn't complete parts were left out either by people forgetting or domestic animals eating them. Show that it has versions. The findings in Yemen demonstrate this. Publicize it. The Qur'an has developed over time, like any other book of faith. This evidence is a direct contradiction to the statement that the Qur'an is the literal and unchanging word of Allah himself. This destroys its legitimacy.

The *ahadith*, the written reports of Mohammed's sayings and doings, are all based on hearsay. They were transmitted orally for about two hundred years before being written down. We need to show how this would not be accepted as proof or even legitimate in a court of law. The law of the *shar'ia* is based on inference and arbitrary application of some agreed-upon principles. We should show this as a weak foundation for any system. All over the Middle East you have the call to prayer blasting out over loudspeakers five times a day - we need Voice of America and the Voice of Reason blasting out from over radio speakers, and television speakers and through the internet and inside the bindings of printed material smuggled into Islamic countries. We need to ensure people to have access to alternative ideas. We need to fight The War of Information the same as we did against Communism – another dogma which had been bent on world wide domination.

We need to show them Islam is the problem not the solution. Show them Islam is a house of cards, is intellectually weak and is as fragile as an eggshell when a person can use logic and rationality without fear of reprisal. Many won't be convinced, but many will have doubts."

"Sounds good, but what government is going to do that?" Dafna said.

"If governments don't do it, private citizens can and should. The future is at stake. You know I'm not exaggerating. We have to fight Islam with Information and Culture and weaponry – with everything at our disposal. Which brings us to the third pillar – that of Fasting. My idea here is to starve them."

"Everyone needs oil," she replied.

"We may need oil, but they need everything else. They have 'desert' economies and I'm not talking about the climate. The culture can't produce much of anything. Hell, they don't even produce their own oil! The West had to come in and set up oil production for them. We still keep things running for the bastards. So starve them... make them fast for military goods and spare parts for their equipment and all kinds of valuable exports. Restrict them all. Starve them mentally as well – eliminate student visas so that they don't get a good education and then return home to use it against the rest of the world. Reduce them to scarcity for everything except sand, oil and violence. We need to isolate them economically and let them return to a seventh century way of life. After all – isn't that what they want?"

She laughed. "I don't think that's what they have in mind. What do you have in mind about *zakat*?"

"Well, by almsgiving that I mean 'financial warfare'," Ben said. "We need to continue to disrupt the financial networks terrorists rely on, we need to seize assets: real estate, bank accounts, other financial instruments, when we find participation in funding terrorism, whether it be by groups or individuals. Turn it around and use the assets to fund anti-terrorism work. Use their assets against them. We need to stop funding terrorism by giving money to the Palestinian Authority. We also need to stop giving aid to countries which implement *shar'ia* or which support the imposition of *shar'ia*. This includes Egypt, Pakistan, every one of them. Of course we need to put our efforts into reducing dependence on petroleum and need to become more efficient if we can't. We need to make sure people understand that their Sport Utility Vehicles support the Saudis' efforts to spread Islam around the world.

That brings us to the fifth pillar – the *hajj* to Mecca. All healthy Muslims are required to make a pilgrimage to Mecca if the can afford it financially. Islam has Mecca – the center of Earthly life for the *ummah*. It must exist and be ritually clean for the practice of two of these pillars - ritual prayer and the *Hajj*. This is a single point of failure, if I can borrow an Information Technology term. Mecca needs to be held hostage. This maybe the only thing real piece of leverage he can hold over stateless Muslim terrorist networks. If they know that we will damage their holy site and other sites should another 9/11 come about – then we may prevent an attack from happening. Instead of the MAD (Mutual Assured Destruction) policy from the Cold War we need a policy of CAD (Corresponding Assured Desecration.) Islam is the foundation of all of this violence and terrorism and Islam is the justification all the terrorists use. It's the glue that holds the disparate forces together. To strike a blow at a nameless, faceless network you must focus on what is concrete & fixed. Here's what I propose:

You make a list of sites sacred to the terrorists. Publish it with the promise of desecration in retaliation for another terrorist 9-11. When the attacks continue you send a wing of fighters and C-5 transport planes over the list of sites. The C-5s are filled with pig parts and pig blood and pig shit. You destroy anything attempting to shoot the C-5s down. Invite all kinds of media along for the ride. Announce it ahead of time. Live feeds to al-Jazeera. Then with the whole world watching and filming you let the pig shit rain down on the Mosques. Now Allah, being the omnipresent macho presence, as he claims over and over in his Qur'an, would never allow this desecration to happen. He'd intervene for something that drastic. When the world sees that Allah can't stop the pig shit from polluting the holy sites, the people will be shaken in their beliefs. Surely Allah will punish them... then the silence of the pigs. The horror. Cognizant Dissonance. Watch them try to explain that one. Do you think they will continue to pray five times a day in all seriousness when they know tons of pig shit keep raining down on Mecca and nothing happens to the 'evil doers'?

Then do it over and over. Every time they clean it up. No one has to die – but the beliefs are shaken. It is the beliefs that must die – not the people. For the worst of them, like bin Laden and Saddam, its better that they live, actually. They need to be paraded around, ridiculed. Beliefs must be killed, not the people.

Also - eliminate all travel visas from Islamic countries. Identify and deport all non-US citizens who are from countries in the

Middle East or whose governments implement *shar'ia* or support it in principle."

"You say that people don't need to be killed. But what do you do with the hard core – the ones which will never change or accept anything but Islam?" Dafna said, she seemed to be getting restless.

"Well that's the sixth pillar – Jihad. You know what we need to do there. Pick the right fights and show no mercy. People are going to have to die. No way around it. But the point in all of this is that the hot war is only a piece of the entire effort. It's not even the most important. Killing the belief pulls the weed out by the roots. But to do this and to get the word out, we have to live. Getting killed in some New Orleans restaurant won't get me there," Ben said, watching the waves lick the shoreline. He looked over at her. "We need to stay alive and get the word out. We need to live to fight the real battle. The battle of containment, like the cold war. The battle of ideas, of ideology, of ideas."

"You're right," she said, "killing them isn't the answer."

"This is how we have to defeat them," he said, pointing at his head, "If comes down to it I'll kill again. But I realize now that I must do my little part and have patience – that's all. The world isn't going to change according to my schedule."

She looked at him, then stared out to the flat line horizon, across the Pontchartrain once again.

"What are you thinking?" he asked.

She leaned over and whispered into his ear.

"I think you're right. You need to hand it over to the Federal agents," she finally answered.

"Hand me that laptop if you will. I need to contact someone." Then he got busy.

Chapter 66

Ben saw the smoke just as they entered the mouth of the Tchefuncte. He twisted the old throttle to its limit and had to settle for whatever extra horsepower the clanging two stroke could give him. It seemed another ten decibels louder but nothing more in speed. As they approached the boat house, Dafna shifted her attention back to Ben instead of the smoke, turning a darker solid and building into a thick column. She kept shooting him urgent looks from the bow.

Ben took the corner hard at the boathouse, bringing it down to half throttle. He didn't slow perceptibly as they sliced through the mirrored surface of the water in the slip, bumping against its rear with a thud. He killed the engine as they bounced off the bumpers. Dafna steadied herself, then leapt up onto the concrete floor, running over to the wire spool.

"It's gone!" she shouted.

Ben stopped mooring the pirogue. He pulled himself up with his good arm, carrying the laptop bag in the other. He ran over to her and saw that nothing remained on their makeshift table.

They ran out to the courtyard space. The rental car from the airport had its tires slashed. The passenger window was a web of broken glass with a dark void in the middle, billowing the thick, oil-colored smoke they'd seen coming up the river.

Then Ben heard her scream.

"Doctor!"

He turned to her, instinctively following the angle of her gaze to Remlevski's body, lying prone over the few begonias he had put around the base of the picket fence. One of his arms rested on his back in an unnatural position. As they drew closer, they could see the inanimate blankness in his face. His eyes, already taking on the drained hue of faded watercolors, looked up. His mouth was gaping wide. The base of his skull was missing. They had put a gun in his mouth as he knelt with his arms behind his back.

She looked at him, "We've got to get out of here. We don't have any time."

"How did they find us? So fast…"

"Some sort of tracking mechanism. Must be in the case," she said.

"How do we get out of here? The cops will be here any minute. We need to get out of here – figure out what we're gonna do next. " He took a few steps in the direction of the boathouse, scratched his head. "The pole barn."

He ran over to the equipment shed. Remlevski kept an old Chevy pickup in there.

He opened the door and felt for the keys.

Nothing.

He looked behind the sun visor and under the driver's side floor mats.

Nothing.

He began to get desperate. He shot a glance over the hood and saw Dafna going into the house, leaving the front door wide open. He went back to searching. He looked in the ash tray, the glove box and under some of the junk on the bench seat.

Nothing. They were screwed.

He looked over at the house again. He could see her backlit form running down the center hall. She held up the keys, dangling them in the shaded sunlight of the porch. She ran down the stairs in double time. Ben pushed his laptop to the passenger side, got out and fully opened the wire gate behind the truck as she blew past him and mounted the driver's side bench seat. She fired it up and cleared the shed.

"They've set the house to explode. Propane filled the house – it was hard breathing in there."

"If that's the case, leaving the door open won't save the place," Ben said.

She was driving erratically, like a like a Roman taxi driver in rush hour. Ben was flailing at everything, trying to keep himself from banging around the cab. She had it floored, fishtailing down the lane, still accelerating. The old truck surprised him. He blinked during the bright flash and then they both felt the concussion as all the propane filling the house exploded. From the rear-view mirror he saw the expanding black-orange fireball, rising above the trees as it curled in on itself. She hesitated at the asphalt, then took a right onto board-flat Highway 22. It would intersect with Route 1077 in less than two miles and from there they could get on Interstate 12 without going through Madisonville.

"We're going to need new plates, " she said between breaths, "they'll be looking for this if they're any good at all. When they could figure out what vehicles Remlevski had, they'll know our plate numbers," she said. The authorities would be able to find them in a hurry.

Suddenly he began to feel tired. The enormity of the situation began to sink in. They had the weapon again. He and Dafna had no clue what they looked like, what they were driving or which way they had gone. They had no way to track the terrorists. They had nothing to stop them if even if they could. The pistols were gone – either in the rubble of the house or in the hands of Remlevski's killers.

Ben's mind brooded on images of the old man, lying there dead. *He had probably saved my life and paid for it with his own,* Ben thought. They had killed one more of the good people of the world. *Another victory for Allah, the Bloodthirsty. In some ways, Remlevski was lucky,* he thought. His survivors would have enough of him to identify and bury. He hadn't been so lucky with Nick. He thought back to the time when he'd taken delivery of Nick's remains.

He stared at his brother's ring, twisting it on his finger. All these deaths but *stay tuned people, there's more to come!* They had the weapon. And they would use it as soon as they could. He and Dafna had no way to stop them now.

"I've got to get in contact with the FBI," Ben said. "It's in the hands of terrorists. I've got to tell Daniels everything I know. Now."

She gave him an empathetic glance for a few seconds.

"Do it then. This is your country and your people. You have to do everything you can."

He considered what she said.

"They're not just *my* people. They are just *people.* Okay? That should be enough. This tribalistic way of thinking has to stop. We're going to end up killing everyone in the name of 'Tribes'. The United States is going to pay a incalculable price for the sake of tribe: the Islamic Tribe. And the ironic thing about it is the fact that the United States is the Anti-Tribe. We have always been about inclusion, about leaving the historical baggage behind in the old country and getting on with the bright, shiny future. Sometimes that's been a bunch of empty words, sometimes we haven't lived up to I, but the trend in this country has always been to the positive. Towards inclusion. It's a juggernaut. But you know, come to think if it, that's one of the reasons we're the favorite target for the fourteen-hundred-year-old tribe known as the *Ummah* – the Muslim collective conscious. It's time the world gets past the old groups. It's the Twenty-first century, for God's sake! We can reach around the world instantly. Fed Ex brings every mailbox in the world within a three-day trip. The internet and phones make everyone even closer. But we still have these old tribal distinctions are they're going to be the end of us all, pronto, if we don't get our shit together here." He pounded the dashboard several times in frustration.

"You'll never get the Muslims to think in those terms. Their ethos rests on the separation of the *Ummah* from the Others. It's the

Bedouin gestalt made even more vicious in religion. Without it they're lost and they know that."

"Us vs. Them will bring Us all to The End," he said, "You can't rehabilitate psychopaths and sex offenders. Unfortunately for us, their prophet was both. Mohammed still has 1.2 billion people caught up in his narcissistic universe, fourteen centuries after his death. Until we can destroy that bubble and destroy the grip of fear he still has on them, we'll never be able to rest." To do this we have to stay alive and keep fighting. This will be a long term project, longer than the Cold War. The jihadi arm of Islam will never be able to defeat the United States and Western Civilization through force. But through misdirection, obfuscation – *taqiyya* is a word for it - they are fighting a second jihad. They intend to chip away at the civilization itself and use itself against itself. The fruits of Islamic culture are rotten and always have been. Did you ever wonder why they buy western weapons? Or fly western planes into western skyscrapers? It's because the combined GDP of the Islamic collective, if you exclude oil, is less then the output of Finland. Nokia can kick the Islamic world's ass. They are destitute and bankrupt if not for oil. That's why they won't win the hot wars. Rome wasn't built in a day and neither was it destroyed in a day, but when the people grew fat, spoiled and ignorant and lacked the will and the means to defend themselves, the Visigoths walked in and took over. Most great civilizations fall because of internal problems. That's why we need to stick around, Dafna. That's why you and I need to stay alive -- someone needs to get the word out. What we hear from the politicians and the media and all official sources so far amounts to 'Islam is the religion of Peace.' We need to make sure people have another set of voices to help guide them to real sources of history and information – to make sure that we're not ignorant about the War Against Worldwide Jihad - that's the war we're in – not the War Against Terrorism. The people of the United States need to realize that. Me dying for personal revenge won't help everyone at risk and it won't help my wife and kids either."

He noticed she looked tired; her complexion turning to a thin, gray gauze.

"Innovation in their religion is a sin – their prophet said it plainly," Dafna said.

"You don't change the belief – you kill it – not the tribe. That's the only way this thing can end. Disrupt, disrespect, discredit the system every way we can. But in the meantime we need to play it smart and stay alive for our kids. This will take a long time."

"Religious beliefs are entrenched in a person deeper than anything else. "

"Then it must be weakened, shown to be false, confronted at every turn, frustrated and denied until it dies inside the people. This is the only way to defeat it. Killing people will not kill the beliefs. But I do realize that many people will have to be killed to protect Western civilization until the beliefs die. Islam as a cult is only fourteen hundred years old. History shows that cults come and go. Pagan Roman religions lasted as long. It's a matter of time and persistence. But patience and focus are two difficult things for people in the United States. We need strength of purpose, perseverance and a long term view. Much longer planning than 'what am I going to do Friday night?' This will take a couple of generations at least."

"Then I'm afraid for you," she said.

Chapter 67

Agent Jack Daniels shifted nervously back and forth in his chair, but he didn't have to worry about anyone noticing at 7:45 pm. But that was the thing, you see, the thing that bothered him most. It was Monday, June 30th and in a few days from now it would be the 4th of July. He and Adams knew the attack would happen then. He looked at the message again: painted on the screen in big bold letters:

> Jack,
> Lost the suitcase. We think the original owners came and got it back. Not sure how. Must have tracked it somehow. Have no idea where they're going at this point. Will call you with more details at 20:00 Central time. Send me number where I can reach you.

Adams had paged him about a half hour ago, telling him to check his NetMail account. He looked at his watch: seven forty-five.

He didn't have much time. No way he would take the call in the office. They recorded every line, for all he knew. If not that, then the Chief, if he had really turned, would be monitoring his line specially. What to do?

With what he suspected, he should in no way get the Chief involved. The paranoia frayed his nerves. He looked around, checking the office for the twentieth time. He had no time to think about this. He had no time left at all.

He clipped out the email address, deleted the old note and started a new one in reply. He typed:

> Call the front desk of the Regency in Union Station.
> Don't know the number, but I'll be there at 20:00 CDT.

He clicked 'Send', deleted the copy and cleared out his NetMail trash can. That wouldn't stop anybody, really, but it made him feel a little better he left, while the FBI security system logged his exit out the door and recorded his image. He had less than fifteen minutes to get down to Union Station and take the call. That was the short-term plan. After that? He had no idea.

A Plague on Both Houses

O ye who believe, fight those of the disbelievers
who are near you, and let them find harshness in you,
and know that Allah is with those who keep their duty to him.
Allah – Qur'an 9:123

Chapter 68

All afternoon the water had fascinated him. He had never seen so much of it. True, he had been at sea for three months, but that was not useful. Not drinkable. Men couldn't drink sea water. But all of this, they could. So much of it. Everywhere he looked. Indeed, to retrieve the case they'd traveled on a bridge over at least 45 kilometers of it. All along the highway, as the sun set behind them. Water in abundance.

Abdullah let Abu do the driving while he rested and let his mind wander. He could afford to relax now, after all those days of tension. He looked up out of the window and admired the billowy clouds . The air itself was thick with water, creating a hazy, pink and blue sky, which colored all the bodies of water they traveled past along the way to the base and the other brothers. Shakha Da left him to his thoughts while crossed into the Florida panhandle along Highway 10.

Abdullah brooded on why Allah had been so generous in this land, with these people. Allah had given them so much water. And the land. Green. Flowering. Overflowing. Truly a garden as he had only imagined them before in his mind's eye. It looked like paradise on Earth. But why give all this to the undeserving? *Allah knows best,* after all. Wasn't that what all the wise men said? Who was he to question? Even the Harbinger of Things to Come amounted to nothing in God's estimation. *Allah Ta'alla knows best.* He had heard this all of his life. He had always used it, like a bucket of mud plaster, to patch the holes in his thoughts or in his faith. *Allah Ta'alla knows best.* Simple and true. No need to worry about it. Nothing to argue about. He submitted to His will long ago. It didn't matter why or how as long as Allah willed it. That one, simple phrase and his fear of hellfire had served him well. Now he and Abu and the other brothers were on the cusp of the last battle. They *would all fall martyrs in the Cause of Allah and because of this they would meet again in Paradise. The Qur'an guarantees this; the words of Allah himself, brought down to the Prophet, may peace and blessings be upon him, through the Angel Gabriel.* He was very close to his final days, when he would kill many of the *najis*, the *kuffar* and in doing so, would cleanse himself of all sins. God *is all-knowing and merciful for allowing him this*, he thought. He looked over at Abu Shakha Da and smiled, then returned to his daydreams, setting his gaze on the golden-green reflections of the trees on the mirrored surface of the water.

Chapter 69

Ben continued to work on his laptop as the rolled up Interstate 55 somewhere in Mississippi. Remlevski's Chevy had been a surprise. Despite all the noise and jostling suspension, the truck had been doing well as it made the gradual, but inexorable climb toward Saint Louis. Ben had been getting a strong, reliable signal so far along the highway. The connection hadn't failed once. His notes and his dog-eared copy of the Qur'an took up most of the space on the seat. He'd been trying to figure out more about the two groups: where they were, how many there were and any other important tidbits that might be in the NetMail messages he'd bookmarked. He'd lost his power cord somewhere and the battery had a little less than an hour's worth of juice remaining. He put it into 'hibernate' mode, disconnected the phone and dialed. *I'm racking up a huge roaming bill. I wonder if AirWarez will pay for it*, he mused.

The thought of the company brought to mind Eitan and Ofer. He had too many things to think about. Too many things to do. And only about an hour's electricity in the laptop battery.

He and Dafna needed to get the story straight. In the back of his mind he wondered if he would be free of all this. Ever, even best case he doubted it. Could he ever be free of it? Would they track him down after the dust settled? The FBI -- would they ever leave him alone after this? God knows who or what shadowy organizations knew about him out there – who knew what they might know or might try to do to him if they figured out who he'd been working with.

He worked through it all, in spite of all the sirens going off in his head. Things couldn't continue the way they were going. Someone had to stop them. He knew he was the only one who had all the pieces. He had to finish this.

He fired up his Java developer toolkit and hacked away furiously at the keyboard. He didn't tell Dafna a thing about what he was doing, but her curiosity registered in the looks she threw his way. He didn't have enough battery power or time left to explain. She didn't push it.

He modeled his new app on all the common smileys people attached to their messages in the new AOL Instant Messenger chat windows and other places. The little scene went like this: a smiley sat there and waited. Another smiley bounced up alongside the first, carrying an old, black bomb with its fuse burning. The second smiley shoved the bomb into the other one's mouth. The second smiley bounced out of sight. The first smiley sat there, same as before – oblivious. The first smiley blew into twenty bloody pieces, fly out of the box and out of view. Then the scene repeated.

He gave it a lopsided smile and closed it. He brought up another one, let it run and then checked his account. It worked. With that verified, he opened it up the code again and hardwired it to Jack Daniels' address. He recompiled it. *Almost ready - just have the note to do now*, he thought.

The phone started ringing. He had to switch mental gears. Someone from the insurance agency had the decency to return his call.

He sat there for a while, stewing. Dafna could hear the gears in his head turning, even over the industrial-strength road noise in the Chevy.

"What did they say?" she had to shout above the wind, coming in from the open windows and the 90-decibel G-chord resonating out of the tire treads.

"I called him at his house. My insurance agent. He told me 'you're screwed', basically. They won't honor the policy on the house. Some bastard in Madison, Wisconsin found a way to wiggle out of it."

"How?"

"According to them, the FBI classifies the destruction as 'an act of terrorism'. Westerling tells me the company updated their policies after 9/11 to state that acts of terrorism, like acts of God and acts of war, aren't covered by homeowner's policies. He says they've *clarified* that in all policies, both private and commercial. Told me to check the revisions they sent out in March. A lot of good insurance does you. The policies, and all their weasel clauses went up along with the rest of my house."

He looked out the window to watch the sign for Yazoo City, Mississippi rush past.

"What are you going to do?"

"I have no idea. Even with the inheritance, I can't afford to carry a mortgage for my current pile of rubble and take on another one for an new place-- at least not for equal value. I *am* screwed." He looked out the window again. "I need to call Daniels now. It's been over fifteen minutes. He should be at the Regency."

Dafna shook her head.

Ben dialed. The Regency desk clerk answered promptly on the second ring. Sure enough, Daniels was waiting at the front desk.

"Ben – good to hear you," he said, "the shoot-out is still all over the news. They killed…"

Ben missed the rest of it. "I'm having trouble hearing you. Wait a second," he said. He cranked his windows up and Dafna followed his lead. The air conditioning wasn't working and immediately the cab air closed in on them. Ben noticed it, but it didn't put him into phobia mode like it would have less than a week ago.

"What does Chief know about this?"

"Who knows? He knows what I know up to now."

"You've got to work around him. Can you get help from outside your office? Working with Chief would be a mistake for obvious reasons."

"That could mean the end of my career – you don't seem to understand how things work in the machine," Daniels said.

"We're talking about something more important than office politics, believe it or not. Do you really want to go through proper channels and be a day late on this? We have three days. If we don't figure this out in time the terrorists set it off. And that will end a lot of careers. And lives. You have an idea just how bad this will get, right? They're going to release a bio-weapon. Once it's out of the can it will be like a wild fire – uncontrollable. Don't let your personal career path determine the fate of a nation. We're talking about a million lives here. You and I are responsible now. We know."

Daniels didn't say anything.

"Did you hear me? I said 'We're responsible now.'"

"Yeah, I hear you - you sound like my father." Daniels paused again. "Look - the whole agency is in an uproar. They want to know why Chief asked for surveillance on the restaurant. They killed one of them while they were checking the place out."

"That's number one of about a half a million if you and I don't get it this done. Sacrifice something here. I have – my house is gone. Insurance won't cover it because your agency classifies it as 'an act of terrorism.' But what would that matter anyway if this weapon gets released?"

"Allright; let's get the party started then, I'm pretty sure I can get what I need if I have some kind of proof. "

"Listen: We have photos of the suitcase and its contents. I'm sending you a package – to your NetMail account. I've sent a note in the cipher to both NetMail accounts – the one for the group that destroyed my house and the other group. I'll forward copies. When they open the notes, you'll be paged with the DHCP IP addresses they're using and also the mac address of each machine that accesses the notes. When you get the pages, you're going to have to get a team to trace them."

"Allright. I should be able to do that," Agent Daniels said.

"Also, I sent the note posing as ArAzahad33 -- the one the Chicago group used. I told both the California group and the weapon courier, the one using ArRad13 that I was separated from everyone in New Orleans and that I want to hook up with their group to finish this off. I asked for a time and place. Said I was on my way, like I knew the city. When we get an answer you need to have people ready to take them out? Understand? Could be anywhere in the country, but my guess would be one group's in the Anaheim group will take out L.A. and the other group is going to Manhattan. Makes sense, right? The two largest cities in the U.S."

"I'll call you back later," Daniels said. He didn't sound enthusiastic anymore. He sounded more like he had the day Ben walked into the Market Street office unannounced.

He had been driving for a hours time now and didn't like the way she kept looking worse. The color had drained out of her and she had a fever. While they had stopped in Memphis to switch drivers he'd bought some Over The Counter medicine in a local Walgreen's along the service road. It didn't help at all. The fever still consumed her, the heat producing a thick sheen which coated her face and neck and which the road wind couldn't evaporate fast enough to wipe away.

They had crossed into Missouri a while back and she had lain down across the bench seat. Her skin began to take on the texture and color of driftwood and she started coughing regularly. Her head, resting on his lap, became a furnace and he began to sweat almost as bad as her because of it.

She had something bad. He had no idea what it was, but knew it where it had come from. *Why did she have it and he didn't?* Then it dawned on him. Steadying the wheel with his bum hand, he reached into his pocket and pulled out the prescription bottle Dr. Remlevski had given him for the gunshot wound.

"Take this," he said putting one of the 100mg Ciproflaxin pills into her mouth. She didn't say anything, swallowing it between coughs, which had already gotten juicy by then. She had fluid in her lungs.

"Ben, I have to tell you something," she said, so low the sounds of the highway drowned it out. He knew she said something by the way she moved her head. He rolled up the window briefly so he could hear her.

"Ben, I have a confession."

His winced involuntarily at the words. *What else?*

"I worked against you back in New Orleans. At Remlevski's. While you were asleep. I need to tell you now, before I can't any longer. I feel like I'm going to die."

"You're not going to die," he stated.

"I told the doctor to put a device in your wound. It's a tracking device and a microphone. They will be able to turn it on and off to listen to you when you come into range."

"What?"

"I'm sorry, Ben."

Then she was out.

He drove on with a head full of thoughts, all trying to push themselves to the front of the line. *He would never be able to get himself out of this. Ever. And Daniels hasn't called back. Time was running out. Even he got the help he needed -- all the help in the world – it would not be enough. They wouldn't be able to find the bastards in time.*

A Plague on Both Houses

Allah permits you to shut them in separate rooms
and to beat them, but not severely.
If they abstain [from providing sex],
they have the right to food and clothing.
Treat women well for they are like domestic animals
and they possess nothing themselves.
Allah has made the enjoyment of their bodies lawful in his Qur'an.
Mohammed – Hadith Tabari IX 113

Chapter 70

They entered the apartment with great fanfare. The brothers shouted, throwing their arms up in joyous celebration. The plan was coming together no matter what the Infidels did. God was on their side and the vision of Abdullah, clutching the suitcase in the doorway, was the clear proof.

After a few minutes of hugging and lively chatter, Abdullah asked for an appraisal. The bright young cell leader laid it all out for him. They had all just come together that day. They had been making the final preparations according to plan. They just had to make it through that day and the next.

"Everything is going according to the original plan?" Abdullah asked.

"Yes, our three fellows here in the apartment all still have the jobs. They've done excellent work for the last year and a half. Sami has even been promoted to a foreman of sorts." Sami smiled.

One of the brothers brought a tray of hummus into the room and the leader gestured for Abdullah to take a seat on the floor as they made a closed circle around the coffee table.

"Yes, and showing up every day taking orders from the Jews and Cross worshippers was more sacrifice than you'll know. I worked like a dog under them," he said, "It was humiliating.

"But you kept it up; you went to work every day and now you have the access we need," the leader said. He dipped his bread into bowl and scooped some of the humus into the fold.

"All three of us do, yes. We all have access to their staging area. We have their trust," Sami reported, proud of his accomplishment.

"Truly excellent. This is even better than what we had planned for," Abdullah said, dipping his bread into the selections on the platter, resting on the coffee table. It was good food. Now that he felt safe, he relaxed and realized his hunger. He ate quickly, speaking between dips.

"Which one of you has been trained on handling the biological agent?"

"I have," one of them said. His cropped hair and lack of a beard made him look like a boy. By the look of him, he wasn't far removed. "I have the room back there set up for Biohazard Level 3 conditions," he added, motioning with his head.

After the meal, Abdullah fired up a laptop and connected to the Internet. He wanted to give things one last look before going silent. He accessed the account and saw two new messages. One of them was from al-Warraq, dated late last evening. Abdullah paused.

It couldn't be.

He thought back to the meeting in New Orleans, replaying the events in his mind. He saw al-Warraq lying by the kitchen door, the back of his head missing.

Maybe he had been wrong.

It had looked like al-Warraq and in the heat of battle he had mistaken someone else for al-Warraq. Perhaps it had been one of the other brothers martyred in the gun battle. If that were true, and if he had the other canisters al-Warraq might need help to set them off. The codes? What if he had the other set of canisters?

Abdullah decided to open the note. It had the cipher, just as it should. It also had a GIF file that showed a Muslim smiley bombing an infidel smiley. He watched it to see what it did once, then disconnected from the connection, but kept the note on the screen.

"Abu," he shouted, craning his neck towards the din of the television set, "Come here, I need you." Shakha Da came in wearing a happy expression. All of the brothers were excited. Shakha Da raised his eyebrows quizzically and smiled.

"Get the holy Qur'an I've been using. You know where I keep it, yes?"

Shakha Da didn't say anything. Abdullah found paper and pencil in the interim and began to decode the numbers on the screen as soon as Abu Shakha Da brought him The Book, carrying it carefully in the right hand, wrapped in a cloth.

"Isn't that sacrilegious, I mean, using the Noble Qur'an itself as a coding tool? Those are the words of Allah Himself," he asked.

"These are English words in Roman characters. The recitation – al Qur'an - was given to the Prophet, may peace and blessings be upon him, in pure Arabic by the angel Gabriel and God Himself. *Arabic*, Abu. This language is not good enough nor is it sophisticated enough to carry the full meaning of Allah's commands. And we are not using complete *ayats* entirely. We've taken only words from here and there. The Infidels would not expect us to do this. We do it to circumvent their rigid thinking as well. The Crusaders and blood-sucking Jews would never suspect it. They are too limited to see this, in spite of all their attempts at clever deceit. That's why we decided on it."

"I still don't like it. It doesn't seem right," Shakha Da said.

"English words are not the words of Allah. They are the words of *al-najurum* a dirty people."

"Then let us use their words against them, as we use their tools and money and everything else then. Words are powerful weapons."

"They will be condemned by the same words on Thursday we will deliver Allah's retribution and then again on the Last Day, when they will be judged and used as fuel for Hellfire," Abdullah said, brightly.

It took a little while to decipher the message. Abdullah read it aloud to himself when he had all the words on paper:

> Brothers
>
> I am separated from our other group. I am coming to join up with you, since it will take too long to find them. Tell me where to meet. Tell me in numbers I have a GPS - I can be there tomorrow by midday. Don't abandon me – I wish to die in Allah's service. .

"Do you know the one named al-Warraq? The one based in Chicago?"

"I know of him," said Abu Shakha Da. "But I am from the California group – we never saw them or communicated with the other cell, for that matter. We only dealt with you. The security protocol, you know..."

Abdullah stared at the note. He thought about the body in the restaurant – turning it over in his dark mind's eye. al-Warraq died in the restaurant. He was pretty sure of that. He couldn't take a chance. The note must be treated as a fake, with serious implications. He must assume the enemy knew about the coding system after all. Now they were trying to pose as one of the brothers, to find them all before it was too late. And he had opened it – in an unprotected location. He had opened the castle gates in a sense. They would be able to pinpoint his location if they had enough power to do so. Abdullah had to assume the worst.

He knew what must be done. He closed the laptop and walked out into the main room of the apartment. The four of them were watching pornography tapes. One of them was drinking wine out of a green bottle.

This infuriated Abdullah.

"Have you taken leave of your senses brothers? We've come this far, we're this close and you're polluting everything. Look at that filth!" He screamed, pointing a bony finger at the screen.

"Abdullah – brother - calm down," the cell leader said, "Relax. Have you forgotten that martyrs killed in Jihad are guaranteed a place in paradise? It doesn't matter what we do in our final hours. The prophet, may peace and blessings be upon him, said this many times. The Qur'an validates it. We are guaranteed." he smiled the smug smile of one who has it all figured out. *The idiot.*

"What if something happens? What if we don't succeed in the operation? Then you have consigned yourself to taste hellfire!"

They straightened up at this. The cell leader asked, "What do you mean by that?"

The sounds of moaning women and forbidden music coming wafted out from the television, filling the room with their stench.

"Turn that filth off," Abdullah said.

They turned it off.

"What do you mean 'if we don't succeed in the operation'?" the cell leader repeated.

"I just checked the NetMail account al-Warraq – the one working with you out of Chicago and who coordinated your cell – used to communicate with me."

"So what?"

"He sent a note late last evening."

"And?"

"He shouldn't have been able to - I saw him on the floor of the restaurant with a big hole in the back of his head."

Involuntarily they rose from the sofa as if pulled by a puppet master's string.

At this point two more of the Florida brothers came through the front door. They had a couple of western women in tow. Both were dressed in shiny, colorful clothing. The hem of their dresses did not conceal even the majority of their thighs. Their hair, in shades of light brown and gold, was in full view and they appeared to be drunk, like the brothers they came in with.

Abdullah looked at them, mouth agape. The bar hoppers looked at him, surprised, then looked at the carpet, ashamed.

"We have been compromised three times now, " Abdullah said. *Someone would have to be punished for this.*

The women looked Abdullah up and down, amused. "Who are you?" she asked while chewing gum, "Hey baby, what's going on? I thought we were going to party." Her date didn't answer.

Abdullah did.

"What's your name *sharmoota*?" [whore]

She was annoyed. She looked at him with a curled lip, as if she were trying to avoid smelling someone's fart. "I'm Rochelle, not that it's any of your business, sheik."

Abdullah laughed at her.

"Oh you'll get your party, Rochelle," he said, still laughing, " you'll party with all of us... Brothers! Collect what we need." He looked around, growing impatient exponentially at the lack of reaction. He pulled out the Glock Pepito had given him on the boat and stroking its length on the cream-white smoothness of Rochelle's breastbone he screamed in Arabic," Let's go, now! you deaf ones? Have you taken leave of your senses? We will be staying at this whore's house for the last days. Let's go! Any delay places us in the hands of the unbelievers and therefore in the care of the *Shaytan* himself. Do you wish to remain in the hands of *Shaitan*?"

He struck the dirty bitch on the forehead to emphasize his point.

She thudded against the floor, writhing and bleeding.

They started moving after that.

War

Chapter 71

He didn't know the floor number, but he knew the isolation chamber was underground. They had given him an electronically-sealed 15 by 20 rectangle to pace in. The leaden silence was more oppressive than any set of steel bars could have been. As he paced around the circuit, he realized the emotions he cycled through – the frustration, the anger, the anxiety over Dafna's condition, the worry over his house, his life and his family – all these feelings - weren't accompanied one of the old familiar ones. He felt no panic creeping up behind it all to put a knot in his stomach and cause his heart and the base of his head to pound like it used to in situations like this. Where was it? He lingered on the idea for awhile, amusing himself with it. He should be freaking by now, pounding at the door and pushing the call button to try to talk them into letting him out. At the very least he would sweat himself out of the panic. But the old familiar feeling escaped him. It even embarrassed him to think about it. His father had died right there next to him and he couldn't do anything about it. They had been trapped in a box. Up until that moment he had carried a model of that box around inside his head, letting it limit him. The incident happened years ago, when he had been equipped with the tools of a child. He had carried the box around ever since, never dealing with it squarely. The realization embarrassed him now. He had dwelt on little things all this time. Trivia. Fleeting moments in decades past. He had allowed it all to set the rules – he had allowed it to set the limits on him for far too long. Aside from his father's death he had really had a pretty easy life. If you looked at it globally, that is. The world had real evil in it and he hadn't been up against that in the past. He had never known the real threats that dictators and disease and death threats and demagogues created for all the other young boys around the world. And some of them had lost their fathers, too.

It happened all the time – every day. He had always been safe and his problems, in the scheme of things, had always been small. Really. That is - compared to other young men out had to face. He had been spared any real evil in this world up to that day, 9/11/01, when his brother Nick died in the South Tower. Now he knew True Evil. He had stared it in the face.

He had no idea what to do next. He was in unknown territory; even the air pressure felt strangely negative to him. He dismissed that as a physical feature of the isolation room he was in.

The weird popping in his ears came from the air filtration system. After all, they had him in a fish bowl, watching him for signs of Death. So far, he had been strangely spared. So far, so good.

He tried to look through the slats of the vertical blinds, hung on the outsides of the band of picture windows running along the front side of his chamber. He couldn't see anything outside. Funny – not a 'problem' He supposed his new window on the world had everything to do with freeing himself and Dafna from the hooks in the meat locker. Dafna…

Dafna. He looked at the round, institutionally black-and-white dial on the wall clock and watched the needle-thin, red second hand jerk its way toward the '12'. The docs had put him in isolation as soon as they had checked her out and heard his story. Since about an hour out of Saint Louis she'd been in dire straits. She started coughing up the bloody sputum by that point. He had picked Saint Louis University Hospital because he recalled hearing about their research into biological pathogens. Or he'd read it in the paper. That or fact that it was the first hospital he'd passed on the Interstate as he came into town. But he'd chosen well, after all, he'd saved her in time. They had known what to do right away. Evidently they had a sort of bioweapons readiness program or something to that effect. It had been a madhouse at first, up in the Emergency Room, but once they put him in the Fishbowl they hadn't come back to see him since. They left him in the silence to deal with the trauma. He did better this time, and used the adult toolbox to work on himself. He would have to wait, but it didn't bother him. She was in good hands. They had gotten back in time.

About an hour later, a youngish, thin doctor type finally took a peek at him. The point of his slightly crooked beak parted two of the vertical slats and he peered in, birdlike. He carried a clipboard and made some scribbles. Wouldn't be a surgeon after the residency, though. His hand shook as badly as if he'd just downed a full-sized latte from Starbucks as he scribbled some more notes. Ben thought his hand jerked almost as bad as that second hand on the clock. He played at making a few notations, glancing at Ben and different points in the room occasionally. *Looking around for what*, Ben didn't know. *Signs,* he supposed. *Ominous signs. Maybe pools of contagious blood and vomit? Some other manifestation of God's wrath? Who knows?*

The doc-in-training reached for the intercom, mounted in the drywall between the last of the windows and the magnetically-locked door.

"Adams. Ben Adams, correct?"

Ben pressed hard on the button -- a white, plastic square under the speaker grille.

"Yes."

He made more notations on the chart than a 'yes' was worth, looked up at him fleetingly, then reached for the button again.

"How are you doing? How do you feel?" he asked, not showing much concern for the answer.

"I'm fine. When are you going to let me out of here?"

He smiled, "Not for a while, sir. Your friend is very ill."

"Do you know what she has? Is she going to be okay? How is she doing?"

"She has a form of *Yersina Pestis* - Pneumonic Plague," he sniffed a bit, repeating, "pneumonic - that means - 'lung based'. After you told the attending ER physicians she had potential exposure to a biological agent, the team narrowed the list of pathogens considerably." He looked up from his notes again. "Thanks for doing that. You saved us a lot of valuable time. And starting her on the Ciprofloxacin *may* end up saving her life. "

Ben nodded. Then: "What do you mean – *may*?"

"Look," he said, "Plague has three natural forms: bubonic, septicemic and what she has – pneumonic. The bubonic form has a mortality rate of fifty to sixty percent if untreated. In the middle ages, Plague pandemics killed 13 million in China and up to 30 million in Europe. That eliminated a third of the population."

"The Black Death…"

"It was called the Black Death because of the darkened swellings of the lymph nodes, buboes if you will. Between 1347 and 1351, at least twenty-five million people died in Europe. The Black Death is excruciating. They died from a disease which can make human lymph nodes in the groin and other places swell to the size of apples before they finally burst."

Ben looked like he was going to be sick.

The resident continued, "And the bubonic form is the least virulent. I suppose you know this already, but your friend has something far worse." He blinked several times and swallowed, staring at Ben. He had ran out of notes to make.

"What's the mortality rate for lung-borne plague?"

"If untreated, natural strains approach 100%."

Ben looked at him. He seemed to be waiting for the question. Ben obliged, "but she has something worse? Worse than that?"

"We're only guessing at this point. A weaponized strain of air-borne plague bacteria will be multi-drug resistant most likely. It's too early to tell. But she's in good hands. They made an immediate diagnosis. They've got her on a regime of serious antibiotics," he said, adding, "if that doesn't work, nothing will."

He had no bedside manner. No wonder he was checking things off on a chart in the sub-basement of the hospital. *A real empathetic one, the bastard.*

Ben kept it going, nonetheless.

"It can't be all that bad. Look at me. I don't have it. Why is that? I think it's because I was taking the Cipro for my wounds a good day before we were exposed. A hundred milligrams twice a day. I'm free of it."

"We think it's too early to say definitively. We'll have to keep you here until we're sure. What we're up against. We can't allow this thing to get out into the wild."

"How long do you think you're going to keep me here?"

"Forty-eight hours. At the minimum. I'd be surprised if you get out even then."

"Look, I've got tickets to Disney World in two days. Non-refundable. Not to mention a ton of stuff to do... I have urgent business to take care of understand? I can't really go into the details, but it's important. I don't feel sick at all. Look at me." he gestured, arms opened wide, "there's nothing wrong with me."

The doc chuckled at this.

"I don't make the decisions around here, Sir," he said, shaking his head. He suppressed a laugh, looking down the hallway. "A technician will be coming around to check up on you, along with one of the doctors. They're going to enter the chamber to collect some data and check your vital signs and hook you up to the monitors. We'll need to take some samples for testing as well."

"I'm sure they'll put you the same regimen."

"They gave me something when the put me in here," Ben said.

"They'll probably put you on a drip. If you're okay in two days we should be able to let you out of isolation."

"Let me talk to Dafna," he said.

"Your friend? Sorry, sir, I'm afraid she's incapacitated. She's in and out. The fever comes on strong," he stopped himself, "sorry. I didn't mean to alarm you. Don't worry. She's stable. They've put her under Intensive Care. They're taking very good care of her."

"Can I use the phone? Let me call her then?" he asked jutting his thumb back at the wall phone next to the hospital bed.

"I don't think she can talk to you now. Ask the other guys when they come down to see you, okay? It won't be long now?"

Ben walked over to the edge of the bed and sat for the first time.

The doctor and the technician had been with him about ten minutes when he mentioned the x-rays. They had done a work up of his shoulder and hand when he had first come in, carrying Dafna like a dying bride through the parting doors and into the Emergency Room.

"What did you find in my shoulder?" Ben asked. The doc was still looking him over with what seemed like genuine curiosity.

"Would you like to see the images?" the new one said.

This doc was strangely chipper about everything. It seemed the more morbid and virulent the subject the more upbeat he got. *This one would make a good pathologist but a bad mortician -- too enthusiastic*, Ben thought.

The doctor the plastic squares from the spring on the clipboard and held the plastic up, over the bed, under the nearest florescent rectangle illuminating the room. Ben could see what looked like a silhouette of a pocket watch inside the outline of his body. "Looks like a pacemaker," he said, "but whoever put it in should be sued for malpractice. They didn't hook it up to your heart properly." He made tsk, tsk sounds with pursed lips. "Terrible."

"Give me a piece of paper and something to write with," Ben said.

The technician flipped a piece of chart paper over and handed him a pencil.

Ben wrote:

Take it out of me.

He held it up so they both could see. They stopped what they were doing and straightened up for a second.

"Take it ….."

"SHHHHHHHH" Ben sounded out. He wrote again:

That's not a pacemaker. My life is in danger.

The attending doc humored him and took his turn:

Are you joking? What are you talking about? What is it? Why are we writing all of this down?

Ben replied:

It's a bug – spy bug. And a tracking device.

Could be a bomb to take my head off too. Don't know.

Got to get it out ASAP.

then:

You r crazy. No way.

Ben thought for a moment. He reached for his wallet and pulled out a card. Then he wrote:

Call Jack Daniels – FBI @ 314-555-1212 cell phone <u>only</u>. He'll corroborate.

National security.

Doc:

It's 3:30 am

Ben:

Do it now. ASAP

He woke up when he heard the blinds rattle against the window. He blinked rapidly, trying to get his eyes lubricated enough to focus them. When he did, he could see Daniels looking in at him, still rapping against the glass.

He raised himself slowly, then swung his legs out bedside and planted them on the tiles. He walked with a little difficulty to the window. The last four days had taken its toll. He winced when his upper body moved, despite the painkillers they'd given him after they cut it out of him. At the time he'd insisted it be done with a local. He wanted to be aware of what they might say. He didn't want them to give it away, after all. He didn't want Eitan and company to know that *he knew.* He hoped that it worked, but the old man always preached Murphy's Law and would be looking for something like that.

Contingencies.

Funny how they hadn't had much of a Plan B when it went down at the Crescent. Killing everyone in sight and blowing the place up were never really much of a 'Plan B'.

He looked at Daniels while he tried to mouth something unintelligible through the glass. Ben pressed the square button on the intercom once again.

"How you doin'?" Ben said. He pointed at the speaker, prompting him. He gave the 'okay' sign, but put his finger up against his lips as a warning."I wouldn't know. No mirrors in here. If I look as bad as I feel …How's Dafna?"

"I don't know. They didn't tell me much on the way down here."

"They don't tell me anything at all, so consider yourself lucky," Ben said, adding, "the last thing the doc told me was they'd have to keep me for two days minimum. To watch for signs." He over his shoulder at the clock. "I've got forty-three hours to go."

Daniels didn't press the button this time. He stood on the other side of the barrier for a moment with a empathetic look on his face. Ben walked back to his bedside, picking up the yellow legal pad and a black felt tip marker. He returned to his place at the glass.

Get something to write on. Don't say

anything – they can hear.

"You want me to get some news about Dafna?"

"Yes."

"Okay, I'll be back in a few minutes, just wait."

"It's not like I have a choice, now do I?" Ben replied.

Daniels stomped off briskly toward the light spilling down the broad, dun-colored terrazzo staircase at the end of the hallway. Dafna's room was next to it, on the left. He pressed his cheek against the glass to get the angle he needed. He could just barely see Daniels standing at the end of the hall in front of Dafna's windows. He paused for a few moments, watching the drama in her fish bowl. Then he turned and walking more deliberately, returned his spot in front of Ben's window. He wrote while he spoke.

"She doesn't look good," he said, at the same time holding up a piece of paper with these words:

What about the suitcase?

"Did anyone upstairs give you a prognosis? What are they doing about it?" Ben said, scribbling this message as he spoke:

Two of them – terrorists have one – told Dafna.

Ours - ??? no clue. Has FBI traced email? Anything?

"I don't know what to think. They said she's stabilized, but they're not saying more than that - if you read between the lines I think they're worried." Daniels said. He held up:

Got the IPs. Southern California. Somewhere on Van Nuys Blvd – Anaheim area. We're narrowing it down.

"Did anyone upstairs give you a prognosis? What are they doing about it?" Ben asked, scribbling as he spoke.

Ben wrote: What about the other account?

" I don't know what to think. They said she's stabilized, but they're not saying more than that - if you read between the lines I think they're worried," Daniels said.

Daniels wrote: don't know.

"How does she look? Can you see into her room?" Ben asked.

Ben wrote: Look ... when I leave I'm out of here. I'm done.

Agent Daniels hesitated for a moment, thinking about the implications of 'I'm out of here'. Then he shifted back to the conversation as his marker squeaked against the paper. He was pressing too hard. He spoke: "They've got her in isolation - intensive care. She has windows and blinds just like this room, but I can't see much of anything. I looked in, but they have a curtain drawn."

Daniels gave Ben the evil eye. He held up:

What?! BullSHIt!

gesticulating at the paper with a rigid pointer finger.

Ben spoke, unfazed by the display, said, "What does that mean? Intensive Care?"

He wrote: Got a life to live.

"Someone is by her side pretty much all the time as far as I can see. She's got the best of care."

Daniels: We <u>need</u> you. Not over yet!

Ben didn't say anything. Instead he scribbled and held up:

So does my family. More than you do. You know everything I do – <u>use</u> it!!!

Jack wrote back:

Not just about the terrorists - spies in US. Help us.

Ben: Not my problem.

Daniels: Is your problem!! Bioweapon makes no one safe? Remember?

Ben: Not my problem. Israelis won't kill us - don't worry re: them. Find the other case before they use it. July 4th. L.A. & ??? New York again? WMD = 5 million dead ! Worry re: that – not me.

Neither of them said a word. They kept sending notes back and forth.

Daniels: Need to get both weapons & get Mossad holding case. worked 2 yrs on this. got them if they r holding case during bust.

Breaking the silence, Daniels said, "how do you feel?"

"I don't think I'm getting any worse. The attending physician says I have to stay in here a minimum of forty-eight hours. Can't talk them into anything less. She's got a virulent form of the pneumonic plague. They aren't taking any chances with me," Ben said.

Ben wrote: get them how?

Daniels : Wear a wire.

Then he said, "To be honest, I'm glad they're not. "

Ben: No wire – boss –Eitan – checks for it.

A look of recognition ran across his face. He wrote another line:

wait – use their stuff

"Yeah," Daniels replied.

What stuff?

Ben: A Sharpie like you has camera phone, right?

Daniels whipped his phone out from its cradle in his inner lapel pocket. He flipped it open to show the lens.

Ben: take a picture of this.

He lifted hospital night gown and reached under.

"Uuuuuggh," Daniels sounded involuntarily.

Ben tugged at his side. He pulled at a wad a rags held against his side by strips of medical tape. Carefully and slowly, be unbundled the mess. He held the thing up against the glass. Agent Daniels fired off some snapshots, taking a new picture each time Ben changed the angle of view.

what you think? Hope glare isn't bad. Find the frequency, Kenneth.. you got it?

Daniels held up:

?

Ben: use his own stuff against him. Israeli made? probably

Daniels: ok – got it. I find out – come back – we make a plan

"Anyway - I should be going," Daniels said. He faked a yawn, adding, "see you later, my friend. I'll check back in with you soon."

"Good thanks. I'll see you then, man. Take care," Ben said.

He sat down on the edge of the bed and took his time, carefully putting the device back against his skin. He sealed it up under a mass of rags and waited.

A Plague on Both Houses

Allah's Apostle said, "O women!
Give alms, as I have seen that
the majority of the dwellers of hell-fire were you women...
I have not seen anyone more deficient in intelligence and religion than you.
Mohammed – Hadith Sahih Bukari:V1N301

Chapter 72

Lexie and Rochelle lived in a twelve unit plywood dump a quarter of a mile off the main road behind the local Wal-Mart. The complex wasn't that old but its condition verged on neglect. None of this mattered to Abdullah. It suited him well as a matter of fact. It stood at an intersection and the two streets had unobstructed lines of sight. They would be anonymous here, since a mix of all types of people came and went and no one seemed to care. It was a transitory neighborhood, filled with migrants and all kinds of people who didn't know their neighbors and couldn't care less about it. The one thing that bothered Abdullah was the location of the whores' apartment. They stayed in the one directly in the middle of the building. It was in the middle floor, sharing walls with tenants above, below and to both sides. The thin walls could be a problem, but Abdullah would make sure they kept their guard up and their noise down for the few remaining hours.

Back at the old apartment, the brothers had packed up everything but the T.V. at the old place in a matter of an hour at the old apartment. They had stayed for evening prayers, then watched a rerun of some hopelessly shallow and corrupt Western comedy while some of the brothers took turns with the women. Abdullah and the one who had brought the women back to the apartment about ownership. The brother had insisted that the example of the Prophet, may peace an the blessings of Allah be upon him, as well as the examples from the rightly-guided companions, may the blessings of Allah be upon them, showed the he alone should have the women to himself. After all, he argued, it was by his guile that they had been claimed as spoils of war. At this point, despite the lack of blood, they were in a state of war and in the middle of an assault on the *Dar al-Harb* the House of War. The women belonged to him.

Abdullah, being the acknowledged leader, counter-argued that the war hadn't truly begun, so the women weren't his exclusive property, backing his position up with examples from the Sunnah and from the *Shar'ia* as well as the rulings of the various imams he could think of which supported his side of things.

After bickering back and forth for about twenty minutes they reached the conclusion that it didn't matter anyway, since the women would be killed when they left the apartment for the final time.

So Lexie ended up leaning over the bathroom sink, her hands tied to the p-trap beneath it while the brothers satisfied themselves from behind. They made her stand since they needed her room for the preparations. The brother trained in those matters was already taking steps to convert the room into a makeshift Level 3 Biohazard lab.

Meanwhile, Rochelle had the luxury of being tied to her own bed as they raped her.

Abdullah had one of the first rounds with Lexie and was still bringing up his underwear and trousers when the Weapons Technician interrupted him. He turned away modestly as he should, since no man should look at the private parts of another according to law. The technician, a thin, small man with bloodshot eyes, stood impatiently at the door. When Abdullah was decent he continued.

"Brother this place is not acceptable for our purposes. We need to make a decision, right now," he said.

Abdullah turned to look at him. He wasn't much of a man, he thought, this bio-technician. His mother could probably grow a thicker beard.

Abdullah asked him for an explanation and looked down his nose at him.

"The work requires better facilities than I will be able to put together in the present situation. We need to have level 3 biohazard conditions while I unload the canisters and also while I load the delivery devices. In these closed conditions and with the materials at hand I won't be able to bring us to that level of safety."

Abdullah nodded as he spoke, staring at a point on the wall. He pretended to consider the difficulty of the situation, then said, "Do the best you can with what you have; *inshallah*, God willing, our plan will be successful. It's in Allah's hands and Allah knows best."

The weapons man looked up at him with slight disapproval. "You don't understand. We *need* to protect *ourselves*. We have a highly virulent pathological agent in there," sweeping his arm backward for effect, "If we don't take the necessary precautions we could all end up dead before we have a chance to deliver the weapon. I'm not sure how fast it works."

"Seal the door then." Abdullah offered.

"That won't work. If I go in and out we will all be exposed regardless. If we vent the room to the outside we could spread the contagion before our plan goes into effect. They have well-trained epidemiologists in this country. Consider that. If the weapon begins to infect the neighbors too soon it will give away our location. Local police or federal agents will knock on the door before we're ready. Again we lose."

Abdullah brushed past him, going out to the kitchen. He walked through the main room, which looked like a $25-a-night motel in Fort Lauderdale during Spring Break; sleeping bags and blankets were strewn everywhere; the coffee table was heaped with half-empty bowls, overflowing ash trays, magazines and assorted trash; the couch and chair loaded with unwashed and disheveled young men, getting greasier by the minute in the stifle of the closed-up apartment. Abdullah walked past it all, stepping over the newspaper and empty cans of Coca-Cola and crunching the stray pop corn kernels under his bare feet. He entered the kitchen, digging around in his laptop bag while the technician, who had followed him, kept complaining.

"We should have stayed at our apartment. The old apartment was better. I had the room set up right, with the HEPA filters. We had it isolated and would have had no problems then. You made a mistake bringing us here. It's not too late, let's go back and get the room set up properly."

"We couldn't stay – I accessed the NetMail account and gave away our position. It put us all at great risk."

"We're at risk here," the technician said, "I can't guarantee that we won't all be exposed even if I can get it to Level Two conditions."

Abdullah turned to face him, holding his pistol once again.

"We've all agreed to a martyrdom operation. What did you expect in the end?"

"We have two ways of ensuring safety for the brothers. First, don't open the canisters. Second, you open the canisters and load the dispersal equipment while you are sealed in the room. You remain sealed in the room until we are ready to leave. That leaves us with only one real option." He smiled slyly.

War

"I will surely die," the technician said staring at the black circle, nine millimeters wide. Abdullah broke the silence.

"You are an educated man. You know what 'martyrdom operation' means. What did you expect? What did you think about, idiot? Your future glory and celebrity as 'the great Jihadi' who fought the great *Shaitan* and lived? Did you think you would spend your latter days reliving it on al-Jazeera? Martyrdom means death. As Sheik Osama bin Laden said 'We love death, while they love life.' Did you think this was all a mind game? Something to be considered in the abstract? Nothing will be more real to you or more meaningful than your own death, brother. We will all ascend to paradise together, just two days from now." Abdullah smiled at his own images, but kept the gun trained on the technician.

"Our only guarantee of paradise comes from killing or being killed for the religion of God on the battlefield. That is from the commands of Allah himself in Qur'an 9:111. I will not be counted among the blessed if you close me up in that room. I bring Allah's curse down on your head for that," he said, spitting symbolically at Abdullah's feet.

"You are a Muslim trained in the ways of the western man, the infidel, but know little about Allah's way. The prophet, may peace and blessings be upon him, said: 'Five are Martyrs. The one who dies of plague, the one who dies of an abdominal disease, the one who dies of drowning, the one who is buried alive and dies, and the one who is killed in the cause of Allah.'" This comes from both Bukhari and Muslim's *ahadith*. You would have done better to study the Qur'an and the life and sayings of the prophet, may peace and blessings be upon him. That would have been worth more than filling your head with the useless rubbish the West has to offer."

"The one who dies of plague: how is that a martyr's death? That makes no sense if you think about it," the technician countered.

"Are you disputing the prophet?" Abdullah rumbled, through gritted teeth. The technician could barely hear him over the blaring of the Television in the other room

"Do you want to die right here? I should kill you now. Allah knows best. In the Qur'an it says 'if you do not fight you are a hypocrite. Allah promised to punish hypocrites severely and put others in their stead." he put the muzzle to his forehead and pushed down hard on it, saying "From what you've said already, I should do the same right here, right now. How difficult can it be to load the spreaders?"

The technician began to stammer," N-no one else is trained in the procedure. It needs to be done correctly to ensure proper dispersal of the agent. None of you has been trained. You need to be t--trained to handle it," he said, beginning to stammer.

"Give the glory to Allah, you fool. You will see him soon, if he wills it. Allah allowed this to happen so that his people would be given the means to destroy the westerners. You have very little to do with it. Allah has already decided how this will go. You mean nothing. I will kill you where you stand."

Abdullah leveled the piece at the technician's head as he scrounged around in the refrigerator, his hands shaking as they gripped pickle jars and wedges of cheese.

"What do you say? Do you die a martyr or disgraced where you stand?" Abdullah posed.

"I will do it," he whispered unevenly.

"What did you say? Say it loud enough to hear you womanly bitch. I should kill you now anyway. You weaken the ummah with your fear."

"I said 'I will do it' - go to hell you bastard!" he yelled. Tears welled up in the technician's bloodshot eyes.

Abdullah smiled maliciously. "You've found strength now. Allah is all-wise, knowing," he said waving the gun a the refrigerator door, "get what you need out of there for the next two days. Check to make sure the room has everything you will need in the loading procedure. Then seal yourself in the room. You won't leave the room until July fourth. No one leaves this apartment until then except the two who work in the park."

Chapter 73

He walked out of that basement exactly fifty hours after he'd first carried her in. They had disinfected his clothes and scrubbed down the laptop bag and everything else he had, including his wallet. They let him go, but wouldn't let him look through the blinds to see how she was. They said it would 'disturb' him. He laughed at this as he walked down Grand Boulevard, towards the viaduct, passing under the brightly lit archway at its southern terminus. Sodium arc lamps brightened the pre-dawn sidewalk quite well but did nothing for the darkness in his mind.

He tried to minimize the threat with the proposition that the death toll would only be half what they had intended, but it didn't work. He knew half of millions is still millions. The Israelis had the other suitcase, thank God for that. What they wanted for, God only knew, but Ben did know that at least in their hands the people of the United States wouldn't suffer and die.

Was a suitcase worth Dafna's life? Not to him.

As he walked across the bridge span he let his mind wander across the span of time and events they had been through together. It had only been a few days, but seemed like much longer. He could never repay her. He had no doubt he loved her, but he had made a promise to Grace on a rainy June day many years before. He intended to honor it.

Semper Fidelis – always true. It should apply to marriage as strongly as it did for Marines.

He walked along Grand Avenue shadowed in the penumbra of his thoughts until he reached Lindell, where he turned right. The Greisedieck Brothers' building was about twenty-five blocks down, past the point where Lindell became Olive. He didn't care. The walk would do him good. Life. He cared about her, wanted her to live. She had saved his life, but he couldn't return the favor. His heart hurt. He knew something about life. He had helped bring it into the world. He was a father. He had helped bring people into the world. But now he had also taken them out. He thought about the killing he'd done. He stared at the hole in his heart. It didn't bother him. In fact, he didn't feel anything about it. This surprised him. Maybe it had to do with emotional shock – who knows? He felt a weird separation from himself, a fragmenting... He had killed out of love for his brother but in the end it was nothing – not even a cold comfort to kill for a person that was nothing but a memory now. Revenge killing did nothing. He should honor them, but remember that they were intangible now. The past. He realized then that Grace had been right, as always. He *had* cared more for the living than the dead. He made another promise, right then, as he looked down from the bridge looking directly into the exhaust stacks atop a coal train's engines, shaking the piers at the apex of the bridge as they rolled on. He made a new promise. He would disconnect himself from the hatred as much as he could, because hateful blood lust damaged the heart and did nothing to improve the world. In the end it would kill mankind if things didn't change. He had to do something about this. He had made a promise years ago to love, honor and cherish. He intended to fulfill that every day he had left. With a vengeance. That would ultimately win out, of that he was sure. He would make sure his children knew they were loved and that the world *potentially* can be a good place. *Make of it what you will. The will to love.* His girls needed to know they were loved but also what they were up against. His dying or emotional absence would stunt their abilities to grow into the strong and beautiful people they were meant to be. He made his decision. He cared more about his girls than the dead. That is the way it should be; the living have potential – anything is possible. The past is fixed.

Living in the past will never work and never has.

He knew the global jihad will ultimately fail because of this simple fact, but he also knew it didn't release him from guard duty. He had to get the word out... turn the tide... he had to get the bushel basket off the lamp so that the Truth could light the room.

The walk cleared his head. He was going to need all the wits he had when he walked into that building in less than an hour. He fired up his phone and sent the text message to Agent Daniels. It was time to settle accounts.

When he reached Jefferson Street, he turned south for a couple of blocks, then turned again, heading straight down Market street. Daniels should be waiting for him at the FBI building, he thought. After a minute of so he could see someone leaning up against the iron fence along the street. It was too dark to be sure at that distance, but who else would be modeling the latest athletic-cut Brooks Brothers jacket at five am in downtown Saint Louis on July second?

He assumed he could safely bring the list down to one.

Full circle in less than a week, he mused, *what a long, strange trip it's been.* The Dead were right after all.

He was walking up to the same glass shoebox with the patch of bluegrass and the iron fence, but this time he would be well received. Daniels was waiting for him. He tried to break a smile. He had been right after all and he had done some good and had disrupted the terrorists' plans. Now only half the people would die, but he couldn't be happy or satisfied no matter how he looked at it.

War

He was glad to see Daniels. He had been the only one besides Dafna that had helped him through all the madness. Ben would do this thing one last thing for Daniels and for his country and then he'd be finished personally. He untangle himself. Nothing more he could do anyway– except wait for the death tolls on TV in a couple of days. Like he had the week of 9/11. This time he would start July 5th , from his hotel room at Disney World. People would start getting sick that fast. Dafna had. He and Grace and the kids would still be at Disney World when CNN and the rest of the Information Façade would crank up the machine on this latest terrorist attack.

Daniels came up to meet him, carrying a pad of paper again. He had a paragraph pre-written:

> Okay - we have the freq. of the device. I'm working with a group out of HQ – DC. Bug got a lot of attention. Plan: go in there, get them to talk about the suitcase. Get them to talk about what they've been doing to get it. Find out where the suitcase is and how they plan to get it out of the U.S. Get him to say as much as possible. We can use it to make our case against them.

Ben shook his head, beckoning for the pad and marker. He wrote quickly, causing the pen to squeal against the paper.

> Won't work. He scans for this stuff.

Daniels wrote:

> He's not going to scan for <u>his own stuff.</u>

Daniels underscored the last part of the message several times for emphasis. Then he moved on:

> He'll let it slide this time. You sure it's in the same place?

Ben: I've got it taped up on my shoulder. Hurts.

> It will work. It's under a wrap. Sounds same?

Daniels replied:

> What about Plan B? Never know what he'll do. You say: Contingencies.

Ben:

You got any ideas? I'm open.

Daniels held the paper up. Nothing. then Ben reaches for the pad.

Yes. Plan B. But I need to connect to their network.

Daniels:

Let's go in the office. I can get you a line.

Ben:

No. might have enough time to see where it came from. Don't have much time: watching?

Ben sat on the edge of the fence footing, dug around in his bag and pulled out his laptop. He pulled out a pigtail and connected the phone to the modem card. Daniels sat down next to him. Daniels looked down Market street to see the beginnings of color in the dawn sky, behind the Arch – a sky of muted watercolors near the horizon. It was early, but even so, they didn't have any time. Ben knew they only had this sunrise and the next to find the weapon. So did Agent Daniels and everyone at FBI HQ, which had cranked up a war room and had teams in Manhattan, D.C., Los Angeles all frantically searching for leads. They had the IT chipheads working on the data from the website and from the NetMail accounts. So far, they didn't know where to look really. They could only guess and someone bet the most bang for the buck would be in one of those two cities - New York or D.C. They spent all the resources on those two places.

Daniels watched Ben connect and bring up several windows. He clicked on a few things and a couple of blue bars ran across a pair of status windows. Ben repeated it a third time.

Daniels wrote:

What are you doing?

Ben opened a notepad window and typed:

I'm starting up the web cam apps on three PCS. Now I'm giving you this laptop. Don't shut it down. It's connected to the cams – see the windows?

War

Ben had three little windows up in the monitor, each showing a different scene. Two of them were in cubes along the windows in the Greisedieck Brothers' building. Daniels had watched the place long enough to know that. He guessed they were Ben's and Ike's cubicles.

The third window displayed an empty office. The lights were on. Papers were spread out on a mahogany desk. He was already at the office. *Doesn't he ever go home or sleep?* Ben thought.

I've set them up to stream to you. sessions are recorded. plan B. Lucky he's not in the room. He's around.

Jack didn't write anything, instead he gave a 'thumbs up' and smiled, tentatively. He looked tired.

Ben wrote:

What about the others?

Daniels:

?

Ben:

Terrorists. Do you have location from the IPs and mac addresses yet?

Daniels:

Getting help on that. HQ has 100+ people on it.

Ben stood up and looked towards the jagged skyline cast off from the downtown buildings. He breathed heavily a few times, trying to strengthen himself. He turned to Daniels, looking up at him from his seat on the fence's concrete footing. Ben pulled his ID badge out of the bag, letting it slide off his shoulder to the street. He handed the laptop to Daniels, who stood up.

"Plug it in," he said, "don't want to loose power before the big show." Then he started on down the street again, never looking back.

It always comes down to someone taking the long walk, he thought. He felt the dread building in his middle, scratching his innards as if he'd swallowed a ball of nettles.

He entered the lobby of the Greisedieck Brothers building just as the clock behind the guard desk turned to 5:22. He stopped to sign in, per off-hours procedure. The guard took note of his condition.

"Get hit by a train?" He chuckled at his own wit. Original.

"Something like that, yeah," Ben replied in monotone.

He headed toward the stairway as he always had in the past, but then turned and pressed a button in the elevator bank. He was getting too old for that sort of shit – too old and tired. He decided to take the elevator that morning just like any other lazy American would.

He stepped out of the elevator into the glass box around it.

Cameras everywhere.

He swiped his magnetic card and it let him through.

He relaxed supposing they'd save his execution for a less conspicuous place, should it come to that. *Gallows humor*, he silently observed as he walked down the half-lit hallway on the interior side of the cube farm. He kept looking around and straining his ear for sounds of Eitan. He lurked somewhere close by, to be sure. Ben could be sure of that if nothing else.

He saw the shaft of light from Eitan's office spilling onto the gunmetal gray carpeting. It took the shaped of a parallelogram, distorting the angles of Eitan's doorway as it spilled out. He decided to go to his desk first – tidy up a bit before Eitan realized he was there and came for him. He would be deluding himself if he thought they didn't know where he was. Of course they did.

He glanced at his wounded shoulder, wondering if they had figured out the device was no longer inside his body. Could they tell by the sound? Dafna had said it was a bug and a tracking GPS device. What else? Probably also had mini-charge to blow his head off. *Note to self: get it off shoulder ASAP. Need shoulder later.* More gallows humor.

He sat down at his desk and checked out the equipment. The monitor was off, but the CPU fan hummed. He checked the position of the web cam.

Good angle.

He got up and turned to check on Ike's camera.

Eitan stood in the doorway.

War

He wasn't smiling.

At that very moment Agent Daniels was at his desk as well over in the FBI field office. He had hooked Adam's PC up to a power supply and was making sure the disk had enough room to store the files. Three simultaneous streams brought the thing to its knees. He wondered if this would prevent them from getting the proof. If the laptop couldn't keep up part or all the files could be corrupted and they might miss crucial pieces of testimony. They would be worthless.

He debated whether or not he should sacrifice one of them to save the other two, but stopped himself. The one he closed would probably be the one they needed. He agonized over what to do for a long period of time, until he saw Ben in his cube. Window number two. A bit jerky, but the picture would do. He decided to leave them all running. He dialed Washington on the line they'd set up in the war room.

"Yeah? Hello…"

"Daniels in Saint Louis here."

"Daniels? You must be psychic."

"What's wrong?"

"Our device went blank about two minutes ago. We just finished the trace checks. It's out at the source, understand?"

Daniels looked at the screen. He could see Ben swiveling in his chair and standing up to face Eitan. The bandages looked undisturbed.

"They've got it blocked inside the building."

"It's obviously a shielded location. We're screwed here. We got nothing."

The war room was telling him their own devices didn't operate in the building. They had identified the device, figured out the frequency and had tapped into it, hoping to turn it against its owners.

Now it was worthless.

But Daniels pressed on, undeterred.

"That sucks... but we have alternate feeds. I've got three streaming webcams up. I just verified them." Daniels said, rechecking to make sure window two still worked. It did. We're still tapped in."

"You're on your own Daniels. Good luck."

Daniels hung up.

Ben stepped into the office behind Eitan, who closed the door behind him. The old guy never took any chances, down to minutiae like open doors in an empty office. Ben sat in his usual chair, nearest the wall. He was looking at Eitan, but listening for the fan on his desktop PC. It hummed. Good. Out of the peripheral vision from his left eye, he could see the shape of the web cam, sitting atop Eitan's oversized monitor. Another good thing. He and Daniels could still get it done. Eitan began to speak, choosing his words even more carefully than usual.

"Ben, it's good to have you back safe and sound. How are you?" he said, very smooth.

"I'm a little worse for wear, but I'm alive."

"I like to think every day above ground is a good day, wouldn't you agree? I think we can both appreciate that now." He smiled like a suburban lawyer who just had one hell of a product liability case dropped in his lap.

Ben nodded and chuckled a bit. He couldn't help it.

"Most people in this world wouldn't appreciate that statement in the same way we both can. You've come through a trial by fire and you've done well, Ben. I want to make sure you realize that."

Ben changed the subject.

"Dafna isn't doing well, Eitan. She'll probably die." he stopped there, checking to see Eitan's reaction. Pity? Remorse? Empathy? He couldn't tell what the pregnant pause meant, but he knew now that the bug must be useless. Eitan hadn't done his compulsive electronic sweep. It must not register in the building, he thought. Then Eitan shifted the program and got down to business.

"I know her father like a brother. Better than a brother, actually. I'm talking about the same understanding we share now, yes? But over a lifetime." He paused, seeming to let his guard down a moment, "what does she have?"

"The docs tell me it's the Black Death. They wouldn't let me see her."

Eitan bowed forward and clenched his fist, striking it lightly against his forehead.

"It's gets worse than that – it's in her lungs and very aggressive."

"Antibiotics?"

"She's not responding well enough." Tears began to well in Ben's eyes. He blinked them clear and noticed Eitan doing the same. "God help her," he added.

"This has nothing to do with God, but in their minds it's all about God!" Eitan's voice rose in anger. "May their Allah's curse be upon them for what they do!" He took a couple of seconds to collect himself, then started in on Ben.

"We need to go over the details to see if we can find the others."

At that point, he noticed his computer was on.

He reached down and turned it off.

Ben had to do something right away.

He began breathing irregularly.

He stood up, clutching the side of the desk while he leaned over it, gasping for air.

Jack Daniels drove through every red light until he reached the intersection of Ninth and Market. He waited for this light to change, since it was in the line of sight of the Greisedieck building and didn't want to give them a warning. He gunned his car through the intersection between the telephone company buildings and turned the corner, making a right on Locust. He stopped the car and ran over to the accordion-style gate blocking the entrance to the old storefront they used.

Fumbling around with the keys in dim light, he finally opened the lock. Could he make it in time? They had no more options. He could feel it sliding out of his grasp. He locked the entry behind him and ran up through the darkness. They wouldn't get another chance. This was for real.

"I need to get out of here," Adams forced out between breaths.

"You're having a panic attack? After what you've been through? What's wrong with you?" Eitan said. He was incredulous.

"I gotta get out of here now. Now." Adams staggered toward the door, knocking over the other chair, but getting out before Eitan could swing around the desk to stop him. Adams doubled over while his breathing came back to normal. "Claustrophobia," he explained.

Eitan knew about Ben's condition from the obligatory company psych profile, but… he'd been in the room at least three times before without incident.

Eitan didn't like this at all.

"Take a few moments, then we'll go back in and go over the details," he commanded.

"I'm not going back in there," Adams insisted.

"Yes, you are," he insisted back. Eitan trusted no other location, even in the building. He had the extra measures put in his office. Executive privilege-- you might say.

"I've been through hell this week. They hung us on meat hooks down there in 'Nawlins. They were going to kill us. I'm not going into another box like that, ever! The locker and your office are the same size. I'm not going in there!" Adams shouted.

Eitan looked around. No one else was in their section yet. He looked at his watch: 5:47. Some of the early risers would be showing up soon. He had maybe twenty minutes to finish this. He had to get the assessment from Adams and the other items before he could proceed. Adams wouldn't be forthcoming in an emotional state - he'd leave something out and it could be material to the operation.

"We'll leave the door open. That will help," he offered, gesturing back inside.

"No way," Adams said. Then he bolted down the hall, turning into his aisle. Eitan came after him. He moved fast. Eitan debated whether he should take care of this now or wait. They had no time left – 4 July was tomorrow. He needed to debrief Adams now; Eitan had to have the information before his handler called for the latest and probably last update on this matter.

Every moment counted now.

He could number the hours remaining on his fingers and toes – probably on Adam's digits too, even if he was missing a few. He didn't have time to bullshit around with someone having a panic attack. He had misjudged Adams. He had overestimated him, but if he could get what he needed in the next few minutes it wouldn't matter.

He took up his position at the cube door again, blocking Adams. Adams sat down in his own chair. He looked disheveled and a little more than off-balance.

"Have it your way then," Eitan said, if your feeling better, let's get just go over a few details. It won't take long."

This seemed to relax him.

"I'm all right now," Adams said, "thanks for understanding."

"I understand that you are irrational in your fear of closed places, but you need to find your composure. I need to hear what you have to say."

A flash of surprise and anger ran across Adam's face. Then he relaxed. "What do you need to know?"

"Everything from …" he stopped for a moment, "turn off your computer."

"But…"

"Shut up now! I said 'turn it off'. I don't have any patience left and our time is running out. Tomorrow is the day. Now shut it off. You are my friend, Ben. You know that. We are on the same side."

He leveled a .22 semi-auto pistol at Adam's head.

"Turn it off now or I shoot you where you are."

Adams complied.

Eitan cocked his ear, scanning. He hear nothing except for the cooling fan for the computer in the next cubicle. Keeping the gun on Adams, he reached around and turned it off. He wanted to leave nothing to chance. Adams looked deflated – he wondered, but then put it out of his mind. He had to hurry now.

"Now tell me the details about the case you opened: the keypad, how you opened it, what was inside and the events after that."

Adams described the case to him in detail, then told him everything he remembered about the terrorists. He had a keen eye for detail. He would have fit in at The Office very well, but for one thing. The claustrophobia had him by the balls. He would have never amounted to anything in Israel.

Daniels had started all the equipment up and had it trained on the widows across the street in record time. He turned up the laser microphone and put it squarely in the center of the aisle between Ben's desk and Ike's old desk. He had checked himself over and over: *tape rolling, cameras recording, laser microphone powered up. Everything operational.* He listened to the output as the laser picked up the infinitesimal vibrations from the windows of the Greisedieck Brothers building as Ben and the Israeli went over the details of the case and what had happened in New Orleans. Daniels checked the recording process again. Everything was running. From the sound of it, the quality of the recorded conversation was crystal.

Somehow Ben had put the old man directly in the sweet spot where microphone could pick the evidence off the glass and for posterity. And for the courts. Life could turn on a dime. He'd thought they had lost it all back at the office, when the window into Eitan's office had gone dark. *Oh this was just as good*, he thought. Daniels patted himself on the back.

They had it all recorded. With his evidence, the Bureau would finally be able to get the warrant they'd wanted for three years. Now they'd be able to bust the ring wide open. They'd get at least five to ten agents on premise and no telling how many more if they moved fast enough.

This was once-in-a-lifetime.

A career maker.

He owed Adams big time – this alone would put him in The Big Time. Together they had beaten the Mossad – the world's best -- at their own game.

Daniels had at least thirty minutes on tape. They had them. Ben's involvement in the whole thing would be excused – he could show it was coercion by just running the tape, when the son of a bitch pulled a pistol on him.

Daniels stopped congratulating himself when he heard it.

Someone in the room.

Someone behind him.

Metal sliding against metal.

Then a voice.

"Pardon my French, but what the fuck you think you're doing, Jack?"

Daniels didn't have to look. He knew who it was.

War

"That's everything I can think of," Ben said.

"Are you sure?" said Eitan.

"Yes, and I know the stakes. These are people in *my* country we're talking about. This is my home after all."

Just then Ofer came through the doors.

Empty handed.

He waltzed up the aisle.

"Miss me old man?" he said.

"Like I miss the case of gonorrhea I had back in '79" Eitan replied, not missing a beat for once, "did you hand it off?"

"Yes, one down, one to go," Ofer said, "was he of any help?"

"I think so, our handler will appreciate it. We're working on the other one too. New York and Washington are most likely."

"So you don't have the case anymore?" Ben asked.

"Nope. The handler has it."

Ben didn't think it wise to pursue the line any farther. Not that it would do any good.

"You've done very well," Eitan said, "You should pursue a career in this line of work." He smiled – sarcastically?

"What are you going to do now?" Ofer asked, non-confrontationally for once.

"I think I'll stick to what I'm doing."

"Not here you won't."

Ben tilted his head, "I'm sorry…?"

"Get your things and go," Eitan said.

"You're firing me?" he laughed haltingly, confused. He looked at both their faces for signs that it was a joke.

"Yes, as you know Missouri is an 'At-Will' state. That means I can fire you for most any reason or no reason at all. You're no longer needed here at AirWarez. Thanks. We'll send you the remainder of your earned pay in two weeks," he said, then added, "I assume your mailbox at home wasn't destroyed in the explosion?" More smiles -- wicked this time.

"You bastard" was all Ben could manage to say. He shook in fury as he gathered up the pictures of Grace and the kids, along with his cell phone charger and a few papers. He brushed by the old man.

He stopped and turned back to get the one picture of Ike with some old girlfriend and his dog, Woofer.

"You're a good man, Ben," Eitan said, "Please don't take this personally. This is just business. It has to be done. To protect us. "

Looking back over his shoulder, he didn't say anything to Eitan. "Good luck to you, too. I hope you find the other one before it's too late. You don't have much time."

"I know," Ofer said.

"By the way I need to turn in one more piece of AirWarez equipment," he said, unbuttoning his shirt. He reached under it and pulled off the device, wrapped up in the rages and still taped to his shoulder. He opened up the package and pulled it out. "This belongs to you." He tossed it at the old man, who caught it.

Eitan didn't say anything.

Ben walked out into the light of a new day – impossibly bright and shiny for the circumstances. But then again, only he and a few others could see the thunder heads gathering over the nation. The whole thing was out of his hands now.

It was over for him, except for the part of protecting his family from the bioweapon. He had a day to figure that out, if he could find a way, that is.

He looked up at the abandoned building across the street and thought about Agent Daniels. He had failed him. They didn't get it recorded.

Ben started back up the street, back the way he came, toward Market Street. He needed to call Grace and tell her he was safe. Explain things. Tell her he cared more about the living than the dead. Tell her he was still alive. Tell her he had been wrong - again.

Where to start? He had put them in one hell of a mess. They couldn't go home. He didn't have a job. The insurance company refused the claim. He didn't know if they could ever recover. Where to begin?

He decided where. He looked at his watch. It was July 3rd.

If he remembered correctly, they about five hours to get ready. He could meet them. They'd go to Disneyworld anyway. Why ruin that too?

He pulled the tickets out of his wallet and checked the flight time. Grace and the kids could still get to Lambert Airport from the Lake if he called her right then.

War

Agent Daniels stood among the surveillance equipment, mind racing for a way out. Chief stepped into the light and he could see the 9mm in one hand, and the stainless steel suitcase containing the Soviet Bio-Weapon in the other. He had a clear shot and Daniels had no where to go.

"I said: 'What are you doing, Jack?'"

Daniels tried to read him, but it was pointless with Chief most of the time. This time was no different in that regard, but in every other way it was.

Chief was working for them.

Chief had the weapon.

Chief was going to kill him now.

"I'm finishing up what we've been trying to do for the three years. And I did it. I've got it on tape, sir."

He regretted having said that – *did he just close the deal?*

"Well done. Gold star for you today," Chief said. He laughed, but kept the gun on Daniels.

"Who are you? Are you really FBI or something else?"

"I'm FBI – I'm legit. You know I have twenty-two years in. That's real."

Still he had the gun on him.

"Bullshit. You're not FBI. You're working with the Mossad. That's CIA territory. You're a spook and now you're gonna kill me. Adams was right about all of this, you know. Said you weren't to be trusted. Said Ike told him that. Now you're working against your own country. They're right after all."

"I don't work for the Mossad, Jack, the Mossad works for me. Ike worked for me. Adams was working for me all along – just didn't know it. I'm CIA."

"Great. Now the CIA pimps out foreign spies and kills off FBI types like me. What a wonderful world."

"I'm not going to kill you. I came downtown to pick up a delivery." He shook the case a little. "When I'm leaving I see someone's gotten into our stake-out through the gate and I came up here to make sure who it was. You shouldn't be up here. Sorry about the gun." He said, lowering the weapon. "This is all classified, you understand? We appreciate your resourcefulness and tenacity, though. You've helped flush it all out for us. You made things happen. People have noticed."

"Wait - the CIA can't operate domestically. That's our job, the FBI..."

"9/11 changed the rules of the game, don't you agree? The FBI is a crime fighting organization, you know. It doesn't handle espionage well. It's not supposed to. So we have a problem with this new threat. What do we do? We need to outsource until we can get rolling. So the CIA contacts me, signs me up in December, 2001 and hooks me up with a network to run. The Patriot Act gets passed and helps with the arrangement."

"You're still working with Israelis – foreign agents."

"Buy the best and fuck the rest, pardon my French," Chief said. "You want to win this world against global jihad or do you want another 9/11? The Israelis have fifty-four years' experience dealing with these Islamists. It makes sense to keep them around for a while. They get results." He shook the case again, "See what I mean?"

"There's still another one of those out there, you know."

"I know."

"I went over your head, we've got a war room set up at headquarters and two teams out in the field in D.C. as well as New York. We don't have a lead on it, as far as I know. We're just extrapolating."

"I know and by the way, I don't hold it against you. We have some of the Agency's techies on the dead letter account as well. We'll know where the locations they read the notes from in short order."

"That's the key. FBI is working on it too and I've got the IP addresses that Adams supplied."

"We know. They're comparing notes as we speak. We may still be able to stop this from happening. Now grab your tapes and let's get out of here. We have less than a day to find them and take 'em out."

"All right, Chief, " Daniels said, gathering the tapes and flash drives up into the crook of his arm.

The phone woke Agent Daniels up. He'd been laying on the couch in Chief's office for a couple of hours to try and get some rest while the boys in Washington checked the NetMail access records. Jack and the Chief had been reviewing everything from Adams in the meantime. He realized must have fallen asleep at some point in the early morning when the phone went quiet. Now the shouting from the earpiece jolted his mind out of the therapeutic spin cycle it had been in.

"Daniels… Agent Daniels…anybody there? Hello?"

"Yeah…" he managed, not moving his mouth enough.

"We have the records now. We can see that someone definitely moved from the Black Sea, through the Med."

"Adams pretty much told us that. The website."

"Then we see a pattern of New Orleans and Chicago. After that it's Anaheim and"

"New York or Washington? Is it one or both?" Daniels asked.

"Neither…"

Pestilence

Pestilence

The punishment of those who wage war against Allah and His Messenger,
and strive with might and main for mischief through the land is:
execution, or crucifixion, or the cutting off of hands and feet from opposite sides,
or exile from the land: that is their disgrace in this world,
and a heavy punishment is theirs in the Hereafter.
Allah – Qur'an 5:33

Chapter 74

Abdullah bin Malak al Zalam led the prayers as the sun came up. This time he didn't muffle his voice. It no longer mattered if the infidel could hear them, as they were leaving immediately afterward.

Doing the *salat* one last time a sense of fulfillment and closure to his mind. The universe was in order. He thought back to those months on the sea, when this had all started. It seemed like a lifetime ago. In a sense it was. The journey across the waters had been the end of his earthly life – when he put it all behind him. Now the transition would be ending and he would die a martyr. He would be raised to heaven on the last day. The Garden waited for him – he was sure to have a place now. Giving up this life amounted to nothing; a small price to pay for the reward. And Allah always keeps His promises.

Abdullah congratulated them one by one after the prayers. He kissed each one, extending his sincere wishes of Allah's blessing over one and all.

Then it was time.

As a group, they checked over the list of items needed: identification badge, firearms, biohazard suits. They put these items into their collection of company-issued tool boxes and canvas bags. After that, they all put on the blue gray jumpsuits issued to groundskeepers and put the identification badges, complete with Hispanic names, around their necks. The two legitimate employees left, taking one extra *jihadi* with them.

The plan had been worked out months ahead to the smallest detail, but Abdullah was well aware troubles always present themselves in the details. His mangled leg reminded him of this fact everyday.

Abdullah had the real employees them go out to the truck and start it and close all ventilation. The intense humidity wouldn't be a problem for an hour or two and they'd only needed fifteen minutes to reach the park.

When he heard the truck running, he donned the headpiece of his suit. He opened the door to the preparation room and cut through the plastic. The technician had the two devices up on the table ready to go. He walked over to where the technician lay, curled in the fetal position by the corner window. His skin had the color and shine of putty coated with oil. His drool made a bloody ring in the carpet. Abdullah pulled the pillow out from under his head, which thudded onto the floor. He doubled it up around the Glock 17, pressed it to his head and fired twice. He didn't know if this would leave the technician a martyr or not, but *inshallah* – if God wills it. God is merciful to his believers and Allah ta'alla knows best. As always. He didn't give it a second thought.

Abdullah walked back to the table and set the pistol down between the other weapons. Each weapon had about twelve-kilograms of plague bacterium in it but the canisters and delivery system brought the total weight to at least twice that.

He took them down one at a time, as quickly as the suit would allow, placing them both in the same plastic box with wheels. He had their assurances they'd be able to get the cart past the guards without question.

He closed the lid and sealed it. Then he lifted a metal can with about five liters petrol out of the truck bed and made the climb back up the wooden steps one last time.He watched them drive away, heading toward the Kissimmee Wal-Mart about half a kilometer down the road.

He doused each room as thoroughly as possible. When this was ready, he took a pillow from the couch and walked into the bedroom. Rochelle laid there, still stretched between the posts by the ropes they'd used. It smelled like sex and urine in the room even with the strong smell of petrol everywhere. She had a look of terror on her face, seeing him in the moon suit with the gun one hand and the pillow in the other.

She tried to scream through the gag. She struggled, but it was no use. Her eyes bulged and her swung her head violently back and forth as he placed the pillow over it. He pressed it down hard to stop her movement. He fired into her head. She kept twitching spasmodically for a second until he put another round in her head. The other girl, Lexie, bucked up and down and tried to scream out as much as the other whore had.

Abdullah wasted Lexie exactly the same way he had done Rochelle - two shots to the head through the pillow.

He opened all the windows, started the fire in every room and locked the door behind him. He bounded down the staircase and leapt into the truck bed as they took off. Now they would drive to the parking lot and wait until the appropriate time. The employees went early, since they needed as much time as possible to attach the devices and make any necessary modifications. No one would be in the parade staging area that early in the day and scrutiny at the gate would be at its weakest too.

He took off the moon suit, since he was already dressed in the groundskeeper uniform. He let them moon suit blow in the wind for a minute of two to get rid of any stray plague bacteria still clinging to it.

Chapter 75

Acting Special Agent Daniels shifted around in the coach seat some more. His legs kept itching and were restless. They give passengers just enough room to fit, albeit uncomfortably, in coach. He did have an empty seat next to him. He would have thought the first flights would be filled. The War Room had booked the flight for him as he and Chief drove to Lambert. They had also begun the process of mobilizing the Center for Disease Control in Atlanta, FEMA, [ARMARIID] the state and local law enforcement and emergency agencies and everyone else who deal with catastrophe. The park had its own enforcement agency and they were put on notice. The last access came from Kissimee. Anaheim and Kissimee could mean only one thing.

They had planned to take out Disneyland and Disneyworld.

Adams was out of pocket. He kept trying to reach him until he remembers Adams left his phone attached to the laptop to do the web cam connections. Long night – his mind felt like it was Ash Wednesday, the morning after the all-nighters on Rue Bourbon. *He didn't have a phone to call, remember?* He made an in-flight call to the War Room and asked them find his wife's number. What soccer mom out there would be without? Daniels didn't know her name, but how many Adams from Saint Louis could there be?

The War Room was also going through employee records to see if they could identify likely suspects before they insisted on locking the park gates.

A Plague on Both Houses

Fight in the cause of Allah those who fight you,
but do not transgress limits; for Allah loveth not transgressors.
And slay them wherever ye catch them,
and turn them out from where they have Turned you out;
for tumult and oppression are worse than slaughter;
but fight them not at the Sacred Mosque,
unless they (first) fight you there;
but if they fight you, slay them.
Such is the reward of those who suppress [Islamic] faith.
Allah – Qur'an 2:190-191

Chapter 76

When the time came to enter the park, Abdullah couldn't have been more relieved. He'd been sitting in the cab of the truck for hours. It was a busy day for the park, which helped the cause in several ways. The guard staff would be either pre-occupied, overwhelmed or off for the day, celebrating with their own families. All the extra people would help spread death to many more. *Allah will be greatly pleased*, he thought.

They'd made it through the first ring of defenses without a problem, the gatekeepers watching the parking lots barely looked at them, waving them on with impatient disdain. *Too many cars to look at properly on a busy day, may Allah be pleased, he thought. Americans are more concerned with efficiency and convenience than anything else – except maybe the question of how to separate the poor Islamic world from its oil. Well, very soon they would have a whole new set of problems to worry about.*

The walkie-talkie attached to his waistband went off.

"I'm coming out to meet you now."

"We're ready," Abu replied in English.

"Meet me at the end of the parking lot, nearest the Main Tunnel entrance," the metallic voice said.

No one in the truck said anything. They all got out, grabbed their gear and walked in lockstep towards the tunnels.

When they met up with him he said, "Let me do the talking. I will keep speaking in Spanish as we walk through the doors. Queue up to show your badges. We only have to worry about the one at the desk. Ahmed will wait in the inner hallway. He'll dispatch the guard with the taser, if necessary, just like we went over back at the apartment. Don't worry, *inshallah,* we'll be in without a problem. Don't do anything stupid," he said, surveying the group, "just relax. They won't know what hit them until it's too late."

"No one give us away. We've waited years for this, brothers. *Allahu Akbar…*" Abdullah said, though matter-of-factly and under his breath so as not to draw attention to himself.

"*Allahu Akbar*" they all replied reflexively. *Allah is greatest.*

They entered the tunnel antechamber in seemingly random jumble, all the while speaking Spanish gibberish. A lower-class Anglo was on duty, vacant in expressing and sitting behind a desk to the right. The vestibule for the Utilidors, as they called them, was a rectangle about seven meters wide and three deep. Whether or not the guard had a gun Abdullah couldn't see. The brother with the taser leaned against the tunnel wall in a spot impossible to see from the guard desk.

They each filed past the guard, who checked to see that they all had badges, but nothing more. He didn't ask to look in the toolboxes or canvas bags. He nodded and waved them through as if it were a burden more than anything.

They were in without any complications.

They walked down the hall a short distance and stopped at a door on the left. The one who actually worked here lead the way. He opened the door, going inside quickly. A group of men putting on the life-size costumes of Mickey Mouse, Goofy, Pluto and Donald Duck turned around to look at them. The last of The Brothers locked the door and stood by it as the others took out the actors with the Taser or with iron rods or heavy metal wrenches or hammers from the tool boxes. They beat them all at least to the point of coma.

"Careful! You're getting blood on the suit!" one of the brothers shouted, this time in Arabic.

They took them all out in a matter of seconds.

They worked silently, efficiently, pulling the costumes off of each one of the lifeless bodies and dragging each one by the feet into the back area of the locker room where they quietly finished them off.

It didn't take long to bludgeon the infidels to death once they got busy. They stuffed the bodies into the larger lockers and returned the green room. They took their moon suits out of the canvas bags and put them on. They secured the guns to the front of the suits by Velcro straps and then divided into pairs, each helping his partner slide into the costumes. Then they got to work on stage two of the plan.

A Plague on Both Houses

The term 'civilians' does not exist in Islamic religious law.
There is no such term as 'civilians' in the modern Western sense.
People are either of Dar Al-Harb or not.
Hani Al-Siba'i,
head of the Al-Maqreze Centre
for Historical Studies in London.

Chapter 77

People packed the streets in Disney World, making it hard for Ben Adams and his girls to get from one ride to another. *People are funny,* he thought, *they think they need pack themselves together to have fun. Just like sheep. The more crowded the conditions, the bigger the 'event'.* Well, it was Independence Day, July Fourth after all. People naturally wanted to come together to celebrate. People need to feel connected to others in something larger than themselves whether it be good or bad. That day the crowd had to be over fifty thousand. It was probably the biggest day of the year at the park. What better way to spend it than wedged between a sweaty and rude throng under the unforgiving Florida sun?

The density of people added to the humidity and heat – all of them breathing the same air. It made it seem thick as potato soup and just as refreshing on a summer's day. Ben noticed he had to work harder to get the oxygen he needed while snaking through the crowd. But the children didn't care, they panted too, but waited without complaint in the lines all morning. Their happiness infected him.

Grace and the kids had packed as soon as he had made the call back in Saint Louis. Ben had walked back up to the FBI office, but it wasn't open that early and Agent Daniels had disappeared. He went back down to Union Station and called Grace and she took him back. They made their plans to reunite t at Lambert Airport four hours after. He hadn't heard from Jack. Maybe Daniels had figured out a way to get them after all, but he didn't want to know bad enough to call him. He had decided to take up the pen instead of the sword. He would live longer that way.

He thought about Jack's card, still tucked away in his wallet. Thanks to the miracle of modern communications he could turn Graces' phone on and give Jack a call.

He decided to stay in the moment, with his family and wife, making memories. He didn't want the evils of the world to intrude, at least not for a day or two. After all, he'd done everything he could already anyway. Leave it to the professionals, he thought. That should be enough. He could call Daniels and find out later and not be the worse for it.

Back to making memories in this clean, orderly, sanitized version of some child's dream. No monsters here – only the good dreams. At least for a while.

Marrying Grace was the best decision he would ever make. He regretted that he'd pretty much destroyed their lives in the material sense but he was surprised that she didn't seem to hold it against him. Maybe she did, but she wouldn't let it spoil the trip. A good sense of priority and timing – two of her better qualities. She held his hand in the lines and sat by him on the rides and her eyes told him good things. They said she loved him despite the fact that he was an idiot.

She would keep loving him. Grace and the kids mattered -- everything else could be replaced.

He knew he still had to fight *al-mu'minum*, the True Believers, but he could do it in a way that would also keep him alive. There were many ways to bring the enemy down besides killing. The world war against global jihad was going to last long time, maybe longer than the Cold War, which lasted forty-five years. It is the same struggle. The struggle of a belief in individual rights and liberties pitted against a totalitarian, collective movement.

Ben stopped his mind at that point.

He could fight the battles later. Mohammed was truly evil and even thinking about him poisoned Ben's mind. He resigned himself to the fact that the world would still be a shit heap when he returned to it. He re-joined his family in that happy place and left thoughts of Mohammed behind. The parade would be starting any minute now and they jostled among the cast of thousands to try and get to a spot with a good view.

A Plague on Both Houses

Fight those who believe not in Allah nor the Last Day,
nor hold that forbidden which hath been forbidden
by Allah and His Messenger,
nor acknowledge the religion of Truth,
(even if they are) of the People of the Book [Jews and Christians],
until they pay the Jizya [protection tax] with willing submission,
and feel themselves subdued.
Allah – Qur'an 9:29

Chapter 78

Special Agent Daniels, Chief and the other local FBI agents and the park's own security force fanned out as they reached the entrance. The plan consisted of closing all gates until they could stop the terrorists and take them into custody. At that point the team members from the Center for Disease Control along with the Army's Medical Research Institute for Infectious Diseases (USAMARIID), out of Fort Detrick, Maryland would assess the contagion threat. At that point, FEMA could either release the other agencies and the people or in worst case, turn the entire park into an isolation chamber. The gatekeepers complied with the orders and sealed all entrances and exits. Those who had respirators put them on. Jack and Chief were among the lucky ones that had them.

"Now what?" Daniels shouted through the mask, "They could be anywhere within two square miles."

"Go to the castle first," Chief said, muffled. Rivulets of sweat already ran down the slope of his balding head.

"What if they aren't there?" Jack said.

"Then we'll be at the center – shortest distance to everything."

They ran up Main Street, shedding the jackets and exposing their shoulder holsters. People along the street got out of the way when they noticed them coming, but too many people crowded the streets and blocked Daniels, preventing him from making a good run. He began to pull away from Chief and he and the younger Disney guards reached the castle steps first.

Ben could see the parade starting farther down the road, as the garage doors opened and the floats began moving out of the staging area, which had been disguised to look like mountain granite, the color of salmon. The clapping started and the sound system cranked up a happy tune. A ripple of anticipation ran up through the crowds, seven to ten sweaty people deep on both sides of the street. The parade route would come up through Liberty Square, then around the castle and down Main Street, cutting the park roughly in half. Liberty Square was about a third of the way along the route. Anxious people trying to get a good view kept bumping and rubbing against Ben to get a preview of the floats, about sixty yards away at that point.

The first float had the Princesses motif and had live actors as Cinderella and the Prince dancing a waltz inside a plastic dome. Smoke machines added to the effect. Other characters walked along the edges of the floats, waving to the crowd and engaging some of the kids next to the cordon ropes with their ad-libbed antics.

Kristen and Sarah squealed and pointed, looking back at Ben and Grace to make sure they were having as much fun. Ben smiled and laughed to himself, finding Grace's hand to give it a squeeze.

Ben had a better view of it all as the floats came closer. The second float had Snow White in the bubble and the seven dwarves walking along side it. Smoke came out of it too, hanging in the still, heavy summer air of early afternoon.

The third float showcased Sleeping Beauty and had Mickey and Friends walking along beside it. He squinted at it, still about fifty yards away. He noticed it didn't look the same as the first two floats. Something was wrong with the smoke machine. The smoke seemed to be more uniform and flew differently – like the dust out of a beaten rug. The characters were all there, skipping along…

Mickey didn't skip.

He walked along with a bad limp.

Ben's smile fell as the words flashed through his mind,

> "By the rat He punished you unbelievers and again by God's example you will be punished through a rat. This July 4th it is we who will be dancing."

He remembered Chicago said that the night they had come to the house and killed Ike. He looked at the dust coming out from under the float and the way Mickey limped up the street.

And he knew. He grabbed Grace's hand, pulling her closer.

"Grace, give me the phone, now!" he shouted above the crowd.

She looked at him, surprised and aggravated, but pulled the phone from her purse, having to wiggle and twist it out in the close spaces of the crowd. He fumbled for Daniels' card as the phone came up through its startup routine. He dialed. Daniels answered on the first ring.

"Jack?! Where are you?! I know where they are. They're here!" he said.

"Ere are you?" Daniels sounded strange, like he had his head in a toilet bowl.

"I'm at Disneyworld, I'm in the Magic Kingdom, in Liberty Square. They're here Jack! they're using parade floats to spread it!"

"Get outta there," it sounded like. The poor quality of transmission and the noise all around Ben made it hard to understand.

"Did you hear me? Where are you?" Ben shouted. The people around shot dirty looks at him. He was causing a scene.

"We're here Ben. we're on the way. I'm here. We know – I'm at the castle. Coming to you. Which one?"

"The third float – Sleeping Beauty. Mickey is one of them. Probably the others – Goofy, Donald and Pluto," Ben shouted.

"Okay-" then the disconnect.

He grabbed his forehead to try and organize his thoughts. He checked the float – it was still about forty yards away. The smoke didn't seem to be blowing in their direction. He thought to check the wind. Licking his finger, he held it up while looking at a flag over by the Hall of Presidents. No discernible wind. The flag agreed. Then it fluttered slightly toward the back of the park, in the Northeasterly direction. He grabbed Grace by the shoulders and turned her so that she faced him.

"Grace, listen to me, this is life and death, " he said.

He had her attention.

"Take the kids and go to Main Street. Get inside somewhere closed up – a bathroom or something."

"Why –"

They're here, understand? They're spreading it from that float," he pointed at the parade, "you've got to get to a sheltered area down by the main gate. Cover your mouths and noses as best you can and don't remove the covers until someone tells you it's okay. I love you. Go."

She didn't say anything, but bent down and pulled the girls up.

"Let's go," she said. She forced a wedge through the crowd. Ben watched them until the people blocked his view of them.

He forced his way up to the rope and took another look. Thirty yards away. He peeled his shirt off and tied it around his nose and mouth as best he could. Then he jumped over the rope and ran towards them. The faces along the way displayed the spectrum of expressions -- mostly confusion and surprise. The floats stopped when they saw him coming. A young girl who worked as a parade handler tried to stop him but he blew by, knocking her over. The bastard inside the Mickey suit knew something was wrong and turned to meet him. All the characters around that float turned to face him at that point. Ben crashed into Mickey, knocking him to the pavement. The crowd roared and screamed, not knowing what to make of the scene. Mickey's head came rolling off, revealing an unknown person covered in a white biohazard suit.

People closest to the action began screaming and running in random directions, spreading the panic up and down the line. Ben tugged on the head piece, trying to pull it off. Pandemonium burst out through the park in a shock wave. Someone started shooting. Ben couldn't see who – he had to take care of the jihadi first. He got the head covering off. The terrorist from The Crescent. The one to arrive with the suitcases. The one with the limp and the strange permanent bruise on his forehead.

They had succeeded in releasing a thing far worse than The Black Death into the crowd.

Grace had a girl in each hand -- Kristen on the right and Sarah on the left. She ran with them as fast as their little legs would take them. She had to settle for that rate of speed, since she couldn't carry both of them anymore. She had hoped Ben was wrong, but when she saw the men in respirators run past her, in the opposite direction toward the parade, she knew it was true. She had to get the children as far away as she could. She had to find something to protect their lungs. Her mind raced faster than her legs as she pulled the children towards Main Street. *God help us all. Don't let my Ben die,* she prayed.

Acting Special Agent Daniels had a clear line of site down to the floats. He could see the terrorists trying to free themselves from the costumes. One of them fired into the backs of the fleeing crowd to buy more time. Daniels considered, but was still too far from them to take a shot at a dead run. But he closed the gap fast. He stopped. A civilian had one of them down, still in his suit, and was punching the life out of him. Another one of them opened fire. Jack took aim at another shooter, trying to outflank him on the left. He raised his piece. Daniels fired three times, hitting him once in the chest. A bullet whizzed by, too close by the sound of it. He fell to the ground and rolled up into some landscaping for cover, getting behind some fake boulders poured in concrete. Daniels could see Ben scramble over to the one he had just shot, getting down behind the body and taking the weapon. Shots flew everywhere and some stray people had been hit. Daniels couldn't see the one in the Mickey suit – the one Ben had been fighting with at first. He looked around. Then he saw someone crawling under the third float. It was him. He could distinguish bits of Mickey's hands and feet scurrying along under the skirt of the float. The terrorist bolted for tram when he made it to the front of the float undercarriage. Daniels watched him jumped on and start it up, swerving around the first two floats and picking up speed. The dust flew out in every direction. He was trying to spread the disease as much as possible. Jack couldn't do much – the others still had him pinned down. He took a shot but missed. Other law enforcement types joined the fight.

The terrorist driving the tram floored it, careening up the street toward the Hall of Presidents. Dust kept flying out from underneath the trailer bed. The actors still trapped in the float bubble beat against its sides in sheer panic. Daniels looked for a way to break out of there. Someone had to get that float stopped.

Ben had been laying behind the dead guy's body for protection. He had his weapon now. He looked around to see what he was up against. They were all shooting at him and Daniels and the rest of the force that had come along. Ben didn't want to risk moving until he had a good reason. From what he could see they were all pretty much pinned down.

Out of his peripheral vision he saw the tram began to move again. The leader had gotten away from him when the shooting started and was now driving off, spreading floating death all along the street. He had to be stopped. The more agent in the air, the worse the toll would be. Many people were already dead -- they just didn't know it yet. He hoped he wasn't one of them. He'd been lucky once but hadn't been exposed to it at the present level. He didn't think the shirt around his face would help much.

He took a chance when the others regrouped and began laying down fire. He rolled over to the right and crawled about twenty yard, making it into one of the buildings. Now that he had cover, he half-stood, running through the adjoining rooms until he could get out on to the street with some cover. He stayed as close as he could to the buildings, trying to close the gap with the float, which was moving erratically. The bastard had been hit or he had lost control. Either way, the terrorist jumped off as the tram before it plowed into the Hall of the Presidents. Ben ran up close enough to be able to see him duck into it through a hole in the wall.

First things first.

He reached the float, stopping for a second to readjust his face covering. He realized it would be as effective a sieve in stopping something as small as the pathogen, but he couldn't wait for better protection. He crawled under the float, still spewing dust.

He wormed his way up to the spot where they had attached the device. A crude-looking metal box, fashioned out of sheet metal, seemed to be the hopper. It was bolted to an electric motor and a blower of sorts, looking like a hair dryer more than anything. He held his breath and started pulling at the wires spliced in the main line running down the center of the undercarriage. The motor stopped and the dust began to settle. He wriggled back out from under the float and took off his mask, still holding his breath. He left it lying on the street and went looking for the terrorist in the Hall of Presidents.

He entered through the hole in the wall, feeling out of his element; crouching, trying to stay quiet, sweeping the gun from side to side. He listened for sound. Nothing. He checked the pistol again to make sure it would fire if he needed it to. The place was strangely silent, in the middle of it all. He could hear sounds outside, but nothing inside. Focusing his concentration to pick up sounds, any hint of sound, inside the building, he heard nothing.

He approached the main auditorium door at a wide angle, crouching down to look around its edge. He scanned. Rows of seats began about ten feet inside and curved slightly running across the breadth of the auditorium, mimicking the arc of the outer stage wall. *What was behind the curtain?* He moved down to it. He listened again. Nothing. Was he crouched down, waiting for him among the animatronic likenesses of great men like Washington, Lincoln and Truman? It would be an ironic twist of fate for a thug and believer in totalitarianism to hide among the defenders of liberty. He took a peek under the curtain, holding his breath, waiting for the bullet to his head.

He wasn't on the stage.

Ben scanned the auditorium one last time before returning to the antechamber. Maybe he could found another way out, he thought. He looked around the room and saw another door, close to where the tram rested. He made his way to it, backing along the wall and past the oil portraits. He opened the door, waved the gun around and listened. He couldn't hear anyone, but decided to go down into the basement. He read the plate on the other side of the door, "Stairway #10 - Hall of the Presidents." as he closed it silently.

He went through the door at the bottom of the stairs as carefully as before. It opened to a long, curving hallway. It was some sort of utility tunnel.

He could see parts of the costume and the moon suit a little farther down the hall. It was well lit, spacious and empty, as far as he could see. He ran along the outer wall towards the costume. Bare walls in either direction – no where to hide. The corridor ran about a block before it changed direction, angling back to the left. It went about a quarter mile before it changed in the other direction. He took off down the hall, keeping to the inside wall and trying to minimize the echoes of his footfalls and his breath, which to him seemed as loud as if he were breathing into the intercom at full volume. He couldn't slow it down. The adrenaline wouldn't let him.

He was scared shitless. His feet got heavier as he dwelt on this. Then he had the though, *Maybe I should let the professionals take care of it. Where could the guy go, after all?* But he knew it was up to him again, as it had been all along. *He had been the fulcrum on which the whole thing hinged. From the beginning. He had to take another long walk. Shit. The guy had to be caught. He had to pay. It was up to him.*

Ben had to make sure of it. He came up on a doorway on the inner wall, labeled "Stairway #12 Ye Olde Christmas Shoppe" and looked inside at the stairs and landing. He tried the door. It opened. He listened. Didn't hear anything. He closed the door, silently.

He decided to keep going down the corridor.

It ran on for another two blocks around the turn, then angled sharply to the left again. It seemed to be an octagonal shape. The tip of the gun made a terrible, clattering echo as Ben pointed it around the angle, striking the open access panel along the inner wall. Instinctively he ducked down. He squatted for what seemed like a minute – listening. Satisfied he hadn't caused any harm, he turned his attention to the blank darkness of the open scuttle hole. No lights. He could see a crawlspace terminated at this end. Pipes and cable and conduit ran along the walls.

He heard something inside.

Scratching noises in the darkness. Far away – out ahead. He corrected himself, *No, that wasn't it, really. More like dragging noises.* Someone crawling through the pitch.

He knew who.

He formulated a plan. He would run along the corridor and look for the next access box. Then wait for him to come out. *Good plan.* But he had no guarantee that the tunnel didn't branch. It could join a shaft too, and the bastard could simply climb up to the street somewhere and make his escape.

He didn't see any other way. If he wanted to stop the son of a bitch he'd have to follow his trail. He'd have to climb into the thing and crawl through the confined blackness himself.

He got in, put his pistol in his waistband, took a deep breath and started crawling. In a matter of seconds he left the relative comfort of the lighted corridor behind him.

He started off slowly, tentatively, trying to get a feel for it. He could tell by the echoes that he had two feet at most on either side. He bumped his head once and that slowed him down more.

He crawled for at least a couple hundred yards, stopping to listen every ten yards or so. As long as he kept hearing the noise, he started up again. Ben could hear him up ahead, transmitting pings, which ran quickly along the lengths of pipe as he struck them. Ben was gaining on him, despite the slow pace of crawling by feel.

The noises were getting louder and stronger. Ben had no reference point, but he was guessing the terrorist might be fifty yards ahead. Some light spilled in around the edges of a new access panel.

He waited for a moment until he could hear the crawling again and then he passed by it. The crawlway got narrower now. Ben had no extra side-to-side room – he could either go forward or backward. The space was now only as wide as an adult American man. It was about four feet tall. If you had light, you might be able to run down it while bent over, but that was impossible in the darkness and he had no way to check for sudden changes in height.

The terrorist started grunting and moaning up ahead. Ben thought back to that night his father died, when they were trapped in the elevator. He remembered feeling helpless in the dark – afraid and alone. He had avoided elevators and enclosed spaces all his life. It had been as dark as this. He couldn't see anything at all. The darkness magnified sounds in the emptiness, until the blood hiss filled his ears and his pulse filled his chest. He could hear that now, too, his pulse that is. The fear welled up in him and he felt became singularly aware that would be up to him. He was afraid and alone once again, but this time he wasn't helpless. He realized this had to be done.

He kept crawling.

The crawlspace followed the obtuse angles of the corridor and Ben smacked his head hard as it changed. He pinged the metal pipes with his head, just as the one listening just ahead of him had done.

He stopped up ahead.

Ben stopped, rubbing his head and listening. He tried to control his breathing as it started to accelerate.

The silence stretched out for what seemed like a minute. He used the time to feel for the angle change.

Crawling noises up ahead again.

Ben started back up again.

Crawling noises stopped ahead.

He froze.

A flash, then gunshot.

Deafening reverberations.

He could feel the bullets disturb the air as they whizzed past. He flattened himself, head sideways against the floor and arms shielding his head.

Another blast, then another. He winced each time, waiting for the inevitable sting.

But nothing hit him.

Now he was both blind and deaf. But he could still feel his way along so he forced himself to move forward. He stopped as the corridor light streamed back into the crawlspace less than a street block away up ahead.

The bastard climbed out and ran off before Ben could pull his weapon out. He couldn't tell which direction he ran but he didn't think he should go out the same hole. The terrorist might try springing the same trap he had thought about earlier. He had to find another way out first.

Ben started crawling backwards, picking up speed until he came to the last access door he'd passed. The tunnel opened up at that point and he enough room to turn and directly face it. With both feet he kicked at the metal square as hard as he could, using the back wall as leverage. The door flew open and he wasted no time tumbling out head first. Immediately, he rolled and pointed his gun in the direction they'd been crawling.

Nothing. He got up and ran along the inner wall, like he had before.

At the next angle change, he peeked around the corner. He could see two doors up ahead, the first was a restroom, the other a side hallway. He hear footsteps and ran after them. Ben passed stairway #13 and kept going to the end of the hall. It was stairway #16, the one leading to Adventureland and Frontierland. He flung open the door at ground level to see if he'd take fire. Nothing. He ran up the staircase, two at a time, and burst out onto the pavement next to the Enchanted Tiki Room, now deserted. Ben scanned the area and spotting movement over in the area by the next amusement ride. He ran towards it, changing his angle to keep the utility box and the electrical shed supplying the ride between him and his target. He came around on him from the right and saw the limping terrorist weaving between cars of The Magic Carpets of Aladdin. He spotted Ben when he glanced over his shoulder. He turned and fired prematurely wasting his ammunition.

Ben took cover behind the copious metal around the power shed.

"Give up!" Ben shouted.

The terrorist replied with another shot. Ben leveled his weapon and took a shot.

Then another.

The terrorist changed direction. He ran into the center of the ride machinery, taking up a position behind the center column where the arms rose up and extended over to the cars where

Ben countered the change in angle by running over to the control panel.

He could see him over there, mind turning – looking for another way out. Ben looked down for a second and pressed the red button, starting the ride. The arms began to raise and lower the cars as they rotated around the center column. The terrorist had a bad limp and couldn't move fast enough to get out of the center circle and the cars, blurring by now as they continued to pick up speed, effectively trapped him in a closed circle.

He swiveled again to respond. Ben could see him squeezing the trigger in a strange, stroboscopic effect as the cars flew past. Nothing came out of the gun. He had no more ammunition. He squeezed the trigger but it did no good. He was out of ammunition. He tried to fire several times, then shouted something and frantically looked for a means of escape.

"Stop," Ben said in Arabic, "it's over. You are finished."

"It will never be over, " the terrorist screamed over the roar of the cars. Ben started walking over to the perimeter of the cars. The terrorist became agitated and forgot about Ben's weapon as he panicked, trying to time the cars for an escape. .

Ben was walking over to perimeter when Ben squeezed one off missing him. He limped off behind the central support column and leveled his weapon again. Ben ran to the edge of the ride, pointing the gun at the terrorist, who kept hiding behind the supports. The flying carpet cars trapped him. Ben could see him timing the lower cars.

"Stop now. It is finished," Ben shouted in Arabic, trying to say it over the screeching of the cars.

"Go back to Hell where you belong, son of a dog. You'll find the whore that bore you there, " the terrorist shouted back.

Ben ran into the center, right behind the next low-flying car. He barely made it in.

The terrorist charged him.

Ben fired, point-blank, hitting his right thigh. The force of it made Abdullah stagger backwards into the path of the next car. It caught him square against his head and chest and teed him off, like a

Big Bertha driver, lifting him twenty feet in the air, throwing his body end over end, now reduced to a shattered bag of bones, until it landed headfirst and crumpled onto the pavement, and finally came to rest; no longer rigid and defined as the living thing it had been seconds before.

Ben sat down next to it.

Chapter 79

He came to between surges of the fever. His cough had an unnatural rattle and he shook violently as he tried to clear his lungs. His face and the rest of his visible skin, had taken on the color of putty as was coated in an oily sheen. Ben finally looked up and realized the two men standing over him were Agent Daniels and the one they called Chief.

"Good new, Ben. The doctors say you're gonna live," Daniels said beneath the surgical mask.

"Lucky you," Chief added.

"Don't think so," Ben rasped.

"The worst of it is over now," Daniels said.

"How long?"

"You've been sick for three days."

He looked past them, across the expanse and finally it registered that he laid in the middle of a vast assortment of sick people, arrayed in regimented rows, but showing the variety of shapes, shades and sizes – *all conceivable kinds present and accounted for, sir….* stretched out in many rows of the black-and-white checkerboard floor of the dining hall of the Cinderella's Castle, which for now served as a makeshift hospital. His mind was too cloudy to count.

"Grace? Girls?"

"They're going to be all right. You saved them from exposure, remember? You saved most of the people here, you know. They didn't get to release even half of it," Chief said.

"You did good. You did them proud, Ben," Daniels added.

"How many? Dead?"

"So far, about four thousand."

Ben thrashed his head.

"That's worse than 9/11, but *only* by a thousand," Daniels said. He shook his head and expressed his disgust, "It could have been a lot worse, if you think about it. You made a difference, you know that?"

Ben heard it, but kept his eyes blankly set on the arched ceiling. He made a noise.

"The USAMARIID biohazard units have come in along with the Department of Homeland Security and have detoxified the place. FEMA just put the seal of approval on things. In a day or two they'll begin to release the people who have no traces of infection." Chief said, smiling, "and I'm glad to say they're in the majority here. More than forty thousand of them."

Ben tried to smile, but it was for show. Dying would have been easier than living at that point. Breathing hurt. He couldn't move and felt like he was slowly rotating on a roasting spit, spinning and burning simultaneously.

"We don't know the exact details. We're all in isolation here, Ben. No one can leave until the CDC gives the okay, but we expect that soon, maybe another day. They'll begin releasing us in stages as fast as they can process us."

Ben didn't say anything. He closed his eyes.

They sat for a moment or two, looking around at all the sick and dying. Most of the patients were lying on the ground, but they did have IVs running the available Ciproflaxin and other prophylactic antibiotics to everyone he could see. Chief began to notice the growing stench of bacterial corruption at that point.

Ben spoke again.

"Dafna – she okay?"

"I'm sorry Ben, she died yesterday," Daniels said.

Tears began streaming down the sides of his face. He convulsed, sobbing. His phlegmatic lungs pushed up a mixed mass of bloody and green sputum that he choked on as turned his head to try and spit in on the ground.

He heaved and shed tears silently for a long while. They waited for him to settle once again.

When Jack felt enough time had passed he said, "Ben, we do have some good news. I got the agency to lean on your insurance company and they've agreed to partially cover your house damage. We can make up the balance with funds appropriated in the Patriot

Act. One of the provisions allows Federal agencies to pay restitution after acts of terrorism and my contacts up the chain tell me this is definitely one of those cases. You'll have enough money to rebuild."

"You've attracted a lot of attention," Chief added.

Ben looked up at them.

"This ain't over yet. Not even close."

"Just rest," Daniels said, "We're gonna need you. We need as many people like you we can get. We have many more battles to fight in this war. We need your help. Stay alive, brother." He reached out and squeezed Ben's hand.

Then they left.

Ben lay there, staring up from the floor at the gothic arches and stained glass of the castle. The setting reminded him of Saint Roch's where he had failed to make peace with all of this during the months he'd tried. It seemed like a good time to try again.

Not being a religious man, nevertheless he began a prayer.

"I thank you for my life, O Lord, and for the time I have left on this Earth.

Help me make the best of it.
Help me make a difference with every day I have left,
Protect and guide us all of our days,
Save us from ourselves, Lord
Help us grow out of our stupidity.
Save us from this plague
and deliver us from this evil .
Amen."

Acknowledgements

The author would like to thank and express support and appreciation to the following people and organizations:

Jihadwatch.org: Hugh Fitzgerald, Robert Spencer and Marisol Seibold

Ali Sina and staff of faithfreedom.org

Geert Wilders and Theo Van Gogh

Dave Horowitz and his Freedom Center: http://www.horowitzfreedomcenter.org

Diana West of The Washington Times

Foehammer of foehammer.net and thousands of bloggers, creators of sites and contributors to sites who point out the link between Islamic theology and the actions of jihadis and the Islamic world.

blogger Fjordman

Debbie Schlussel of http://www.debbieschlussel.com/

Michelle Malkin http://michellemalkin.com/

Sheik yer'mami of http://sheikyermami.com/

DC Watson author of *Truth is not bigotry (Sometimes It Just Hurts)*

Daniel Pipes http://www.danielpipes.com

http://thereligionofpeace.com

http://www.memri.org/ and its translators

The Muslim Student Associaton (MSA) and their compendium of Islamic texts posted publicly which makes verifying the scale and scope of the threat a simple task: http://www.usc.edu/dept/MSA/ The author encourages readers to go to the site and verify citations from the Qur'an and Ahadith used in this story.

The signatories of the Saint Petersburg declaration, among them:
Walid Shoebat, Nonie Darwish, Ayaan Hirsi Ali, Ibn Warraq
and Wafa Sultan

Bruce Bawer, author of
While Europe Slept: How Radical Islam Is Destroying the West from Within

Mark Steyn, author of *America Alone: The End of the World as We Know it*

Andrew Bostom author of *The Legacy of Jihad*

Oriana Fallaci author of *The Force of Reason* and *The Rage and the Pride*

Bat Ye'or, author of *The Dhimmi: Jews & Christians Under Islam*

David Pryce-Jones, author of *The Closed Circle*
Brigette Gabriel, author of *Because They Hate*
Raymond Ibrahim, author of *The Al Qaeda Reader*

Michael Savage
Congresswoman Sue Myrick of North Carolina.
Congressman Virgil Goode of Virginia
Congressman Tom Tancredo of Colorado

Members of the world wide intelligence community and armed forces, who are the 'rough men who stand ready to do violence and ind doing so, ensure my peaceful night's sleep' as Orwell puts it.

Pope Benedict XVI, who insists on reciprocity from the Islamic world.

To the people who read drafts of this story and provided feedback and suggestions – a big thank you. – as well to my commercial artist friend who designed the cover of this book. Well done.

And lastly the legion of People who take the time to research and think about the inextricable link between Islamic theology, law and practice and its tragic influence on the world, who are kindred spirits to those who also speak of these issues at the risk of personal reputation or physical threat. Such as Italian convert Magdi Cristiano Allam.

About the Author

Zack Highstreet is the pseudonym for a forty-year-old suburban man, ordinary in every way. He'd be unremarkable if you passed him on the sidewalk. *A Plague On Both Houses* is his first novel and he'd like to live to write another. He takes the lessons of Theo van Gogh and Salman Rushdie as serious as the next terrorist attack.

A Plague On Both Houses rose out his need for an answer to: "Why do they hate us so much?" He found the answer in the canonical texts of Islam: the Qur'an, the Ahadith and the *Sirate Rasullah*, or *The Life of* Mohammed.

Zack earned a bachelor's degree in Journalism and a Masters in Information Systems. He has worked for local newspapers and in the Information Technology industry as programmer/analyst, database administrator and as a Technical Lead on many projects. He lives with his wife and children in a house behind a white picket fence in the middle of a quiet, safe Midwestern town.
You may correspond with him at a_plague_on_both_houses@hotmail.com

www.ingramcontent.com/pod-product-compliance
Lightning Source LLC
Chambersburg PA
CBHW031143050726
47495CB00018B/457

* 9 7 8 0 6 1 5 2 2 2 8 4 4 *